AMI T

The L   Men

THE_LITTLE_MEN

Pic Credit: Shubham Garg

Printed in India.

ISBN: 978-93-342-3570-8

Preface.

Before reading this book, there are a few facts one needs to know about the Indian IT industry to understand the context and setting of the novel *(for ones who don't already know this!)*. The Indian software industry has witnessed fantastic growth in the last two decades, earning significant GDP for the country owing to a great business partnership with the US, primarily. It has resulted in colossal benefits to both countries on the following accounts:

1. Indian currency is around 85[1] times cheaper compared to the US dollar ($1 ~ 85 rupees), which means outsourcing software projects to India is much cheaper for the US, and earning in dollars is much more valuable for India. Relying on dollars helps IT companies clock excellent revenues and

---

[1] *As of 2025.*

profitability year after year. They earn in dollars and pay their taxes and Indian employees in INR.

2. Unlike India, the US has 6 time zones. Indian Standard Time (IST) is 11.5 hours ahead of US Central Standard Time (CST). This means when the offices close in the US, the offices in India can open, and vice versa, ensuring a great degree of round-the-clock support for the US businesses.

3. India is a great pool of bright, English-speaking young engineering graduates who are as hardworking as they are good at mathematics and can be relied upon as logical solution providers.

4. Both the US and India are democracies, so there is mutual respect and stability in this setup. Both countries find a lot to learn from each other, making it a healthy win-win partnership.

5. India has excellent internet connectivity due to a dense fiber-optic cable network, making data exchanges between both countries easy. As a result, numerous BPO (Business process outsourcing) operations have shifted to India.

6. The Indian Government supported software parks with various schemes, tax rebates, and subsidies over the years, allowing an ecosystem to be developed over time.

The Indian IT industry has revolutionized the job scenario in India as well as in the US. *'Bangalored'* is a term coined to explain the loss of a job in the US, which got shifted to India (*to Bangalore, an Indian metro*) owing to cost-saving reasons. Since the growth of this relatively new industry has been rapid, it has been subject to several ups and downs over the years. The cultural impact of this industry on the Indian diaspora has been tremendous.

After Bangalore, Hyderabad, and Chennai, Pune is one of the largest IT hubs and is home to several big IT companies. There are more than 5 million Indian software engineers (*and this figure keeps increasing year after year*) supporting global businesses directly or indirectly. Every year, several graduates from engineering colleges are hired, often in large numbers, to join IT companies. This story is of one such newcomer in one such organization, which happened to be part of the churning resulting from the global recession of 2007–09.

This book isn't about the industry or the recession entirely, but knowing these things will help you enjoy it more! After putting things in perspective from my end, I would like to invite you and make you privy to the world of *'The Little Men'*.

For the readers.

When I started writing, I wanted to write about the recession, but then midway through, I realized that the people and the reasons for the recession are completely inseparable. Hence, I trashed it all and started writing about the recession through the lives of people.

'The Little Men' is an insider's account of a year spent by a newcomer in the Indian IT industry, a blend of facts and fiction based on real events and some people I met in the backdrop of the IT recession of 2007–09. It explores the idea that a recession is not always just a recession of demand; it can simultaneously be a recession of hope. Drilled down from the macrocosm of the industry to the microcosm of one person's brain, it is a recession of ideas, culture, and innovation. If, at times, the death of an idea or a dream can cause the death of a person, then similarly, the death of an idea or a dream can be the death of industry as well.

Narrated through the eyes of 22-year-old Amitarth, a fresher in a software organization, we find the protagonist in a shy techie who experiences everything that he sees emotionally and with a curious mind. Recession is but a backdrop, a reflection in his life as he struggles to make sense of the events in his life and as his mind and heart conflicts.

Life takes a turn when he realizes his dreams don't align with the great Indian software dream, and while there already are conflicts of interest between the protagonists, there is something even bigger plotting against them at the same time. Does he stand any chance of saving the two people who are dearest to him from themselves?

It's also a story of his team as they see their lives getting inevitably tangled and altered due to something uncontrollable and big, something nobody really understands.

The journey of these little men then becomes analogous and synonymous with the journey of an industry, a sine wave filled with heartbreaks, disappointments, and setbacks yet simultaneously throbbing with hope and resurrection.

Yet, by no means is this a boring account of monotonous economic concepts. This is a valid story primarily about people, their dreams, their friendships, ideals, and love. Yes, it also is about recession and survival, but more importantly, it's about growing up!

I would like to dedicate this book to Lord Ganesha for the strength and inspiration; to these fantastic cities—Pune and Bangalore; to my teachers who taught me the alphabet; to my parents and grandparents for reading me the bedtime stories; to uncles and aunts who gifted me books; to my friends who always egged me on to write; to my brother and kid who helped maintain my spirits in the face of disappointment; to my wife for her infinite patience as I nagged her incessantly for feedback; to my past experiences for the life lessons; and to this industry, that gave me a kickstart.

Finally, special thanks to the late Naniwadekar Sir, who gave me complete access to an entire library filled to the brim! While browsing through those books, at some moment I won't be able to pinpoint; the writing bug bit me.

There's a quote by J.D. Salinger from '*The Catcher in the Rye*': '*What really knocks me out is a book that, when you're all done reading it, you wish the author that wrote it was a terrific friend of yours and you could call him up on the phone whenever you felt like it. That doesn't happen much, though.*' If, after reading this work, you feel somewhat similar, you can let me know at the email address shared. I promise to reply!

Thanks a lot for your time.

Ami Tikekar *[littlemen.biglives@gmail.com]*

Little men with little dreams,

All struggle to make some sense;

Of their life that offers them no respite,

And coming to terms with pain and pretense!

How things do matter, no one understands;

But all jump right in with half a stance;

Survival is the call of the day;

Whether they will succeed is part of chance!

Never giving even a passing thought,

To what we were born to be and what's our core;

Of what would have made us happier,

And made us love ourselves and our work just a tinge more.

And so life moves on,

With a thousand sorrows,

And we turn out to be survivors,

With no tomorrow!

Not that we give a damn about the moment,
Just half-glad that we are still half-alive;
We'd rather fill ourselves with longing,
Than dream a dream and really strive.

Just a shoddy lookalike,
Of all that we could have been;
All we try is to size our goals with every failing,
To match an uncertain future,
That we wish remains forever unseen!

Prologue.

I know two things about bubbles. One, they tend to rise upward. Two, they burst! When one invests in a bubble, well knowing the above two things, that is insanity!

But I can understand why one would want to. This world and all things within it need a direction. The favorite direction, for some reason, universally loved, is *'up'*. If something, anything, travels up fast, people would invest everything despite their good sense. It is our collective sickness.

Quite a time for philosophy! I stood on the terrace of our plush five-story office, looking down the parapet wall and watching the busy road below. It was 10.30 a.m., and I assumed people on the road, driving their cars, were too absorbed to notice the beautiful shimmering, blinding sunlight reflecting over car roofs ahead of them, but that light somehow seemed less positive to me today.

I missed her viciously; that vacuum inside me was a sickness, rotting me from within. We three were wheels within wheels, and the entire system had reached a dead wall. We don't progress anywhere from here—only downward. And it wasn't just our lives alone. Wasn't the entire world spiraling downward? There was no hope within or outside.

I stared down intently.

Damn, if I do jump, it will hurt badly! That doesn't scare me. But what does scare me is that, just when I am about to hit the office floor and splash it red, mid-air, I regret it and panic. That's the stuff nightmares are made of. I just don't have the guts. I am not Prabhu, nor am I Mitali.

My phone rings. It's my manager. It rings and rings and rings. I don't answer. Finally, it goes silent, followed by the loud beep of an SMS.

'*Please meet me asap.*'

I gaze at the message numbly. It is inevitable, isn't it? One way or the other, I can't avoid her. I don't want to go back to my floor and meet my manager. That's the last thing I feel like doing. The phone beeps again.

'*And please don't leave before meeting me!*'

Project manager again!

I look down. If I do jump, I can avoid the meeting! If I do go down, one way or another, it is all Prabhu's fault. Should I write a note blaming it all on him?

But then maybe the blame wasn't all his. *Lehman Brothers* is going down on its own, isn't it? Maybe I can't blame either—neither Prabhu nor Mitali.

It's my mistake; I let those crazy bastards in my head. My head felt dizzier than ever!

1.

March' 07 (a year ago):

Facebook, Twitter, Amazon S3, Amazon EC2, and Hadoop had already been launched in 2006. Google had purchased YouTube in November 2006. In January 2007, Windows Vista was released, and in March 2007, 3D Systems had released the first 3D printing system under $10,000.

India's software industry and BPO-KPO sectors were steadily growing.

My father opened the main gate of the company guest house. I followed him inside. There was a boy standing by the gate, as if waiting for someone.

"Hello." I ventured an acquaintance with the stranger.

"Hi," he replied back, lowering his chin until his giant forehead cast a shadow over his eyes. His eyes pierced mine, and I could sense doubt in them.

"You are joining FORDIT too?" I shook off the queer buzz in my head whenever I met any stranger and tried to ask smilingly. Our recruiter, FORDIT Tech. [2], was a mid-sized, fast-growing IT organization that specialized in embedded system technologies and

---

[2] *They went with the tagline* 'Translating technology into solutions' *and had offices in several major cities, but our joining was in Pune.*

was one of the respectably new[3] players in the market if the performance of its shares was anything to go by. But our joining had got delayed due to mysterious business reasons.

"Yes," his expression remained paranoid.

"Let's keep these bags inside and then you two can talk," my father intervened.

"Let me take yours, sir." He took the bags from my father's hand, which took me by surprise.

"Thanks, buddy. I am Amitarth Kumar. What's your name?" I asked him as we all walked in.

"Prabhu… Prabhu Mohapatra."

"And you did your engineering from?"

"Bhubaneswar."

My room was on the third floor. As we carried our four bags to my room, I saw a couple of guys in shorts walking towards us. I knew them all too well. One of them was a peer from my engineering batch, Abhinav Kashyap, a dude with a French beard, a sardonic smile, a nasty temper, and an abnormally big bottom for the shorts he was wearing. The other guy… well… had plenty of his own reasons to frown upon me.

○●○

---

[3] *celebrated a decade in 2006!*

We three were from the same small town engineering college in Maharashtra and got mass recruited from the college campus for our first software job in Pune.

We had no idea or experience whatsoever with the residential facilities in the city. So, we enthusiastically formed an Orkut committee[4] comprising new joiners from our college across companies. I met Rohit V. on this committee. Four to five people from our college decided to buy a flat and stay together as we knew each other even though we were from different sections and branches.

As it turned out, Rohit started dictating his terms regarding the kind of flat, rent, location, and other factors, to a point where the rest of us were left with hardly any say on the matter. I had had enough of bullies in my college life, so despite his repeated requests and numerous phone calls for involvement, I wisely opted out of the gang. He took it as if I had ditched him halfway.

Well, each has his own version of the story... and this is my version, so... let's make peace with it.

○●○

"Hey, hi." Abhinav greeted us. Rohit just gave a nod.

---

[4] *before Facebook, there was Orkut!*

"Hey," I said palely.

Abhinav was the kind of guy one so routinely came across in any engineering college—a person one would instantly regret meeting. I had seen the likes of him through all the four years of college—participating in various competitions, being someone who was all too eager to be the group daddy, a familiar but unfriendly face on our campus. He was a *know-it-all* category of arrogant showoff who genuinely believed that anyone who disagreed with him was an idiot. He had no patience with people with differing opinions and basically lived on two kinds of emotions—vanity and hatred. This may sound a bit extreme to normal people, but to him, it was the only way to lead a fulfilling life, where His Majesty must have the right to dominate people and people must bow down to his every command. Those who went against his vanity would become the rightful recipients of his no-holds-barred hatred. These two emotions were enough. One would feed off the other.

We all walked into my room.

"Perfect," my father said, looking around. It was an AC room, fully furnished and shining in anticipation of its new resident.

"This room is amazing." He looked at it with his eyes glistening with the rightful pride that his son had finally landed his first job, thus an entry into the corporate world, and a certain happiness that his efforts to come to see me off were worth it.

"Okay. You guys freshen up; I will catch up with you tonight. The dining hall is on the second floor." Abhinav briefed us and walked out with Rohit behind him.

All the while, Prabhu stood in the corner, intently looking at me.

"You are a shy person," he said with an edgy finality to his words.

"Impressive, Sherlock, but it's too early to know me this well," I said, smiling.

My father left in an hour, leaving me on my own.

I vividly remember this day, as this was the day I left my city and my parents for the very first time!

○●○

I freshened up and went down, only to find myself in a sea of unfamiliar faces eating together at the only and rather long dining table. What added to my misery was that most of them were girls!

Ohh nooo!! My stomach made that gurgling sound. There's nothing to deny. I am shy when talking to girls. Really shy!

But what always made matters worse, as it was in this case, was that most of these girls were really good-looking, which left me completely tongue-tied. Some guys instinctively project confidence while I, at best, could only project my nervousness.

I stood there, feeling out of place. As I took just a second more than I should have in deliberating on where to sit to attract the least attention from the crowd, all of them looked up at me simultaneously with curious glances. They were at least 20 people.

I stood with a sinking feeling in my pit as I knew I was short on time for my next move. All that was expected was for me to pull out a chair and sit down quietly without tripping or making any awkward gestures.

Fine, I can do that. It's simple.

I said *'Good morning'* politely and sat in the first empty seat that I could grab. Just that it wasn't morning; it was evening, so all the girls laughed like the tinkling of silver bells, making me feel like an idiot.

Worse, I had sat beside what looked like the prettiest girl in our batch, and that meant I was in the eye span of every guy on the table.

Those were not *clean* gazes. I wonder how girls tolerate it!

We had our introductions over dinner, where I stammered a couple of times. But the girl's name was Pooja Sagar, and this was one of the only things my embarrassed mind noted. She was an NRI[5] from the Middle East.

---

[5] *Non-resident Indian*

There were many pretty faces in that room, as there always are, but there was something striking about her. She had refined features, a meltingly toothy smile, an angular face without the sharpness of a paper knife, and jet-black locks. Her smile had an innocent way of making someone chatting with her feel good about himself or herself. But what set her apart were her eyes— the most expressive pair I had ever seen, and they twinkled with meaning as if winking at me for some secret joke that only both of us knew.

Abhinav and Rohit were already quite a group with the girls. They were having trouble shutting up. The girls giggled as full stops to unending repartees of zero wisdom. Other guys pitched in, and I was left behind feeling completely uncomfortable.

Now, I should have done the same thing, but years of shyness had taught me that shy people are too self-righteous to stoop this low, either too self-righteous or, well, maybe too shy.

"I know. I know. It's amazing, right?" A voice emanated from behind me. It was Prabhu. He stood beside me, looking at the newly formed group.

"What's amazing?"

"What isn't? Look at that. That proves that lust is faster than friendship." He said it sardonically.

"You need to tone it down a bit, buddy." I said, looking away.

"What's amazing is the fact that groups are formed at lightning speed and that everybody likes it, though it's not likable at all. You and I don't stand a chance, bro." He replied casually, taking a bite of his ice cream. I felt sick inside.

○●○

It was night, and I tried hard to talk to people. But we all know how it normally is. People want a bite of the group, not of the losers.

So, I met a couple of geeks who just had to include words like Symbian, Java, cache, and compiler in every other sentence. I met a super-shy version of myself who couldn't stop smiling, just because people approached him for small talk. I met some people who acted like NRIs because they had appeared for the *GRE*[6] and were awaiting the results.

All this while, Prabhu was with me. It's a silent bond sometimes. Birds of a feather know they must flock together. As Prabhu would reiterate many times later, '*We were square pegs in round holes.*'

I met some guys who looked smart and slick and sounded agreeable but were too independent to be grouped. And then there were some who were neither here nor there.

It was difficult to find a similar frequency, a like mind, a friend.

---

[6] *Graduate Record Examinations. On clearing the exam, person can study at some college in the US based on their score, which often then leads to a job in the US.*

○●○

At night, Prabhu came to my room and said, "The guys are drinking in Abhinav's room, and the girls are drinking too. Do you drink?"

"No, I don't." I said, slightly scared.

"Neither do I. But we are supposed to be up by 7 o'clock tomorrow. 9 o'clock office," said Prabhu, concerned.

But we knew it didn't matter. The majority formed the rules, and we were outliers.

The next day, our pickup buses arrived early. We had our breakfast at the table, where girls and boys chatted. We could see some couples already, and Pooja sat beside Abhinav. I shook my head in frustration as I scribbled.

> *Trapped in the cobwebs of my mind,*
> *My vision falters at every step.*
> *I don't know what to make of sunlight.*
> *It stands for hope I never met!*

"What's this?" Prabhu asked as he peeped into my notebook.

"Nothing. It's just... I... I scribble stuff." I shut my book immediately. "Some poems... stories. Nothing serious. It makes me feel better."

He smiled. He was a pudgy fellow, not bulky but bordering on the line between healthy and fat. His face was soft, and so were his eyes. I couldn't find a single rough edge in his frame. It was all curves and rounds.

"So, what are you thinking?" I asked Prabhu.

"Your name should have been Amitabh, which is homophonic to your current name but with better recall." he said, pondering. "May I call you Ami, as in, from *Mon Ami*, which means *'My Friend'* in French?"

"People normally prefer to call me Amit," I said.

"But it's not *'We, the people'* here; it's *'Me, the I,'* right? I prefer Ami," he said, making a face. I suppressed a chuckle.

"So, you did engineering in the electronics stream?" he asked me.

"Yes. How did you know?" I asked, surprised.

"You told me. I am an electronics engineer too. I, too, told you this yesterday, but you were busy watching the girls. So, I figured it wouldn't have registered. By the way, I am working on coding a source-to-source compiler."

For the first time, I noticed that he stammered a bit while talking, as if unsure of the next word that might come out.

"Working as in?"

"I am working on a compiler to translate source-code of programs written in one programming language to another." But he himself seemed half-convinced. It wasn't such a terrible idea for 2007.

I wanted to say, "Oh, c'mon, you don't need to show off to me. I thought we had an understanding."

But all I said was, "You look sensible. Leave such things to Balaji."

Balaji was one of the nerds I had talked to, a day before. He was a bit too showy for a geek and was already solving computer bugs in C-programs for girls and giving them *'tips'* for writing error-free code in his nerdy voice. He would always be with the other one, Sasidhar, who was just as geeky but a degree less when it came to showing off.

○●○

The next two months were full of inductions, trainings, and new learnings throughout the day. Prabhu and I used to hang out together, totally invisible to the people around us.

There was something profoundly wrong with this guy. He was full of nerves, a sudden temper, sudden depression, a sudden show of warmth, and sudden bursts of enthusiasm.

We would spend our evenings in the cafeteria on the top floor. Our cafeteria was divided into two parts—one half was indoors where people could sit, and the other half was open to the sky, where we could walk to the end to stand at the parapet and see the busy road down below with the never-ending traffic. This open-to-sky half would often be sparsely populated. Hence, it was our favorite standing spot. Evenings with cool Pune breeze would make him philosophical.

"I think she is interested in you."

"She who?" I asked, consuming a bite of my rum ball.

"Pooja."

"Whatever made you think that?" I asked.

"I see a glint of interest in her eyes every time you talk at some point in the training class. It is as if she genuinely wants to listen to what you are saying."

"You sure?"

"Yeah. I mean, you won't be able to see it. You can't, but I can."

I wasn't sure if that was believable. She would stay with Abhinav throughout the day, listening to him chat non-stop and smiling. I could understand that she needed people around her; not being in a group is considered unharmonious. It was a matter of public notice that discordant chords don't ring well with her.

Meanwhile, the girls were all ga-ga over Rohit and his hairstyles, which he had changed three times in the last two months. It was a big group of twenty-odd people, with the nucleus being Abhinav. They would either be flirting with each other or passing nasty comments on people who weren't in their group.

That was the group dynamics—either you were in, or you were garbage.

People trying to show off individuality were quickly written off as *'irritating'*. The shysters were written off as *'boring'*, and it was an insult to even talk to or about them.

As for me and Prabhu, we were written off as the *'gay couple'* as we would always be together. We were one of the favorite topics for cracking jokes at the lunch table for the group. We could see them laughing at us, sneering, and jeering at our *'inability'* to talk to girls. The boys were asked to stay away if they didn't want *Crazy* Prabhu to molest them.

So, in the lift, if it so happened that Prabhu and I were present and Rohit and the girls happened to walk in, then Rohit would just jump apart dramatically, look at us, and scream, "Stay away from me, please! I am straight." The girls would burst out laughing... and yes, even Pooja.

I mean, this behavior was so unlike hers. I would genuinely feel she had the presence to make the deadliest of people feel alive. It was a rare quality, and it would contrast unhappily with the qualities of the people she chose to spend time with.

But she wasn't really the judgmental type; nope, that wasn't her. Her existence was settled on believing in the hidden good in people, even if some of her beliefs were pure floo-dust. Left to her own devices, she wouldn't hurt a fly, but then I guess being part of the mob has its own demands—one of which was to laugh at the freaks. But I wouldn't mind her laugh at all, pretty as it was unkind; it would still make my heart skip a beat! And then there were others, all equally nasty. They would crack jokes at us every now and then. We were like a never-ending supply of jokes that had ceased to stagnate. There would be discussions within our earshot that I looked straight, but it is so difficult to differentiate the *'twistedness'* in one's sexuality. The girls would tch-tch and giggle, and all of this happened just within two months.

This had increased to such a degree that Praneet, the individualist in our batch, approached me once and said, "I think it's better if you guys stay apart. What's the need for encouraging such rumors?"

But I knew these rumors had a base. Prabhu was so crazy that no person in his right mind could ever tolerate him for long. People just couldn't see my incentive to be with him. He had a talent for irritating people in seconds.

○●○

Everyone in our batch was taught the basics of the C and C++ programming languages, along with SQL and HTML.

Then the batch bifurcated, wherein computer-science engineers were by default chosen for training in programming languages like Java and Dot-Net, which would lead them towards *coding* and thus development in some projects, and other stream engineers were absorbed in embedded systems and related maintenance projects.

I guess it's a natural selection in some ways; the Comp-Sci guys were more inclined towards coding than others and so were preferred for it. But every engineer worth his salt, from Mechanical to Civil, would dream of getting development as it promised nerdier work and more scope career-wise.

As an electronics engineer, I was option-lessly absorbed as a tester in an embedded systems project for an MNC giant of a client overseas after spending a month and a half on the bench.

The project was located on the ground floor.

Prabhu was shifted as a tester to a project called *INSITE* on the floor above. Now was the time to actually work to get paid.

○●○

Every evening at around 5 o'clock, we would meet in the office cafeteria on the top-most floor and enjoy a rum ball while discussing the daily titbits of the day. It was almost a routine. Prabhu would always wait till I completed my part and then, when asked about his day, would divert the conversation. He didn't want to look like a loser to his friends.

The evening Pune breeze would soothe his hurt of the day, and he would open up to share his subtle dreams, which he would find very difficult to share or even describe.

"You know what? I think I should really be writing a code for trans-compilation[7]; I told you about. Did you read this book, *Open Sources*? It talks a lot about cross-compilation [8]and open-source software systems[9] that people generously donate for the benefit of society at large. This is a revolution that Linus Torvalds started... " and he would happily carry on telling me the story and history of Linus Torvalds.

"You are an engineer, a person responsible for bringing a technical revolution in the country... Why the fuck are you working on testing? Ask them for development. Development is like fuck, and testing is like kissing after it. No one cares about kissing after sex. How long will you keep on kissing, man?"

I wondered what would happen if I demanded development from management that way.

"And what are you working on?" I asked him to gain some encouragement from his example, but *'That's not important'* would be his abrupt way of cutting the conversation short.

He had no rough edges. Even if he were to shout, he would never be able to appear threatening, so I knew he would never

---

[7] *Translation of source code in one programming language into source code for another programming language.*

[8] *Process of creating executable code for platform B(the target) while compiler runs on platform A (the host).*

[9] *Where source code is donated and freely available for re-distribution and modification.*

become a boss in his life. He could get his way only through manipulations, and he was undoubtedly great at it.

○●○

Every evening, we would leave the office at around 7 p.m. by bus and would reach Aundh at around 7:45 p.m.

Then we would saunter down the streets as neither of us would like to go home.

"Why don't you go home?" He would ask.

"I get bored. I am living with my cousin in a rented flat, and he is this fat, bald guy who only worries about getting me to pay money for the bills. Plus, he is dishonest and messes with the calculations a lot. He lies to me as well. I hate to be with him, as all he does when I am around is hog the TV remote so that he can watch his channels. Everything he does is basically to get money out of me." I told him with a disgusted look.

"Wow, he seems like a charming guy to me. He is my role model. I want to be just like him in three years," he said without batting an eyelid.

"Shut up." I was amused.

His sense of humor was more weird than sarcastic, but it wasn't as fake as that of others in our batch. People would try hard not to be themselves in order to impress others, without ever really liking the other person. Everyone wanted to be noticed, but nobody wanted to notice.

"Why don't you go home?" I asked him.

"I live with my sister and brother-in-law in an elite apartment called *Grapevines*. But I think he hates me. My brother-in-law, I mean."

"How can you say that?" I asked.

"For one, he shouts at me a lot and asks me to get out of the house immediately if I have any dignity left inside me," he replied.

"And you still have doubts?" I asked, raising my eyebrow.

"Oh, come on, he can't really hate me. He is my brother-in-law, married to my dear sister. We are like family. He just likes to fake it. The thing is... " He paused to buy peanuts. "Do rupaye me sirf itna hi... Kya bhaiyya lutte raho IT-walo ko *(Hey Man! Only this much for two bucks? Keep looting IT people),*" and then looked at me. "I hate him. He is a bald, arrogant, average guy working for an IT company as a manager. There is nothing special about him. He has no life and no ambition except earning money and eating out. He is half dead. Not even remotely likable."

"So, you don't like everyday people?" I said, smiling.

"Of course not. I like people who win Nobel prizes or at least keep trying to win one. I like interesting people. The reason why I like you... " he said, pointing that peanut cone towards me. "...is because you are lonely. That's interesting to me—something different, you see."

"Hey, don't treat me like a guinea pig. I thought we were friends." I said, feeling a bit humiliated.

"Come on, are you a girl? Then why do you talk like a girl? We both know I like your brain, and you like mine. We are both twisted in our ways. The fact is, I am more honest about it while you are shy. So obviously, the world hates me, and it's still unsure about you. Don't worry; someday, when your mask wears off, they will hate you too. Chill!" He exclaimed happily, munching the last of the peanuts.

"Let's go sit at that bus stand," I said.

"Yes. Let's."

From where we were sitting, we could see the glass-tinted walls of a gym that was newly opened in a multi-story apartment. It was 8 o'clock that night, but people were still running on treadmills for dear health.

"Girls teach in those gyms you know, so people pay extra to join them. If I start teaching as an instructor in these gyms, they will have to bring down the fees from 2000 to 200. Everybody wants a girl. You want one too. But your politeness impedes any progress," he said.

"Whatever. I am just not boyfriend material. I am not smart like Abhinav or a dude like Rohit. I am just a loser wasting my time with another loser like you," I said, looking down and feeling sorry for myself.

"Yes, you most certainly are a loser, but Madhura likes you," he said, looking at the buses moving on the streets.

"What?! How do you know that?" I asked, startled.

"You remember the induction program we had before joining our projects? Madhura was in my group for one of the tasks. For that task, we were supposed to meet at Harish's place at night to finish it. After the work was done, I walked her down to her home." He waited to see if I was interested.

Obviously, I was.

"Then?"

"While going back, she told me her story. She used to be harassed by a boy in her college. She had a boyfriend recently, but all he wanted was to use her physically. Being as frail and weak as she is, I can't imagine why the dude would want to. But anyway, that's beside the point. She left him because she wanted a sensitive guy who could understand her. Her father has lost his job currently, and he has the responsibility of getting her married. She had something about her that just sucked me in—a whirlwind of emotions," he said merrily, his eyes twinkling with craziness.

"So, where in all of this, did she say she liked me?"

"Weren't you listening? She wants a silent, sensitive, and understanding guy as her boyfriend. That's you. You are the only one in our batch who's sensitive and understanding," he said, looking at me.

"You are unbelievable," I said, covering my ears with my hands.

"Hear me out. You write poems; you write stories. You are the most genuine guy I have met in my life. There is something very truthful about you. Just impress her with all this and become her boyfriend." He paused.

"Okay," I said, considering his line of thought, "Then what?"

"Then you use her." he said without blinking.

"You are disgusting," I said, giving him a dirty stare. "Why don't you do it? You can be her boyfriend too."

"She is like my sister. I cannot marry her. You can."

"And you talk this way about your sister?" I asked, really angry.

"Forget what I said. I just said what you wanted to hear. The point is that you both are made for each other. Think about it. Imagine her walking with you on these romantic moonlit streets, her hands in yours instead of mine—your pudgy friend. How does that sound?"

"Why are you holding my hand?"

"Just to give you a feel. Make her happy, buddy. That's all life is about. Tonight, when you go home, I want you to imagine her as you would your wife, and no, not the sex part. As soon as you open the door to your house, imagine her running straight into your arms. Can you hear her saying, *'I was so lonely, dear. I missed you all day long.'?*

Then imagine yourself kissing her nose, which goes red, and she runs away to the kitchen to bring you a cup of tea."

"Wait a minute. Wait a minute. I can't take it anymore. Are you making fun of me? Because this hurts a lot."

He looked at me with eyes full of disbelief. "I know the world hurts you and I, as a friend, can't do anything to save you from it. But I am the only one trying to make your life easier by giving you some hope and some belief for the future. So, what if it's just an imagination, a flight of fancy? They, too, will come true for you someday. I, as a friend, want them to. Until fancy makes you happy, it is more valuable to us than reality. Never forget that. *The world means nothing unless we see it in our own way.*"

I didn't understand it then, but what he was asking of me was to run away from reality. But, as painful as the reality was, running away from it seemed like a very appealing option to me.

"Learn to dream, boy! It will be best for you to detach yourself from reality for a while. Stop accepting reality with all its dirtiness and disappointments. Instead, shape it to be as beautiful as your imagination."

With that, he gave me his first smile of the evening.

○ ● ○

I went home that night with dreams in my head, only to open my door to find my fat cousin half-naked, waiting for me to pay the electricity dues.

After an uneventful dinner alone, I managed to snatch the remote at midnight and continued to watch TV till 3 o'clock in the morning.

I never understood why I could never sleep early, even when tired. I tried to think if Prabhu made sense. I tried to contemplate if a girl was what I wanted. I tried to think if that was the reason behind my consistent yearning, longing for *something* that would fulfill me.

But I can't like or love somebody if I don't know the person, even though her eyes did twinkle a lot. Oh darn, those eyes! I had no idea whether I was asleep or awake, or whether it was an intermediate medium between the two.

I decided to talk to her the next day and try to find out whether she was a person worth dreaming about. Finally, at some point, by dawn, I dozed off. So much for my plans, but I never actually managed to talk to her because of my shyness, and I never found out how she was behind those eyes.

Somehow, I never met Madhura after the induction, and it never led to anything as we had thought. She was happily married after a few years. But those eyes of hers stayed with me.

I scribbled:

This isn't the first time, dear;
I have missed many a flights.
Waiting up for hope and yet sliding down,
Blinded by the tunnel-end lights.

As Prabhu said years later, "You should have tried. What was there to lose?"

I don't know. I guess I didn't want to disappoint myself by discovering that she wasn't the one.

This was my complex lacuna—expecting perfection everywhere and believing every story told to me, as long as the story had elements of hope, even if far-fetched.

2.

July'07:

It was Prabhu's birthday that day.

I was working on some small code in the morning that required me to work for a couple of hours in the embedded systems lab. I started late in the morning, saw myself in the lab mirror, and tried to figure out how I was looking.

That day, I didn't meet Prabhu during lunch as he was not in his cubicle. Only in the afternoon, after my work was done and successfully passed over to the team lead, did I get time to pour a cup of coffee for myself from the vending machine and walk up to Prabhu's floor.

It was a big project area, with around 300 people. His location was in the last row, somewhere in the middle, by the window. That led to a very complicated nomenclature for his location.

He was sitting in his seat, looking at his computer screen, scratching his head.

"Am I disturbing you? Too busy revolutionizing the cyber-world?" I asked, smiling and sipping my coffee.

He looked up at me with relief, as if he could see rays of sanity emanating from me, which might be his very first since morning. "My asshole team lead never gives correct instructions. Since morning, I have been doodling with crap, which leads nowhere.

Let me kick his ass. Just wait for me here," and Prabhu stormed towards his team lead as I followed him, curious to see how a rookie kicks his team lead's ass. Prabhu stood by his seat for 5 minutes and, sure enough, returned with his own ass kicked.

"That bastard wants me to try harder. He says I am an idiot for not figuring out how to insert the auto-implementation feature into the code by now."

"Wow, Linus... It looks like you had a rough day. Anyway, I came for something more important. Many happy returns of the day, dude," I said, patting the big guy.

"Thanks, mate. Before I forget... " He opened his drawer and brought out a big box of sweets. The box was almost full, which meant no one had wished him since morning, and his eyes amply told he was genuinely touched that I did.

"Hey, this calls for a party. I think we would have our own little private bash at some nice restaurant," I said.

"Good restaurant? Are you crazy? I don't have money. We'll celebrate at our regular rat-biryani stall. Eat all you can." He said, looking around, "We'll take Puru too."

Rat-biryani stall was the name given by us to a small Chinese food place, near Bremen Square, that served chicken items at ridiculously low prices. Chicken Biryani for thirty bucks was our favorite.

Since we couldn't imagine any meat item served at that low a price, we reckoned that he was serving rat meat. But it tasted okay and was cheap, so we were good with it.

"Why? Did he wish you?" I asked because I seriously doubted it. Purushottam Mahanty was a fellow Bhubaneswar classmate of Prabhu, and both could never see eye-to-eye over anything. Both were assholes in their own right. Puru, as he was fondly called, was full of himself and, when not drunk, did some fine poetry on women's breasts and nudity. He even recited it to girls who understandably failed to see the *'aesthetic'* value objectively and almost always confused it with obscenity. Hence, he was kept at an arm's length by them. He had similar problems with Prabhu, whom he thought was a big dick, to be fired immediately from the office. Both constantly irritated each other.

"Of course he didn't. That's the point. I will still prove my magnanimity by asking him to accompany us to our lavish party."

"He wouldn't accept the invitation without the booze."

"Then we will get him booze. This is our day. We refuse nobody nothing," he said cheerily, quite enjoying his fantasy of being crowned *'king of generous parties at shitty places'*.

So, we approached Puru, who gladly accepted our offer of free booze, and he even returned the favor by wishing Prabhu a happy birthday.

"How is this asshole so generous today?" Puru asked me.

"Beats me!"

We went to the location beneath the banyan tree, where a couple of chairs were placed in front of the small biryani stall.

"Let's get you booze." So, these guys bought a bottle of cheap liquor for 100 bucks.

Puru immediately started with the bottle, as we ordered biryani and ate it while constantly analyzing what we were served.

"I think it is some other animal today," Prabhu said, chewing the meat and looking at me with apprehension. "I think it is human meat today."

"Do you think I am in the mood to care?" I blurted out, my mouth stuffed.

"That's my boy," he said, swallowing the remainder of *'whatever it was'*.

Before long, the evening transitioned into the darkness of the night.

"What's the bill amount?" Prabhu asked the stall owner who was probably from the north-east.

"₹ 200, sir,"

"Good. My wasted friend here will give you the money," he said, pointing at Puru.

"Let's go," Prabhu said to me.

"H-hey, wait..." Puru opened his eyes and tried to speak, but he was too drunk to argue.

"It's okay. I paid for your drinks; now you will pay for our food," Prabhu said, getting up from his chair.

"Arseho... " But Puru couldn't even complete his sentence.

We started walking away.

Puru was too drunk to even talk properly and suddenly started to chase Prabhu, trying to catch him. Prabhu knew how murderous his grip would be now; he ran for his dear life. I stood thoroughly embarrassed and yet in splits as these guys chased each other for 20 minutes on the street.

It was a comic sight for us but not for the people around, who could clearly see the sadistic pleasure we were deriving from this exercise.

So, these two ran and ran till Puru lost his balance, slipped, and fell into a dirty puddle on the street.

"Wait. Is he dead?" I ran behind Prabhu.

"How does it matter? Pay the bill or run for your dear life like me. I don't have any money," he said, grinning.

"What the... I don't think I have either. Let's check Puru's pockets."

Puru had passed out in the puddle, blissfully dreaming and grinning simultaneously. We rummaged his pockets and found five hundred bucks, with which we paid the stall owner's bill. Then, as we started walking away, he called us back.

"Aren't you forgetting something?" The stall owner asked.

"I don't think so. I never tip." Prabhu went into aggression mode in an instant. The guy was very touchy about money.

"I meant your friend." He looked at us incredulously.

Since it was getting late and neither of us wanted to take Puru back home, we decided to get him aboard a bus and let him go home by himself.

"But shouldn't we accompany him? He is only half awake. I don't think he can make it to his home safely."

"Of course he can. Stop undue caring. This is Puru we are talking about. If I know him even a little by now, we shouldn't worry even a penny about him. He will reach home safe and sound. Trust me!" Prabhu rarely looked this confident about anything.

So, we got the guy on the right bus and asked the conductor to just push him down the bus when his stop came. Puru, meanwhile, was still smiling about something and reciting a poem of his. We trusted him to crawl back to his room from the stop.

When we were done, we went home and slept peacefully.

The next day, I got up as usual and went to the office. I was just about to start work when I received a call from Prabhu.

"Hello," he sounded frightened, as only then would he whisper on the phone.

"Hi," I said while simultaneously replying to a daily status report mail on Lotus Notes[10].

"You know what happened?" he asked in a hushed voice.

"No, I don't. Please update me," I said, still checking my emails for today's work.

"Puru hasn't come to the office today. So, I called him. He says he's in the hospital. He was so tired that he passed out on the phone." He was talking very fast, an old habit of his when very tense.

"What happened?" I asked. I suspected a prank.

"I have no idea. I think we should visit him."

I wondered what could have happened. I had this disturbed feeling the entire afternoon. Just when I was about to call Prabhu to inquire which hospital Puru was in, I got a call from Prabhu.

"From what he said, apparently last night, Puru tried to molest some lady on the bus. The crowd on the bus thrashed him. I never expected such a lowly act from Puru." I could imagine him shaking his head over the phone.

"Well, I must say he finally lived up to my expectations," I said, sighing over the phone. I felt bad about myself. I should have felt guilt about leaving him alone on the bus, but I felt none.

---

[10] *Enterprise email system owned by IBM earlier. It is now purchased by HCL and known as HCL notes.*

We visited Puru at the hospital.

He lay on the bed, his body covered in bandages, his eyes fixed on eternity; tranquil yet shaken. He looked at us with an affection we knew we didn't deserve. We heard his version, and it seemed he had no intention of molestation; he was just trying to ask his home address to the lady. But since he was drunk, the lady misunderstood and started shouting.

"You must have touched her at inappropriate places," Prabhu said, frowning.

"I don't know. But I do remember touching something soft," said Puru.

Anyway, people didn't wait before breaking all hell loose over our well-intentioned molester. Before he knew it, people were merrily pummeling him to a pulp. Now that we knew the truth, we decided to bury the episode and seal our mouths so that the story never reaches the office.

But surprisingly, someone leaked the story to the girls, and from then on, Puru was completely banned from any kind of batch social outing that involved girls.

○●○

That evening, we were standing on the office terrace, looking down the rooftop parapet. It was a huge open circular terrace, vast like half a football field, the rest half of which was our indoor cafeteria. Prabhu asked me again if I was upset over something.

I was upset, but not sure why.

"You are again having one of your loneliness attacks," he said, looking into my eyes. "I can figure it out when I see that far-away look in your eyes."

I gave him a weak smile and kept watching the clouds drift away. I was feeling very alone—an abyss inside me that nothing could fill. A distant dream came into my eyes that nobody else could see—something that made me very sad. Something nobody could understand—least of all myself. During those moments, Prabhu would look at me incredulously as I traveled alone in some faraway land.

"Come back. Come back," he said, waving his hand in front of my eyes.

I looked at him, amused.

"Come back, where?" I asked with a smile.

"Back to this heaven—where girls are waiting for you to approach them and save them from monsters like Abhinav. You are an artist, man! You deserve to be here, on the earthly plane," he said.

"I am too tired to wire myself back to reality. Nobody waits for me here." I looked at him with tired, empty eyes.

"You break my heart," he said in a crestfallen tone, as if I had stepped on it.

I kept looking far away at a whitish-orange cloud that looked alive to me. It was something I wished to merge with and vanish one day, just to escape from reality. To be done with the worries of life, disappointments, and frustrations.

"Do you know Mitali?" Prabhu asked me.

"No. Who is she?" I said, still looking at infinity.

"She works with me on my project. She is supremely white-skinned and has gray eyes. The white ghost... remember?"

"Oh yes. Mitali Acharya. She is very thin and white and looks like an angel. Dirt avoids settling on her skin because it's afraid of maligning perfection; it's almost impossible to miss her. Her skin makes her conspicuous in any group of brown-skinned people. What happened?" I asked, immediately interested. I had seen her around Prabhu's project floor.

"I have been talking to her about you," he said.

"What about me?"

"You know, you are not the only one lonely here. Beautiful, geeky ladies get lonely too, as she did. Big deal! Stop being so full of yourself," he said, banging his fist on the wall.

"What's her problem got to do with me?" I got to the point directly.

"Now we are talking," he said, moving forward enthusiastically. "It has everything to do with you. I have been trying to put you in her—I mean, in her thoughts. You see, every girl has these dreams of her perfect man. If she starts seeing a person colored in the colors of her own dreams, she will love that person. That takes time. I have been doing that for you, feeding chunks of you to her fantasies. Don't ask me how I know all this about girls. Some US research... What do you care?"

I saw that face and smile and knew I was in the vicinity of pure evil.

"Brilliant. Now I understand why we are such close friends," I said, smiling.

"She is innocent, man. Just like a child. Don't break her heart, or I will kill you. It is supposed to help you both. Meet her and dig her. Don't get into that friendship mess that you always try to get into. That hurts girls more," he said with phony sincerity.

"But what exactly have you been doing?" I asked him.

"I have been trying to sell you to people—correction, I'm trying to sell your idea to people; to portray your innate awkwardness, shyness, and absent-mindedness in a way that will appeal to girls."

"So basically, you have been pimping me out?" I couldn't think of another way to phrase it accurately.

"Please don't insult me by using an extreme word like that," he said, covering his ears. "Appreciate the subtle difference. I am not

selling your body (*that is too crude for a guy of my capacity!*); I am selling
your idea. Hence you can, at best, call me a mental pimp—or better
still, your soul pimp."

This guy was surely God.

"You are awesomeness personified!" I said it with affection in
my eyes.

"Thank you. I have been speaking to her since the day we joined
the project. She is awkward and innocent, just like you. She is too
geeky, so nobody speaks with her. This is where I jump in. I drilled
a hole in her first, gained her confidence by being all ears and heart
for her, and tried to be her buddy and confidante in this cruel, cold
IT world. I found ways to meet her to clear my doubts and to ask
really complicated, irrelevant questions. But it makes her happy.

By the way, did I mention she is four years older than us? She is
my mentor."

"No, you didn't. You have this talent for forgetting to mention
the most important facts," I said, disappointed. "She is too old for
me."

"Is that so?"

"No, I'm just kidding," I said, smiling.

"Now it's time to pour you in—drop by drop. That has begun
already. I have told her everything about you—about how you are
the sweet lamb lost in the band of programming wolves. On how
you feel the need to be defined beyond the variables one defines in

a regular C program. On how you need to find your identity in this world of chaos—of finding your inspiration that goes beyond just technical efficiency. Then how can I miss your personal information and background?"

I was losing myself in those words. "And?" I asked.

"And I saw a glint of interest behind those glasses of hers," he said triumphantly.

"A glint, huh?" If somebody portrayed someone to me like this, there would be plenty of glints in my eyes too.

That night, as usual, I couldn't sleep because I shared the same room with my crazy cousin, who liked to keep the fan turned off, and I wasn't used to sleeping in an oven. So, unless I was very tired, falling asleep was difficult for me. Around 1:30 a.m. in the night, I started feeling sleepy and patiently waited to doze off, but instead, my phone rang. It was a message from an unknown number.

The message read somewhat like this: *'The alethiometer needles are equally spaced over the dial. But are we ready for the fourth needle to show us the truth, and is the truth ready for us?'*

WTF!

Then another message arrived: *'Can you see fog in the night, a rainbow of my plight, pleasure of sight, and color of delight?'*

And then one more: *'Do you think Leonardo da Vinci saw the Mona Lisa while painting her, or do you think it was his imagination of a perfect beauty?'*

These were supremely incorrect questions to be asked of a sleepy dude in the latter half of the night!

'Fuck you, Bastard. I am going to kick your ass if you send me any more messages.' was all I replied to that number, limited by my vocabulary. The messages stopped after that.

That killed my sleep. I went out of the room and watched TV until 6 in the morning, after which I was too tired to hold anything except sleep in my eyes.

I got up late and went to the office.

The entire day, I dabbled in some low-end work and worked like a dog on some tasks that needed no more intelligence than that of a dog. I just killed time and somehow worked till the evening.

I waited patiently in the cafeteria for Prabhu, but he didn't arrive. I called him and had him come to our usual spot on the terrace.

"Hey, you know what? Some strange things happened last night. Someone kept sending me random messages."

"Like what?" Prabhu asked.

I read him the first message.

"Funny. Let me respond," he said, taking my phone away.

He typed in a message, but then he saw the number and the received message, and something about it made him stare at it for a while. I could see his face flush with color, and with it, his memory returning. He didn't send his message.

"What happened?" I noticed a conspicuous change in his demeanor.

"Umm... nothing."

"Whose phone number is it?" I asked, now suspicious.

"It's really not important. Let it be."

"So, you know the person?"

"I do. Don't you have any work to do? Let's meet later," he started walking away from the ledge.

"Should I call this guy?" I asked, knowing he couldn't escape this time.

"Don't. Okay, you got me. I know you will find out somehow. This is Mitali's number," he said, looking at me and minutely noting my reactions.

I tried to look mildly shocked. "Oh, so care enough to explain how she got my number?"

"Frankly," he said with a grimace. "No, not really. You take matters to heart."

"What's the deal, big guy?"

"The deal is this. I went to her home yesterday evening. I joined her on the office bus and went to drop her off at her home while talking to her all the while. You know she gets involved with anyone quickly. She lives alone, as nobody even talks to her, and she couldn't find any roomies. I went to her home. She cooked us dinner. While talking, we didn't realize it was past 11 p.m. Since it was too late, she let me stay, and she slept in the inner room."

I could see loopholes in his narrative, but merely to edge him on, I said, "Okay, so... "

"Guess what the topic of our discussion was?" He continued, even though I had already gotten a clue. "*You!!*"

"Oh really? So interesting!"

"You know what's even more interesting? I believe she is single, and apparently, the description of the man of her dreams matches you. I talked to her about your personality traits, your background, your nature, etc. She said she is not looking for a serious relationship, and if you were fine with it, you could be her boyfriend."

"What? Did she say that? She actually said that? Oh... " I felt choked and out of the air, but I dare not show my interest yet.

"Then?"

"Then I left in the morning, worked all day, and here I am drinking coffee with you."

"What about the damn messages?"

"Oh yes, she asked me for your number sometime in the night. I told her that I had already talked to you about her and that you have her number."

"You are lying. She wouldn't allow you to sleep at her house," I said with a degree of firmness.

"Excuse me?" he said, putting down his cup. "She wouldn't allow *you*. But thanks to me, now she will. Never doubt my ability to get through and make a way. By the way, do *you* remember how *you* replied to her messages?"

I showed him the reply.

"I know what you sent. You are such a halfwit!" He looked up from my mobile, smiling at me. "Oh dear!" and smiled some more. "You sure know how to prick a balloon. Her ecstasies and fantasies were all rudely brought down to earth and properly buried by your poetic replies. Can't you make out from the language that it's a lady? I mean, even a child will figure that out."

"I am no more a child, and when the fuck did you give me her number?"

"Didn't I? So sorry."

"No, wait a minute. I don't think you have the balls to do something like this. No, my friend, I think you are exaggerating again," I said, shaking my head.

"You will be very sorry if you don't believe me this time," he said, raising his eyebrow. "Anyway, I need to ask her; if she's okay to compromise a bit and manage with an imbecile?"

"And also ask her why she lets people like you in her house." I spoke.

"If a person has the knack of controlling minds, he can be anywhere he pleases. Learn that, and you will never be unhappy again," he said.

"Sometimes I don't understand a word of what you say."

"My words are meant to be implemented, not understood. I am not a man of words like you." He had a knack for closing his repartees with something even more quizzical.

○●○

That night, as I went home, I had just one thing in mind: to make sure I had a good meal and a decent sleep.

I was tired of my half-dreamy sleep full of weird nightmares and frustrating endings. Me falling down the building, me failing an exam, me trying to run away from people trying to murder me with swords and knives, me trying to write a code without error to clear the test that would save my job, and many other erstwhile dreams that always ended with my getting up the next morning with a painful headache and an even painful heartache.

Something should have changed over the years, but it never did. God should have listened to me by now, but somehow, I never got a response. Every day was a battle, and every battle was lost. I had given up my dream of living life with dignity, honor, and self-confidence. I was riddled with doubts over my ability. I was running a race I knew I had already lost.

And these days, sometimes, when I slept at night, I would subconsciously pray to God that I would never wake up. That somehow, I would lose myself in that darkness, and my consciousness would not see the light of the next day. A petty way of escape, I know, but still an attempt towards trying to maintain a degree of dignity while leaving this cruel and competitive world—in the sense that I, at least, fought till death gulped me down. Only I knew I had chosen to go down the darkness—a bleak exit but still an escape.

I would choose it any day, anytime.

I didn't feel like waking up, I didn't feel like going to the office, and I didn't feel like living even a second of my lowly meaningless existence. And yet, I had to!

I ate some crap at our usual ultra-cheap Chinese stall and went home to find the TV remote captured by my cousin. Having been left with no other choice but to sleep, I closed my eyes on the bed and tried to escape into the comforting darkness and looseness of sleep, slightly wondering what dream I would see tonight.

Sleep just wouldn't come that easily. So, I got up and walked by the window and watched through the windows of the flats in the apartment in front of us—blurred and fuzzy images of people living their usual mundane lives with satisfaction. Partly bald men with potbellies chatting on their mobiles half-naked, women cooking in the kitchen, half a dozen windows glowing in the rapidly changing neon lights of TV as people watched some mind-numbing favorite sitcom of theirs, pretty girls with cute bums looking at me suspiciously as I looked back at them; lives of half-dead people for whom good life meant nothing more than money, cars, clothes, a cozy home, and sex.

I chuckled to myself, knowing I lacked all the above items in my life. But I knew I hated those people, and I knew the only reason I liked Prabhu was because I hated them.

I also knew we would never find solutions to whatever our problems were. I went back to my bed and closed my eyes. I was tired of the world just as the world was tired of me. I just prayed a bit that my sleep would never end and took my leap away from consciousness.

○●○

The dream I had that night was fluid, and it kept changing. I found myself sleeping on the road in the rain with nothing except my inners and a countdown alarm beside me, which kept ringing every now and then, supposedly to wake me up for the office. I saw my cousin sitting in the rain watching TV, clutching his remote.

He kept yelling at me between commercials to pay the damn electricity bill of 5,000 bucks. And then I saw myself feeling cold at my heart, which had stopped beating, short of blood and hope. I needed life, I needed blood, I needed hope, and I needed the bloody rain to stop. After the alarm rang for the nth time, I brought forward my arm to hit the snooze button, only to find that this time around it was indeed morning.

My head had this weird pain again as I got up half an hour before my bus time. I held my head with both hands to let the blood flow resume. Prabhu had messaged me in the night.

But his message was terse. *'Get pure-white chrysanthemums to the office. It's her b'day. And wear that pink shirt of yours. She likes pink.'*

What the fuck! I didn't have a pink shirt. Is he under dope at all times? I called the guy. He would never pick up his phone in the morning. It was the time for his dead slumber and today was not going to be any different.

I put on the best-smelling clothes from the cupboard as none were washed or ironed, sprayed some from that long empty bottle of deo, checked whether I had enough money for dine, wine, and flowers divine, and I was off, running on the streets searching for some damn shop that would give me those white chrysanthemums. I was running so fast that my shirt was already sweaty. I knew a certain shop that would be open at that time of the day; one where a bald man with a bow, mustache, and suit like that of a waiter would stand on the street with his table full of flowers. I never thought he would find a customer in me. It was an embarrassing place to be caught standing. And yet, this was the guy I was searching for today.

Obviously, owing to the wonderful law of Murphy's, that guy hadn't turned up today with his flowers. So, I went around the square in an auto, searching for some shop that sold real flowers. Believe it or not, I found some white chrysanthemums as soon as I heard my company bus leave the stop.

Faced with a clock that always ran faster than me, I raced towards an auto to catch up with the lost time. But these pre-paid autos waited till they were entirely filled with people, and so I was left with plenty of free time to count my curses.

I reached the office stylishly late—by around 50 minutes—and my body was pierced by the dirty and judgmental gazes of people on our floor as I walked past them to my seat. I avoided looking at my project manager, but I knew she would never miss this crime of mine. I avoided the infrared lasers in her eyes by not looking at her.

Prabhu didn't come to the office that day as he wasn't well, nor did I broach the topic when I called him. I went up to *INSITE* umpteen times to check if Mitali still sat where she was supposed to.

She sat there quietly like an angel, working, and I wondered if I should wish her and give her the flowers as per the plan. That would have been hell weird. I chuckled a few times, imagining the expression on her face if I had.

But as I was leaving for home late that night, I cleaned my drawer. I took another look at those fast-withering flowers. They wouldn't last the night, and they weren't mine to keep.

I picked them up and went up to *INSITE*.

The stations were empty; people had left. Ensuring no one was watching me, I placed them neatly on her desk and returned.

Next morning, before she arrived at the office, they might get thrown away by the cleaning staff, but they would leave a scent of my presence and of their own purpose in her life, no matter how paltry, no matter how aimless...

○ ● ○

Every evening, we would roam the Pune streets purposelessly, talking with each other.

We would see the buildings, the people, and the lanes and eat and drink any damn thing we would feel like in those three hours, just because we had money in our pockets. That was a freedom only money could buy! We would speculate endlessly in which building and on which floor the girls of our batch might be living, what they might be doing at that very moment, whether we had any chance of ever talking to them, and what we would do if they actually did talk to us.

Prabhu was an encyclopedia—a giant trash bin of useless information. He had seen every A-B-C-grade movie in every language. He had read all the books I knew the names of, and still, all he was interested in, was talking about my love life.

"You know Priyanka (*from our batch*) is the one who likes you. She has innocence in her eyes. It's not Pooja; it's Priyanka you will marry, I tell you. That girl has a slutty laugh. You are lonely—too lonely sometimes—and if you don't find a girl like her quickly, even I won't be able to save you. You are sliding down, minute by minute. The world is out there waiting for you, full of girls. But you are a slave to that shell of yours. And I, my friend, can't fulfill all your needs."

"Actually, you can!" I said mischievously.

"Umm, yeah, in a way, you are right; I can. But I don't wish to seduce a vulnerable friend like you, and you can surely find better asses than mine. Abhinav and Rohit are out there having fun with Pooja, and here we are standing outside their building, unable to figure out the floors they live on. What a pair of losers we are!!

One of these days, I would love to see you just grab her by her waist and kiss her without saying a damn word."

I gave out a nervous half-laugh, knowing I would never be able to do something that brash. I lacked his guts and insanity.

"You have this tight system of rules that bind you. Just get drunk one day, break that whisky bottle on Abhinav's head, and without thinking or blinking, tell Pooja you want sex. She is so sophisticated; she would sleep with you simply out of politeness. She hates saying no to people who demand anything forcefully from her. I can't see any other reason why she would hang out with Abhinav. Forget sex; do you even have the guts to ask her out for a coffee?"

"Stop giving me ideas, man. I am a shy guy, as I have always been. I just don't talk with girls. I would never be able to do so without looking at their assets. I can't look them in the eye because if I do, I have this overpowering urge to kiss them. I can't be gay like Rohit and feel nothing while talking to them. Nor would I like to violate my code and do something untoward that I would regret later."

"Yawn!" He gave me a bored look. "You know what your problem is? You overthink. If you like someone's ass, just go ahead and touch it. If there's one thing you need to learn from me, it's my impulsiveness. C'mon, let's try it," he said, giving a small clap.

"Look around; let's find a girl you like; then you go and touch her ass. It will make you feel better, trust me."

"I will never do that. I am not a creep like you."

"Listen to me. A hungry man lusts for food, a thirsty one for water. Are they sinners too? You are hungry and thirsty, my friend. What's your problem if you get what you want?" He said it in a frustrated tone. "You know in many ways; you are everything that's wrong with our society. You are not a go-getter. You never do what you want. You live a half-life full of fears, rules, codes, ethics, shyness, shame, and all that bullshit. You mean well, and you get shit. I mean dirty, and I get shit. What's the difference between you and me now? We are both losers, but at least I am happier than you. I never stopped myself. I never denied myself the stuff I wanted."

"Stop giving me *gyan*. You know, as I know, I will live longer. Patience is the key to success. Someday, my day will come."

"Fuck you and your long life. Today is your day. It's now—here!! There's the girl of your dreams waiting for you. She's the path to your happiness, and you know that. What stops you from not being a loser and asking her out? She wants your help. She wants you to save her from wolves like Abhinav, and here you are, acting like a sissy farting out random philosophies at me just because I have the time to listen to you," he was making sense. "There's nothing wrong with it. You are the underdog, remember? Get her *'under'* you and fuck her like a *'dog'*. Then get over it and do something meaningful. For God's sake, stop stopping yourself!"

"But I don't want sex. I want a companion—a friend who is a girl. I want to know her before I touch her."

"That's not possible," Prabhu said, shaking his head. "Boys don't want friends when they think of a girl."

"I do!"

"No, you don't!"

"I want a meaningful relationship, a romance, and real love and affection, not just sex."

"You are talking like a girl right now. I really feel like kissing you. Okay, maybe you have a point, but you also want sex, correct?"

"Maybe."

"Someday you will get her. When you do, promise that you won't forget me!"

"I promise!" I said, smiling.

"So, then, we can have threesomes?" He raised his eyebrow.

"Fuck you!" I showed him the finger.

He didn't mind that at all but then he went from happy to somber.

"By the way, there's something important that you should know," he said. "I am leaving my sister's home this weekend. My brother-in-law kicked me out."

"You will be leaving?" I felt something break inside me. Is he serious? What will I do without this guy?

"Apologize and bury the conflict. Where will you go at such short notice?" I said breathless.

"There's no conflict from my end, dude. He thinks I am a loser, and he seems unable to tolerate me in his house anymore. He and my sister are fighting over me now. Finally, today it was she who told me to get lost. I wouldn't want their marriage to suffer because of me. So, you see, I am short on options. Unless of course... "

"Unless of course?"

"I could move in with you at your cousin's house."

I gulped. My cousin would never allow it. Besides, Prabhu was not a safe reference. He was bound to cause problems one way or another.

"What's taking you so long? I will pay any rent you want me to pay."

"It's not about the rent, dude. We're full, and you know my cousin is an asshole."

"So then, you move out and stay with me. We will move somewhere closer to the city." Again, I gulped. I wasn't sure I wanted to move in with this guy. I liked my night's sleep whenever I could manage to fall asleep, and he was a sworn maniac. How long can one be a party to someone's insanity before losing one's own sanity?

"I don't think it's a good idea. I am already well settled, and this place is closer to the office as well."

"So then, what? Are you saying we are roaming like this for the last time?"

I felt my heartbeat weaken.

"C'mon, dude, you know it would be disastrous for both of us. We don't have anyone except each other."

"The only options I see are that you apologize to your brother-in-law or move somewhere in this area," I said with finality.

"Then, basically, I have no options at all. Do you know the rates around here? I can't afford it. This area is just for rich people like you. And tell me, who will move in with me if you don't?"

"I can't afford my place either. Half my salary is gone in the rent. But I can't leave this area."

"Fine. I don't wish to force you," he said solemnly. "I guess it's goodbye, then!"

And he did move away that very same weekend.

He called me before leaving, but I was asleep and didn't hear the ring. Later in the day, I called him.

"How did you get it so fast?"

"What do you care? You didn't even help me find options, and you didn't help me with my baggage."

"You know well; I have been busy and tired."

"Everyone's too busy and too tired when it's my work. Anyway, as you know, my sister's a project manager at Wipro. She pulled some strings and got one of her juniors to rent me this flat. I would be sharing it with another guy."

"Cool. When can I visit?"

"What for?"

"To meet you and see your new home."

"Come whenever you get the time and are less busy and tired."

"Oh, c'mon. Stop being so finicky."

"You can come now if you can. Call me when you reach the stop. I would come to pick you up," he said and cut the phone.

I could sense bitterness in his voice and heart, and so even though I was tired, I went to his place that very evening. It was a good 10 miles away. I called him from the street once I reached his area, and he appeared promptly to guide me to his flat.

○ ● ○

Prabhu kept chanting about the pros of his area and how blessed he was to have found such a heavenly abode. The locality of the apartment did look good, the lift seemed to work, and so I, for a moment, cursed myself for not moving out of my cousin's place.

"And you have no idea how cool my RP *(Room Partner)* is," he said, tapping on the door of his flat on the fifth floor.

In a moment, the door was opened by a half-naked guy in nothing more than shorts.

"Hey, Aditya!"

"Hey!"

He had a very unremarkable yet sharp face with a pointed frame. He looked freshly bathed and had an eating plate in his hand, which I later realized was for worship.

"Seems to be a very religious guy," I whispered to Prabhu.

"You bet. He, too, works at Wipro. I moved in last night. He was so affectionate and friendly, and he invited me to sleep in his bedroom. He said I reminded him of his brother. I think I have finally found a friend and a companion... ahh," he sighed, and so did I.

He was clearly hurt by my behavior. But aren't there reasons for everything?

I roamed around the house. It was a cool 1 BHK. The rooms were spacious, and the house was airy. We stood on the balcony, checked out other flats, and chatted until it was dark and gloomy outside.

"The place is good." I confirmed my judgment. "And so is your roomie," who was still standing in front of a God frame with that plate in hand. It was like an hour now. "But I need to leave."

"Tell me something. Can you sleep here tonight? It is fine, I mean. Adi will not have any problems."

"That's fine, bro, but I need to go."

○●○

For a few days, Prabhu couldn't stop basking in the greatness of his newfound angel. But slowly, with time, this chatter kept on subsiding until he stopped talking about him completely. These days, he avoided any topic whatsoever of his relations with his roommate.

"We fight a lot. There's really nothing much to say." He would end the conversation with a casual shrug.

After a few more days, things were back to normal.

"Don't take his name. I so want to kick his ass," he said, slamming his cup of tea on the table so hard that some tea spilled over his hand. "*Oyeee*, why do they heat it so much?" He wiped his hand with the tissue. "You know, from now on, we will be calling him a bastard. Call him by that name."

"But, dude, he is your angel, your brother. I thought you slept with him every night. Is he not good enough anymore?" I said it with a nasty smile.

"Stop messing with me, dude. That thing is just too sentimental. To top it all off, he's a thief and a sadist."

"Look who's talking?"

"I am an iota better. I don't steal money from others' pockets, and at the very least, I don't make holes in people's underwear with incense sticks."

"What the hell are you talking about?"

"I thought he was religious. Bull shit! As soon as we started having these arguments, I began noticing my inner wears ridden with these holes that can only be done by those incense sticks, ones this jerk burns day and night. So last night, I confronted him."

"What the hell? You accused him of making holes in your underwear?"

"...and that he should stop this show of purity and religion in front of me. I can't tolerate hypocrites. And I can't tolerate him because he is dumb and clueless as to why he does what he does. Suffocating me with smoke all day under the guise of religion, then using the same incense sticks to make holes in my clothes at night."

"C'mon, you are taking it a bit too seriously. A few small pinholes here and there are harmless."

"I don't think you understand the situation. Let me explain. I use that cloth to cover my butt," he said, actually groping his butt. "I don't like holes in it!"

"I get you. How did he take it?"

"He said nothing."

"Nothing?"

"Nothing. But the very next day, I found my innerwear burned down near the stove. He purposely didn't throw it out so that I could see them."

"You mean... you don't mean to say... " I asked wide-eyed.

"Yup. He is a pyromaniac."

"Oh... "

"I got so pissed off that, in front of his eyes, I broke his phenyl bottle in the hall. Now our house is permeated with this weird, suffocating smell. It's impossible to stay there. But both of us are so angry that neither of us will clean up the mess."

"But... but... how will you breathe?"

"The question is not how we breathe or whether or not we breathe. The question is who breaks down first."

I took a moment to digest the situation and find some logic in the scenario. I failed to find any.

"So, what's your next move?"

"Talking to the house owner and getting this bastard kicked out. If he's a psycho, I am no less."

"Good for you. He did turn out to be your brother after all."

○●○

"Ever wondered where that milk has come from?" Prabhu asked with mischief in his eyes the next day, as he saw me intently eating my cornflakes in the cafeteria.

"It has come from some dealer's dairy," I said, eating my flakes with a crunching sound. Though they were soggy, it felt amazing when they made my teeth happy with something to crunch upon.

"No, I mean the source."

I didn't answer. I knew being a sadist he would find some way to make anything I find enjoyable sound disgusting.

"This milk has come from some animals' breasts. It's not that clean if you were to imagine its journey. You seemed to be enjoying it, so I just thought I should let you know."

I put down my spoon and looked at him with tired eyes. "What's your problem?"

"My point *(except, of course, to disgust you)* was that once you block your mind from thinking in the directions that are disgusting, you stop making yourself guilty. Then it doesn't matter what you do."

"There's no reason to feel guilty about drinking milk."

"Is there not? You are, in effect, drinking the right of some baby donkey or baby monkey, and you argue there's nothing wrong?"

"Baby calf. And I have paid the money to the dairy owner. It's his sin now," I said, smiling.

"There you go. As long as you can justify your sins, they aren't sins. Any disgusting act of yours, if justifiable, no longer remains a sin. So, there are no sins for people who care enough to justify them. In other words, you are a sinner, and I am not. You see, you keep feeling guilt for any action you take. That's a trademark of the sinner. I never did feel any such guilt."

"That's because you are shameless,"

"And you are shameful. Look who's happier. Now that we have reached a consensus on who's black and who is white, let me tell you that you are everything that I hate about this world. If you are a slave, I am free; if you are evil, I am good; if you are sadness, I am delight; if you are darkness, I am light."

"Bravo," I said, clapping my hands. "I am done. Let's go."

"But seriously, think about what I said," he said as we picked up our bags.

"Yes, I get it. I will try to be less shy from now on."

"Not just that. Think about the fact that I am the son of God and find some way to worship me."

"You are not God's son. You are the devil's father. The only way to save this world is to put a cross through your chest. So, appreciate the fact that I am a normal guy and don't care about the world," I said, smiling.

He saw me finishing the bowl and waited some seconds until I had consumed the last spoon.

"I talked to my house owner," he said. "I told him what a danger my roommate is to civilized society. I explained the incident to him and concluded by saying that the guy should be rehabilitated and treated psychologically. I was most considerate, the way I put it."

"Alright, what did he say?" I said, trying to speak without spilling out the milk from my mouth.

"He said I was paranoid. Aditya has been living long enough in the apartment, and he never had any problems. Since I was the one with a problem, I should be the one to get out. He called Aditya, and they both had a long chat about how I, in actuality, was a bigger problem to civilized society. The bastards really fucked my ass figuratively. Then the owner gave me an ultimatum to leave the place in a week."

"Why would he say that? This is an injustice. What would you do now?"

"I don't know, man. The house owner believes every word of my roommate. If it's my word against his, I lose."

"So, when are you leaving?"

"I am not. I finally lost my cool and said I was not leaving the apartment, no matter what. You should have seen me in action. I was shouting and shrieking, and they were completely taken aback. I said if Aditya didn't leave the apartment in a week, I would approach the police against both of them for mental harassment."

"Incredible, dude." I was amazed.

○●○

That night, Prabhu called me. I didn't pick up his call. He was in the habit of randomly calling me at night if he couldn't sleep. I know—selfishness at its extreme.

I slept without putting further thought into the matter. I woke up late, as usual, missed the bus, and somehow dragged my ass to the office. The work was scarce today, and, to my surprise, I found no missed calls from Prabhu's desk. I finished my work comfortably before lunch and called him at his desk. Nobody picked up. I called him on his mobile. It rang, but he didn't pick up.

Strange, I thought. I called him back many times during the day. No one picked it up.

But the very next morning, he called back. "Bro, I am in trouble. I can't come to the office for a few days."

"What did you do now?"

"For once, it was not me. This time around, I was on the receiving end. I am in the hospital."

"What the... " I cried out aghast.

"I know what you are thinking. No, I didn't try suicide. That bastard Aditya tried to burn me down along with my bed."

"Stop kidding."

"No man! The other night I gave him a piece of my mind and went to sleep. I woke up sometime during the night due to smoke in the room and found myself on fire. The bastard had set alight all my clothes too, along with the bed. I started shouting. Then Aditya rushed in with a blanket, put it on me, and under the excuse of dousing the fire, he beat me to a pulp. Later he called an ambulance, which then took me away."

"Awesome. I so want to be like this guy. He is my idol," was what I wanted to say. But instead, I said, "Hmm, you should have taken the *'Pyromaniac'* angle into consideration. Did you tell the owner?"

"Aditya is working hand in glove with the owner. I wouldn't be surprised if it was the owner's suggestion to scare me away."

"Good that you aren't scared. So, are you approaching the police?"

"Are you insane? I am shit scared. I just threatened them with the police, and they burned me down with my clothes. I can't imagine what would happen if I actually did approach the police. I will be discharged tomorrow morning from the hospital, after which I plan to sleep on the railway platform unless, of course, you generously let me stay with you for a few days."

"All the people are back at the flat. Where will you sleep?"

"I will sleep in the toilet if you so want. But please don't let me stay on the platform," he said, sobbing.

"Dude, grow up. Borrow whatever money you need from me and stay in a lodge till you get something else."

"I have my sister to borrow money from. All I need to do is let them assault my dignity. But I expected you to stand with me in my hour of need."

I knew I should have. But it was too risky to help him. I wonder whether that's the reason why we never get timely help when we most need it. It's too risky to help a drowning man; he may take us down with him!

○●○

Prabhu found another accommodation near Nal-stop at an ultra-cheap rate. It was nowhere near as good as the previous one.

First, the locality was an issue. He lived on the first floor of a shabby independent house with clay roof tiles. The bottom floor was inhabited by the owner, who was a rickshaw driver. To top it all off, Prabhu shared that apartment with another guy—also a rickshaw driver.

Even for a guy with Prabhu's reputation, this was a new low.

"Why do you need to live in a slum? Isn't your salary getting deposited?"

"It's honestly not that bad, but yes, it is cheap, and I need the money. I need to send it home."

"Better stay on the railway platform and save all the money."

"It's illegal, and there's an issue of personal safety. Lots of psycho serial killers roam the city streets at night. I don't want to fall prey to their cold, ruthless, murderous instincts."

"You are paranoid about everything these days. Why are you sending the money home?"

"Mother needs it." He said it solemnly.

"But your father would be working, right? Or is he retired?"

"My father is no more," Prabhu said it so intensely, that I felt something die inside him.

"You never told me..." I suddenly felt sorry for him.

New perspectives give us an eye to look at the possible reasons for insanity, which in turn makes our sympathy feel less guilty when it rolls out.

"Long story! I will tell you sometime when I find you ears enough." He ended the conversation abruptly.

○●○

Our empty hours in *FORDIT* would often be long and lonely. Work would either be too hectic or it would be a long vacuum where we wouldn't know what to do with our time.

Such moments were increasingly sparse, though.

The cycles of stress and vacuum were erratic, each of uneven lengths, leaving us often in a state of psychological disorder. And we were completely cut off from our batch. They would never look at us. They would never talk with us.

"Sometimes I think it's entirely our mistake," I said to Prabhu once, in moments of reflection over our traumatic present. "We are anti-social, not them," I said. He looked at me blankly. "Why can't we just go out and talk to people? Why? What stops us from not being ourselves?"

Prabhu strained his ears to understand the meaning of the words coming out of my mouth. Sometimes he would be in a trance—just not himself.

"Yes. It has been my fantasy too. What would happen if we went to sleep one night, got brainwashed and reprogrammed, woke up in the morning, and started talking to everybody? How would it be if we just woke up as a different person every damn morning?"

"Exactly. We build walls around ourselves and think we are residing in a fortress—deeply protected from the hurt of the world. But before we know it, we are the slaves of our own minds, and the fortress becomes our torture chamber. When will we be free? Freedom from our own selves?"

"I need salvation, man! That's the only thing I need now," he said, looking at his toes gravely. He was in his sandals today and sitting with his legs stretched on a chair in the terrace cafeteria. We would always prefer sitting outside, in the open, away from the chatter.

The evening horizon was filled with gray clouds, and the cool wind reminded me of the lonely evening times when, as a kid, I would stand alone in the window of my home with my father away. There would be no electricity, and mother would be away cooking alone in the kitchen. There would be no one else.

I could silently feel the warmth slipping away from my heart and being replaced by a dull sadness. A state of being completely vulnerable; ear-splitting, silent screams of your mind going unnoticed for lack of a company that may fill you with warmth.

I knew Prabhu was going through something similar, but perhaps more tragic. His hollow eyes, gazing at the infinity of his toe, held many stories, some of which seemed too horrific to share.

"Do you really want to know about my father?" he asked me.

"I do."

"I want to tell you badly, myself. Please don't hate me after this." He took a long pause. "I killed my father."

"Are you crazy?" It was a jolt for me.

"Not literally, dude. But I was the one responsible for his death."

He paused again, trying to put his hurt into words. "See, it's like this. I was preparing for IIT JEE [11] from one of the best possible coaching institutes of the time. He was retired, and his entire hopes were on me—that I would do well and carry forward the family baton. But I screwed up—missed IITs by a good 1000 ranks. My father died that very week due to a heart attack. It was due to the stress of a sudden disappointment. He had been a heart patient for a while. I should have known. I let him down at the wrong time."

I looked at him sadly. How does one console a person who has lost his father? This guy had been living with a lot of guilt.

"Stop being paranoid. How do you know it was you? It could have been anything, you know. Mere coincidence," I said.

He smirked and said, "It's too sad to be a mere coincidence, man!"

It was surprising how he had managed to hold himself up after the blow. He seemed to be reading my mind.

"I couldn't. I was young. I went crazy with sorrow. I was in the hospital for six months, where they gave me shocks night and day to tranquilize me. I wasn't crazy like this, you know." He paused and then looked up again. "This is the new me, and I don't like it one bit," he said bitterly. I looked at him. His eyes were unclear and

---

[11] *Indian Institutes of Technology (IITs) are the best engineering colleges in the country. The only way to get in, then, is to crack JEEs (Joint Entrance Exams), one of the most difficult examinations in the world.*

confused, yet resolute. It is amazing what grief does to people, I thought. No wonder he hated guilt. It had destroyed him entirely.

"It's also the fall from grace that hurts, man. I was reduced from being a numero uno to a petty nobody. My sister hates me. Mother loves me, but that's just because I am her son, even when I know she has every reason to hate me. That hurts bad." And yet he had no tears or emotion in his eyes. Something inside him was dead.

"If only I was less logical. If only I was less intelligent. If only I could convincingly lie to myself that *'I wasn't the reason my old man's dead'* without knowing it's not true, I would be a happy man today."

He looked at me and smiled. "You don't always choose a complicated life, man. Sometimes you just get one, and you live with it. That's all life is!"

There is a reason for insanity of every kind.

My gaze softened as it met his. I knew we understood each other perfectly.

"What about you?" he asked simply.

"What about me now?" I asked with tired eyes.

"I find you intriguing. You are tall, lean, and have an air of a martyr. You have a good frame; try putting some flesh on it. Your face is non-scary, so smile more; it might go well with that softness in your eyes." He paused and looked at me again. "But don't smile too much, as I really don't know if you brush your teeth."

"I do," I lied, embarrassed, remembering all the times I woke up late and compromised on my brushing. He didn't notice.

"You appear like a lost child. Girls like lost children."

"Noted. I can manage that. Yeah," I said, blinking.

"Just work on these two things then—smile more, brush often, or maybe it should be the other way around," he gave me a nod. "And yes, you have personality issues."

"I know."

"Want to tell me why? I can see the GUI[12], but it is important to know the backend story. You know mine." Maybe he anticipated some resistance from me.

I took a deep breath to lighten the stress of narrating things that I didn't feel like. Opening up suddenly seemed like a bad idea, so it was a good enough reason to do it.

"My father's an alcoholic, and my mother is physically and mentally abusive. I used to be academically strong, but I completely lost my will to study and concentrate when we faced acute financial issues during my undergrad, leading to severe bouts of depression for me. Obviously, I fared badly, which led to a less-than-average engineering college, and now I am here only because the economy is doing well, and IT companies need people." I took another breath to re-control that overwhelming stammer that came with

---

[12] *Graphical User Interface.*

this monologue, but I continued, "I also have anxiety issues, which I have always had, and I can express myself best through poetry. It's like a therapy. Anxiety is also because I had done well for myself in previous years and slipped in the past few. I shouldn't have—grades went away along with whatever self-respect and reputation I had garnered for myself."

"Let me say the rest. You take life too seriously," he said, looking at me with concern.

"But don't we all?" I asked, feeling violated.

"Matter of fact summary—Fall from grace," He gave a nervous sigh. "I hope you have a hanky in case you feel like crying. I don't have one. It's a touching story; you earned yourself a meltdown. Good job!"

"Hey, that's a true story," I said, smiling.

"I like you," he said suddenly.

"Thank you," I said, giving him a nod. "I have been trying to like you."

It was a handshake through the eyes with a general feeling of resonating rhythm between us. Effortless stuff!

"You know what? Enough of wallowing in guilt! I love you, and I must find a girl for you before I die. This is one thing I will do in my life if nothing else," he said, getting up.

"Chill, mate! I don't need a girl."

"You don't know what you need. Everybody needs a girl. Decide for yourself when you get one. Dump her if you find her boring," he said in a steely voice.

"It looks like you found your life's purpose." I said, well-knowing Prabhu would stop at nothing this time.

○●○

It started the very next day. As soon as I reached my desk after breakfast, I got a message from Prabhu.

'She is in pink today. Looking absolutely ravishing!' He was talking about Mitali.

In an hour, another message came.

'Standing at her desk. She's bashing me for giving the outlay variables wrong. I smell her perfume... ahaaa... Damn, she smells hot when angry.'

In an hour, another came: *'She's talking with her mom, I guess. Her nose turned cherry red. Good lord, she's livid.'*

I knew what he was trying to do. He wanted me to think of her, imagine her, and fantasize about her. That was his solution to everything—dream about it.

In the evening, he declared, "This can't work. I am asking my manager to shift you to my project *INSITE*. You need proximity."

"That's impossible. My manager would never let me go. I am a person she has invested lots of energy in. Besides, I have learned a lot in my project. Your project will be something totally new. It will be too much hard work for me."

"Do you want the girl or not?" he shouted.

"I don't. C'mon, she's just a girl. I am not going to change my project for some random chick."

"She is not some random chick. She is your Noah—your savior. Things will work out. Just promise me one thing—when they do, you will let them flow and won't sabotage it. It would be fun, I assure you."

"I don't get you! I seriously don't." Why was he hell-bent on hooking me up?

"It's simple. You don't need to stretch but promise me you won't stop yourself when things start rolling. We seriously need some highs in life, man," he said with earnestness.

"Wait a minute. I must ask you this question now. What do you get out of all this?" Things were starting to get too weird in my life. Any person helping me so much was way too suspicious.

He was silent for some moments, then asked me instead, "Are you happy with your life?"

I stood transfixed. How does one answer that? I could not think of anything.

"That is a very important question that must be answered. I know you are not. Maybe something missing from your life is the affection of a girl. We need to find out. So, treat this as an experiment. What I get through all this is some spice in my own life. Fair?"

"Hmm... sounds fair."

"Good. Now you will play along, and we will hopefully have some fun in our dull, dead life riddled with boredom. Pay attention. I want you to think about her. Truly, deeply, and completely think about her. Her tiny little actions, her way of looking at people, her way of looking at you, her favorite cuisine, her favorite pastime, her favorite book—every damn thing about her. Loving a girl is an art, and there is only one way to do it: be obsessed with her. You must excel at obsession to earn her attention."

"Will I be able to do it?" I felt my legs shaking with excitement.

"Trust me, you are a natural!"

○●○

I started paying more attention to her.

Since their project was located just above our floor, sometimes when I would stand in the corridor of our floor, I could see her come out alone and go to the cafeteria.

She would always look preoccupied with her thoughts, her head always unconsciously tilted and her eyes looking somewhere through the floor. It was as if she were walking in a trance.

She had regular lunch hours. I would try to make it to the cafeteria during those hours. It would take her around 25 minutes to finish her lunch. Though she was a slow eater, she would not waste a moment more after she was done. I would leisurely spend an hour or more chit-chatting with Prabhu or my project mates. And yes, she would always be alone!

"She has an aura about her that just repulses people, not unlike you. People feel strongly uncomfortable and tense in her company. She is seriously awkward, man!" Prabhu told me once.

She did have an awkward stance when walking and an unusually sharp gaze with ruthless gray eyes. Those eyes were merciless, and that reflected in the way she would look at people. Her stare was clinical, mechanical, and slightly scary.

And it wasn't just her eyes, but her voice too. It was screechy and intolerant, like an owl.

"How do you get along with her?" I asked Prabhu once, perplexed.

"I get along because I ask a lot of questions, and she genuinely likes to share her knowledge. She loves Unix and loves talking about it. But she isn't a showoff—that is the one thing she is not."

She was surprisingly strong too—tall, lean, but strong. Her sense of dressing was not too primitive either—decent jeans and top. Her hair was long and would normally be nicely curled together in a long ponytail.

"She is actually a very nice person if people care enough to know her. Just like you," said Prabhu. "There's something very normal and unassuming about her. But unlike you, she is completely comfortable with herself."

Prabhu told me she was meticulous about her routine.

"I am always interested in finding out what makes a person tick—yes, the person's clock signal. FYI, her clock has a highly consistent frequency. Basically, what makes her tick is the momentum given by her previous mood pulse. This means she is a person of habit and is much closer to being a robot mind than we are. I envy her," Prabhu said.

"Is she a nerd too?"

"Yes, she is, but with much better personal hygiene. For one, I know she is one girl you won't find boring. Since all nerdy girls are nymphomaniacs, you might get lucky."

"That's a stupid stereotype."

"It is a stereotype for a reason. Learn to be a little optimistic in life," he said, raising his eyebrows.

○●○

But the more I looked at her, the more I thought that she belonged to no stereotype—she was awkward, gooey, and freakish in her own unique way. I would visit Prabhu many times in the day just to catch a glimpse of her working at her workstation. Sometimes I would see her looking at us. She would never acknowledge it.

Never once did I try to approach her. Never once did I try to hear her voice. Never once did I try to attract her attention. But I guess there are things that one cannot control after all.

That evening in the cafeteria, I asked Prabhu, "What's happening with *'Project Drip'*, mate? Am I in yet?"

"Patience, my man! We are almost there."

"Where exactly are you planning to take this, dude?" I asked, slightly dizzy at the way things were shaping up.

"Wherever you want it to go," he looked at me and smiled.

"Ultimately, we have found a girl perfect for your journey towards happiness."

We finished our rum ball, threw away the paper plate, and walked towards the lift. It was evening, and probably, for normal people, it was a good time to leave the office.

"What's pending for you now?" Prabhu asked.

"Not much. Just need to delegate my work to our offshore bosses and ask the ticket owner to reply to my queries from the previous ticket. Half-hour work, tops. What about you?"

"I need to meet my project manager next week to ask him to switch me to another project. I cannot keep working on my present one," he said.

"You change your mood every minute. Do you have any project in mind?"

The lift opened, and we walked in, as did scores of other people, including Mitali. I suddenly noticed she was standing ahead of us.

"That's yet to be decided. Anything but this! I am bored, and the learning is almost nil here," Prabhu said, but I wasn't listening. I was looking at her.

She stood in the corner by the door, silent and completely aloof from the environment. It was as if she had no sort of feedback mechanism with the mortals in the lift. Nobody cared enough to look at her, nor did she care enough to look at people.

But what was surprising was that, unlike in our case, friction was completely absent. I felt the world was built in such a manner as to be indifferent to her, and she was completely comfortable with it. There was no tenseness in the air, not even a remote possibility of possible interaction, and not even resignation. It was as tranquil as a crow sitting on the cow's back—as if she were a different creature totally. And I knew if at all it was possible for anyone to attune to her frequency, it could only be me—just me!

"Why are you smiling?" Prabhu asked.

"I am not," I said, suddenly conscious of the lapse in my facial muscles.

"Yes, you are."

"Don't shout. I am right next to you." I tried to hush him up, but he was too sharp to miss the reason behind the smile.

"Why are you smiling? Tell me why." He raised his voice while looking at her, and I just broke down into a hysteria of delirious smiles that just wouldn't stop no matter how hard I tried.

It had started to happen increasingly. Nervousness is sadistically clever at finding ways of gushing out in all the wrong forms at all the wrong times.

"What's so funny? Is there somebody here who is making you smile?" He said, looking around, leaving nothing to subtlety.

Everybody was looking at us now—everyone except her. She just tilted her head up silently to look at the floor number we were on.

In seconds, the door to the lift opened, and she got out.

Glad she missed our histrionics!

3.

Mitali's version:

I got out of the lift and heaved a sigh of relief. God, guys can be so embarrassing!! In particular, that idiot Prabhu!

I just don't get it sometimes. What do they want? Young teenage boys from small cities in their early twenties working in an IT organization, confusing attraction with life-long commitments and wasting their time and energy on fantasies they are never likely to realize.

I could see the tragedy and the lack of clarity, but also the desperation, frustration, and vulnerability behind it. I had gone through it all and more. I also knew how it would end. I knew all the future stages.

Why won't I? I was one of the 2 million-odd [13]faceless crowd, working in one of the numerous software organizations in India, working night and day behind the same desk, trapped in the professional responsibilities that stay with you 24 x 7. I was a lost identity, a petty nobody lost behind the screen doing a kind of work that had nothing to do with what I had learned in engineering, and I had been doing it for more than 4 years. By any standard, that's an era.

---

[13] *As of 2007.*

In the software industry, it can be a bit too long. It reflects on your mental health. And I was 4 years older than these guys. Do they have no sensitivity to maturity and scale? I felt sad again.

These freaking moods! I was just 26, and I could already feel the dark circles behind my once bright gray eyes. It was ennui and boredom and a sinking feeling akin to a person trapped underwater desperately trying to come out.

I reached my desk and sat down with a slump. People were leaving already. My stupid project manager left at 7 p.m. I just don't get why he gets paid so well for working so little. I mean, we all need to grow, but we engineers are always the ones to slog.

I swung open my drawer and pulled out the cleverly hidden bottle of anti-depression pills. I took a couple with my coffee, which had gone cold, and sat back to relax.

Christmas would soon be on its way, in a few more months. Year-end meant a time for audits, long nights, and long telephonic status calls. I sighed. Things were way too predictable in this project.

And management never gave releases—freedom from the project. Every year-end, they would give surprise releases to less ambitious people who never asked for it instead of the people who actually did. Every year, I would be disappointed.

The reason for my non-release last time was that it was based on management's perception of who would be a value addition to the project. People would whisper that it was just a clever way of clipping the wings of talented people so as to control the ever-increasing rates of attrition. They didn't want the jumps to be easy. By giving people shitty work, the company ensured that they turn out to be unsatisfactory candidates in the job market, and thus the company was spared the expense of training the new people. The policy, as it seemed, was to make the ambitious, efficient, and smart ones slog by giving them no opportunities to build their careers.

It was only today that Prabhu asked me if he would get a release from this project so that he could search for a new one.

Funny!! Because I have been trying for it for the last two years. I am stuck with this job. Finding a job outside is difficult with the kind of work I do. There's nothing on my CV.

But I didn't say anything. I just smiled politely, looking him in the eye. I hope he caught the sarcasm in my eyes. Sometimes I leave so much to subtle semiotics that I start getting suspicious if I am the reason people don't completely get what I mean. But the truth is to be perceived, not explained.

Maybe if he continued with his present level of inefficiency, he would be given a release. It depends on the requirements of the project.

Do I talk to myself too much? Maybe. I do like arguing with myself. At the very least, there is no way I could lose the argument. It's a relaxing feeling.

The cubicles were all empty now, most of them anyway. People would just come and leave without wishing each other. It was a very cold feeling—so much for the team spirit. Most of the guys were married or were in a relationship. I could tell so as everyone had a photo frame of their family on their desk.

"When are you leaving for home, Mitali?" Deepa, my teammate, asked me. She was filling her purse with tissues that she had stolen from the restroom.

"Can't you buy some outside?" I asked, disgusted.

"It's free here. I need them while traveling back by auto to the city. There's so much dirt and pollution on the road that skin goes all dusky and oily," she said, locking her drawer.

"Turn off your system too. You forget to shut it down every other day. Why do I need to remind you every time? With this entire power-saving theme going on in the company, I think it's better you don't forget. At night, the guard comes around and notes down all the systems that are on and reports it to the manager the next day."

"Oh, c'mon! Who does that? I don't believe it!" Deepa said it in her usual cheerful, carefree manner. "And leave the office early. It's Friday night. Happy weekend!" She applied lipstick and left.

Oh, yes... Friday night... There's this pressure of doing something out of the ordinary on a Friday night. No wonder people were leaving early. I had to wash clothes and study a programming book on Java as usual.

○●○

I saw Prabhu returning to his desk in a hurry. He saw me looking at him.

"I would just make the report on the status of work and send it to you in no time after which I plan to call it a day," he said, pulling his sliding chair back.

This guy was seriously dicey. But he was the only one who tried to talk to me. Sometimes it doesn't matter who it is; I just needed another human being beside me.

"So, what are your plans for the weekend?"

"Nothing much. I will watch a few movies on my computer and will probably sleep very late at night. Then I will get up sometime in the afternoon tomorrow with a heavy head. In the evenings, my friend Ami and I plan to meet at Deccan Square. We will just chill out, maybe watch a movie, roam around, eat roadside stall food, and have a good time. If possible, I also plan to wash clothes, but that would require a serious exercise of will on my part. So, most likely, you will see me wearing this same shirt on Monday," he chuckled.

I smiled back weakly and whirled my chair to face my screen. But it sure sounded fun.

"What do you guys talk about?"

"About nothing and everything. No subject is taboo—not even building time machines. We just see people, discuss some philosophical things, and get nerdy with crazy ideas. We like walking around new lanes and seeing new things. Maybe both of us will be appearing for the *CAT*[14] exams for MBA next year, so that is another thing we talk about."

"Sounds interesting," I said and sighed. What's with *CAT* exam and engineers?

"What are your plans for the weekend?"

"Not much. Study."

"The reason I ask is that maybe, if you are free, you can join us if you like. We are really simple guys—no complications. We will simply get together and have a nice relaxing time."

"I appreciate the invitation, but I don't go out much," I said, shrugging my head.

"Yes, I notice that. You don't open up much. But we are an interesting company, and Ami knows a lot about Linux. We have memorized the entire *MINIX* code in that Andrew Tanenbaum book and plan to twitch it to make a new operating system.

---

[14] *Common Admission Test.*

Building an operating system is every Comp-Sci engineer's dream, and we are not even Comp-Sci engineers." He giggled with mirth. "There are just around 150 operating systems [15]in the world presently. Wouldn't it be cool if ours was 151st? You can assist us if you wish."

"All very interesting, but you won't get time for all this when you get even more involved in the project and the pressure increases. And the organization is not interested in paying you for building an operating system. You are just meant to resolve tickets, and if you're still left with free time, then resolve some more. Just do the work you are supposed to do."

"And yet you study Unix, Java, PHP, C++, and whatnot," he was looking through me. That glance should have made me uncomfortable, but it didn't.

"I do it because I must." I said it tonelessly.

"Maybe I can visit you sometime... like last time."

"It would be better if you don't visit me now. My house owner dislikes strange guys coming over," I made some excuse.

"But we live so near, don't we?" he said with pleading eyes. I shrugged.

He left soon afterward, and I was the only one left in the office.

---

[15] *Approximate count of non-distinct operating systems in 2007, considering all variations and distributions.*

The lights were off, and as I sat in the chair, looking through the huge glass pane behind my cubicle at the distant lights of the city, I thought the evening seemed strangely lonely and empty.

These lights melt with a sense of déjà vu and nostalgia. How many times have I sat by this very glass pane with Neeraj, and watched the city lights glow? Sipping coffee while watching his intelligent, bright eyes reflect the dim colors, and his words meeting brilliance. Beautiful times! But he was gone, and I missed him—nobody would understand how much, though. Sometimes I wished he knew!

I picked up my purse and lifted myself up to walk away through the long, lonely corridors towards another long weekend.

○●○

On reaching my place, I entered my room, filled with books.

There were some on the bed, some on the table, and some in the drawer of clothes. If the tidiness of one's room is a reflection of the tidiness of one's mind, then probably I have a lot of cleaning to do—externally as well as internally. However, the silent brooding side is just one aspect of my personality.

The other one is the romantic, vulnerable side, which people find very easy to manipulate and take advantage of. I have always been carried away by dreams and the hope that someday someone will come into my life and save me from myself. It happened just once—when Neeraj became my life. But when he moved away, like all other joys, I was reduced to a wrecked ship that badly needed a mast and a direction.

I plan to give my existence meaning by getting better work in my professional life. But then, there are complications.

○●○

My parents have three kids. I am the youngest. My elder brothers were both bright guys. We grew up in a fiercely competitive atmosphere at home, competing for the top ranks. The best rank was respected, and so was the person. My parents were rigid in their beliefs about loving us more for our medals than for being ourselves.

My brothers were *IITians*, doing top-notch jobs in the best of the organizations, and I trailed them merely trying to follow in their footsteps, trying to match their high standards.

Something had derailed in my life.

It's amazing how much it hurts to be neglected and ignored by one's very own parents in the company of brighter siblings. So, the bond had gone weaker over the years. They didn't know who I was as a person, and they never seemed to bother enough to know what went through my mind. Hence, they weren't on the list of people I approached when in trouble and let me also tell you that list isn't very long—Neeraj featured first on that list.

○ ● ○

Neeraj and I were collegemates. We completed our engineering at the same college in Pune, albeit in different branches. We met first during our placements. As destiny would have it, we found ourselves clearing the aptitude tests of the same companies and then attending the interviews with the same interview panel. We would smile at each other every time, and then we would even screw it together—the interview, I mean. It was eerily certain that we would perform similarly.

Finally, when I got placed in *FORDIT*, I found him to be selected too. Though we shared complementary wavelengths, we couldn't have been more different in our outlook. I was more bookish, while he was more outgoing. As they say, opposites attract, and the sparks would fly often. We had our training together and were assigned to the same project and team.

We would chat a lot—about our disappointments, dreams, hopes, and uncertain futures. I never realized how involved I was with him. He was always more ambitious, though. A year ago, when he got an offer from a better project in this same company but with the location as his hometown, Delhi, he decided to switch.

As soon as I heard the news, I realized how alone I would be without him—it was heart wrenchingly painful. Also, it dawned on me that I had never made any other friends except him. He was my world. Hence, the very day he left Pune, I proposed to him. Since it would be a long-distance relationship, he said he would need to think about it.

And there was another minor complication—we were from different regions. He's a Punjabi, while I am a Gujarati. So, there you go!

We would talk to each other every weekend. After six months of convincing him, he said that he had no problem with a relationship but that his parents might never agree for their marriage. He's trying to convince them though, and hopefully things would turn out fine. I don't know what to say. It depresses me. So, lately, we never talk about the convincing part—we just chat. Not that it would be a smooth sailing with my parents. They would roast me alive. But I was ready for it. Was he too? I was not entirely sure.

That is just because he's not as needy as I am. He has a life, his own set of friends, and a very positive outlook towards life. But he is in love with me, and that is all that matters.

He is my best friend. One that could be trusted, relied upon, and taken for granted. I can't see how love can come before friendship. I mean, friendship is about being there for each other, generating a comfort level, and knowing the person inside and out before trusting them with your heart. He is the only one there ever was!

○●○

I again received a message from Prabhu. *'Can we meet outside?'*

Most certainly not, you psycho!

My last encounter with Prabhu was freaky. I had been assigned as a mentor to him to guide him through his initiation into the work. Prabhu had been incredibly difficult to teach—he was no better than a monkey. In fact, monkeys can be trained, but not drunk monkeys.

He used to keep looking at me strangely and would approach me to ask silly questions. My team lead had asked me to be very generous and tolerant with juniors. Slowly but surely, he worked hard to gain my confidence—first, through his words and then, with his uncanny intuition. He had the knack of sensing the vibrations of people, I believe. He always had the right words to say. He would often understand when I was sad, lonely, angry, or bored.

Something in his aura was very relaxing and forgiving. I realized he would always come to my desk to ask me questions at those moments—whether he had any or not. A listening ear is so hard to resist. I would talk a lot with him, scold him, laugh with him, and try to change him. All this while, I thought he was the one interested in me. Then he says he was not. It was his friend.

"Do you see that guy by the door waiting for me for lunch? You won't believe... " He stopped and looked at me. "Maybe I shouldn't say... leave it."

Basically, all the project spaces in our entire building had glass doors and walls, so it was possible to peek in and peek out easily.

"That's fine. You can tell me," I said, smiling.

"Okay." He looked into my eyes attentively. "No, leave it... bad idea!"

"Okay, leave it!" I said. He expected more coaxing, maybe.

So, then he directly got to the point.

"It's nothing bad, you know. I was only unsure how you would take it," he said, lowering his voice. "The thing is, he keeps talking about you. Nosy bastard! But I believe he likes you," he kept looking at me keenly.

"Oh!" I wasn't really expecting this. "Oh!" I took a moment to stabilize myself. "Tell him, I am committed."

He looked at me with those irresistible, heartbroken eyes of his.

"C'mon, he doesn't need to know that. If I were you, I would enjoy the courtship and attention. After all, aren't fans difficult to find?" Prabhu said.

"Won't that be just cruel and deceptive?" I said, staring at him incredulously.

"Listen! Is your boyfriend around?"

"No, he is in Delhi."

"Long-distance relationship?"

"Yes."

"When was the last time you met him?"

"6 months ago."

"And are you getting married anytime soon?"

"Probably not."

"Next year?"

"Umm... not sure."

"I thought so. You look so lonely. What are your thoughts on casual dating?"

"People get serious."

"What if he does not?"

"Then it can be harmless fun."

"Exactly my view. Pardon my opinion, but as it is, you have no friends in the company. That's the truth. Won't a good-hearted chap be fun to hang around with? Think about it," he said, looking at me with eyes that knew what they were talking about.

"I hardly know him."

"I will tell you everything. He is adorable."

"What's his name? Let's start at the beginning."

"Amitarth."

"Quite a heavyweight name," I gulped at the thought of saying something unpronounceable.

"Well, whatever his parents aspired to while naming him that, it's yet to materialize," he said, eying that guy's super-lean frame by the pillar outside our glass door entrance. "Someday he'll reach there. Till then, please do me a favor and call him Ami."

I nodded in relief at my effort saved.

They both went for lunch.

I wasn't convinced. But Prabhu was adamant.

"It would be fun... F...U...N... What more reasons do you need? Aren't we all bored here?" He wanted me to give Ami a chance. I sure thought the guy looked decent. Mildly cute, perhaps!

That entire night, Prabhu sent me messages about the need to open new doors in life—the need to break apart and come through, to get a kick from each and every day in life.

"Why not? Why couldn't every second be magical? Why shouldn't we be enchanted every damn moment? Don't we live just once? I am telling you; you must give him a chance."

○●○

Finally, the next day, he told me that he was coming to my place, and he did, post dinner.

"He is a saner version of me, a person who believes in the magic of a moment with all his faith. I think he deserves to know you."

I should have told him not to come. The house owner doesn't like it.

"Just have some fun in life. It may be at his expense, but then he will have some fun in his life at your expense. After all, what's to lose? Nobody is serious here."

I took a moment to let his words sink in. After all, if things didn't get too sticky, everything was okay. Need is not a sin. Morality is both a luxury and a burden for everyday people. There was slim chance of Neeraj ever finding it out. I would never let it reach that level.

"So, what do you say?" He looked at me with those insane eyes. I was suspicious of Prabhu's over-enthusiasm. Did this guy actually exist? Or was Prabhu playing some sort of prank on me? Things were too good to be true.

"I want to know if this guy is actually interested. Right now!"

"That's easy. Let us message him from your mobile. I believe he has your number, and I will see his response. Send a message that only a girl can."

So, I sent him a message and waited for a response. There was no reply.

"Send another," Prabhu said.

So, I sent him another. No reply.

Then one more. No response!

A reply came after 15 minutes.

'*Fuck you, Bastard. I am going to kick your ass if you send me any more messages.*'

We looked at each other, appalled. Nobody knew what to say.

I spoke first. "You lied. You lied all the way."

My eyes were blazing.

"Now don't jump to conclusions, dear. Maybe he didn't have your number. I thought I gave it to him. But I am getting so absent-minded day after day. I'm never sure these days."

But I didn't believe him. I didn't believe a word of what he said then on.

I had to find out for myself. It had to be foolproof.

"I would have to sleep on your couch tonight," Prabhu said, looking at his watch. "It is past midnight. I won't find any means to go back."

"I don't care, dude. This is a girl's place. You can't stay here. Besides, this is Pune. You will find one thing or another."

"I will leave by early morning. Nobody will find out."

"You don't understand."

"You need to be a bit adventurous in life. I promise I will move out before morning. Trust me, I want no trouble myself."

I don't know why I said yes, but I did.

Probably, I had a reason!

○●○

After he slept on the sofa, I took his mobile and sent a message to the number he had last sent the messages to.

'Get pure-white chrysanthemums to the office. It's her b'day. And wear that pink shirt of yours. She likes pink.' I auto-timed the message so that it would reach him a day later post-midnight.

○●○

Prabhu went away in the morning, and I had another routine day at the office. The next day, I got ready quickly and went to the office.

And then I waited!

I waited by the entry door of my project floor, from where I could watch the lobby of the project floor beneath. I waited 30 minutes. I knew the guy was not at his desk; I checked while coming up.

Was he ever going to be on time? 30 minutes turned to 50. His project manager was not going to be happy. Or was he sick or something? In that case, there was no point standing by the door. I thought of asking Prabhu if his friend was okay.

Suddenly, I heard the footsteps of somebody rushing in from the big door at the front. There he was!

Unbelievable though it seemed, I saw a lean frame of a guy in formals with a backpack running through the corridor. His blue shirt was already wet with sweat, and his hair was disheveled. He ran as if his life depended on it. And in all this mayhem, he had managed to get three sticks, which led to three ugliest-looking chrysanthemums at their ends. But it didn't matter. I smiled at the naivety of it all.

He looked up suddenly. I rushed inside.

I sat down at my workstation. Prabhu was yet to come. So, it was all true—every word of it. In spite of myself, I felt an exultation in my heart that I knew was meaningless. There was no way it could lead to anything. What was I going to do?

But then nothing happened. Suddenly, everything stopped. I never got those three chrysanthemums, and I never heard about him again. Today, it has been weeks since that incident.

Suddenly, my phone rang, and my flow of thoughts was interrupted!

I hoped it would be Neeraj. It was not. It was my team lead.

'Mitali, there's been an incident. Really urgent.'

I should have never picked up the phone. All problems arise on Friday evenings!

Ami's version:

"Dude, she is staying in the office for the night. She went home but was called back," Prabhu whispered breathlessly on the phone. "A ticket she was working on, bombed in production big time, and now she has to re-test the code and submit the results tonight itself. The problem is that there is nobody on the floor. She pleaded with me on the phone to give her company, but you know I can't go back to the office and stay all night. It is too lonely in the office today, and she sounded scared."

I glanced at my office computer watch. It was 9.40 p.m. That meant the last bus to leave the company would leave in 20 minutes. I didn't feel like going. It was the weekend again. Another boring set of holidays with the same old set of people in my room.

But I knew I had to leave now. If this bus leaves, the only mode to go home would be the cabs, but cabs were only for people who had special permission from the project manager, which I could only have if I had any critical work.

The cost-cutting drive was on, and they were trying to save every little dime they could. Though this could have been an extreme coincidence, we couldn't see hand-wash in toilets. Even if that couldn't be directly correlated to those melancholy clouds of depression that hovered over us or to the cheapness that our company displayed routinely, it was still very unlikely that the project manager would not interrogate me if I dared to do the blasphemy of boarding a cab without being part of any *'value-addition'* to the team. Cabs charged hefty money.

So, I had started packing my stuff in my drawer. Headphones to be kept in a drawer—check, printouts of the C++ and UNIX tutorials that I wanted to take home for study—check, shut down the computer properly—check, pack my bag—check, lock the drawer—check, umm... what else? I was about to call Prabhu to ask if he wanted to join me, but before I could, the mobile had rung.

Apparently, he had left early.

"So, is your work over?" he finally asked to jolt me back to reality.

"I don't know. There is just too much work today." I lied.

He wanted to say something but stopped, and I could only hear his heavy breathing on the phone.

"You would take a cab, right?"

Oh yes... How was I going to get home if I did wait? I took a moment to think. But, hell, no thoughts came to mind.

"That's fine. I will." I lied, well knowing I can't.

Mitali's version:

It was 11 p.m. I knew from the start that something was wrong with the day. It had been too quiet... too relaxed. Fridays are never this relaxed!

I furiously typed on my system. I had to get it done before 2 a.m. and leave by cab. But cabs are dangerous. Only the other day, there was news in the paper about a young married woman—a software engineer—who was raped and then killed by the cab driver. It's scary!

I asked that idiot Prabhu to join me in the office, but he bluntly refused. What a jerk!

I looked at the entry door of our project space—I was the only one left—more or less. I looked at the distance between me and that door, and the area in between was uncertainly lit—some patches with bright spots and some completely dark. It was funny in one way and very scary in another. I needed to concentrate. But I couldn't. The deadline was 3 o'clock in the morning—that's when the US guys would leave for home.

The code just had to be pushed to production before the start of a new business day, but I was in no mood to work tonight.

○ ● ○

I can't just work all the time. I have my moods, my life, and my fair share of gray spots.

There were just too many thoughts in my head, and I made the mistake of uploading the wrong file of variables in the outlay job. That meant a wastage of another 20 minutes until the job was completed, and I would need to run another instance. Shit!! But I needed these thoughts so that I could keep my mind away from the other scary thoughts. I was always afraid of the dark—my rich fantasy imagined all sorts of creatures and bad things in that darkness. So here I was, alone on the floor, working in darkness.

The automatic lights on the floor switched off, and there was only one left working on the top of my head. It must have been very picturesque and photogenic, I know, but I couldn't possibly have taken a picture of myself sitting there alone.

I needed a break... my eyes... they hurt... all watery from the intense stare at the system. I rubbed them with my palm and took out my hanky to wipe the glasses. I don't know if eyes are built in a way to stare at a computer system routinely—10 hours a day. Sooner or later, the eye problems are certain to catch up. The least the companies could do was distribute carrots for free. I chuckled at the thought. But seriously, why can't they? I mean, they can always keep carrots dangling by the coffee machine. Or at least carrot juice instead of caffeine.

Ohh crap! I shouldn't have thought of coffee. Now I must drink it! That's the curse.

I pushed my chair back lethargically and lifted myself up to slowly move my feet towards the coffee machine outside our floor by the stairs. It was a machine shared by two floors—ours and one below us.

I knew the corridors were dark, and everybody had left.

Slowly, as I reached the machine, I noticed a form standing by it—taking a cup of coffee. The person looked tall, and as he turned, he stood very silent—so eerily silent that I felt a chill up my spine. He must have noticed me because, as I came closer, he retracted but didn't leave. I switched on the lights near the machine—wouldn't want any sudden molestation in the dark by some watchman.

It was Amartirth *(or whatever his name was)*. Possibly, the last person I was expecting. It was a shock.

I couldn't read his expressions.

Was I supposed to greet him? Was I supposed to act unfamiliar and cold? I wanted to ask why he was staying back. I just wanted to ensure it was a coincidence. That would have been comforting for me.

As I tried to move closer to the machine, he stumbled away clumsily, stepped on his own shoes, and, whilst avoiding tripping, somehow managed to get half the coffee on his shirt. I suppressed my smile. I never knew I had such an effect on people. His reactions were so blatantly unsubtle that it was a joke.

He scampered away hurriedly. But strangely, I felt safe in the office now.

○ ● ○

I returned to my desk and started working. The problem wasn't going to fix itself. The whole confusion was about the business objective. The business owner had been unsure of the requirements from the very start. He had no idea on what he wanted, and the volatility of the requirements was too high. In the end, what got implemented and tested was diametrically different from the solution that the stakeholders earlier had in mind.

The funny thing is, somehow it was my fault now!

So, there was a mail waiting for me in the mailbox, asking me to do the entire system testing with three additional test cases.

Hmm... that would take time!

My team lead had little or no sense of responsibility in such matters. I was expected to take care of the problem end-to-end. So, after the testing, I was to call the business owner and make sure he was okay to deploy the code in production.

And then I was to leave for home.

My Saturday was ruined already. I would be sleeping the entire day once I reached home. It was difficult to muster enough strength to wash the clothes and study. The spillover effects of a night out at the office are just too huge.

I looked at the glass door entrance to our project floor. That door was still far away. But then there was a figure silently standing by it, drinking coffee as he kept looking at me! I stopped breathing for a second, only to chuckle to myself an instant later.

It could have been only one person. Some things are just too *'in your face'* to be termed mere coincidences. The happy fact was that I wasn't complaining!

He stood there for a long time.

Two hours later, I was still working.

Ami's version:

She was working alone at her workstation, under that solitary light that brightened her cubicle. It was so beautiful that I felt like clicking a picture of her working alone in that light—like a silent ballet dancer dancing alone under the moon—but with nobody to appreciate. People talk of poetic justice, but there was a certain poetic sadness in this case—something akin to a tragedy.

If only she knew that someone was watching her perform in that poetic moment! If only she knew someone was watching her mesmerized.

But how could she possibly know? That was the tragedy. I was cleverly hidden in the dark behind the pillar near her project floor entrance.

I kept watching her till my coffee was over, and then I got another.

This cycle continued for a long time—it felt like hours.

Finally, I just couldn't stand it anymore. I needed a break. I needed to get a grip, and my head was kind of spinning. I was too sleepy and drunk on too much coffee.

And then, just as I was about to throw the cup and leave, she looked up straight at me, just for an instant. It made my heart stop.

It was an accident; it felt like one. She wasn't expecting me.

No, it was more than an instant because there were moments filled with silence and instant recognition on her end, and maybe it was also relief. Before I could read more into it, she was back at her work, and I don't know if I imagined it, but I thought she was smiling.

Mitali's version:

I kept working for a long time. Finally finished the deployment. When I looked at the system clock, it showed me 3 o'clock.

When I looked at the door, he wasn't there. I sighed.

God, I was famished! I wondered if he had left. The in-door cafeteria on the top floor would be closed for sitting purposes, but the open-to-the-sky cafeteria would be open. I just took a sandwich and a rum ball and walked out to the giant open-to-the-sky moonlit terrace of our office building.

He was standing at the very end of it, by the parapet, looking down, silently munching.

The Pune skyline of tall high-rise buildings around him seemed to engulf that small frame of his, as the shimmering lights from the glass walls of those buildings complemented and contrasted the night sky.

His form looked so lonely and aloof against that giant backdrop that I felt a deep sympathetic pain just looking at him. It's an instant connection sometimes.

I stood on one side of the terrace too, lazily ruminating as I tried to chew and swallow that almost inedible and cold sandwich. I should have got it heated in the microwave. When in the night filled with stars, your chain of thought is broken by that inedible and repelling lump that just wouldn't go down your throat, it means the sandwich has to be bad.

He was done with his munch and was looking down; his mind was somewhere far away. I wondered where. He wouldn't have told me, even if I had asked.

Then suddenly, he looked to his right to notice me looking at him from a distance. He wasn't the least bit surprised. He kept looking at me unhurriedly—not with a stare but just a look. Maybe I was the one staring. I looked away, trying to hide my shock and interest.

He moved his eyes again to look down at the abyss. There was so much distance between us and so little communication, but on that moonlit night, if that lonely frame of a man had asked to kiss me, I wouldn't have refused.

If only he knew he wasn't the only one lonely and that the world is filled with people like him, searching for something or someone, sometimes their own selves. If only he knew he was standing right next to one of them, maybe just maybe, he'd feel peace.

Sometimes I feel people are ill-equipped to deal with pangs like these. If everybody in the world is looking for someone, or for that mysterious, soul-filling thing called love, why is it that they don't find each other?

People try to fill this void inside by overworking, overindulging in food, hating people, or running after money, when all they need is a hug after a hard day's work.

Don't we all? I guess I needed one.

People often confuse things with happiness. Maybe I would buy myself a Rolls-Royce tomorrow, but that car would be just another thing without that special someone to accompany me on a long drive. A basic level of comfort with the people we care about and who care for us is what happiness constitutes.

But that right person is slippery; he evades me, maybe because he runs to find his own Ms. Right. We all just chase each other; if only we took a moment to wait, maybe we would find each other. But we never stop, do we?

Heck, what was I thinking? I need to control my train of thought. They keep derailing when I am over-tired, and my philosophical bent of mind would choose such moments to interfere the most. I needed to come back to my dreary, tired existence and think of going back home. But what about this guy? I looked at him.

He just stood still without a worry in the world. Does he have no home to return to?

Maybe I should approach him and ask if he needs a lift (*would convince my project manager somehow*). I knew he had no way to go back. There was no mode of public transport available that late at night (*our software park was way out of the main city*), and he won't be allowed to pay the cab with his own money.

I had spent enough time in this company to know that one can't get a cab for standing at one place drinking coffee and watching over some girl.

So, I walked towards him without an iota of idea of what and how I was supposed to say what I was supposed to say.

But then, before I could inch closer, before my very sight, he bent down and started panting, somewhat akin to a dog trying to vomit some gibberish that it might have eaten. What a simile! I cursed myself. He was in visible distress. He unbuttoned the top buttons of his shirt, and when it didn't help, he tore open the whole shirt. I ran towards him. His eyes were bulging out of the sockets.

"Hey, are you alright?" I tried to get him up.

His eyes were blood-red, as he made a pathetic attempt at smiling.

"I am perfectly alright, ma'am. Could you please call the doctor and Prabhu? Or leave it. Don't worry, I will be fine." He kept a brave face.

"Cool," I said, smiling.

But then he had another chasm, and he started rolling on the floor.

"Of course I am not alright, you dumb... Can't you see? My heart is pumping like a steam engine, and I am suffocated. I might be having a heart attack or something. Please get me some water, cold water. Heck! Get me a doctor first." He kept doing those rolling stunts with a constipated face, and he was sweating like crazy.

Okay, this was one of those times one is not ready for. I felt my pulse quicken as I ran towards the people inside the cafeteria for help.

Ami's version:

I have blurry images of the frenetic and confused activity that took place in the next 2–3 hours.

As I lay on the floor, I saw people rushing towards me. I could hear them debate as they tried to figure out the number to call. There was a 24 x 7 ambulance facility we had access to, thanks to the money paid by our organization towards the Mediclaim for its employees and their dependents.

There was a delay of an hour as people hurried clumsily to carry me down the floors to the ambulance and then to the nearest hospital mentioned in my Mediclaim.

The only thing I noticed—the one that really stuck with me— was that Mitali hadn't accompanied me in the van. I felt a pain that hadn't just to do with the malady of the moment, which led me to close my eyes, wishing I would never wake up again. But then, since when was death so merciful?

I opened my eyes as someone frantically shook me to wake me up. It was the doctor!

"Your heartbeat has gone above 120. What did you take?" There was a weird mechanical heartbeat sound in the room; maybe it was the ECG machine.

"Can you hear me? What did you take?" the doctor shouted in my ear.

I hadn't consumed anything substantial or out of the ordinary except the coffee, which I had been drinking non-stop.

My lips muttered, "Coffee." I took a moment to count, and my smile kept broadening as the count kept increasing. "At least 17 cups," the sheer magnitude of that number brought a grin onto my face.

The doctor looked at me for a moment to ensure that I wasn't joking, then shouted instructions to the nurses. "He's delirious, dizzy, dehydrated, and has heart palpitations... excessive intake of caffeine leading to an acute diuretic effect."

Moments later, I felt multiple needles in my arm, but I was too tired to care. I closed my eyes and passed out due to the sheer ennui of my mind. I woke up at around 10 a.m. the next day to find myself tranquilized and with needles in my arm to pass in saline.

But I was alone! Where the hell was Prabhu?

4.

Mitali's version:

I called Prabhu the next day. "How is he?"

"How is who?" he asked me back, his voice sleepy. It was afternoon.

I rolled my eyes.

"Ami, of course. Who else? Didn't I tell you last night that he had a stroke of some sort, and you were to accompany him to the hospital? I didn't go only when you promised that you would be on your way."

There was silence.

I asked him, awestruck. "Don't tell me you didn't go either! That would be just horrible." I felt my breath stop as I could hear his breath over the phone. It was a breath of an intense search inside one's head for an excuse.

"I thought it was a dream," he whispered on the phone. "I really did. So, I just slept off."

"What!! Are you kidding me?" I shouted on the phone, my voice going hoarse and whiny as I cut the call.

But then I called back.

"Yeah yeah! I am on my way. Don't shout. Searching for my toothbrush. I need to stop looking like a patient myself first. It's a Saturday afternoon for God's sake!" Prabhu cribbed.

There were sounds of action, and something breaking over the phone.

"By the way, I am ready to meet him."

"Meet him as in...?" he paused, and so did the crashing sounds.

"As in, meet him in general. No big deal. In a friendly sort of way."

"With what intentions, may I ask?"

"To get to know the guy!"

"Cool." I could sense glee in his voice. "Now we are talking!"

"Yes, yes! But first, ensure that he isn't dead already. Let me know."

Ami's version:

"She called me at night. I couldn't come," Prabhu looked at me.

"Sometimes I wonder if she even knows me," I said, looking at the ceiling fan whirling above me as I lay on my hospital bed.

"She does, dude!" Prabhu said, pleading. He was sitting on an uncomfortable steel stool near my bed.

"Even if she does, I have no confidence in what you have told her," I said, still looking up.

"Why don't you meet her and clear it up yourself?" Prabhu said, trying to reason things out with weird hand gestures. He was losing coordination with his body parts slowly. I couldn't help but suddenly notice the weight he had put on.

"Why would I? I don't even know what the stuff is—myself," I said.

"Oh, just talk it out, will you?" Prabhu said. "And remember, she is but the means and not the end. Your end is happiness. It's the destination for both of us. Be happy. Don't get too serious; just use her, and don't expect much!"

"Firstly, I don't believe you. Secondly, you never once fail to disgust me!" I said, closing my eyes. Our search for happiness was turning into a pathetic mess.

"All I talk about is life and the bare-open core of it. It is disgusting as it is. Fine, a day later, it's Monday. We go and talk with the Mademoiselle. Let's clear some air. For good or for bad, I think you must take a step forward now." He made sense.

I was discharged soon, and Prabhu helped me home.

○●○

That night again, I kept hearing the snores of my cousin. It had been weeks since we had last spoken. We used to have nominal conversations over bills and money, but then that was about it.

Sometimes, I wonder why people are so money minded.

He was 30 and about to get married. He had purchased a flat for 20 lakhs in Kothrud to be moved into after marriage.

All he wasn't able to find, though, was a girl!

He was going bald and paunchy, plus he had lost all his romantic instincts. So now, why marriage? Why ruin the life of some girl when he could have easily purchased sex? Sometimes people are too dumb to know what they live for, but I shouldn't concern myself with somebody else's problems. I had my own.

○●○

That Monday, at around 11.30 a.m., Prabhu called me at my extension.

"Ready?" he whispered.

I licked my lips, which had gone dry. I hadn't been able to sleep, and I hadn't taken a bath. My throat was parched, and my work wasn't done.

So, no! I wasn't ready.

"Yes? Cool! Come by in exactly 10 minutes at my desk. She would be free then," and he banged down the phone.

I looked at my team. Everyone was working. Importantly, no one was looking at me, so I just moved out.

I reached Prabhu's desk. He nodded at me and asked me to wait. I kept standing. He took a moment to just sit straight and close his eyes, then he sighed, locked his system, got up, and went to Mitali's desk.

He stood there at her desk and bent down to talk to her. Then he turned towards me and nodded again. That was my call to approach her.

She looked at me, her gray eyes nervously transfixed on my face. I walked towards those eyes, timing myself to reach them within 5 seconds.

It was at that moment that I realized that I had never taken the entire matter seriously! I had never considered what I would do if she indeed agreed to be together. I had no idea what I was to do next, except to sweat like a cucumber.

That isn't a good feeling; it feels like the earth is shifting below your feet. I was not prepared to go and talk!

What was I to say?

Both Prabhu and Mitali were looking at me very seriously as I moved ahead. Never before had I been so intensely aware that I hadn't bathed and that I wasn't breathing. I went straight up to her. She was still sitting in her chair. I extended my hand. She kept looking up at me but hardly noticed my hand.

It was then that I noticed that she was looking very pretty in blue, the color of her dress nicely contrasting her eyes.

Oh, awesome! Just the thing needed to stress me even more. Then my brain just blacked out!

"I like you..." I muttered, "Your..." No word came to mind. Probably, I wanted to say her dress. "Umm..." Or maybe her eyes, but wouldn't that be too indecent? The silence of the moment was stretching to infinity, and it was killing me.

She looked at me wide-eyed. Her eyes expected an answer.

"Brain... your brain! I love it!" I closed my eyes because of the pain of embarrassment; maybe I wanted to say, '*her mind*'. Also, elementary pleasantries like '*hello*' or '*hi*' were completely skipped.

I looked at Prabhu. He was looking at me aghast. In fact, everybody on the project floor was. It wasn't just my brain, intoxicated with fear and nervousness, that was playing games with me. People were actually staring at us, at the pitiful sight of a sweat-clad guy standing in front of a shell-shocked Mitali.

I felt the cubicle walls cave in on me. Before I knew what I was doing, I picked up my bag and fled.

Just like that!

○●○

I went down to my desk and worked like a bull; no, a dog seems more appropriate! I just had to ensure that no more thoughts came to mind. By evening, there were no calls from Prabhu's end.

Then, by 6.30 p.m., suddenly, the phone rang. It was Prabhu.

"Hey, coming to the cafeteria?"

"No way," I paused. "There's just no way I am coming up ever again. I would need to pass your floor."

"Tell me something; how do you do it?"

I knew what he could be talking about. "I am a natural, I guess. Things just happen," was all I could mutter out as I clutched the phone tighter.

"Yeah, I mean acting like a total idiot and still emerging a winner! You are a genius in that sense."

"What are you talking about?"

"She smiled after you left, and then she just couldn't stop smiling the entire day. Apparently, something about the lameness you manifested was cute! Hahaha, who would have known? Girls are weird. She wants to meet you again."

"Well, God and girls work in strange ways, I guess," I said, smiling with deep relief. What were the odds? When times are good, no matter how one falls, one lands on one's feet.

"But dude, seriously, you ran away. Everybody saw. What scared you?"

I don't know, or maybe I did. Only one thing came to mind.

"It must be her eyes." I stuttered as I said it. Those gray eyes sparkled as they stared. All day, I was trying to not imagine them looking at me wide-eyed with so many expectations.

There was heavy breathing on the other end, and the voice said, "I like your answer. You are doing well—surprisingly well, in fact. So, you get to decide how you meet her the next time! But don't keep her waiting," and he hung up.

○●○

The next few days I gave it some thought, and then one fine morning I called Prabhu from my office extension. It was Friday again, the busiest day of the week, and people were busy planning weekend getaways.

"Hey, it's me!" I whispered.

"Yes, yes, I know. Shoot!" Prabhu asked in a busy tone—busy mornings of a new business day are a hassle for the soul.

"I have decided the time, date, and place for the next meeting," I whispered breathlessly.

"Oh, don't tell me you have!" He started whispering too, in excitement.

"This Saturday!! Dinner first, and then a movie at Deccan. What do you think?" I tried to bring whatever animation I could into my voice.

"Cool," he said. "I would ask her on *IP Messenger*[16]." A second later, he returned. "Messaged!"

I had to wait only a second for an answer.

"She says, Sunday afternoon, lunch at Deccan, and no movie. It is not a date, seemingly," he said, laughing.

"It isn't?" My eyebrows rose automatically.

---

[16] *Serverless lightweight Messenger for LAN. No cloud, Secure & High availability.*

"Of course it is, dude! The very fact that she mentions it means she has been thinking along those lines or has already. Congrats!" he chipped out merrily.

"Yeah, right!" I said, baffled.

"Don't be late."

○●○

I waited at the pre-decided hotel at exactly 11 a.m.

The day was nice, and the hotel was busy. A gentle breeze fluttered the umbrella over our table. I had worn the cleanest of my clothes and had taken a bath. Obviously, one can't afford to make the same mistakes twice. Prabhu had told me to wear sunglasses and to call the shots while ordering food.

'Be a man!' He had messaged me and had also called me multiple times since morning just to remind me of the same.

Sunday had started and so had my date. I woke up happy and smiling. Today was the day, I thought, nothing can make me unhappy.

As I sat by our reserved table at the venue, waiting, I tried to empty my mind and not act nervous.

"Don't be yourself. Be suave," Prabhu had said.

He had also asked me to be geeky and talk about computers and computing languages. "Start with C. By the time you reach C++, you are to hold her hand. I will pray to the God of masculinity to strengthen your balls. Reserve the table and don't act cheap."

She came on time, as promised. She was dressed in a sleeveless white top and jeans. With her hair nicely curled back and the color of her specs complementing her eyes, she looked like the Greek goddess of love, Aphrodite. Why would someone dress so incredibly for me if this wasn't a date?

As she approached the table, I stood up and smiled at her.

She smiled back, but before I could even say *'Hi,'* she spoke out, "Hey, I don't want any misunderstanding; hence, I would like to clear up a few things at the very onset. This is not a date, and it can't be one, as I am committed." She smiled again.

My face paled as I shook her hands and saw her sitting down. The date was over, as it never was one!

"I felt like inquiring about your health and apologizing for not joining you at the hospital. So, I thought we could meet. I hope this didn't disturb your Sunday plans." She said it politely.

I tried to smile, but probably all I could manage was a wince.

My mobile vibrated. It was a message from Prabhu. *'Did you reach?'*

'Why didn't you tell me she's committed!!!!??' I replied.

"So, how are you?" she asked.

"Great. Should we order? I am hungry," I had lost my interest in the conversation that wasn't meant to go anywhere.

She appeared shocked for a moment but soon found her grace. "Sure. Good, you regained your appetite. What would you like?" she asked, scanning the menu.

"Whatever you are ordering for yourself, please order for me too," I said, yawning. Who cares!

My mobile vibrated again. It was Prabhu. *'She's bluffing, bro! Some idiot must have smiled at her a few times in college, which she mistook for commitment—typical withdrawal-from-reality symptoms. It's an insult for girls these days if everyone has a boyfriend and they don't.'*

Hmm... a possible theory to explain the anomaly.

"You didn't sleep properly?" she asked again.

"I am a late riser."

"So, today's meeting did disturb your Sunday plans," she said. "By the way, I was thinking of ordering a sandwich. Are you a vegetarian or not? I am vegetarian."

"I eat everything, not choosy at all. But please order a veg. sandwich for me today."

"Why? Trying to be chivalrous? Don't want to make the lady feel odd? Don't even try," she winked at me.

"Chivalry would be a waste of my time, wouldn't it? You are committed," I winked back.

She went solemn. "Not really. It won't be a waste, except in that sense. Everybody appreciates kindness and courtesy."

We called the waiter and placed the order.

"So, tell me something about your boyfriend. He's from Pune?" I asked.

"Neeraj is from Delhi. He was my classmate and a fellow joiner at *FORDIT*." There was a glow on her face, as if someone had inquired about her core competency. It was like asking a dog to bark and a fish to swim! She kept speaking about him merrily for 10 minutes.

After a while, I messaged Prabhu. *'Dude, need to recheck if it's a bluff. I am not so sure!'*

What sort of a date was this? Why would any guy be interested in a girl's chat about her boyfriend? She was tactless, for sure.

'I suspect it is more one-sided. She wouldn't be sitting there with you if it wasn't. She's lonely as hell,' Prabhu replied back. I sighed.

Yes, maybe she was, but to be fair, who isn't? I looked around. The sun was obscured by the grayish-white clouds floating across what was otherwise a brilliant blue sky, and hence the sunlight had dimmed. The wind blew more pleasantly than ever, ruffling the umbrella on top of our table. She was still chirping about her boyfriend. I paid no attention to her words.

I kept looking into those eyes of hers—sensitive, calm, yet lonely and vulnerable. They reflected her feelings perfectly. As she spoke, they kept shifting, but at all times, they were sensitive to what I thought or whether I was paying attention. They were asking for a third-person acceptance of her choice—a pathetic substitute for one's emptiness, if you ask me. She knew there was a void, and she was filling it with stories. What was she, if not like me?

I smiled at her for the first time, as one would on finding a long-lost friend.

She smiled back. "What?"

"Nothing. Great guy," I said, smiling. "You love him a lot!!".

"Thanks." Her face lit up. "And hey, I forgot to ask you. How have you been health-wise? You gave me a scare that night."

"I am okay, as you can see," I smiled, sunnily.

"Excess intake of caffeine? Hmm, that's amusing," she said, stirring her tea. "I always wanted to ask this—for my own satisfaction. Somehow, I find you to be a guy I can be honest with." She paused to look deep into my eyes. "Why did you stay back that night?"

My eyes met hers. It was unfair, that question. I knew I couldn't lie to those eyes.

"Why do you ask such questions? I never asked you the real reason why you are sitting here." I said.

Her eyes didn't have it in them to take that amount of surprise and not react. She blinked a couple of times but then smiled.

"What do you mean?" was her brave attempt at ignorance, though her eyes spoke otherwise.

"I mean nothing." I smiled at her. "Our food is here." She knew exactly what I meant.

We ate quietly. She kept looking at me every once in a while— she was yet to recover from the surprise. I couldn't help but notice that we were silent, yet we were having the best conversation we possibly could.

"Do you want anything else?" she asked me finally. I shrugged.

"Bill, please." She motioned at the waiter.

I stiffened. This was the difficult part. Prabhu had warned me about it.

If I shared the bill, it would prove that this isn't a date— *'which we are against proving'*. I could almost hear Prabhu's whisper in my ears.

If I paid the bill, it would mean that it was a date from my end— a stupid signal to be sent—after all I had just heard her harp about her boyfriend.

'And if it's a date, it's a must that you receive a goodbye kiss,' I heard Prabhu again. *'Either she gives, or you take.'*

Such a loser! I closed my eyes.

The waiter came back with the bill.

She saw the amount and paid it. "It's a treat from me for not being able to join you that night, though I should have," she smiled sweetly.

"It isn't a big deal, you know; it really isn't," I smiled back.

"C'mon, after all, we do know each other in some ways," she said solemnly, avoiding my eyes. She seemed to have the habit of going from happy to somber in an instant.

As we left the hotel, I wanted to grab her hand and walk. I wanted to be with her—for her.

I didn't feel like leaving, as I could sense so many things left unsaid.

"How do you plan to go?" I asked. It was an unnecessary question.

"Maybe an auto or a bus. I don't stay too far, and it's just 1 o'clock," she said, looking at me.

I don't know why, but it felt like she didn't want to leave either. She turned to say *'bye'* as we saw an auto approaching.

"I had a nice time," she said as she looked at the auto, then looked at me. The auto passed us, but she didn't stop it.

Instead, she looked at me and asked, "Hey, how about a movie?"

Now it was my turn to be surprised. Where did that come from?

My hesitation got the better of her. "The thing is, I won't be able to study even if I go home. I know you must be busy, but..."

"Sure," I nodded heavily. "A movie would be awesome, yeah." How many flimsy excuses was the lady going to give, and how many did I care for?

"Which one would you like to see?" I asked.

"What kind do you see, normally?" she asked.

"I am not a huge film buff. Normally, any English action movie works. Good special effects are enough. I enjoy comic films too," I grinned.

"Nice. I like watching romantic movies, but I also like spectacle movies with a storyline," she said.

"What is your favorite romantic movie?"

" *'Gone with the Wind'*—A timeless classic."

"Should we go for a romantic movie then? There would be quite a few playing at E-Square," I asked, hopefully. Hope being, I might end up being the lucky guy with the supportive shoulder to cry on.

"Well, I was thinking more along the lines of Harry Potter," she frowned.

I might have given the impression of being slightly disappointed because she thought it important to justify her preference. "Films these days are less about romance and more about vulgarity and sex."

Oh, really?

"So do you mean to say that vulgarity and sex are acceptable if there is enough romance?" I looked at her. "Well, I always wanted to ask this to a girl!"

"If things are romantic enough, then there is no separation between the two. Sex is but the means to an end in that case."

"And what end is that?"

"Manifestation of one's affection towards the other," she said, blinking at it. We were already on the topic of sex without any hint of doing it, though. Sad!

We bought the tickets and went through the ordeal of sitting through the extremely soporific movie. I was bored but she liked it.

"It is kind of nice!!" she chirped. We got the corner seats. She laughed, smiled, and reacted at most of the scenes. It was like looking at a small girl who had never quite grown up. I bought us popcorn. She gobbled hers and then also mine. "I am sorry. I am a bit gluttonous about popcorn. They are the stressbusters during the movie."

What stress! The movie was all yawns.

When we got out of the theatre, she was happy. "This was the best HP movie yet!"

"Books are better," I said cynically.

"Don't compare it with the books; otherwise, the moviegoing experience goes for a toss. It was a good movie in itself!" She said in the tone of a movie reviewer.

Maybe! I wouldn't know.

It was evening. We wandered along the crowded Fergusson Road aimlessly, watching people pass us by. It was just people for her, but couples for me—teens having a good time. I wanted to hold her hand desperately—to touch her, as you know, means to an end.

But I didn't have the spontaneity to do it. The strain would rather accumulate in my case, and I didn't have any popcorn with me either. Finally, I decided to be a straight shooter.

"Hey, I wanted to ask you something," I whispered in her ear.

"Yes?" She turned and faced me.

Even before I opened my mouth, I knew I was going to screw it up.

"This may sound weird, but will you slap me if I touch you?"

There!

Her eyes widened, and they had the same intensity of innocence and lack of mercy as the last time they had stared into mine.

"That would depend on how you touch me," she said, "and where!"

How does one touch a girl without making her slap you? It should be playful but not... well, lustful.

"I mean, there is a difference between how you'd touch your sister, your friend, or your girlfriend, right?" She brought forth her hand. "Here! Touch it properly. Keep it clean. I am just a person. Try not to make me uncomfortable." I couldn't help but notice the quiver in her voice as she said it.

She should have found a better excuse to hold hands. I couldn't help but smile!

I grabbed her palm in mine, and we continued walking down the street as if nothing happened—nothing, except a smile that stayed with me even after I slept.

5.

June '07 (3 months after joining FORDIT): Apple iPhone launched. Netflix online video streaming service rolled out to all customers. Dropbox founded.

The lady sitting in front of me asked. "What is a code?"

The panel consisted of two ladies and a guy.

I assumed the other lady was from HR.

I took a moment to structure the answer.

"Code is a set of commands written in a programming language that performs a function. Developers do the coding—it's the process of creating a new functionality. But nowadays, most development is incremental—small tweaks to an already developed code."

"What do testers test?" she asked me again.

"They have to find the errors in the new code written by the developers and check if the code is working fine with the entire system once plugged in," I said.

"How do they do it?" she asked.

"By testing the test cases on the functionality of the code, an example of a test case is: if the switch is on, the fan should rotate. The code says it should happen, but is it happening?"

"And who writes these test cases?" asked the guy next to her.

"Testers."

"Who verifies these cases?" that same person asked again.

"The business owners of the ticket—the guys who understand the business behind this technological need. They have an extensive experience in the business. A ticket is their request for a change in the present code owing to some change in the business requirements. On testing the code, testers and the business owners give their green signal or sign-off, and the code thus gets plugged into production or real-life business scenarios."

"What if the code bombs *(fails)*? Whose responsibility is it?"

"Of the tester. Because he didn't test it well enough to find the error in the code. The developer should be happy if the tester finds errors because that would have prevented a future calamity, which can also cause a loss to the organization."

"Okay, so developers are the guys who code, and testers test that code. Glad you are aware of that." The lady smiled.

After this, she asked me some basic SQL queries. I answered them to the best of my ability.

"He is giving decently correct answers," she whispered to the lady next to her. "Fundamentals are fine; communication isn't too bad!!"

She got up and shook my hands. "Rest of the things can be taught on the job. It's almost afternoon now. Enjoy your noon. Join us for the status call in the evening." She turned to face the HR. "Do I need to drop an official email on this?"

I had spent a month and a half on the bench, and so getting absorbed into some project felt great. Tension subsided and relief gushed in.

The lady who shook my hands was my first project manager (PM).

That evening, I reached the ground-floor meeting room I was asked to come to.

"Our team is waiting for you in the conference room for a meeting. Just walk inside and be seated. I will be joining you in a moment." My project manager smiled a plastic grin at me. "Introduce yourself, and yes, Amit, welcome to the team!" She winked and went to her desk to get some printouts.

Okay, so behind the glass door of that small room were seated the first team members of my professional life. I thought of waiting for my PM before entering the room. She should be the one to introduce me, ideally. But she would take time, and I didn't want any disobedience from my end.

I opened the glass door and peeked in. All the people inside looked at me. They were sitting around a table. I looked for a chair to sit on, but all were filled.

One of the guys (*he was one of the interviewers*) spoke out, "Please get a chair from outside and also an extra chair for Kanchan."

"Umm... Kanchan?"

"Our PM... You forgot to ask her name during the interview," he and everybody else smiled at me. "Come quickly; the call is about to start in 7 minutes," he said, pointing to the clock.

I wondered what the call was about. But I rushed to take the chairs in—met our PM by the door.

"Rush, Rush! Take a coffee if you like." She entered. "This is Amitarth. Our new teammate. He would be loosely tagged to Bhoopal to help with the Crux II assignments. But, if need be, he will help Raj with the Crux I assignments as well."

"Hi!" I smiled. All nodded.

There were at least six people seated in the room, including one girl. They all looked from different places.

"Okay, we still have 5 minutes," Kanchan said, checking the clock and sipping her coffee. "Team, could you please introduce yourselves?"

The guy in my afternoon interview started first.

"*Bhoopal Rao*—been with *FORDIT* for 3.5 years—currently serving as a team lead for Crux II assignments." He might have been 26, sported a mustache, was thin but short, and sounded nerdy and South Indian. Being from a central Indian state (*Maharashtra*), I had never ventured to the south of my state—only towards the north. So, South Indians, encompassing all four states, were an alien creed to me—almost not from the same Earth. I say it in as innocent a way as possible!

"*Rajan Vamsi*—been with *FORDIT* for 3 years—currently serving as a team lead for Crux 1 assignments." Again, a South Indian accent. He looked 26 and had a mustache. He had a kind of paunch one can get only after overconsumption of either beer or rice—I wondered which was it for him!

"*Piyush Kanodia*—been with the team for 2 months." His smile was the widest, and he gave me a knowing look. He seemed to be from one of the batches in 2007 and looked the same age as mine.

"*Jaya Dutta*—been with the team for 1.5 years." She was the only girl on the team and a Bengali—the accent just gave it away.

"*Suman Nandamoori*—been with the team for a year." Again, a Southie guy. He had a booming voice and a genuine smile. He seemed like a happy-go-lucky person.

"*Yogendra Patil*—been with *FORDIT* for 3.5 years. Bhoopal and I joined the project together around 2 years ago." He had a deep voice and did not seem to be from the South.

Except Piyush, almost everyone looked 3-4 years older than me. Kanchan, of course, looked much older; she was in her late thirties.

"And you know me," Kanchan smiled at me. "I guess it's time, Bhoopal!" she said, disposing of her cup. Bhoopal started dialing.

She turned to apprise me. "We are having a status meeting with the onsite managers. Our project is completely offshore *(except for developers who are onsite)*—we talk with our clients directly. As the pressure increases in terms of assignments, you will be having status calls every evening with the clients for the assignments you guys are working on. Great, right?"

In normal onsite projects, people would share assignment outcomes with the onsite manager, someone from our own Indian team working from the U.S., who would act as a coordinator between the technical team and the clients. But for this project, testing-related work being completely offshore meant that no one from our testing team was earning dollars on-site, and the team was coordinating work with the clients directly through status calls.

The call connected.

Our client manager's name was Bob. After my brief introduction, I was more of a mute spectator throughout the call. Bhoopal was the chief spokesperson.

I asked Piyush, "Why does Bhoopal speak for everyone?"

He whispered, "I guess that's because we are not so confident speaking English. Kanchan is particular that we don't cut a sorry figure."

"So Bhoopal is that good at English?"

"He's equally horrible, but technically the most competent amongst us, so Bob is slightly more patient with him. He kind of respects him. However, even after so long, Bob still faces difficulty comprehending his Telugu accent," Piyush chuckled. "With time though, we are all supposed to start speaking for ourselves."

"And Kanchan?"

"She is good at managing people, but like most managers, her technical knowledge is not all that good. So, she avoids speaking on calls. In some ways, Bhoopal is indispensable for her and us."

○●○

After the call was over and Kanchan walked out, everyone seemed relieved. Suman had the most enthusiastic voice. "Coffee time, guys! Bhoopal, you spoke for a bit too long, man!"

Bhoopal said, "What to do? Bobby was in the mood to talk."

Everyone seemed very friendly with each other.

"Are we all on the same team?" I whispered in Piyush's ear.

"Basically, we are all on the same team but get to do different kinds of assignments under Crux I & II modules. Correspondingly, we make use of different custom tools. Every assignment often has a different business owner. Bhoopal gives a summary and status of all assignments we are working on, along with corresponding business owners, to Bob in the everyday status call."

"Why are you still speaking of work to him? Boring him to death the very first day, eh? *Kyaa rey* Amit, don't ask so many questions in the very first hour. Let's go for coffee," Suman was certainly the loudest member of the team.

"You didn't ask Kanchan to join?" I asked Suman.

"Bhoopal asks her every single time to join us, and each time she says *no* under the guise of some work. She only hangs out with

Prakash, the PM of the neighboring project. *Achha hi hai na!* We don't want our fun times at coffee to get converted into team-building sessions," Suman spoke out loud, oblivious to the fact that she might be around, or somebody might overhear.

We took coffee from the coffee machine and sat down close to each other on the pavement.

"So, first day! Do you remember our names yet?" Suman asked.

They all looked at me. I recounted everybody's names. They were impressed.

"Good memory," Suman complimented.

"So, is there a lot of work on our project?" I asked, hesitantly.

People looked at each other and then grinned at each other, and slowly everybody's eyes turned towards Bhoopal, who was grinning too while sipping his coffee. "Why don't you ask Suman? He can answer you the best."

Jaya smiled the most, "Yeah. Suman is the hardest-working member of the team. Ask him,"

Suman retorted. *"Arey kya rey tum log—majak udate mera!"* He looked at me. "The thing is this: I have been part of the team for a year, and till now, I haven't worked for even a day."

"So, what do you do?" I asked, wide-mouthed.

"I play online cricket."

He saw my eyes widen. "But isn't your workstation right next to Kanchan?"

"So what? She knows." He got defensive in like a second. "There is no work for the project they hired me for."

"So, like, everybody just plays online cricket here?" I looked around at people in disbelief.

"No, man! We all work like dogs! Not everyone is as lucky as Suman," Raj snapped.

"Are you all Tamilians?"

"We are Telugu, except for JD, who is Bengali, Yogi, who is Marathi, and Piyush, who is..."

"A Hindi-speaking guy from Bhopal," Piyush added.

"So, then most of you are from Chennai?" I asked, sipping my coffee.

Relevant people looked at me awestruck and said, "Dude, we are from Hyderabad. People from Chennai are Tamilians."

Being a guy who had never crossed the river Krishna to explore the other side, I remarked with the typical nonchalance of a geographically challenged ignorant, "What's the difference? Basically similar, right?!"

"Dude, I'll punch you. We are way better than the Tamilians. How could you even compare?" Suman said, flashing his fist.

"Oh, okay. I wouldn't know." I said, drinking the last drop from that cup in my hand. "*Potayto, Potahto*".

And then Suman just lost it. "You are such a punchbag, mate. Let me pour some coffee on you," he clutched me in his arms and literally poured some coffee on my head.

We kept talking for a long time, till after what seemed like an hour. Kanchan herself came out to persuade us to return.

"Team, I am not going to do this every time," she said, and that was what she would say every time for most of our coffee breaks then on, before driving us inside.

In our project, developers *(mostly non-Indians)* were onsite, and we were all testers. They would give us a code to test based on a ticket initiated by some business owner. Now, in layman's terms, the way I understood it, my job was to test the code that controlled the functionality of an industrial engine, and I would test if the code worked as they, the business owners and the developers, expected it to.

The module for the newer version of these engines was headed by Bhoopal, and the module for the legacy or the older version of engines was headed by Raj. The codes for both these versions were completely different, and so were the tools used to complete the assignments.

I came to know my team in ways other than professional, understanding them beyond their roles. They all were people, actual people with personalities, contrary to what was expected out of them professionally.

Suman was the guy I instantly made friends with. Something about his dark looks, rectangular face, loosely controlled disarming smiles, twinkling eyes, and moist but booming voice was intimate and genuine, but the only thing that stood out of the ordinary was his height. He was 6'2. If a girl nudged away her stereotypes, with time, she would probably find him handsome. His intelligence would show when he would be able to sense the right time to stop, and so would his passion when he wouldn't be able to.

If Suman was the Joe next door, JD was the girl next door's cranky sis. She was the kind who would look better fat. She had a chubby face, was of average height, and was bright. There was an alertness about that face that would only get enhanced with some fat around it. There were times when she was soft and quiet, but that was only when she had softened enough to forget reality momentarily. I had often seen her consume calcium tablets and scratch her nails. She wouldn't have turned heads when she walked, but I guess she would certainly hold someone's attention when she talked.

Rajan and Piyush were both plump and short in equal measures. The difference was that while Piyush was plump uniformly with well-accentuated muscles, Raj's aura of plumpness was mainly due to his belly. While Piyush was fair and square-faced, Raj was wheatish, round-faced, and mustached.

Bhoopal was dark with an angular heart-shaped face, trimmed mustache, and triangular eye sockets, with the sharpest and calmest eyes of us all. He spoke slowly, took time to choose words and ponder, and would often say things that automatically brought clarity to the situation, whether he chose it or not. His presence was a steady flow of energy and purpose, and problems would resolve themselves when he was around.

Yogi was slightly plump again, with big eyes and an unassuming grin. He was a trifle shy, but with an air of unbridled affection and a certain numbness towards technology.

"Dude, you and I are the last of the survivors on this floor," Suman said to me the next day. I looked at him wide-eyed.

"What is the difference between us and our world, Sherlock?" he asked. He was speaking of our project floor.

"Umm... We are poor," I said hesitantly. But I knew it was the wrong answer. Everyone on that floor was poor.

"Idiot! I didn't mean it that way. We don't have a paunch while everybody else has it," he said. "Look around. We are an endangered species."

Suddenly, it was as if I gained new perspective; everyone's paunch protruded from their bodies until it hurt my eyes. "People are so ugly, mate." It was seriously disgusting.

"I know. We have somehow survived the onslaught of fat on our bodies. Tell me, why is it that we don't go to the gym to keep ensuring so?"

"You forget. I get up at 10 in the morning, while you get up at 9.30 a.m. We got to be in the office by 11 a.m. If it's a choice between sleep and the gym, sleep wins," I explained.

"Okay, so how many times do you shag every day?"

"What??" I was shocked.

"How many times?"

"I don't... you..." I tried to smirk as if I had been asked the most ridiculous question ever, but the words just got stuck in my throat.

"Dude," he said, staring deep into my eyes.

"What?" I asked.

"How many times?"

"I don't, man!" I blurted out, feeling violated.

"See, the reason I ask is that the second-best way to burn calories is to shag it out, and I know you are lying. Every software engineer shags."

"Is that how people deal with frustration here?" It sure sounded like a made-up fact.

"That's the only way people deal with frustration everywhere. Here, they also deal with boredom and the lack of growth in the way mentioned," he winked at me.

"Oh c'mon!" My eyes almost popped out at what he was trying to say.

"Yes!! That's how I stay thin."

"Don't tell me that you shag under your workstation. You sit right next to Kanchan, with only a thick pillar between you."

"Why can't I? Nobody comes there. She can't see me. It's the safest place there is! And I get a high from the thrill."

"Dude, you are scary!"

"I was joking, mate!" He laughed at the fact that I took it so seriously. "I don't do it under the table; I use the restroom. Now please don't ask me who I imagine," he said, winking.

"I will not. You'll creep me out," I said, rolling my eyes. "You are a sex maniac."

"Well, everyone is! I ruined my college years that way—blind chatting on Yahoo dating rooms. Bloody addictive."

"But why the office of all places?" I said, throwing my hands in the air. I hated how everyone around me was turning out to be a psycho.

"Well, the company doesn't expect anything better than that from me," he said sighing. "That's what I get paid for. By the way, you should totally know how I lost my virginity."

"No interest! Can be anyway!"

"How do you know it was not in the office?" He smiled at me enigmatically.

I don't know if he was speaking the truth.

With Suman, you never know!

○ ● ○

Suman seemed to have abandoned any ambition to grow in the organization. He would just waste an hour in the cafeteria every morning, come to his workstation by around 12 p.m., and then continue his marathon online cricket sessions. His would be the first IP message to ask the entire team to come for lunch, then for coffee, which would easily stretch for an hour. JD would be the first to answer any message of his.

He had already spent a year without any work, but he seemed least worried.

"One can always tell some story to recruiters, *rey*. I keep studying. The work we do is basically dead-end work, so none of us is going to get placed anywhere. Look at Bhoopal and Yogi; both have been searching for jobs for a year now. They keep attending interviews with small companies whenever their placement agency calls, and what happens? Nothing! The jobs out there are for some marketable and employable skills, not for the niche work that we do. So, it doesn't matter if I work or not; what matters is to convince the interviewer that I know C++."

"But I never see you study."

"I do study online articles. I also applied for jobs but haven't received any calls yet. I will only consider Hyderabad-based opportunities."

"You want to move back? Girlfriend waits for marriage?" I smiled.

"At this salary, even the gardener's daughter won't marry me. My mother has high hopes for me, man. Nobody in our entire family has even completed graduation, let alone engineering. I am the first, and my grandmother is insanely proud of me. In fact, she wants to see me get married before her eye operation. There are weird concerns in her mind that she may not be able to see after the operation, so she keeps delaying it. If only she knew how lousy I am, she would undertake the surgery tomorrow. I am like the worst engineer ever, but they think I was the only one born after Visvesvaraya, Narayan Murthy, and Ramalingam Raju."

"Okay, skip the marriage part. Girlfriend waiting?" I winked.

"Neighborhood aunty waiting, man! The 40-year-old fat cow I lost my virginity to. Bloody, I used to just use the internet in her house when this Shakeela aunty had my flower."

That amused me.

"Well, have you considered JD?"

He was startled, "What about her?"

"Have you confessed that you want to marry her?"

He kept blinking at me. I knew I had hit on something very soft there inside, something everybody, including him, knew and understood, yet willingly ignored.

His voice softened.

"We are just great friends, dude. Besides, don't you think she deserves better? Ya?" And just when I felt I was about to meet the real him, he smiled at me and smirked. "...and frankly, there is no such thing as love. Always remember that... idiot! There's just lust." He started laughing his weird, evil laughter that I assumed a B-grade, scary Hyderabadi gangster would typically laugh before assaulting the hero's sister.

○ ● ○

Yogi and Bhopal were like each other in so many ways. Both had completed their CAD/CAM course from the same college in Hyderabad, and both later joined *FORDIT* at the same time on the same project. Both were of the same age, and both earned equally low salaries. Both spent a year and a half frustrated with *INSITE*, the project Mitali was currently working with. They later struggled and fought their way into our project and were now proud to have spent two years in it without choking themselves.

There were minor differences, though. Bhoopal was a Telagite, Yogi was Marathi, and Bhoopal was technically more competent. Except for that, both were kind of stuck and were trying to jump over the same professional dead end with similar results. Both treated me like a younger brother, with a subtle difference that Bhoopal, as my boss, was slightly more formal.

Yogi was from a small village near Pune and had lost his father in his childhood. He just had his mother, who would keep asking him to get married and to take more leaves so that he could meet her more often, and not just three times a year. Obviously, she hadn't understood the concept of project utilization (*will come later*).

○●○

"Why was Venky so sad today? He didn't even smile or wave at us. Code bombed, or what?" I asked one day.

Venky, aka Venkateswara Rao, whom Bhoopal and Yogi were friends with *(as he had joined with them)*, was a developer in an adjoining project. Venky had risen to the sanctimonious levels of a developer in a respectable embedded-systems based, sister project and so automatically had the hierarchical right to have the last word in every conversation that he had with Yogi or Bhoopal. He was a wannabe finance wizard, as he felt his knowledge of the stock market was at least as good as his skills in coding.

Unfortunately, 8 out of 10 times when they invested with his advice, they lost money. But the trust never wavered.

"Venky is sharp, and his advice is reliable. Markets are volatile due to the anticipation of a recession leading to panic. Stocks rise and fall unevenly. Our research indicates that they would rise, and as soon as we invest, they start falling. That doesn't mean that we shouldn't invest. That only means we have a lot to learn about investing. Besides, it can be a great side business, you know. Sometimes we spend days without doing anything on our end, so why not use them productively to generate a new income source?" Yogi opened up once at the breakfast table.

He had been investing in stocks for like a year and a half now.

"Bhoopal invests too, sometimes." The mention of Bhoopal would automatically add weight to the theory. After all, he was the guy we all looked up to.

The entire day, Yogi would keep watching his computer for news on the market. Every day, we could tell from their faces if the market fell or rose. And for the past several weeks, we had hardly seen him smile, which wasn't good news.

One day, I just couldn't endure sad faces anymore and asked Yogi.

"Do you lose a lot of money?"

"We invest a couple of thousand and lose around twenty percent every day. Not too much, but when we do win, it leads to euphoria."

○ ● ○

The best way to train people, they say, is to make them train themselves. In about two weeks, these guys finished training me in the tools and technology, and as Bhoopal said, "Time to check if our tiny goldfish in the bowl is ready for the lake swim."

"Goldfish with a better memory," Suman corrected him.

"Is this an easy one?" I asked apprehensively.

"This was the one in the pipeline. No discrimination against the new by giving them simple assignments," Bhoopal chuckled wickedly. "Find out for yourselves if you find it easy. Take JD's help."

The assignment was simple yet laborious. It was based on new fault codes and checking the functions where these fault codes were to be included, leading to new scenarios. There were plenty of fault codes, and hence lots of test conditions.

First step: get the test plan prepared and get it approved. Then, get Zachary the developer's *(call me Zach, please!)* help to make sure none of the scenarios are missed, and after that, get the blessings of the business owners. Then came the part where we ran these test conditions and tried our best to be cynical in order to find as many errors as possible. That would be good, as then the code wouldn't bomb in the production, which ultimately will lead to the greater good in the sense that our neck will be spared.

"What's the deadline?"

"That's for you to decide and inform the business owner. Take more time than necessary and submit before the deadline."

I took JD's help at possibly every step. I spent a couple of days on the assignment and submitted the final results.

'Hi, Svetlana, hope you received the results and got a chance to go through them,' I pinged the business owner.

'I did go through them but didn't understand.'

What was not to understand? I was dumbfounded.

'I will explain it to you.' I went through the entire document, discussing it on *Sametime* [17].

'Let's have a call,' she pinged.

What the hell? I have never had a status call alone before. Where was Bhoopal?

Raj was working on something. "He is out. Just call him, will you? Or ask JD if she can help."

I asked for JD's help.

"I can't, dear; I am chatting with the developer on our new code. It's alright. Just call him, or is it her?" I shrugged cluelessly. "Make

---

[17] *Now owned by HCL. In layman's terms, it's a chat messenger.*

172 | *The Little Men*

sure of the gender before you address them. It can lead to some very funny situations," was her only suggestion.

By the time I returned to my desk, there was already a meeting invite in my inbox along with the participants. Every Tom, Dick, and Harry was part of the discussion. My heart skipped a beat. Moments like these make me more aware of my shyness.

I dialed on time and announced my participation after pressing the hash. Everybody wished me.

"Hey, Amyith, how do we pronounce your name? Is it Amy for short?"

I was about to correct her, but female voice 2 interrupted.

"This might take a while, Elaine. Let's get our clarifications first!"

Elaine giggled. I should have asked who the person was.

"Right, Svetlana! So, Amy, could you please explain to us the test document you just sent us? We are having trouble decoding it," Elaine said.

"Right," I said, clearing my throat. "So basically, we have these test cases, which I hope are clear."

"They aren't. Please go step by step," said Svetlana, piqued.

I found myself sweating, and I said the first thing that came to my mind. "I would, but I don't see what's not to understand. Instead, if you could just ask me your doubts..."

"So, are you saying you can't explain the very test document you wrote? Is that what you are saying?" said a temperamental male voice without an introduction, who I didn't even know was part of the discussion.

"All I am saying is that if there is any particular issue, we can..." I couldn't complete my sentence.

"Let's clear this out: are you saying you refuse to explain it to us?" Svetlana said it in a disgruntled tone.

Now was the moment I chose to lose my voice.

"I don't mean that...I just meant to say..." and I went on to explain the test document word by word in excruciatingly painful technological detail. There was a stunned silence on the other end.

"Call your reporting manager, somehow I am lost," said male voice 2.

"Really sir, there is no need..."

"Name's Steve, and I would like to talk to him right now. I hope he understands English," he said in a heated tone.

"If only there was Zach here, he could have shed some light..." I tried an alibi, framing the onsite developer.

"I'm right here, buddy. I am not sure what you are trying to say," said male voice 3 in a Russian accent.

Elaine giggled. For a normal brain that wasn't testosterone-induced at that moment, it might have actually been funny. I didn't find it so, unfortunately.

There wasn't much left to say. I turned around to find all our team members standing behind me; apparently, the tones weren't just heated; they were loud.

"Bhoopal is coming," Piyush said in a grave tone. "Kanchan called him."

I avoided looking in the direction of her workstation. I could survive, I guess, without seeing her bloodshot eyes trying to burn me down.

"Hello...Hello..." The voices on the call were getting restless.

"He is coming," I croaked at the speaker.

I prayed to God to send Bhoopal with Mercury's wings. And there he was, entering through the project door. He took his own sweet minute to reach my workstation.

"Hello" was his sharp, unapologetic voice at the receiver. He was mildly irritated.

"We don't understand what this guy is trying to say," said male voice 1.

"Go ahead!" he said, looking at me.

I started saying the same stuff again, for a minute.

"This has been such a waste of time, guys," said Steve.

"Monumental," said Svetlana, exasperated.

"Can't you guys be a little more elaborate? None of us are able to understand," Elaine said in a patronizing voice.

"I would need to leave, guys. I have some meetings lined up," Zach said before logging out.

"So have I," Steve and male voice 1 both left.

"What do we do about this now?" Svetlana asked, stupefied.

"We will send you an email with a detailed explanation. It should clarify whatever concerns you might have," Bhoopal replied.

So, the first solitary status call of my professional life ended on a disgruntled note. Bhoopal turned to me calmly.

"Never use strong words like *'doubts'* and *'issues'* while talking with the client. They take it as a personal retribution. Use words like *'clarify'* and *'query'* instead. Also, pay attention to who you are speaking with. Business owners can't understand the technical language we were speaking. You have to speak broad business with them, not the code, if you want them to understand you. Talk as you would with a layman, and next time, if things go wrong, call me early!" he exclaimed, breaking into a grin.

I looked back to find Kanchan standing behind me.

"Don't take it too seriously!" Kanchan winked and patted me.

The day ended on a hopeful note, thus.

○●○

The way this project was, work just wouldn't stop coming. Every day I would come with the thought that I would finish work early—that's how I liked it. But things would never end.

As soon as work assigned to me ended and I reported it back, extra work would pile up like a genie from the bottle. Whenever the boss would see me free, some extra work would pop up.

Suman sometimes said it right: I had the most unfortunate location—right in front of the project manager's suspicious eye. I could not bear to see that evil glint of disapproval every time I would be seen relaxing or taking my rightful time off. She would take it personally—as if it were her failure at productivity management—likely one of the KRAs[18] at which she would be judged at the end of the year.

So, we got into the habit of submitting work later than usual— just maintaining enough work efficiency to score an average rating, taking a trifle less work than we could do without stretching ourselves and managing even less than that, as we would fritter away the time—laughing our guts off at silly jokes over the seemingly never-ending coffee drinking sessions.

But we were supposed to be seated and appear busy at least 60% of the time to ensure the satisfaction of our PM. Bhoopal would often refuse to do so.

'We get paid for the work we do for the company. When there is no work, there is no work; don't bullshit! Go home early,' he would tell us.

---

[18] *Key Result Areas.*

Poor Bhoopal! His integrity as a person wouldn't have helped him grow as a leader in this organization. Here, it wasn't important to be busy; it was more important to act busy—basically, the art of perception management.

We were just resources, but we were hardly resourceful. But then, as Bhoopal would say at times, *'There is hardly anything worth being resourceful about. The basic structure in this project never changes. The only way to be resourceful is to increase the speed of work.'*

Why would I do that? To get more work? I don't think so!

6.

September'07 (Back to the present): SoundCloud was founded in August 2007.

Prabhu kept asking me about his life more and more—about what I thought of him, about what the world thinks of us, and if we will ever be able to break the mold and create our own space in the world.

"We are like ants, you see. A meaningless, dreary existence for greater luxury is not life. Killing one's dreams and fitting into the slot is not life. Making compromises for your family and losing the fire inside just because our talent doesn't match up with our aspirations can't be life. Just doing routine work each day and expecting miracles to happen is not life." He paused for breath, a sigh, and a sip of his coffee.

"Life is not so simple, dear!" I reiterated.

But he had a point. How long were we to keep doing what we were doing?

"One day, after slogging 15 hours each day and after losing all your hair and fire in your belly, you will rise up to the ranks of a manager in this organization. By that time, your expectations would have risen. So that would again be beneath you, and besides, it was not even my ambition to begin with. We are nothing but an army of slaves, damn it! But that's not the real problem." He put down his cup and looked at me to see if we were connecting. "The problem is, I expected my work to give me happiness and make me forget my sorrow; instead, all it does is give me more problems and stress in life. I think we should start drinking."

"There is still time for that," I replied quietly.

As we wallowed in our bubble of boredom and dullness in our daily existence, we hadn't noticed the external factors plotting against us. The latest news was that, while Yahoo was performing well in 2007 revenue-wise, it was also facing some real competition from Google in search and advertising. Something seemed off!

There were layoffs expected in the coming times in the banking, pharmaceutical, construction, and manufacturing sectors. God knew how long it would take for the tech. players to follow suit. The impending recession wasn't making things any easier!

"We are not developing any skills, buddy," I said, keeping that same context at the back of my mind.

"What kind of skills?"

"Employable skills, I mean—the technical and communication ones. We lack the personality to lead. We lack the stability to undertake the burden of responsibility. We lack the stillness of mind to keep learning, even in our daily humdrum. In short, we lack the character to succeed." I summed it up. There was really nothing more to it.

Dreams are one thing, but having the will to sustain them is another prerequisite for making them a reality.

"That is true; everybody works hard, but not everybody has it in them to sustain the boredom of consistency." He yawned at the last word. We were flashes in the pan.

"And yet we keep dreaming, don't we?" He smiled at me sadly.

"Sometimes I wonder why!"

I kept silent. He came out of his melancholy in a second.

"Writing anything new?"

I had started to write a lot recently. It was just one of my getaways to acquire some peace of mind. "Some poems. Nothing earth-shattering," I smiled.

"Write a play!"

"Nah, plays don't win Nobel prizes," I said, and we both smiled at ourselves.

"I have a theory as to why India has such a huge population with so few scientists and so little research."

I yawned. Alas, it was not enough to stop him from opening his mouth.

"That is because we Indians don't know how to spend our free time. All we do is spend it on eating, festivals, marriages, and sex. Every great civilization has flourished only after people excelled in art, science, music, and astronomy. We too flourished in B.C. periods. But after slavery, we just lost our scientific curiosity to think for ourselves and to build our own curious minds. That is the only reason we revel in sex, because nothing else pleases our senses more. It is not due to a lack of education; it is our denseness, or, better yet, the blind obstinacy of our numbness, that refuses to let us think. Education can never be a substitute for thinking."

"You are quoting Thomas J. Watson of IBM," I said.

"Great man, great company. I hope I join it someday."

"True. Companies can be built in a day, but it takes years to build a culture. Isn't it?" I was thinking of the culture of our company.

"While that is true, culture can only be sculpted by great men and women—the people who run with the beacon," he said.

As I thought about everybody from our company in my memory, people who weren't great but were people nevertheless, I knew that couldn't be the case.

"I beg to differ on that. Culture can only be built by common men and women—ones like you and me." I said it with conviction—wouldn't bite my tongue on that.

"Point taken. But still, the truth remains that we as a crowd are uncomfortable in a thinking mode," said he.

"Hmm. Beyond the immediate professional and personal need, we surely do find thinking awkward," I smiled. That was true.

"But we aren't average people, are we?" He beamed and winked at me.

Yeah, we weren't average—he and I. We were levels below, struggling with our personal demons. Average people were at least good at average things, while we both sucked at everything. I kept being kind to us and let that thought pass away unsaid.

○●○

That very month, we had a party on a Friday at Suman's house. All the team gathered except JD because the plan was to drink.

I don't drink, but I was the special invitee to make sure the situation didn't get out of hand. Since there was no plan, we kind of just gathered, and people started drinking. It started with beer, then rum, and later whiskey.

I don't know what effect that sort of cocktail has on people, but it sure wasn't pretty in this case. Suman stood up, started shouting, and began stripping. Piyush, who wasn't a drinker himself, started shooting a video of Suman swearing and dancing on the table, gyrating his belly. Bhoopal just sat on the ground and, weirdly, had bubbles coming out from his mouth. I shook him, but he didn't respond, nor did he close his eyes. It was a funny sight. Raj's eyes were bloodshot and scary.

"Shit, they're going to create trouble," Piyush cried at me. "Take the bottles away!"

But drunken brains can have surprisingly accentuated senses.

"Nobody touches the bottle, or I'll cut his balls and hang them on the bloody door," Raj shouted.

"And I'll make sure that person also does a pole dance for us—naked obviously," Suman said with cuckoo eyes.

Bhoopal tried to say something, but only to have more bubbles come out of his mouth.

Suman's roomie came out of his room. "We need to make sure these guys don't create a scene, bro, or else our flat owner will kick us out. Besides, we bachelors don't have a good reputation here. The neighbors keep complaining as Suman keeps ogling at their wives, sisters, and daughters using a telescope from our room window."

That night was weird, as we kept trying to keep the clothes on these jerks.

By 1 a.m., everybody in the room had cried. Everybody had a failed love story to share, a shattered dream, a family they had disappointed and a nagging father *(except for Yogi, of course)*.

"I could have done *M.Tech*, but I didn't have 60 percent in undergrad, which is the minimum criteria to appear for any such exams. Just lost it by a percentage," wailed Suman.

"I still want to do it, but I am too old for it now. I have a soft brain and am not as brainy as Bhoopal," Yogi added.

Bhoopal tried to say something, but only more bubbles appeared.

"I didn't have money to do the *GRE*; otherwise, I could have joined my girlfriend." Piyush sighed sadly.

"Guys, no more drinks, please," I interrupted; it was a false note in the gloomy music of the hour.

"*Chup sale!*" Suman snapped and looked at everyone. "Let's watch porn!!"

"Yay!! Bring it on!" All raised their glasses in the air.

"But the sound should be on mute," Suman's roomie said desperately, not that anybody listened.

It was a crazy night; people just slept off while the movie was still on.

"Thankfully, nobody got nude. Let's just carry them to the rooms inside; I wouldn't want them to sleep on each other like this." Suman's roommate seemed like a kind guy, one that Suman didn't deserve but needed anyway.

We all slept peacefully and woke up in the afternoon the next day. Everybody was sober now and left with a heavy head, but only after drinking a cup of steamy coffee that Suman's roomie so lovingly prepared. Bhoopal seemed to be still struggling with his voice; he just waved at us and left.

We had another weekend ahead of us.

○●○

'Should we go out for dinner this weekend?' I pinged Mitali the next week.

'I have to study.'

'You can bring along your books too. I will watch you study.'

'Not interested!'

'My treat.'

'For what?'

'I like treating you.'

'I don't like free food.' She pinged back.

'You can pay for us both.'

'Very funny. I don't like to squander free food either.'

'Well, we can share the bill.'

'In that case, why not eat at our own places as usual? Why go?'

I took a moment to consider that option.

'You can call me at your place, you know.' I took a moment to rephrase what I was going to ping next. *'I like homemade food, too.'*

'Nice try.'

'Well, I'll not bring Prabhu, so you don't have to cook for both of us. Just me.'

'Are you kidding me!?' I could almost hear her shriek. I chuckled.

'By the way, did I tell you I find you very pretty?' I asked.

'I can see where this is going.'

'Stop playing chess with me. I don't think of the next 10 steps like you do. At least take something at face value.'

'Oh, yeah? I am not pretty, nor am I blind. I can see through your tricks.'

'You are pretty, blind, and dumb,' I said.

'You are an idiot!' she exclaimed, fuming.

Now that's what I call a wild cat. We both didn't type for some time.

'Oh, c'mon! You have an eyesight of -4. Without your glasses, you won't be able to tell a boy from a girl,' I attempted to inject some facts into the conversation.

'I can hear them.'

'Very clever.'

We again stopped chatting for some time to get control of our train of thought.

'So, I can't be dumb, can I? I was right in calling you an idiot,' She concluded her point.

We paused to restructure our strategy.

'All your cleverness comes out only when I make a plan,' I pinged.

'You are an idiot for making such a plan.'

'Okay, you make one!'

Again, a pause. I wondered what reply was to come.

'Fine. Come to my home for dinner tonight.'

I choked over my coffee. I hate jackpots. Now if only I could just stop myself from ruining it…

'What time?' I typed.

'We'll leave together.'

She was serious. I found my confidence slipping.

'Well, how do I come back?'

'You don't! You sleep at my place.' She pinged back.

'I have no clothes with me.'

'You can wear mine.'

I could almost imagine my face growing bluer.

'I am serious. This isn't funny.'

'I wouldn't be so concerned about clothes, if you know what I mean.'

I choked again. This was too true to be a jackpot. I felt chills down my spine.

'We would just be eating, right?' I pinged.

'Depends on you!!'

Hmm...time for an enigmatic reply.

'I would prefer food after play. Play ruffles up the appetite,' I was pleased by my cheesiness.

'Which game do you want to play, Mr. Player?' she asked, naughtily.

'Whichever loses the most calories, <wink>,' I remarked.

'I don't play football.'

'Neither do I.' I was disappointed by her lack of understanding on subtle cues.

'Well, I guess we'll figure it out when the time comes.'

Now we were talking!

'Sure. At what time, then? We can leave even now. My work is over.' It wasn't!

I wouldn't lie that I felt butterflies in my tummy.

There was a pause. A longer one this time. Then came a reply.

'You were conversing with my neighbor. She started chatting a while ago when I left the place to fetch a coffee. Sorry for not locking my computer. Thanks for entertaining her and disgusting me. By the way, do I have to remind you every single time to get a grip, Mr. Perv?'

My face fell and grew pale.

'I didn't know. I was surprised to find you talking in this manner. I hope we'll forget this as a petty misunderstanding.' I just blabbered whatever diplomatic words I could think of under the circumstances.

'Right! So, dinner tonight at 8 p.m.—my place,' came a reply.

I didn't know what to say.

'Who's this again? Enough pranks!' I responded, feeling helpless and confused.

'We leave together. Gotta go. Work!'

She logged out. I looked at the screen, stunned.

Mitali's version:

I chuckled at the whole affair. The best thing I like about online chat is one can so easily pretend to be one's neighbor.

Ami's version:

I waited for her at the bus stop that evening.

I waited for 15 minutes until she came to catch the company bus. She didn't seem to notice me, but I knew she would never miss what she had her eye on.

The corner of that bespectacled eye was a powerfully effective tool. We would never even nod at each other in public, each conscious of her reputation to protect. So, we just stood as far apart as possible, with at least 10-15 people between us.

Abhinav and Rohit were among these people, along with a few giggling girls. I would never raise my eyes to see which girls though—it would hurt me if I saw Pooja laughing at Abhinav's vitriolic jokes on me.

Pooja had turned out to be an unattainable ideal.

All I sought was the closest replacement. But unattainability doesn't mean that feelings fade—instead, they only grow sharper. What I felt for her was inexplicable. She was an invisible part of my mind. I knew she was beyond my reach; so far, even trying seemed foolish.

Yet, unfailingly, there was a connection every time she was around me, a potent possibility that she would respond if only I made an effort to try. I wouldn't dare try though; I didn't want that dim hope to fade.

"Hey!" somebody shouted in my ear. I looked in the direction of that voice. But of course, who could it be? It was Rohit.

"Hey, you didn't wear your pink shirt today!" His voice boomed. People giggled.

It used to be a huge group of at least 8-10 people at any point in time.

"I don't have one." I whispered without looking at them.

"Don't mumble!" he snapped back.

I didn't respond, but I was aware of my ears going pink.

"...and where's your...umm...partner?"

"Prabhu isn't my partner; he is my friend, and he'll be late today. Why are you so concerned?" I snapped back this time. I didn't want to be a guy without a spine in Mitali's eyes.

"You are so sensitive towards Prabhu. I hear you guys are getting married." His voice went shrill with cruelty and sadism; he wanted people to giggle at this one.

There were a few sniggers—from the loyal ones, who would laugh first and then listen.

"No, I am getting married to your sister. You didn't hear that?" I said, adding, "I thought she would invite you!" People stopped chuckling. He wanted to punch me, but he didn't have enough hot impulse to do so.

"Laugh now, assholes!" I mumbled and gave the finger to the group.

192 | *The Little Men*

Thankfully, Mitali's bus arrived. That was enough show of spunk for the week. My whole body was trembling with tension. I saw Mitali enter, and so I did too.

"That's not even your bus, idiot!" Rohit shouted at me, and there were a lot of guffaws this time. "Don't worry, I wouldn't beat the shit out of you. Get down."

I wouldn't take that chance.

She didn't look at me. I sat many seats behind her, patiently awaiting her response. She didn't even move her head.

I felt tense. Her stop came after almost an hour.

She got up and moved towards the door, not once looking back. I followed her with my bag, well aware of my cluelessness. At the bus door, she casually glanced at me once and then got off. I got off as well.

After the bus went away, we waited at the stop for some time. She just stood silent, and I kept looking at her for some response. I was too shy to ask her about the dinner plans.

After a moment, she walked away, and I followed her silently.

○●○

We kept walking for what seemed like a long time—I was behind her as her shadow. She would keep glancing back from time to time.

Finally, we reached her place and her gate, and that's when she turned to look at me properly for the first time.

"Listen, my house owner is conservative. He does not approve of boys visiting me."

I raised my eyebrows.

"It's not like many do," she said, clarifying, "but he would still freak out if he saw any. You would need to be a bit surreptitious and quick while entering the house. There's a fair chance we might be able to miss him."

"Quite a watchdog, eh? What does he do?" I asked.

"Nothing. An old Parsi retired guy in his late seventies. His wife died long ago. He lives on a pension. Pa's acquaintance. Keeps bothering me from time to time for little things."

It was an old independent place with two small, detached, single-storied blocks: one with a front entry where the owner stayed and the other one at the back with a side entry where Mitali stayed alone. Mitali's block had a front yard with a small unkempt garden that seemed strewn with dry fallen leaves. It appeared that the place had little to no maintenance. The front gate was common to both blocks. Most houses in that lane were independent, and that colony seemed residential and quaint, with little traffic.

We tiptoed towards the door of her room; it seemed to be at the far end of the gate entirely. To the best of our hope and knowledge, nobody saw us.

"Do you not find it a little risky to live all alone? Take a partner, no!" I.

"Actually, I tried to live with other girls, but that was too much stress for my appetite. I like things to be quiet—my way. Finally, I decided to stay alone—even if it appears a little spooky to you!"

"Nah, it is okay." It wasn't. It was eerie.

"Well, I expected my parents to visit me from time to time. They do sometimes—once every quarter. It is too much of a hassle to get them adjusted when other girls live with you."

"True!" I. The rooms were silent, and the light was low.

Oddly, there was little decoration in any of the rooms. Things weren't uncrowded, and yet rooms were empty and simple, a little unclean, with clothes lying everywhere.

But overall, the place was livable—she did make an effort to clean it once every week or so it seemed.

"Are you looking for a photo-frame of my parents, dog, or family?" she inquired, her eyes twinkling.

"Yeah, something of the sort," I said, looking around while trying to keep my eyes from flashing with curiosity.

"I have lots of online pictures—none on the wall. The thing is, I prefer to keep my rooms as uncluttered as possible; I am slightly claustrophobic!"

"So, I guess, maybe you are also commitment-phobic if you like your life similarly uncluttered." I said cheekily.

She chuckled. "You guessed that right. Not always but often. I need a lot of space and air both inside as well as outside me."

What about light? I wondered! She lacked it inside the house, and if my guess was correct, also inside her.

"I will clean it a bit to make you a little space to sit," she said, taking her clothes lying around and putting them all in the washing machine.

"All to be cleaned!" she smiled.

It was evening, and the light kept receding until we could see nothing but darkness through the kitchen windows.

"You could have seen the main road from this kitchen window till like 15 minutes ago," I glanced out to now see an occasional red or yellow light of a vehicle entering or leaving her lane. No other sound broke the silence of the evening.

"Let's close the windows. Too many insects; time to cook," she winked. "Can you cook? I could use a change of taste."

"I can boil eggs. Apart from that, I never really tried!" I closed the windows.

"Hmm disappointing," she said, getting into the mode of Tarla Dalal. "It is the basic art of life, you see. I hope you can cut vegetables at least."

I assisted her a little as I saw her dexterous and unwavering hands go through the raw material like a surgeon in order to make it edible. She seemed to know the soul of cooking. "My entire time here, I have cooked. First, let me get you well fed, and then we can talk. Do you have a kitchen?"

"We do."

"You should seriously try cooking."

"Nah, we are bachelors, and no one is interested. Besides, it is difficult to maintain the accounts."

She kept the food to gather steam, after which there was an awkward pause. She kept staring at the steam droplets inside the glass-lidded saucepan. Everything inside me told me to hug her.

"And now we wait!" She turned towards me, breaking the moment. "You must be feeling odd that I asked you to come to my home today."

I shrugged my shoulders. She sighed at the futility of the explanations she might end up giving.

"You can get refreshed if you want. I too will." She walked away. "Sim the gas after 5 minutes once the color changes to orange."

We ate quietly.

"You cook well!" I complimented her.

"Thanks!" she smiled. "Home food gives satisfaction like no other."

After her dinner was over, she started cleaning the table. "Don't wash the plates. Just keep it in the sink. You are my guest. Make yourself at home. What would you like to do now?"

It was hardly 9 p.m.

"I don't know. How about a walk?"

"Umm... I am not sure if it is a good idea. People see!" She wriggled back on the sofa, playing with her hair. I couldn't imagine what she was thinking.

"If not outside, inside then. Show me your study room."

"Oh yes, my room! It's nothing but a garbage can of books. If you really want to see, follow my lead."

So now I was finally in her bedroom. Her room was exactly as she described it, with half-open books strewn across the table, bed, and racks.

The open one kept upside down on the bed was a book on C++.

"*Bjorn Stroustrup*'s version," she said. He is the founder of the C++ programming language.

"This is the difficult version, right?" I asked, displaying my knowledge and ignorance at the same time. She didn't feel it was important enough to reply.

"Do you have a C++ compiler?" she asked.

"I don't even have a comp."

"Sad!" We waited inside the room for a few moments, wondering what to say next.

"So, what do we do?" she asked again.

"Let's watch a movie!"

"Oh yes. You haven't watched *'Gone with the Wind'*"

"Darn right, I haven't. I love the last line. What was it? Something like, *'Baby, I don't give a fuck!'*"

"It's *'Frankly my dear, I don't give a damn!'*" she said, aghast.

"Whatever!" said I, settling down on the sofa.

"It's a classic, and we can watch it! But don't sleep if you don't want to piss me off."

"I need incentives to not sleep," I said, hoping she'd take my cue.

"I will keep bugging you if you sleep, and if you still don't listen, I will kick you out of my house," she winked.

It was a long movie and seemed even longer on the laptop. Vivian Leigh was beautiful.

"I just love Rhett Butler. Every girl wants a husband like him, but Scarlett is too stupid to notice," she whispered into my ear.

○●○

But then the movie kept going on and on, until I found it difficult to keep my eyes open.

"How long is this movie?"

"Almost 4 hours."

"Damn!"

After another 15 minutes, I just couldn't take it anymore.

"Give me any challenge except this. But please don't ask me to not sleep through this movie."

She gave me an annoyed look. "Old movies are a little slow. Can't you just go with the flow? Keep watching. You will like it."

After yet another 15 minutes, I thought the movie was going haywire.

"So now what? They are going to show us their entire lives?" I asked, my mouth wide open.

"Shut up. They are going to kiss now. It is one of the most romantic kisses in history," she said, sighing.

It was romantic all right, but I was bored.

"Have you ever slapped a guy?" I asked her.

She gave me a weird look. "Why do you ask?"

"I have never been hit by a girl, but I always wanted to, for the fun of it. One of those crazy things to do before one dies. Why don't you try it once?"

"I've hit my brothers before; I hit Neeraj once when he made fun of me." she said, thinking.

"No, I mean slap!"

"I don't want to hit you. Why would I do that? Watch the movie," she said gently.

"If I misbehave with you, you will, right?" I asked in a tense voice.

"You won't misbehave with me. You are a safe guy," and she faced the lappy screen again.

"What if I hit you?"

"Stop being childish," she said. But as she turned to watch the movie, I gave her a small slap on her cheek. She came back in a flash, slapping me.

"Hahaha, that was fun! Slap me once again. This wasn't edgy enough." Maybe I was happy with her touch.

"No, I won't, and please stop threatening me with misbehavior!"

"Look, I can!" I gave her my best threatening look.

"No, you can't!"

Who was I kidding? Of course, I can't. But, to my own surprise, before I knew what I was doing, I leaned forward towards her lips for a peck. I wanted to get it over with before she even knew what had happened.

But she was quicker than me. In a flash, she turned her face away, so I ended up kissing her cheek. It took several moments for her to regain her voice.

"That was stupid, you know!" she said, wiping her cheek.

"I told you I could misbehave!" I spoke in a croaky voice.

"That wasn't misbehaving." Her voice was tense.

"Well!" words failed me. What do I say to that?

"I can misbehave more if you want." I could sense my voice going meek and optimistic as I shrugged my shoulders.

"You can't. You are a nice guy!" she said defiantly, but her eyes said a different story. Maybe a challenge was what was needed.

I stood up, breathing heavily. This was my first time, and I knew I had to misbehave.

But how? It had to be a level higher. Maybe I could touch her chest or hug her. I only hoped she wouldn't end up shouting.

She looked at me with an amusing twinkle in her eyes, as if she could read my thoughts. "You have a very expressive face, you know. The expressions keep changing rapidly, like mercury, along with your thoughts. It is fascinating!" She giggled nervously.

I smiled weakly. It is difficult to surprise people who know how to read your face.

"I think I should leave." I gave up.

"It's 1 a.m. in the night. You can't," she said hopefully.

"I will sleep outside on the sofa."

"That's probably a good idea," she sighed. "I will arrange the stuff."

She slept inside.

○●○

I kept waiting for the dawn, rewinding the situation again and again and imagining what would have happened if I had made a particular choice.

By the morning, I had exhausted all the alternatives. It was 5 a.m., and I went again into her room to see if she was up. She wasn't. She slept peacefully like a baby, clutching a pillow.

Probably for the first time, I saw not frown lines but peace on that face—serenity at its fluid best.

I could have looked at her for hours. There was a strange, lovely glow as she slept, surrendering all her worries while clutching that pillow—was it the escape she seemed to yearn for? I would have given anything to know. But then some mysteries are best left unanswered, like, say, the Monalisa smile.

I inched closer to her face until I could see her closed eyelids and feel her breath. That was the closest I had been to any woman without getting nervous, and as I saw that innocent face, for once, I felt not lust but affection—honey sweetness permeating peace.

I kissed her lips softly, then again. She didn't move but kept breathing evenly.

I wondered if she felt anything.

So, I kissed again, a little more firmly this time, with the hope that maybe her dreams would be happier. She didn't need to know.

"Are you never going to stop?" She said, without opening her eyes but smiling, "It is difficult to ignore for so long, you know, and still more difficult to not respond."

She wiped her eyes to look at me with a half-smile full of mystery, enigma, and affection—it was better than Monalisa's.

"That must undoubtedly be the best way to wake someone up." she said, smiling.

We kissed again, softly. It was my most affectionate touch in years.

She unhurriedly woke up and asked, "Had a good sleep?"

"Nope, barely," I said.

"Rest for some time. I'll make tea."

We got ready by 8 a.m. and waited for the company bus at the bus-stop.

But then, she still stood some 10 meters away from me, just like yesterday!

○●○

I kept pinging her the entire day at the office.

'Would you like to go for a tea?' I asked.

'Nah, I don't like to drink tea after 2-3 times.'

'Too much work?"

'New assignment came.'

'Time consuming?'

'Yeah, sign-off today.'

'Am getting bored—how about a little walk?' I asked, *still persistent.*

'Would have loved to join, but I can't. You know how it is. Maybe in the evening!"

'Yes, I know how it is!'

My day was no different. Work had piled up, and I wasn't in the mood to sit in my chair. It was an overwhelming restlessness. I wanted to share my happiness over today's shared experience with her. But it wasn't meant to be.

That day I waited at her project door as she joined me for an evening walk.

"Can time cure everything?" I asked.

"No, it can't," she said, looking at me. "Sometimes things linger back even after one forgets them."

"True. Sometimes people don't realize how much baggage they carry."

Mitali's version:

When things happen, they can't always be given a name—like the one that happened in the morning. I don't know what it was, but I liked it. I would have been happy almost the entire day, but then it was not to be.

Just as I was making tea in the morning, I checked my mobile, which was charging, to find messages from Neeraj.

'Sorry, I couldn't reply back to your calls yesterday. Been busy. I will call today,' they said.

And then, that's when the guilt seemed to emerge—banging against my insides, much like my clothes banging against the drying container of my washing machine.

How could I have, even for a moment, allowed myself to enjoy it?

I cried in the bathroom.

He did call in the afternoon, as promised. But it was just as detached a call as my status calls with Scott (*my onsite manager*). We inquired, took updates, exchanged information, and cut the call. Sigh!

As for what I wanted from Ami, well, I wish I knew!

Ami's version:

The coming weeks were breathless and filled with utter craziness.

If we met each other on the stairs or in the lift, she would never nod.

If I were with Prabhu, neither would I, but he would get a huge spasm of coughing all of a sudden. It was annoying, but I would secretly thank him for the acknowledgment.

In a couple of moments, she would receive a message, *'Pretty in blue.'*

She would react with a huge dollop of smiles and something like, *'Smart in gray.'*

'Cute in pink!' from me.

'Brilliant in yellow!' from her.

It became slightly less sophisticated over time.

'Sexy in saree!' from me.

'Hot in black!' from her.

'Yummy in brown!' from her.

'Slutty in a tight top!' from me.

Any reason for me to reach her home would suffice. Sometimes I wouldn't even care to make one.

Someday, like today, it would be as simple as *'Should we catch up for coffee?'* I would ping naughtily.

'Why go out? Come home, I'll make it,' she responded.

The events in between flew by like a hazy blur, and before we knew it, we were in each other's arms, kissing, panting, hugging, and undressing as chemistry took its natural course.

"Damn, it's been 3 hours at least," she said, suddenly realizing the theory of relativity effect. "You must be hungry."

"We didn't drink our coffee." I said, smiling.

"Oh, yes!" she exclaimed, getting up surprised.

"Fine, I will come again for coffee tomorrow. Just coffee this time!" I said naughtily.

"No more coffees, teas, studies, or dinners. I know all your games!" she said, tying her hair in a neat ponytail.

After dinner, we laid on the bed in each other's arms.

"What do you write about?" she asked.

"I write about things I can't express."

"Do you mind telling me some of them?"

I gave a brief shrug. "That won't be a good idea!"

"You can't open up even to me? After all this?" she had a surprised tone in her voice.

"Well, what if you know me a little too well, find me boring, then reject me and go away? Do you think I would be able to take it?" I asked tonelessly.

"You can trust me!" she said gently.

"Can I trust you with my heart?"

"Do you have a choice?" she asked, smiling with that irresistible dimple.

"It's right here. But what will you do with it? It's pretty vulnerable, you know." I spoke.

"It makes me feel good that someone likes me so much," she said, snuggling in. "I will use it as a teddy bear and will hug it all the time."

"Can I trust you to not leave it alone ever?" I asked, half-knowing her answer.

She didn't say anything. I could imagine the struggle inside.

"You can trust me to be yours... this moment."

"What about tomorrow?"

When she spoke, her voice was helpless.

"Tomorrow I will lose this. All of this. Everything. Guilt will resurface. I will hate myself for falling for what we have, and I will hate you more for finding me when I needed somebody. Tonight, you can trust me." She kissed me. "But then don't talk so much. Not now."

That's the closest she would ever come to saying she loved me.

I didn't say anything—I only wanted her to understand through my touch, through the interweaving of our fingers. She felt so much softer now.

The night had gone old and soundless as crickets chirped dully. Everything added to the calmness of the moment except the intermittent rustling of the tree leaves and the ticks of the wall clock.

The night belonged to us, along with its silences. The only sound in the world that mattered was each other's breath. They were rhythmic and attuned to each other.

It was the most beautiful thing, hearing her breathe soundly, our breaths intermingling, then complementing, tingling our necks, gently ruffling her soft hair.

As she hugged me completely, I felt she missed nothing in this world, and nothing mattered.

"Tomorrow the world will be full of troubles again, but tonight the moon shines only for us. Hug me tighter," she said holding me and giving me a peck. "Don't let me go!".

I wished that night would never end. I hoped time would stop and the earth would stop revolving.

"I don't want to lose you. You have no idea how much I love you!" I whispered in her ears softly, "Are you comfortable? Should I start the fan?"

"Nope, it's alright." She just held me tighter. "Don't go!"

We were sweating. I gave a long sigh and kissed her forehead as I felt an overwhelming need to reach out for the water bottle on the table. But drinking water wasn't worth it!

She was already fast asleep, hugging me like a baby.

Sometime during the night, ensuring that she was snoring, I whispered something in her ear.

"What?" she groaned, staring at me with half-open, unsteady eyes.

"God, what a light sleeper! Nothing. Go to sleep." I kissed her nose.

Early that morning, I suggested. "You should write too, you know. It will help you get away from things."

She didn't argue that one. "What kind of things should I write?"

"All kinds. Try poems."

"I can't express like you do. A lot of things stay in the mind only," she said, combing her hair.

"That's exactly why I want you to try!" said I, tying my shoelaces.

○●○

"Thinking of her?" Prabhu asked me as he saw me stirring the sugar in my curd vacantly at lunch.

"She still avoids me," said I, based on how she evicted me before dawn. The worthlessness of it all!

"She always will!" he said in an even tone. I didn't like the way he said that. "What exactly do you do at her home?" he asked.

"Nothing much. How do you know?"

"I know everything about you. The question is, why didn't you tell me?"

"It was personal, and besides, I didn't want your comments on it."

"Well, fine!" he said, looking down at his plate and eating again.

"I mean, we do have a good time." I continued, a little miffed at his sudden lack of interest. He didn't react.

"And she cooks really well." I smiled at the thought of food. He said nothing.

"...and we..."

"Will you shut up? I am trying to eat here," he said, miffed.

I stayed quiet for a few moments, more so from the shock. He had never shouted at me before. I kept looking at him surprised. He finished his lunch and walked away soundlessly.

"Hey wait." I ran behind him.

"What for? My opinions no longer count!" he said, walking away.

"Oh, c'mon, will you? You aren't a girl!" oodles of unnecessary hypersensitivity this guy had.

"I am not interested in your love story anymore, and besides, this isn't one!"

"One never knows!" I said dreamy-eyed.

"But I know," he said, looking at me disgusted. "Every great love story requires two innocent souls; your story has only one. You are a fool!"

"Happiness is foolish."

"You are foolish. She is using you. Now, instead of using her back like a bad boy, you start flying over pink clouds, eh?"

"Love and selfishness can't coexist. One ultimately ends up consuming the other." I said wisely.

"Selfishness feeds on foolishness. She feeds on you."

"Stop it!" I said, visibly hurt.

He turned towards me and clutched me by the shoulder.

"Don't you see it? You are her need, not her desire, and you will always and forever be a second fiddle. So, forget about love. You are running breakneck towards a dead end, and if you don't stop in time, you will go splat. Stop investing yourself in her. You will only get hurt!"

He spoke with so much conviction that it hurt my ears, and I knew it was true. But then, weren't we to believe in miracles?

I sighed and looked out of the window at the skies. It did nothing to mend my broken smile. "I know this is stupid. I don't expect you to understand, but I am just trying my best to save something between us—something I know won't happen again to me or to her. She can't see it; I can. Someone's got to stay true to one's feelings in this case, and unfortunately, I am that someone." I said earnestly.

"You can die, and she will smile at it." Prabhu smirked.

"Then I want to die," I went on doggedly. "It's amazing how people let go so easily. It's like this: have you ever met a stranger who, when he or she enters the room, you feel an instant connection with? As if that person knows you and you know that person. As if you were always waiting for that special someone to enter the room because when they do, the room is no longer the same again, and neither are you."

"Are you talking about me?" he asked sheepishly.

I smiled at him. "You wish! I speak about Mitali. I know she feels it too—the attraction and that connection—but she is too practical to notice. I am not."

He threw his hands in the air, " She has a boyfriend..."

"But I don't know if she is happy with him, and if she is, then why was she ever with me? Things change; this attraction doesn't. If she smiles at my pain, then I intend to stay true to myself and see that smile of hers with open eyes. I am supposed to feel the pain until I can't take it. It will make me feel good that I didn't give up. Let's see if my pain breaks her first or me." I smiled with that obstinate, self-destructive glint in my eyes. "If I don't do this, I will never be happy!"

He went silent to look at me with helpless, brooding eyes full of things he wanted to say but couldn't convey; he knew he wouldn't be able to bring sensibility to this situation.

"Listen, it is true that you like her, and maybe she likes you. But consider the odds. You aren't of the same region or age, nor is it that you are crazy rich, so that no differences matter; you have a shaky future, she has a boyfriend who is smarter, and besides," he looked at me. "She is completely cuckoo. Why on earth would you even think of love and commitment with this lady?"

"I don't have an answer for all your questions. But I really want to know her well."

"In that case, first change your professional profile. Become a developer so that she has something to look up to. Testing will lead you nowhere."

"It's called Quality Assurance. Testing is just one of the processes and..."

"Yeah yeah! Save the jargon for the interviewer if you ever get a shortlist on this profile! Even a tea-serving peon is called *'Food & Beverage Consultant'* these days," he smirked." Stop justifying and do something. You will lose her this way. It's inevitable. There is no reason why she should choose you."

○●○

I woke up in the middle of the night with way too many thoughts. It was raining outside, and the breeze was relaxing. I opened the windows and scribbled down my anxiety to calm my mind.

> *'Drinking the pain, till its light white,*
> *I can't think of anything but you.*
> *Take me in your wake again,*
> *I wanna see our dreams come true!'*

Except, it didn't calm me! Craving exacerbated. I sighed and relaxed in the darkness by the window, wondering whether the rain had the power to make a person go to bed.

7.

'It is better to lead from behind and to put others in front, especially when you celebrate victory and nice things occur. You take the front when there is danger. Then people will appreciate your leadership,' said Mandela's wallpaper on Kanchan's laptop.

"Is there something that you'd like to discuss?" Kanchan looked at me as she saw me standing by her table.

"Yes...Umm..." I wanted to put forth my concern as delicately as possible without ruffling any feathers. "Thing is, I have been part of this maintenance project for some 4 months now. I have learned everything there is to learn. So, I was wondering if I could be given a development stint for some time."

"But we don't have code development, or any sort of coding, for that matter, in our project offsite!" she exclaimed, her eyes wide.

"I know, but how about shifting me to some project that has it? It would be a good learning experience."

She smiled at me wickedly. "Why would I do that? I need a resource here. Besides, it all depends on requirements, doesn't it?"

"I cannot work on these assignments' day after day. They are all similar, and they never seem to end." I could sense my voice cracking with desperation and nervousness. I didn't mention my frustration with the pay. Expectation and assumption were that it would increase with the quality of work, though that wasn't always the case.

"Well, I don't see how you have a choice. In today's business environment, and particularly in our industry, it is necessary to be flexible and open to meeting the demands of the business." I knew she was referring to the mild recession that the industry had faced a couple of years earlier and was indirectly threatening me with my job.

"But what about the computer languages you trained me on? I can be a good developer. How would you know unless I am given an opportunity?"

"Opportunities don't exist as of now. Besides, I am only responsible for your growth in this project and not in the organization, you see. You would need to talk to your HR manager about that. But I doubt even he would be able to help you. I can refer you to other project managers, but only if you show me the results here first." She informed me, red-eyed. I knew she was nearing the end of her patience with me and this conversation. "And for God's sake, start shaving regularly. It becomes difficult to even look at you."

I hadn't shaved in the last few days. "My beard gets really rough and..."

She showed me her palm. "Never mind the details. Please ensure you do it."

The conversation was over.

I would find project managers very touchy with the attrition and weak links of the project—dissatisfied people looking for other career options. They would often be least cooperative with such people from then on because all the training and time invested in that person would go down the drain anyway if that person ended up leaving. It would take a minimum of 3-6 months to get a suitably trained functional replacement with similar efficiency to the one that left. Those 3-6 months would be bumpy without the resource, hence the inherent irritation of managers with people having a roving eye.

More often than not, it would lead to cutting the ropes for that resource—closing his learning options on the professional front so that he is stuck with the job and the project he is in.

"Sometimes I wonder if this conspiracy is hatched along with the HRs. Attrition is very high in the IT industry." Suman said after hearing Kanchan's reply. "Instead of improving employee satisfaction to tackle attrition, they take the negative approach and cut the feathers of the bird so that it can't fly away. Do you know what that means? She would never put you in a development role because if you are good at what you do here, she would not want to lose you."

I cringed at this way of thinking.

"Don't scare him, *rey*!" Bhoopal intervened.

"...says the guy who spent a year and a half of his life trying to get out of his earlier project." Suman smiled sarcastically at Bhoopal. He looked at me. "Be careful that she never catches you reading development or coding-related material from now on. If she does, she will make sure you are overloaded with work always, so that there is no time left for any personal development."

Hmm... so the Pareto principle applied here too—make the 20% work like mules while the rest 80% float for a while before getting replaced. I wondered why anyone would like to work on a project that leaves him or her no scope for development. Was it not like raising an army of slaves?

"It isn't like that," said Bhoopal. "The thing is this industry has too many people. You are a drop in the sea. Sometimes it becomes difficult to protect everybody's interests. But if someone sticks around for a sufficiently long time, then the progress is certain. Anyways, the future is in the technology sector only, *rey*."

Bhoopal had this outlook that ultimately centered and rested on technology. I had heard him speak many times about this. "In several industries, the core function is often the one where most people work but are paid the least. Consider an FMCG org., where the primary function is sales. Management, marketing, and HR are the functions that support sales. But ultimately the person who rises to the management through the core is the one most respected."

"But that would take some 10 years, no? Not everybody has that kind of time, patience, and ice in the belly." Suman interrupted in a heated tone.

"I guess it's a choice one has to make. I agree with the fact that a person needs to have a natural progression in sight. But that can't always happen in this industry." Bhoopal said.

"I just want to learn and grow into a role that requires higher skills. I am underutilized." I chipped in.

"Everybody is!!" Bhoopal said it with eyes full of freezing intelligence. "But then understand that this isn't the company's headache. If you want to be a developer, learn to have patience. Things take time!"

The question just was, how much time did I have? My loss wouldn't have scared me much if it didn't have a direct correlation with me losing Mitali—the more that happened, the more I missed her.

○●○

"Damn! I miss her all the time!" I said, putting my spoon down in exasperation. It was snack time. "Like right now, I am eating, and I miss her."

"Do you miss her while drinking tea?" Prabhu asked me, sipping his tea.

"Hell yeah, all the time!!"

He paused himself to raise his eyebrow and reach a brilliant conclusion. "*Damn hormones!*"

"I knew you would say that. Hormones are triggered by my feelings for her." I corrected him.

"I beg to differ. Sometimes it's a neurofeedback—hormones trigger the feelings and not the other way around, not unlike a recession that triggers another recession. It happens! It can make you uneasy. So, I suggest doing some yoga and breathing exercises to get back to normal." He smiled wisely.

"Are you freaking crazy? I love this madness. It's incomparable." I closed my eyes to imagine her beside me. The sweater I was wearing smelled of her too—or was it just my breath? I hugged myself to feel her familiar warmth, her scent, her smile, and her essence.

"You are going crazier!" I heard Prabhu's distant voice in the background, full of glee, or was it gloom—perhaps both.

He had a point.

"Maybe, I guess, we love more those things that we know we will lose someday." I looked into Prabhu's moist, empathetic eyes, hoping they understood what I couldn't express: the fear of losing everything.

He just shrugged and looked away to face his plate again. "Amazing what hormones do to sanity!!" he said *'tch-tch'*ing and giving me that merciless half-smile.

I felt like whacking him.

○●○

There was only one solution to my plight, the only panacea: to see her again. That night again, I went to her home, unannounced and uninvited. I rang the doorbell, and she took just a moment to answer it.

"Why the hell are you here?"

It wasn't exactly the invitation I was expecting!

"I came to meet you." I barged in, smiling.

"But why? And sometimes I wonder how you manage to evade him every single time."

"Him who? Street dog?" I queried.

"My landlord uncle, of course!" Her big eyes gave that cute shell-shocked expression. "He roams around at weird times."

It was irresistible. It would have been unfair not to reward it by kissing her promptly.

"Stop, stop! You animal!!" she said, slapping my cheek, trying to bring out the human in me.

"You tell this now after I come here the nth time?" I was slightly shaken.

"What can I do? It's a new phenomenon. The other night around 11 p.m., I got my dad's call and was feeling claustrophobic, so I came out for a stroll. It is usually completely dark outside in

222 | *The Little Men*

our yard except for the moonlight. While chatting, I saw a figure in white, illuminated further by the moonlight, standing silently near the front gate. I was so scared; I couldn't shout because I couldn't breathe.

I stood paralyzed as the figure noticed me and slid towards me in what seemed like the longest minutes of that night to put its hand on my shoulder and say, *'Beti, do you want water or something? Your face has turned white, like a ghost.'*

The voice made me realize it was my landlord uncle, and the color of my face returned." she exhaled, relieved.

I chuckled.

"Don't laugh. He lost his wife. He gets lonely. It is but natural!" Her pretty nose twitched in indignation.

"Don't laugh; don't kiss. Then, what do I do?" I said, collapsing on her sofa.

"I'll tell you what to do." She held my hand and brought me to her table.

"What do you see?" she asked me.

There were books of all shapes and sizes lying open on the table.

"What do you see?" she asked again.

"Books." I said in a hollow tone.

"Great. Pick that one and start reading." I went to the book. It was titled *'Coding in C for dummies.'*

"...and you know it's not right for you to come here anytime you feel like!" she said. "When are you going home now?" She sounded a little like my schoolteacher.

I gave her a helpless look. "It's late at night. Can I go home in the morning?"

"The reason I ask is, you see, you can't leave with me in the morning, and the landlord uncle normally wakes up at dawn, so..." She gave me a knowing look to help me finish the rest.

I chose my words carefully. "So, I should leave before dawn."

"Good boy!" she smiled and patted my cheeks. "Now I sit here on the bed, and you sit there on the chair at least 10 feet away. You see, I don't trust you... and we read!"

But that's not why I was there!

"I have an idea!" I said enthusiastically, "Let's read naked. Let's check your concentration level while reading."

She gave me the *'you better behave yourself'* look.

"Sorry and *oye*, I can code, alright! I am not a dummy," said I, scanning the book's pages.

"Feel free to prove yourself. The computer is right there. Code anything you want." She pointed in the direction without even looking at me. I spent half an hour on the program and called her to check the output.

"Let's see how you have done." She smiled, compiled the program and ran it.

The screen flickered with the output.

'Are you Mitali? Y/N' She looked at me and smiled. "What is this?"

"I don't know," I said, burying myself in the book.

'Y' she typed and entered. Screen flickered with output.

'You look very pretty tonight. Do you know this? Y/N' She smiled and entered *'Y'.*

The screen flickered again. *What a lovely night! Choose one of the below activities to have a fun time.*

1. Do naked coding; it's synonymous with naked yoga and is incredible fun.

2. Do a belly dance for your audience.

3. Let's play 'strip and stare'—oops 'truth and dare' I mean.

4. Spin the bottle. Whoever the bottle stops on gets to kiss the other.

5. Can't choose.

Press option.'

She gave me a dirty look before pressing *'5'.*

Screen flickered.

'Okay, so can't decide which one's the sexiest option? I guess it's best to kiss the guy around you and let him decide. Y/N'

"CORNY!" she shouted and pressed *'N'.*

The screen flashed again with the output.

'Hi Mitali, are you angry? Y/N'

'Y' she entered cautiously. The program gave output.

'I love you! You know this? Y/N' program asked.

She looked at me for a couple of seconds. I kept reading. *'N'* she entered.

'I do! You know now? Y/N?' program asked again. *'N'* she entered.

'I do! You know now? Y/N?' program asked again. *'N'* she entered again.

'I do! You know now? Y/N?' program asked again.

"Infinite loop," she smiled and pressed *'Y'*.

'Turn right. It's fun to kiss you when you are angry!' stated the program.

"What?" She turned left out of confusion to see my face right next to hers.

"See? I know you in someways you don't." I looked deep in her eyes.

The moment was right there, and I took a sweet second to give her a peck and hug her. We hugged each other for what seemed like an eternity.

"I miss you all the time!" I said when we moved apart. She didn't say anything and just hugged me again.

"Do you?" I wasn't going to leave it.

"Kinda!" she said, looking down. I kissed her neck and lips, but the spark was missing.

At some point in time, we lost our clothes. I worked my way down to her tummy, and as I hugged that warm soft teddy-bearish thing of a lady there, I don't know what churned inside me, but tears trickled down in all sadness.

"What? Why are you crying?" she asked me, shocked.

"I would miss hugging you!" My throat choked with emotion. "Some point in time, when we end, I will!"

I hugged her again and cried like a baby.

"What happened? No, look at me," she said, looking into my red eyes. "Tell me!"

"I don't think I will ever be okay if I lose you." I tried to say it through that thick emotion in my throat as I held her tight. "You see, I am not made in a way to love anyone else again."

"But sometimes we go with the flow and see what happens!" she sighed.

My sad smile stayed. "Do you know what I whispered in your ear that night while you were sleeping?"

"What?"

"I asked you to marry me!" I smiled unhappily, wiping my eyes with her top.

She seemed shocked. "Whaaattt? I am... are you... I have no idea what to say!!"

"Say you are creeped out being with this psycho guy who proposes to you when naked, so that you can't run away either." I said, smiling naughtily through my tears. I spoke her mind, I think—she began wearing her clothes.

"It's 3 a.m. It's time you leave, I guess. You want tea?" she asked.

"I do!" I climbed out of bed too.

"Help yourself and make it for me as well," she said, going to the bathroom.

I went to the kitchen and started making my favorite recipe, the containers and their positions being all familiar now. Meanwhile, I could hear her crying inside the loo.

"Do you like tea sweeter, stronger, or both?" I shouted, shaking the sugar container.

"Put any damn quantity you want!" she screamed back through her sobbing.

I had my tea and waited for her to come out.

"Tea's gone cold," I whispered at the bathroom door.

"I will have it later." She took a moment to answer and started sobbing again.

"Okay, I'll leave," I whispered softly to the door, paused for a moment, and then left.

"Close the door," she whispered back.

It felt weirdly free to speak my mind to her, and whether she reciprocated seemed to matter little. It was important she knew, and now she did. I whistled my way out as the dawn air seemed refreshingly cool and invigorating, but then I saw it too!

The figure in white stood by the entry gate, which I planned to use to get out. I had no idea what to do, and damn, just as Mitali warned, it began sliding towards me.

My mouth went dry as I thought of ways to stop him from shouting *'thief thief'*.

Chances of making a clean escape are rather low compared to what one rather hopefully imagines. The form approached me and paused while I considered my next move.

We stood in silence, staring at each other in darkness—I think he feared bodily harm if he shouted, or maybe he was unsure if I was a thief after all—but this uncertainty would have gotten Mitali in trouble.

I was still near her door. We waited 5 minutes in that sort of time-warp until I could take it no more. It might be fun for him to stand there alone till morning; for me it wasn't.

"Sorry, wrong house, sir. I am slightly confused with the address," I croaked, in a different accent, desperately praying that he would get the harmlessness in my voice.

He didn't say a word.

"I will check the next house over there. Never mind. Go to sleep, uncle. Stop scaring people!" said I and moved out limping, with the hope that he would give the wrong description to the police if he happened to file a complaint in the morning.

○●○

We would keep chatting on *Sametime*[19] all the time.

Soon I knew everything about Mitali's project—people around her, parents, and even relatives. Most importantly, I knew about my competitor.

She was a lonely child, pampered, and yet neglected to a degree. Both parents worked, and she was always an introvert—academically bright but not bright enough and comparatively a little laid-back.

She preferred quiet activities, had sinusitis and a very weak eyesight, and would go out for lunch alone. But in anything technical, she was an aggressive thinker and would take the lead in troubleshooting. She was a little bossy, and her juniors thought of her as a weirdo, so did her seniors—hence, they rarely connected with her outside of work.

Her workstation was tidy, and she had an inherent germophobia. She loved reading books—her only regret was that life is too short to read everything!

Like all girls, she wanted companionship, but she was too proud to ask for it, which was slightly disappointing to me. She still talked about Neeraj with lucidity, which was a trifle unbelievable for me. I simply fail to get girls!

---

[19] *Chat messenger. Owned by HCL since 2018. Before 2018, it was IBM Sametime.*

○●○

"Everybody has a girlfriend, except me. Even you do," I whined near Piyush. "What's wrong with me?"

"Nothing is wrong with you, buddy. It's a happy accident. Can happen with anyone anytime!"

"Nah, it never does with me. I don't know why!"

"Relax. Let it take time. It would be worth it!"

"So one would believe!"

Piyush, too, had a girlfriend whom he met in college. Later, she went to do an *M.S.* in Electronics Engineering from the US while he joined *FORDIT*. She was located in Texas, US.

"Please tell me long-distance relationships never work," I asked him selfishly. I was thinking about Mitali and Neeraj.

"Please tell me they do." he smiled sadly.

I patted his back.

"They do, in 10% of the cases. You are one of those lucky 10%. Hope the rest 90% fail," I said with a tinge of bitterness in my voice.

I was getting weirder day after day—an insecure guy who was forever in paranoia about this other dude he had never seen.

I scribbled vigorously:

'I miss the times before we met,

I miss the times when I didn't miss you,

I tried to convince myself a thousand ways and failed,

That love doesn't always need to get better...

of every man's reason!'

○ ● ○

Full moon decorated that October midnight sky... one of my several night-outs at her place that month.

She was lying in my arms on her bed; the only sound was of a mildly noisy fan above us whirling unhurriedly. We didn't need it. Pune was quite cool that particular October.

"I get bad dreams at night—really bad ones. One of them repeats over and over," she whispered.

"What do you see? Me?" I smiled at my own joke.

"I see that I am in my room; it's night, and there's a tiger prowling outside, so I can't leave the place. I am stuck inside, and then the lights go out too."

"How do you know there's a tiger outside?" Me.

"I just know. I hear its roars, I guess. It's night—too dark to see him."

"So why are you scared? Go to sleep," I said callously.

"Weren't you listening?" she shrieked. "There is a tiger out in the dark, and it's a dream; not everything is logical. Besides, there is a catch."

"Which is?"

"The room is getting smaller with each passing minute. The walls are caving in, thus shrinking the room," she added in a worried whisper.

"So, what do you do?"

"It's a silly dream. I do nothing! But I am claustrophobic, so I wake up and open the windows of my room."

"Your talks are making me claustrophobic. I think it's a full moon tonight. Want to sit outside?"

"I think I saw uncle sleep early. We can go out if you promise to whisper, not shout, and hide in the garden if he comes out suddenly," she said.

We sat on the porch outside her room near the small garden.

The garden seemed alive and full of murmurs—the third entity, our silent companion in spirit. The white flowers of the jasmine tree sprawled the moonlit ground near the porch, and their fragrance pervaded the calm of the night—through the calm of our minds.

She sat there with a paranoid stare, looking at me, oblivious to it all.

"You know gardens were developed to have a safe place; one where kings could explore intimacy in the presence of nature," I said, throwing pebbles at the tree.

"I am not coming into the bushes, if that is what you are suggesting," she said, alarmed. "Dude, don't even think about it!"

"Yeah right, I just made that up." I said, grinning.

She looked at me intently, trying to find something worth looking at.

"It's been weeks; you have persisted with me. Why do you like me? I am not even that pretty, you know!"

"'… *Love*' me..." I corrected her.

"Yeah *that*"

"I don't know." I thought for a moment. "Your imperfections don't matter here. Ultimately, it all boils down to a feeling in my brain—I want to make you feel loved."

"Why?" she asked tonelessly. "Why do you love me?"

I looked deep into her eyes and said, "Because if I don't, I will die."

It was romantic enough, but she was too clever.

"Bullshit. It's just the hormones," she snapped, pricking the balloon of romance.

"Hormones are triggered by my emotions." What to say?

"That's true, but emotions are formed after one does *'it'*," she said, smiling wisely while wiping her glasses with a hanky.

"It's a classic chicken egg story. It is difficult to say what comes first." I grinned.

Maybe she did—she smirked faithlessly.

"Oh, c'mon, I love you." My voice went defensive. "In whatever way one can love the other."

"Look... all I ask is," she put on her specs and gave me that ominous nerdy stare, "whether you really understand what you are trying to say?"

This is the very downside to loving geeky ladies—they want you to think when you feel, and it was impossible for me to not feel around her.

"I know what you are doing. Stop playing that reverse psychology card on me. I know perfectly well what I mean."

"Oh really?" She gave me a cold look through her glasses. "Do you?"

"Come on!" I threw my hands in the air in helplessness. "I do!"

"People get delirious for sex," she justified, "and say all sorts of things. Then they start believing it. You can be one of them. Why do I believe you?"

"But I say this to you all the time. First, you accept it, then you deny it, and now you question it?" I said frowning.

"But exactly. It's just one of those things people say, don't they? Who takes it seriously? Even you shouldn't," she said, smiling.

"Okay... great. So now you want to know why I love you or at least feel that I love you?"

"Yes."

"And would you listen patiently, even if I can't explain?"

"I'll try not to laugh."

I smiled at the futility of explaining light to a blind person in the dark. Words—what do they mean anyway? I took a deeper breath and looked away at those white flowers spread on the ground, contemplating if they would look good in her hair.

No answer to her question came to mind, but I decided they probably would.

"I don't know. You see, I am not so intelligent. But it's just that whenever I am with you, all the things whirling in my head... all the chaos in my life... all of my confusions and all my dreams— misunderstood and unstated, some throbbing, some lost, all of that goes still... entirely!" I looked at her with silent eyes. "The world makes complete sense to me in those precious minutes... And in those precious seconds when you are in my arms and when I feel you breathe and watch you smile—oh, that beautiful smile— I experience peace. Now it can't be explained... I feel God has been most kind to me, and I have lived my life. This is all there is to it.

All that matters. All I care for. The search ends!" I don't know if I made any sense, but I started breathing again.

Her eyes went soft for some time, despite that geeky mind of hers. She sat there speechless and deep in thought.

I picked up a flower and quietly adjusted it in her hairline with quaking hands. "Pretty," said I, and kissed her cheek longingly. " I wish I could offer you more; I wish there was more to this, but this is it! Whatever I am, with my imperfect heart, I am yours."

"Hmm" was all she mumbled, averting my eyes as she hurriedly went inside to keep our teacups in the kitchen. So far, so good— but when her diabolical mind resurfaces, she will make fun of this too. She did return only to arrange for me to sleep on her sofa and then closed the door of her room from inside.

As usual, I left for home early in the morning.

Mitali's version:

Clichéd sentences—they are normally funny, but in this case, I found them disturbing because he actually meant them.

First, the proposal. Now this... I was thoroughly shaken. I cried in the kitchen.

All the sweet things he does and says, Neeraj was supposed to be the one to do them for me, not him! He was becoming way too involved with me, and I was increasingly getting this feeling that I was using him. Not that he would mind, but we would both be in a big black soup when all this ends, psychologically, ethically, morally, and most importantly, mentally.

It has to end, I guess. We both knew it; the sooner the better.

I expected this stuff to fade away with time, not brighten up with intensity with every passing moment.

8.

Ami's version:

One evening that coming week, we stood at the cafeteria parapet chatting over tea, watching the busy road below.

"Neeraj called me today."

"What did he say?"

"Nothing special. He kept telling me about his office, his work, and his parents. He is planning to shift the job at some point. Some cool opportunities have cropped up based on his current role."

I stayed silent for some time.

"How much is his salary right now?"

"And what's it to you?" She looked at me suspiciously.

"Curiosity."

"Why?"

There was no reason to sugar-floss it.

"That can be the only reason why you are with him. Whatever the reasons are, love isn't one of them."

She seemed to take it as an offense.

"Why would you say that? Love is the only reason. You think I can't score a better guy than both of you jokers?"

"Yeah, sure." I smiled.

"If I earn as much as he does and give you all the love and attention you want and deserve, would you not love me more? Come on, be truthful!" I asked.

"You don't understand." She sighed. "The heart has its own reasons, while reason has none. Even if I am with you, I may still stay in love with him without any reason."

I felt my heart sink. "If love isn't the primary reason, no other reasons to convince you would matter anyways."

I was thinking of the fruitlessness of getting money, a job, or a job role. Nothing was going to matter.

"Agreed. But then you forget there is a teeny-tiny thing called destiny involved. Love, as it is, is blind. We cannot always control what we feel towards the other person. I have never tried to analyze why I feel what I feel towards him."

"What do you feel towards me?"

She looked at me and thought for a while. Lack of spontaneity justified what the answer was. "A confidante, a friend, somebody I would always turn to when I am in trouble," she said, wording it carefully.

"So basically nothing." I sighed. I was a friend—a mere friend.

"If only you could understand that your worth is more than a mere nothing." She sighed. "You aren't just a casual acquaintance; you are someone special. But then, there are some things I can never promise you. I will never be able to love you or marry you.

If I could, I would, but I can't. The sooner you get it, the better it is for everybody. You know the inevitability, and yet you don't stop loving me. Sometimes I feel I am using you." I felt her eyes going moist.

I knew she was speaking from her heart. But there was nothing in it for me. But then, if it were true that the heart has its own reasons, then I had enough reasons to persist. Was I in love? The love of a beggar is not respected. What do I do to deserve love?

"We are two very lonely souls who found each other. Why can't we take this as a happy accident?" I prayed for consideration.

"This is not an accident. I was not supposed to be lonely. I was not supposed to waver. I was not supposed to be with you. I wasn't supposed to let this happen," she said, walking away. I didn't stop her. Nothing could have.

As I saw her walk away, I felt she was leaving without a part of her. She was leaving back that part hopelessly in love with me— maybe I imagined it. In some ways, it was equivalent to deserting all my memories.

After a moment, I realized Prabhu was standing behind me.

"She does not love you. She's a bitch!"

"Oh, the less you speak, brother, the better it is for everybody,"

"Dude, focus! What was it that we started it for?"

"Happiness!"

"Which you guys derived by doing *'it'*. Now there is nothing more to it. You can't be together for all time."

"But I want to. I can't live without her." It pained me to see her leave, and it would hurt even more if she ended up with anyone except me.

"There *is only* one way to be with her without being with her," Prabhu said.

"...and that is?"

"You aren't ready for it yet. I will let you know when the time is right."

○ ● ○

"They rejected my leaves again," JD said in a tired voice.

"Aren't you taking a little too many these days? How are you ever going to compensate for 98% project utilization?" I queried.

98% project utilization, which was the project norm, was a way to say that out of the 100 hours a resource is supposed to be available, the company is able to charge the client for 98. Basically, the resource should be working on billable projects for these 98 hours. Sometimes that would leave no time for leaves as personal leaves weren't billable. While we would only bill 8 hours every day to the client, in reality, we would often overshoot it in terms of our working hours, but that was seen as an efficiency issue.

"You know what? I miss Mishti Doi and Sondesh. My mom used to make lots of them," JD said, glancing over her comp.

"What kind of city is Kolkata?" My curiosity was piqued.

"It's homely. I miss it," she sighed, smiling.

"You shouldn't have come here in the first place. It's better in the city of joy itself. Come, look at it. First of all, the food is a problem. Then, no nightlife. But people here are good, right?" I said, debating.

"People are good there too. And food isn't the issue. Yes, to a degree, I miss fish and rice. See, I was transferred from the Kolkata office to here simply because there were requirements here and not in Kolkata. Otherwise, why would anybody come here for that matter?" she said sarcastically.

"Forced?" I smiled.

"Yeah, man!! They threatened me with HR action. Look at my age. I am 26—I did 2 years of post-graduation to land this job. *Badi mushkil se mila hai*, during that mass-hiring phase. I didn't want to give them a chance for reconsideration. Bloody, if they care so much about project utilization, they shouldn't have sent me here. It takes a couple of days to travel to Kolkata and back, and with the salary they give me, I can't afford to buy air tickets," she said, puffing. "So, they directly ship me to this alien project where I feel completely outcast. I work night and day on assignments, which I hardly understand for that matter. I don't have a technical brain, and things are a bit too dry for me as I know it."

"I am sure they think it is a good diversity mix if they send people to different cities," I tried to justify.

"Nothing like that. It is all a game of filling the slots. These HRs are bloody disgusting!" She was livid with rage.

She called Suman. "Let's go out for coffee. Guys, coffee!!" She hammered her cup on the table.

We all went out. It would take just 2 minutes for everyone to gather up on the mention of coffee. People would hastily press windows + L to lock their comp and would hustle out for a nice windy break outside.

"The floor can get claustrophobic sometimes," JD said while sitting on the stairs.

"It's different for you, *rey*. Half the time you stop breathing after you get angry," Suman said with mischievous eyes.

"I didn't ask you, Mr. Smartie-pants. I just got my leaves rejected. What do you expect?" She was still sulking over it. "Bhoopal, why can't I get more leaves? Only 10-12 days a year are not enough. Talk with Kanchan; you know how far I stay."

"You have great expectations from me. *'Talk to her,'* I will, but we know what she's going to say," Bhoopal said, looking at his empty cup.

"It isn't like that, dude. Kanchan needs to be convinced that project utilization can be compensated by others. Say even if she records 96% and we all record 99%, it still will bring the team score to above 98%," Suman retorted.

Bhoopal interjected.

"There is an ethical dilemma in it, can't you see? It isn't right for somebody else to not take leaves and compensate for one who does. It would be against the official policy. Besides, there is something you guys don't know about," Bhoopal said, finally looking up at us from his cup.

"You guys are to maintain secrecy about this and not make any mention of what I tell you now to anyone if you would like me to stay in this organization. It's October now. From next year onwards, the project utilization is expected to go up to 99%." He kept looking at us with twinkling eyes.

We stared back; nobody knew what to say.

"But isn't that just inhuman?" Yogi snapped, "Employee satisfaction ratings will get fucked."

"I was not to tell you guys because news of this kind leads to attrition. But I am doing so, as I want you all to start searching for options. Tough times are coming. There is a lot of hushing up at the top level. We don't have a mere professional relationship, so I am letting it leak," he said in a very relaxed tone. His gaze was set somewhere in the clouds; maybe this time even Bhoopal wasn't sure of the coming times.

"Why do you need to go home, JD?" Yogi asked.

"I have been after my father to search for a groom. I have been in this shithole for a whole two years now, and somehow, I find nobody cares for my future. Year after year, I am not growing any younger," JD said heatedly.

I don't know if anybody noticed the quiver in Suman's hand. His eyes caught mine; he didn't say anything.

"Let's have another cup," Piyush said to diffuse the tension in the air.

"Oh yes, about that," Bhoopal said, looking again at us. "Free beverages will be stopped very soon. News isn't out yet, but 90% chance. Don't ask me how I know."

We looked at him appalled.

"Dude, get lost. We don't want more sad news. Ruined the whole mood," Suman said irritated, dropping the cup.

Everybody started chuckling.

"How do you know all this?" Yogi asked.

"Bhoopal doesn't need to be told. He senses somehow," Raj smiled at him.

Bhoopal just sighed. "Beverages are the cost that the company finds unnecessary. In order to show profits for this quarter, they have been considering this option for curtailing costs. This may happen in December, maybe earlier."

All looked lost.

"So now what? No tea for us?" Piyush asked, visibly distressed. Tea-times were our only stress-relief.

"If you want tea, go buy it from the cafeteria on the topmost floor," JD replied.

"They are also thinking of introducing paid cards to be swiped for a beverage. These machines would be made available."

So, we were to pay for our machine tea now. Oh, man! The world was seriously facing an apocalypse.

"Fine, let's have another cup then. Let's loot the company while at it. They will suck our blood after December anyways!" Suman responded typically.

For once, we all agreed. *Cheers to the crazy times ahead!*

I stood in the huge corridor of our project floor near a small rectangular corporate graphic panel on the sidewall—that was the vision and mission of our organization, which ran somewhat like this: *'To become a $250 million organization by 2009 and to be a competitive and sustained player in the software industry, maintaining high ethical standards.'*

I knew only the first part was important, and the rest were just fillers to make the sentence sufficiently long.

"What are you standing here for?"

I blinked. I didn't realize Prabhu was that near me.

"Hey." I smiled. "Just waiting for the team to join me for lunch."

"Okay. Now tell me something. When was the last time *we* went for lunch together?" He looked at me pointedly.

"Last week once, I guess." I smiled at him.

"It's been two weeks. I eat alone. Alone. You get me? Alone," he shrieked.

I felt like smiling.

"You know there's a difference between you and normal people?" said I.

"And what's that?"

"Normal people work and have a congenial relationship with their teammates. So?" I waited for him to complete the sentence.

"Go on. I want to know what cheeky remarks you have to make," he said, looking at me like a wife would look at her cheating husband giving justifications when caught with his pants down.

"So, they get to eat together and discuss over lunch." I gave him a disappointed look. That was an easy one.

"Let's go for lunch. I want to tell you something. It would take some time."

"Not now. Maybe in the evening."

"Evening you always go out with Mitali." He looked at me pitifully.

"Tomorrow then." I smiled at him while thinking of that saying, *'Tomorrow never comes.'*

"Don't you dare avoid me," he threatened and walked away.

○●○

'Can you just let me know what you want?' I pinged Mitali.

'I would.' She pinged back.

'Whenever you like?'

'I will.'

'What do you want right now?'

'I want coffee.'

'Should I bring it up for you?'

'Nope, I'm going to fetch it.' She.

'Do you mind if I watch you fetch it?'

'Yes, I do. You should work.'

'What if I don't care about work?' I.

'What if you should care more about it and less about me?'

'What if I want to help you help me?'

'Stop bugging me. I am working. Go talk to Prabhu.'

'What do you work for, Mitali?'

'Huh?'

'Read the question.'

'I work because, as an educated lady, I am supposed to work. I am career minded.'

'What exactly do you work for, Mitali? Money? Food? Clothes? House? Car?'

'Security.'

'How much salary will give you enough security?'

'Depends on the inflation.'

'At 10% rate per year.'

'I would need to calculate.'

'I just need a rough figure.'

'Look, I know what you're driving at... I do not work for happiness. I work for money and things money can buy. One of them is safe and tension-free sleep at night. The other is a bed to sleep on. We are middle-class people. No figure is going to be enough for us. More, the better.'

'How long do you plan to run?'

'It's not called running. It's called surviving, and sometimes there is no choice.'

'Do you believe in love?'

She took a moment to answer.

'I do. Completely!'

'What are its dimensions in the security theory you propose?'

'Significant. A good bread-earner will be respected and loved because he would be able to keep my mind away from other worries.'

'Is Neeraj that?'

'He is.'

'Yet, why do you worry all the time?'

There was a significant time gap before she answered.

'We have our problems.'

'I know what they are, so do you.'

'The distance...'

'Nopes. He doesn't love you.'

'Stop it!'

'He has never.'

'Stop messaging crap to me!'

'And he never will.'

She logged out. I kept writing though.

'One can't earn more than enough, as you yourself said. But one can love more than enough, and I will prove it to you. I just want you to understand what you really need, and it isn't a pizza, green paper, cement, or a bed. You are hungry for something that Neeraj will never be able to give you.'

She logged in again for a moment to reply, *'Go to hell!!'*

I smiled. If only she knew I was already there.

"Do all couples do it?" I asked Piyush.

"*It*??" He raised his eyebrows.

"Well, you know... get physical?" I asked, hoping desperately that the answer would be a *'No'*. He thought for a moment.

"Depends on the comfort level the couple shares and their thoughts about it." He gave a politically correct answer. But I wanted the real one.

"But then there is no point in not doing it, right? I mean, that's what the whole GF-BF thing amounts to, right?" I said, debating more with myself than him.

I guess he sensed what I wanted to hear, so his answer was sufficiently diplomatic.

"There is no hard and fast rule." It wasn't like I didn't know these answers. But I needed a third opinion—a sane opinion.

"So, there may be couples who may not have done it?" I rephrased the question in a different manner—clearly inspired by the psychometric tests conducted during our job interview.

"What's the matter, buddy?" He left his work and turned to look at me. He was a well-meaning, unassuming chap.

"Have you done it?" I asked sheepishly.

He smiled mysteriously. "And why on earth would I tell you, sir?"

"Please."

He shrugged. "We have kissed. We used to study together, so it would happen sometimes. We would also..."

"That's enough. Sorry for asking the question. Really am. Silly of me!" I said, embarrassed.

"Can I ask you why you asked?" he asked in a concerned voice.

"No," I said cockily and smiled as he gave me a disapproving look.

"I don't know myself what's with me these days," I sighed.

"Relationships are more than just sex, dude. Trust me, there are more ups and downs in a relationship than anywhere else—lots of expectations, compromises, sacrifices, and patience..." he said, looking somewhere far away.

"Is she okay?"

"Yes, yes, she is all right," he sighed and returned to his laptop without another word. He had forgotten to mention *'lots of pain'*.

○●○

'Prabhu knows what I want. Prabhu knows when I have it. Prabhu realizes when something is missing. Prabhu tells me when I need more. Prabhu understands my needs. Prabhu makes things happen. In Prabhu, I trust,' I read out loud.

"Say that again," he said, looking at me.

I looked at the tissue paper he had given me with these words written on it. Why the heck was I doing this? I looked up for an answer.

"You want me to talk to you again, right?" He reminded me wistfully.

Oh yes! Dude wasn't talking to me. He didn't pick up any of my calls, didn't reply to any emails, and didn't say *'Hi'* when I wished him.

But then why would I want to talk to this guy? I wanted him to remind me of that.

I looked at him—his fat chubby face, his dull greedy eyes, and his soggy pale complexion. Did it really matter to talk to this guy anymore? I had my group now.

He came by to make me realize that he wasn't speaking to me anymore. Otherwise, I wouldn't even notice.

"How is your home life these days?" I queried. He still hadn't let go of his ability to make his life look unsullied, and there was an abnormal calm on the personal front. But the storm was brewing somewhere deep inside, and I wanted to get a little whiff of it beforehand.

"My roommate is a rickshaw driver. He gets some girls every night, and then they do *'it'*. I go home late after they have slept," he said normally.

"Are you sober these days? Whatever it is that you spend your money on," I asked.

It had been a few weeks; I hadn't received his missed calls or random messages in the night trying to share with me his irrational and incoherent paranoia.

"I have no money, and therefore, everything is good. No distractions."

"You spent it?"

"I sent it home to my mother. She is retiring next month from her job in the post office. She needs money now more than ever. Her pension is just 2 thousand."

"Get her here."

"Here, where? Where I stay? Seriously?"

"Go to a better place, dude."

"Can't afford it."

"You are seriously sad."

"And you still leave me alone. Why do you do things like that?" He touched my cheek and looked at me longingly. That was weird. I shrugged off the queer feeling inside me and excused myself as JD called me for lunch.

As we walked away, I saw him standing alone and looking in our direction. He stood there silently till we were out of sight.

"Who's that guy?" JD asked.

"I never told you guys. He is a friend of mine," I said.

"Oh," she said nothing else.

"Why?"

"The thing is, I have seen him standing near our project door lots of times, trying to peek in," JD said gravely.

That was a shocker. I didn't show it.

"He must have come to meet me," I said in a relaxed manner.

"Nope. He just stands, and I saw him while leaving too. I remember feeling it was weird. This is not the only time. I have seen him quite a few times from my workplace as well, him peeking in." She shrugged her head. "He leaves abruptly."

She shuddered just to shrug off the uneasy feeling.

"Since when?"

"Almost a fortnight now."

That was long. Suman changed the topic.

"Someone's just back from home. Did those people get sweets for us?"

Bhoopal had convinced Kanchan to give leaves to JD after she bribed him with sweets.

"There was no time for sweets. I had gone home to meet a guy that had passed the filter of my father," said JD.

She didn't look at Suman; I took the cue, and neither did I. In fact, everybody avoided looking at him. I wondered how weirdly his face contorted, but I didn't want to know.

"What's his name?" Yogi and I asked at the same time. "What does he do?"

"His name is Sudeep Bandopadhyay. He works for a multinational bank, Kolkata, as a director. He did his MBA from IIM Kolkata."

"We want to see his pics," Piyush chipped in.

"You never told us," Suman retorted.

"It all happened in a hurry," JD replied, avoiding his eyes. "And yes, we will all see his pictures when we go down. I got a couple of them."

"How is he?" Bhoopal asked.

"He is well built and mustached. Basically..." She smiled and seemed to be at a loss for words.

"Cute?" Piyush asked.

"Yeah," JD smiled and blushed. "Can say that!"

Suman shuddered. "How much does he earn?" he asked.

JD took a moment to think. "He earns enough."

"How much, I ask?"

"*Kya rey.* Can't you imagine how much a bank's director earns?" Bhoopal jumped in for JD's rescue. "*A lot!*"

"Didn't the guy tell the number just to show off?" Suman laughed sardonically. "Oh, come on, don't say you didn't ask, JD. We all know you. The number is high enough to get you to blush and all, I see."

We stiffened.

"Okay, fine, I did ask, but that doesn't mean I need to tell it to you guys. Some things are to be kept personal, okay?" she said, her ears turning red, but her tone had changed to defensive.

"Yes, I know the secrecy. You never told us you were going to see a guy in the first place. It's all personal, right?" Suman retorted heatedly. Bhoopal jumped in again.

"Who are we to be told, Suman? Some things are to be done tactfully. Think it over; I am sure you will understand. Let's just all have a peaceful lunch first. Loads of work in the office." He saved the day. Nobody else would have dared to resolve the issue.

After lunch, we went down to see the pictures of JD's *'future-to-be'*. There were some customary snaps—like one standing by a silvery car with one hand on its top, glasses on the eyes, and a cheesy smile—to signify that there was a lot of money now and the prosperity was self-earned by Mr. Yours Truly. I guess there was a certain machismo in every such pic—but more to appeal to a girl's parents than the girl herself.

But the cheesiness just went from bad to worse. There were some pics of him in foreign locales—to underline that he had been outside India—and not to just one country but several. So, there was the Eiffel Tower and the Pyramids, Alps, and the Statue of Liberty...

"Stop it, will you?" Suman said, and for once, we all agreed with him as he wasn't speaking just out of bias this time. It was suffocating.

"Okay, fine, this guy is loaded with money. But did you even get to see his face? In every picture, his face is covered under a mustache, heavy glasses, and some kind of cloth on the head."

"He is slightly bald," JD said softly.

"And that's not a problem, you see. Everybody who has so much responsibility is certain to go bald these days," Bhoopal said, playing the fire-dowser.

"Look, JD, don't get dazzled with all the money. If you must marry someone, make sure that guy is good enough as a person and that he will take care of you," Suman said in a heartfelt voice. "After all, how much money does one need to be happy?"

She looked away.

"No, wait, listen to me," he said, looking deep into her eyes. "Don't marry a rich man; marry a good man! He will spend his entire life trying to make you happy!!"

I knew that was a sane advice. No matter whom she married, Suman wanted to make sure she was with someone who would love her and keep her happy.

Maybe JD understood this. She said nothing.

"So, what did he say?" Piyush asked.

"He seems to have kept the decision on hold. He would let me know in the coming weeks," JD said.

"Our guy has been looking out to meet lots of girls, I see. He would choose the most beautiful one. In that case, you need not worry, JD—it can safely be said that you won't be in the top 10," Suman started guffawing, and we all joined in, including JD herself.

○ ● ○

By evening, I had started worrying about what Prabhu was up to. He had gone from weird to creepy in the last few days—I wondered if he needed more electric shocks to regain his sanity. Since I was slightly out-of-touch with him, I was not sure if I had lost my touchpoints.

I called him after the evening status call.

"Hello."

"Hello... Prabhu?"

"Hey, look who called me! The man himself. Wassup, dear?" he asked in a cheerful voice.

"Hey, dude! You fine? Want to meet at the cafeteria?"

"Will join in a sec," he said, and he did.

"You are going punctual, I see," I said, complementing him.

"No biggie! Always was."

"Yeah, right," I responded sarcastically, thinking he meant it as a joke. "You wanted to talk to me about something."

We ordered tea.

"Want to eat anything?" Prabhu asked in a concerned voice.

"Some chips, maybe... But I am fine."

Prabhu went to the counter to get chips. I saw him breathing heavily and looking lost as he was returned the change. He resumed his place slowly.

"All fine? Need money?" I asked.

"I do, but don't worry about it. Things are fine at the moment—I will ask for it if I need it. Why did you ask?"

"You tell! I saw you acting weird and shy about something."

"It is not the money; it is something else. I wouldn't worry so much about money," Prabhu said, sitting down exasperated. "Drink your tea. Will tell you."

"What is it?" I asked, nearing the end of my patience, and expecting the worst.

"Pooja is getting married," he said, sipping his tea. "Next year, April."

I blinked a couple of times. This would take some time to sink in.

It was unexpected, but then, was it?

"But isn't she just 22!?" was the first thing that escaped my mouth.

"Yes, that is beyond the legal age of marriage for girls if that's your concern," he said, stuffing his mouth with chips. "I checked for that loophole."

"She is too young. I thought she would take a couple of years—to know the world, the people, the..."

"She isn't taking that time!" Prabhu sighed.

I sighed as well. "How do you know all this?"

"The news was all over the lunch table of Abhinav's group—they were howling and cheering and congratulating and creating a lot of noise. Everybody who was in the hall at that time came to know. The guy works as a brand manager in Dubai for some MNC."

"When was this?"

"Last week."

"And you tell me now?" I was angry and shaken, forgetting that I was the one avoiding him.

"Relax. It hardly matters," he said, patting my hand.

"Why are you patting my hand?" I asked sharply.

"You can cry. Cry it out," he said, still patting.

"I am not going to cry, dude; leave my hand." But then I did feel something in my heart swell. It was a surprise even for me that this news was so affecting. I felt sad, unhappy, and deeply frustrated. Something inside me wasn't ready to bid adieu to that idea of hers—she was one of those few unreachable dreams.

It was raining outside—just a drizzle, but I wanted to lose the heat. I asked Prabhu if he would like to join. We stood at the terrace parapet watching the vehicles move.

"What are your exact thoughts? I don't understand. Be happy for her. You still got Mitali," he said in a solemn tone.

"I am happy for her—just a little sad for myself. And you know it all too well; I got nobody!" I knew the raindrops falling down our faces would not wipe away the truth written on our foreheads.

"You got me, and you will always have me."

"That's a great thing to say, buddy." I turned to him and smiled.

"Let's go. Lots of work." We turned and started to leave.

"I never asked. How is Abhinav taking this?"

"He is playing it cool, but he is stunned as well—he didn't expect her to agree to the boy her father found for her."

It was a season of heartbreaks, it seemed. But we were never sure if things were ever serious between them, and we would never know.

"By the way, there is something else too."

"Yes."

"Abhinav got an offer to go onsite."

"Are you kidding? Already? In the present scenario?" I was surprised at the consolation the asshole got for his loss. It sure was a season of heartbreaks. Life is fair to the unfair. We both sighed as we finished our coffees.

"Hey, what's a *double-dip recession*?" JD asked Suman.

It was a lazy October morning. We sat on the porch of the company entrance as usual with our coffee mugs, thinking of the best way to kill time. So, Suman and I would just gaze around scouting for hot chicks.

"Hey, look at that Japanese female client who just entered." He pointed it out to me, and I winked back my appreciation. There were some talks about partying and some about booze. But nobody was in the mood to arrive at a decision.

"Suman, what's a double-dip recession?" JD asked again naively.

"How would I know? Ask Bhoopal," Suman retorted.

We all looked at Bhoopal.

"What makes you ask?" He would never answer a question straight.

"It has been in the papers for like a month now. People who read newspapers would know." She gave a dirty stare to Suman, but all cringed. I wondered if anybody read newspapers. Bhoopal smiled.

"The entire world is about to face a double-dip recession. Indian IT seems to be all set to face the full fury of it. The last global recession we faced in recent times was in 1991, and before that in 1981 and 1975."

"So, what does it mean? No jobs? No switch? No promotions?" Yogi queried. The dark clouds had attracted everybody's attention.

"Indian IT had faced a small scare briefly during 2004 when the demand had fallen due to the gaps in our ability to scale up operations and lack of domain expertise and new capabilities; I hope the management knows how to tackle it this time if things get dicey," Bhoopal said defensively. Yogi nodded indecisively.

"Well, there certainly aren't any danger signals from the management, Bhoopal. It's all too quiet," Suman asked, concerned.

"I know," Bhoopal sighed heavily.

There was a silence now, and nobody knew what to say, nobody except Bhoopal.

"Recession is in the mind. It might be a matter of interesting analysis to understand how much of it is real and how much is owing to the collective loss of faith of us all: investors, governments, banks, businesses, and common citizens. We all push the panic button due to limitations in our knowledge and understanding, sometimes directly, at times indirectly," Bhoopal said.

We were looking at him dumbstruck.

"I think all he is trying to say is: Stop overreacting!" JD said cautiously and raised her eyebrows to inquire if she had oversimplified his views.

Bhoopal winked at her patronizingly. "Yes, that's another way of putting it. Let's not spread panic, and let's not get affected by speculations."

"Hmm." JD nodded.

"JD, leave all this. Tell us how things are between you and Sudeep. When's the engagement?" Piyush jumped in to break the perplexity of half-understood ideas.

"Things are not well."

It had been two weeks since the last meeting we discussed Sudeep. I wondered if JD could get through her marriage before this stupid recession hit us. Why board the ship in the face of a storm?

"Why don't you get married? Engagement is stupid."

"*Arey baba*, he is a paranoid guy. A couple of days ago, he called my father to ask why I was standing so close to Suman in one of our party pictures uploaded on Orkut. I had to stay awake all night to convince my father and then him that I and Suman are just friends,"

Suman choked on his coffee.

"You could as well have said that I am your brother," he said angrily.

"Well, we *are* friends!" she shouted, raising her voice.

"But why the hell justify?" he shouted louder.

"Just pardon me, will you? Why on earth do I always sit between you two? I never understand," Bhoopal said, getting up.

"These two sit beside you, Bhoopal, so that they don't catch each other's throats in the middle of their fights," Piyush clarified. "By the way, did Sudeep accept the explanation?"

"I don't know. Father tried to convince him about my character, and he seemed to be getting convinced. He says he wants a girl just like me—homely and intelligent."

Suman started chortling.

"Homely? Intelligent?" He broke out into a fit of laughter. "You duped him well. Let the poor guy find the reality after marriage."

"I am homely, and I am intelligent," she fumed. "And don't mind, but I will have to remove all my pics with you guys from my Orkut account. My *'would-be'* gets jealous already."

Suman looked at her red-eyed, and she returned the stare.

"Can't you be a little firm and tell him to be less chauvinistic?"

"You know well that I can't. I am 26 already. Feminism is a luxury for girls with age not on their side." JD's voice faltered. I hate awkward pauses.

"So, what are your plans? Intelligently scrub the kitchen floors and use your coding genius for cooking the fish?"

"Whatever man!!" JD snapped.

I checked Google as soon as we returned. A double-dip recession meant a recession followed by a short-lived recovery, followed by another recession. The world seemed to be all set for it. I took the last gulp of my coffee and returned to work.

It wasn't my job to think about the recession; I was paid to test codes. I worked for a couple of hours non-stop till I mailed my work to Raj. He wasn't around; he must have gone for a smoke.

268 |

I continued checking the lotus mails for any sign of new work. No new emails were sent to me. But then, it was a Friday. People are supposed to not stretch on Friday, or so they say everywhere. But actually, Fridays are often the craziest!

I looked up from my workstation to see how others were doing. Everyone seemed to be busy, even Suman. For that matter, even Kanchan was at her desk—late for a manager. I hadn't heard from Mitali all day. Maybe she was working too.

I took a moment to relax back on my chair as I continued viewing all these people looking at their monitors and doing what they did best. They were my family—the one I bid goodbye to every evening and returned to every morning. I wished things would stay fine. I had nobody to look up to at home. I thought of taking a solitary walk up to the cafeteria on the topmost floor, only to meet Rohit in the lift.

"Wassup?" I inquired hesitantly, expecting some response. Anger, hate, anything.

He said nothing, didn't even look at me, and just left as the door opened to the second floor. People are weird!

I took a cup of tea before walking towards the edge of the terrace. In the dim streetlights of the night, I saw Prabhu already standing there, looking at the vehicles zooming.

"Life's pace needs to slacken man!" I said, standing beside him quietly. "Everybody is so super-busy these days."

"Tell me about it. Things just keep moving zig-zag with no peace in sight," he sighed. "By the way, something happened this evening. Maybe I guess, it's good if you know."

I looked at him.

"Abhinav proposed to Pooja," he said undramatically. I couldn't breathe for some time. "This evening."

I took a moment to say nothing and one more to regain my breath as the vehicles swooshed past on the road with menacing honks.

"What did she say?"

"She rejected the proposal. Just said she always looked at him as a friend, nothing more."

"Wow," I muttered. "So, Abhinav indeed was after her!" Maybe Rohit was after consoling him and patching things up between the two.

"He had no chance. Her dude earns in Dirhams."

"I don't know, man!" My heart kept sinking. "He took two weeks to propose."

"Let it pass—maybe he thought he would impress her by earning in dollars. We have got enough problems as it is." He touched my shoulders and pulled me back. "You still got me."

"...and Mitali," I whispered and hoped. I wondered what she was up to. "Hey, maybe we need to start searching for new jobs."

"Woah, why?" Prabhu inquired.

"Just in case, I mean, it's recession time!" I said it with doubt in my unknowing eyes.

"Oh, give me a break. What the fuck is this recession anyway? Everybody keeps rambling about it," Prabhu grumbled.

I knew I didn't understand it completely. Nobody did.

We took another moment to enjoy the silence of the moment.

Prabhu's phone rang.

"Give me a moment, please." He moved away to attend the call privately.

Things were going to change in some way, or so everyone believed. I hoped we had the required skills and the luck to survive—all of us—wouldn't want any soldiers left behind. Prabhu, meanwhile, was talking animatedly on the call. I hoped he would turn a new leaf and get into exploring his potential better. He had the gray matter.

"You won't believe what just happened," he returned, humphing. I gave him a curious look.

"Rohit proposed to Pooja too!" He said out loud.

"What the..." I literally shouted, too stunned for words.

"I don't know the details, but he did it in front of everybody on her floor."

I was livid. First of all, he was not supposed to do this. Second of all, he had no sense of timing. Besides, he did it in public, thus embarrassing her.

"He's just a rotten person!" I spit out my rage.

"Needless to say, she rejected him too and chided him for creating a scene. She's never going to talk to him again."

"No wonder. Entirely deserved. She should have slapped him as well," I said, gritting my teeth. "Let's go, mate. Too tired for any more surprises."

I wondered how someone who loved someone could act in ways that hurt the other person. No one would ever do that if they actually meant what they said.

"Wonder what they were thinking. So basically, the situation is thus: Anyone who isn't earning in Dirhams stands no chance," Prabhu said.

I smiled at the sadness of it.

Mitali's version:

"Mitali, how much time should the assignment take? Half an hour more would be enough? Scott's been inquiring," asked my team lead.

Scott was our onsite manager. It was 7 p.m. IST.

"I know. He pinged me as well. Make it an hour," I replied.

'Hey Scott, an hour more should be fine?' I pinged back.

'It should. Thanks a ton, Mitali. Hey, btw, did u see my new pic with Lane and Jacket?' Lane and Jacket were his pups. We shared a mutual interest in dogs.

'Not after the one you last sent, Scott ☺... Been three months now.'

'I would send it across. Take a look.' He sent the pics.

'They are too cute, Scott. Lane's been growing up real quick.'

'She's a natural ☺... daughter of the wild... Anyway, I shouldn't be wasting your time. It's after all a weekend. Have a cool one.'

'You too ☺!' I wrote.

'Simbeth's gonna take me and Diane on a long ride.'

Simbeth was the pony that he gifted his wife Diane on their anniversary. Since then, Diane had been a keen pony rider.

'Have a great time and be careful. I am logging out.'

The day had been a long one. Fridays were the time when people onsite would leave early for a good time out. I wondered where my pony was. I called Neeraj. He didn't pick up the call. I could have spared 10 minutes. It was hardly a 15-minute job, even though I had asked for extra time. Everyone needs a good chat with someone dear at relaxed times. My phone rang; I expected it to be Neeraj—it was Ami.

"Want to join for a small walk?" he asked enthusiastically.

"Can't! Work submission," I said impulsively.

"Alrighty. Let me know if it finishes early. Don't stay back for long," was his optimistic voice.

I wondered why I did that—I was just tired of living a double life and a lie. Neeraj was always the one for me and would always be. I had suffered enough from my incessant moody spells where I avoided Ami and then times when I gave him a lot of time. I knew someone was to be blamed for the stretch it was having on my psyche—the guilt and the moral itch—but it was difficult to say with surety where the blame resided and where the buck stopped. After the work ends, I would call Neeraj—I needed a break from everything.

Ami's version:

I understood well that she never had time for me these days unless she needed me. But then I knew she needed me, and this was a good enough reason for me to hang around. At least someone needed to be truthful to themselves in this whole matter and to one's feelings—complex though they were.

I had called her to get some reassurance that I had somebody—somebody whom I belonged to and somebody who belonged to me. People do have these insane, intense desires to possess and be possessed. Sadly, they end up in one-sided relationships most of the time.

Prabhu looked at me and didn't say anything. He just took my hand and gave it a gentle press. I had to agree that it was reassuring. We went down quietly.

9.

November '07: Kindle (Amazon) eReader launched. Google announced the first beta version of the Android operating system for handsets.

Ami's version:

It was Monday, the first one of November, and Kanchan had called for a team meeting. Team meetings in *FORDIT* had a simple agenda—improving efficiency and productivity. It was post-lunch.

Times were uncertain, and so was the agenda.

Nothing new had come up in the past few months. Looking ahead, there only seemed to be more of the same work. HR team building activities had gone down—maybe there weren't any money left to spare for the same. The team was already working hard to maintain a decent project utilization. Even Suman would be permanently retained in some project, or so it seemed.

We reached on time for the meeting; Kanchan was in the room already, and she gave us a concerned stare. "Where are JD and Suman? Call them too. Let's begin, guys."

They too arrived in a moment. She started as all took their positions.

"First, let's begin with the feedback, hmm? How are things? Anything general you would like to share? It's not every day we get to chat, right?" she said, taking a sip of her coffee. "Why don't we begin with Bhoopal?"

He cleared his throat. "Workwise, we are performing well. Everybody is doing their work satisfactorily. We are working in synchronization with each other—both the domains and corresponding assignments. We complete all our assignments in 90% of the committed time or less." He coughed while talking.

Everybody else gave similar answers in different words. Honest feedback is for honest times.

"Cool. The thing is, we are to tighten our reins. I know we are efficient as it is. But we are to improve at it. Yeah? We are to go *LEAN* and reduce wastage of time..." She took a moment to give us all meaningful stares. "And to improve our efficiency to achieve more work compared to what we do presently."

We looked at each other blankly.

"I have received this presentation from higher management that reiterates the concepts of *LEAN*. It's a management philosophy that aims at working towards adding value to the customer *(as perceived by them)* through everything we do—since this is the only thing customers pay for. For us, it means improving our productivity in the hours we bill the clients. I would share these presentations across. As you are aware, we are set for tough times, and we are to meet our quarterly targets. We are also to reduce our internal costs and expenses. As a company, our focus should be on regaining the share we lose to our competition and to ensure repeat business from our clients. But these are strategic things to be discussed with Bhoopal. By the way, I have recommended Bhoopal to the higher management. He is to be given higher managerial authority from now on. There will not be any designation change immediately—he will continue to be your Team Lead, but he is set for some bigger responsibilities going ahead. Congrats Bhoopal!"

We applauded enthusiastically, and Kanchan joined in. He smiled shyly, too overwhelmed by the suddenness.

"Bhoopal, if you could stay back for a moment, we can discuss your immediate role. Meanwhile, team, please understand these concepts better. We are to work productively at least 80% of the time we spend in the office. That's our moral commitment henceforth."

We went out as the door closed behind us.

Bhoopal being given authority was good news. He was the one trusted by all, technically and morally—an ideal guy to carry the baton. But it also depended on what the baton was.

"Guys, quick!" Suman shouted, "Before the mail reaches our inbox, before our inbox replicates it, and before Kanchan and Bhoopal, the new *'in'* guy comes out with a mission to make us *LEAN,* let's enjoy the few last moments of our short-lived freedom and take a quick coffee break."

All giggled.

He waited for Bhoopal to join us. He didn't come out of the meeting for quite some time. When he did come out, he looked tired and phased out.

"What's the matter?" JD asked as he passed her.

"Nah, nothing." He tried to smile, but he was clearly out of sync.

"Let's go for a party, dude!" Suman shrieked from his place.

"Not today, guys. Let's save this for later," he smiled weakly. "Oh yes, before I forget, we have a team meeting tomorrow. Suman, please send invitations to everybody for the post-lunch session and book a conference room."

Before leaving for home, he promised us a party over the weekend.

○●○

There was a meeting the very next day.

"Six of the eight hours that we spend in the office has to be productive. In the office, we should only do things that add value to the client ultimately." Bhoopal went towards the board to write it down.

"That amounts to 75% of the time," Yogi said. "But Kanchan said 80% yesterday."

"More the better," Bhoopal looked at us. "Currently we are below 50%."

He looked at each of us for a moment, for impact.

We didn't fight that. But unevenness of work was also one of the reasons for this.

"Guys, let's not get confused about this. It is basically to ensure that people build professional skills that enable them to be productive at least 3/4th of their time. We can imbibe the discipline of our onsite counterparts for this. They work most of their time productively; they come on time and leave on time, whereas we spend nights in the office mulling over regular assignments. That is inefficient. Working the *LEAN* way, we can save on the time billed and also on the incrementals, like electricity and supplies."

"Bhoopal, we get it. Why are you explaining so much?" Suman said sarcastically.

"Good then," he said, dropping the marker on the table. "Any questions?"

He looked around. People stared back blankly.

"I have one," I said.

"Yes?"

"How do we measure productivity? I mean, how do we find out if the person was productive or not? He might just stare at his screen all the time. Besides, it's not healthy to look at the screen for 6 hours straight. It makes my eyes water."

"Good question. See, nobody is going to hang anyone if people aren't at their best for 6 hours. But the broad idea is that we need to tighten our schedules and make sure we clock 6 hours of mandatory work in 8 hours. That would mean we need to be at our best and cut long coffee breaks."

"Ahh..." all grunted.

Bhoopal threw up his arms in the air. "It will be strictly monitored by Kanchan. In the time–entry tool, you would need to add detailed comments on work against time."

Things looked depressing.

"We as a team need to work together so that we can survive this hard phase."

"We received another mail in the morning, Bhoopal," Suman said,

"What about that?"

We had received a generic mail from HR in the morning about the resource knowledge validation test to be conducted as a process at least once a year from now on. We sat up in our chairs to pay slightly more attention.

"Company resources are the basic asset of any knowledge-based industry. Our company is thinking on starting this process of regular examinations of resources. But it is as a drive to ensure that the talent mapping is precise, and we upgrade where gaps are identified. Basically, it is also to..."

"This is basically a cost-cutting initiative to ensure that we don't end up retaining more people than necessary," Raj whispered to Yogi.

"I do not agree with that. In these difficult times, we need some tests like these to keep us competitive," Yogi whispered back. Raj just shrugged.

○ ● ○

The previous evening: What happened inside the cabin?

Bhoopal looked at Amit as he closed the door behind him, leaving him alone with Kanchan.

"What are your aspirations in life, Bhoopal?"

He smiled. "We have discussed this several times in the KRA appraisal meetings. I always wanted to grow in the technical field."

"Yes, I am aware of that, and so I would like you to pay attention." She came and sat on the table near his chair. "The world is moving towards management. There is no future on the technology front, at least in our company. We just don't have enough cutting-edge projects, Bhoopal," she said with exasperation. "We mostly have backend support work offsite—doesn't matter which platform."

Bhoopal looked at her, a little shocked by her honesty. He wondered what she was thinking and what was about to come.

"You are a bright guy. I would suggest it is fair for you if you make a transition towards a leadership role. Industry, as we know it, is just too volatile right now. Too much pressure for numbers and for cost-cutting from higher management."

"I wouldn't fit, Kanchan. It's just not my inclination."

"You would. Besides, the technology field is and will always stay open for you. You can always return. But times like these demand that you have some authority to instill some discipline in the team so as to protect them from the things that may slip anytime."

"I understand," he nodded.

She looked at him to see if he did, truly.

"There is something I want to ask you, and this might come across as a surprise." She sighed and tapped her fingers on the table to think of the best way to put it forward.

He said nothing.

"The situation is not good. We are carefully trying to hide our financial vulnerability and weakness from our clients and the software industry. We aren't really earning; we are trying to float. At some point in time, things can fall apart..." She threw her cup into the basket. "...like a house of cards. It all depends on if our major client wants to renew the project contract with us in these turbulent financial conditions. It can happen only if we can give them our services at a price nobody else can."

He stayed mum still. She sighed and continued.

"For those times, I need feedback from you as a senior guy and a close teammate. I would like you to list down here..." She slid a paper towards him. "...names of 3 people who we will have to let go in case the situation gets tricky... you know... businesswise. I need to share these with higher management today."

He just looked at that paper.

"Please try to understand that this is just for the worst of the times."

"Why take names now? Take that time."

"Look, this is for the times when somebody *has* to go. These are matters beyond our area of control, Bhoopal."

"Why me, Kanchan? You take a call. You are the manager. Fire anybody you want."

"*Right-size*," she corrected him. "You mean right-size. You know their technical capacities and their potential. It is better if you take a call and let me know. I would trust your judgment."

He looked down at that paper disgusted.

"Look, I don't like this either, but what if somebody *has* to go? I am giving you a choice to make the right decision. You can use this wisely."

"It is very difficult for me to do so right now. I would have to think."

"I need to submit the names this evening. They haven't given me any time, so I won't be able to give you any."

"Is it that easy, Kanchan? Come on, be fair," he muttered, irritated.

"Times aren't fair," she said softly. "We have to make the best of what we get."

He thought for some time and scribbled down 3 names. The first name was his!

As he was about to leave, he saw her quietly scratch off his. He said nothing; just closed the door to face the people outside, waiting for him.

Ami's version:

So yes, the assignments increased in number, and days began to feel shorter. We were forever in a shortage of time, crunching in an extra assignment at the cost of shorter breaks. Even the loo breaks were monitored, and people would never be free at the same point in time. Hence coffee breaks decreased, and even when free, people would go out for coffee in shorter groups—with whomever available.

There would always be a few assignments in the pipeline for us. Everybody started having 2-3 assignments to be submitted in a fewer number of days. Everybody worked hard to make sure they had no backlogs. But the assignments would never stop.

At the back of my mind, I would always be thinking of Mitali. At night, I would find myself thinking of her in my dreams.

Things had been hectic for me. But the more tired I would get, the more disturbed my sleep would be. Days would never end, and the nights would be wafer thin before starting off another day. The cycle was continuous.

○●○

"Bhoopal, how come we have so much work these days?" I asked him once. "Do we really have so many assignments coming up?"

"We have been greedy about taking up more work and increasing our work pressure. It's an assumption that it might help us renew our contract with the client for another 10 years. The contract is about to expire next year at some point."

"What if all these efforts don't lead to the contract renewal?" He gave me an ominous stare that scared me.

"Let's try not to think along those lines. We shouldn't let a situation like that arise, and let's hope we never find out."

Financials are the key to everything. 60% of the org. revenues came due to an association with this particular client. Most of the projects we had were basically sister projects related to the same client. Too high a dependency if you ask me. But that would also mean that...

"Just because we work doesn't mean we will be saved. Everybody in all projects must work similarly since most projects are interrelated. Besides, there will obviously be a spillover if people freeride," I spoke.

Cost-cutting was just one of the ways to achieve good profits. Increasing revenue was another, and there was a very limited demand in the market for the kind of niche work we were doing except from one particular client.

"You know *INSITE*? That's one of the projects that will be most affected, I guess. The job they do is just a fancy name for data entry. Very redundant," Bhoopal said, "Thank God! I am no longer with that project. That one is doomed for sure, but that doesn't mean we are safe."

My heart gave a wild pang of panic for Mitali, but I stayed quiet. She was capable of taking care of herself.

○ ● ○

I called her during lunch. She was busy, as usual.

"Continue. I may not be able to join. Lots of work," she said in a breathless tone. Sigh... Things were getting wilder, even for her. Prabhu called me to ask if he could join. I did a quick check— everybody was busy. So yes, he could join.

I entered the lift and pushed the topmost floor button.

The lift stopped on the first floor, and Prabhu entered. He shoved people aside and stood alongside me. "Where were you, dude? For the last many days, you were just absent or so it seemed."

Few seconds later, on the third floor, the lift stopped again, and many people entered, including Pooja. People pushed her inside, and ultimately, she ended up standing beside me. She was alone, without any of those giggling or ogling companions, and she stood silently without any of that mirth that I had always associated her with.

I wondered if I should wish her for the fast–approaching wedding. I wondered if it would make her feel good in the first place.

I nodded to Prabhu. Somehow, it felt shy to even speak in her presence.

"What?"

"Been busy," I whispered.

She seemed slightly uncomfortable—–like when a person wants to say something but is out of things to say or is unsure of the way to say it.

Prabhu asked her, "How's the work in your project, Pooja?"

She smiled at us—I don't know—maybe for the first time ever.

"Similar—Tons of pressure and stress, plenty of work. It's mad," she said happily. "How are things going for you guys?"

The lift opened, and everybody walked out. We reached the cafeteria.

"Cost–cutting is reaching weirder heights day by day. No good work in sight," I said in a croaky voice.

"I am sure things will improve. It is just a matter of time and patience," she waved at a couple of girls from her team who waved back at her. As I saw her moving away, I realized I too had something to say once and for all.

"By the way, hey!" I startled her; she turned around surprised.

"Congrats on the soon-to-be wedding. If it's okay with you, care for a coffee with us?"

I don't know what exactly went through her mind, but she didn't smile.

"Thanks for the wishes." She tried to smile politely, but all that escaped was a wistful smirk. "I will catch up with you guys later. They have ordered some stuff from MacD, and I am supposed to pay... so well... must go." She then waved at me.

Prabhu gave me his *'It's a bit rude to refuse a coffee with us, ain't it?'* look.

We didn't talk much about anything, least of all *INSITE*. Why create panic?

Mitali's version:

When will this assignment end? It's been a long haul of stupid assignments, one after the other. Seniority in the team is often exploited.

I called Neeraj. It was lunchtime; maybe he didn't hear the ring in the hustle and bustle of the office. *INSITE* was like a hot stove right now, and I was at the center of it. The people on the sides will escape in some way, the losers and the newcomers both, but I may not be able to. They would get leave from the project by the year-end, and new people would join. The whole project worked on the concept of a pipeline. Some, like me, were retained year after year; ones who would actually try to leave the project.

But in the present scenario, I wasn't sure if it was safe for the people who were asked to leave. It might be equivalent to a pink slip. There weren't many vacancies in any other projects. So, leaving was impractical unless there was a different project to work on— some project where they needed a resource. If I apply independently to some project and get selected—maybe just maybe—I would get a permission to leave *INSITE*.

○●○

That was the very reason I had called Neeraj: to ensure he gets me into his project in Delhi—development of an embedded software support platform for a telecom client—one of the very few interesting and innovative projects in *FORDIT*. It was a small team and a small office in Delhi at that point in time, but the learning opportunity was incredible. I couldn't help but giggle a little at the very thought of it.

That would be the dream come true! The perfect escape and getaway—the staircase to heaven—a road to paradise—the...
The phone rang.

It was a call for lunch from Ami, and I felt guilt again—that sickening feeling inside that I wanted to run away from. I just didn't want to be a part of this anymore.

I made some excuse and went back to work while waiting for a call from Neeraj. It never came. I went to lunch late.

I called him again.

"Oh, sorry, dear! Completely forgot to reply back with all this work," said Neeraj.

"Well, what are you going to do about the thing we talked about yesterday?" I complained in a croaky, nagging voice. I would find it very difficult to not be myself with Neeraj; maybe that's why I was in love with him.

"I am going to get that for you. Just give me some time. I will forward your resume to the boss. Let's see what he says!" He consoled me.

"I miss you!" I said it in the same tone as a young girl would speak to her doll. I really did—a lot.

"Me too." I could feel him smile on the phone. He cut the call.

If only God wishes, all will be okay. Not just okay, it will be great.

By evening, I was still working on the same assignment. The drive was clearly missing. *LEAN* was just for robots!

Ami's version:

I went down to my project floor and found everybody still working. As I moved back to my chair, I saw Kanchan looking at me over her workstation.

It was a disapproving look. I took a glance at my watch—I had taken almost an hour for lunch. Before I could sit on my chair, I saw Bhoopal giving me a look too—it was a look of warning! Any short deviation from the discipline was not going to go unnoticed. My behavior was in contrast to what was expected!

As I sat in my chair, I received a ping from JD. *'Where were you? Away for almost an hour. Kanchan asked twice.'*

I don't understand this. *LEAN* was supposed to be a positive step for a positive outcome. I guess when things get rough, positivity is the first on the list to get compromised.

○●○

In the evening, Bhoopal told us over coffee, "When financial times are tough, perceptions matter a lot. If everybody stays positive and optimistic, then the stock markets don't crumble. Pessimism spreads word of mouth anyway. So, the key to success is to stay positive as an industry and as a team and hope good faith can prevent panic from spreading. Panic-fueled decisions taken to cut the losses often lead to a never-ending decline. Yet, that is what the confederations try anyway, only to fail over a period of time. Of course, sometimes, the fundamentals are wrong too, so I shouldn't generalize."

I don't know where he used to get all these nuggets of wisdom—must be from his stock market misadventures. Things weren't going too well; Venky and Yogi's faces were an adequate testimony to it.

As I left for home that evening—I realized I was missing something— something called an identity.

How long could one be expected to live as a small wheel in the entire gamut of wheels? Where was my own drive to work? Why did I need a push to move every time? Was there even a remote chance that I would ever be given an opportunity to love my job? I had no answers.

The global economy was toying with my life, job, and motivation.

I called Prabhu from the bus. He was still working in the office. Hard times were for everybody. I wondered if I should call Mitali—it had been days since we last met—it had been days since we last talked. We still messaged a lot, but then that was all; it was like talking to one's own self.

I thought I would do so from my home. I called her. She was still in the office—very tired. "Would it be okay if we talk tomorrow? All this crap has drained me completely. Don't have it in me to speak," she.

"Would you be able to go home? It's late."

"I am leaving now." She took a moment and spoke out, "Is it okay if I call you after every 20 minutes to tell you that I am fine? I am afraid of the cabs. If you don't receive a call from me, call me. If I don't pick up your call, call the cab office; I will send you their number. If they don't pick up, call the police, okay?"

Cute! Thankfully, nothing went wrong. An hour and three phone calls later, she was at her place. I had to call her all the three times—exhaustion kept getting the better of her sleep buds throughout the journey.

○●○

Raj was one of those rare people in our company who had ambitions, perhaps the only one within our team. Until then, the lightning of wisdom had not struck others; we were happy in the bliss of our ignorance.

I wondered what his plans were sometimes; he would often sit working late at night—sometimes ranging till 2 a.m.—and would still come back the next day on time. People often sighted him in office over weekends as well.

"I come here if I get bored at home. It's all really simple. I go to Hyderabad once every three months. On weekends I come to check the internet and all. Company is fun," he said when Bhoopal asked him about it over the lunch table.

"You are sad!" JD pooh-poohed.

"What can I say? Work is life." He laughed at his own joke.

"Two ways to think about this, man!" Bhoopal intervened. "Either you work to live well, or you live to work well. Seems it's the other one for you."

Raj said nothing.

"Get married. About time!!" JD said.

"Yes, then you will have things to *do* over the weekends," Suman chipped in, and we all guffawed at the cheapness of it. JD gave Suman a horrible look to stop.

"In a couple of years, when I reach somewhere professionally, then sure," Raj conservatively smiled at us.

Raj was also short-tempered. He never condoned laxness when people had any assignments from his domain. It was all professionalism and efficiency for him.

No wonder *LEAN* found its biggest driver in Raj, though he had his own personal issues with and around it. He would always want his assignment the quickest from us, would give us only enough time for completion, and would never want us to look free or happy. He was good at slogging it out and wanted all to follow his example. No wonder he didn't see eye to eye with Bhoopal over many matters, and most of the disagreements would come over people and team management.

So, if by any chance I got two assignments—one from Bhoopal's domain and one from Raj's—Raj would make sure I submitted his before Bhoopal's. The deadline wouldn't really matter. He would follow up non-stop and would ensure that he hounded my nightmares.

I wasn't sure if he was happy with Bhoopal's rise in management either. He would always feel that he could extract work better from the team and could provide better results more efficiently. Two ways to look at it again—either extract work better or be a better boss.

Lately, he had been at his annoying best. No wonder people avoided his assignments. But the domain quota had to come, and somebody had to do it. So there never really was a way to escape.

Things just went from bad to worse with the pressure, and correspondingly the number of assignments in our inbox increased.

He would never take a no for an answer. Deadlines were stringent, with no headroom for any air. But then the deliverables mattered more to him and to Kanchan and to the management.

○●○

Every day newspapers would be filled with gloom. More and more IT managers from MNCs were being given pink slips—that would save higher—cost wise and loss of technical talent wise.

Core functionaries, if performers, are normally safe in any company even if the situation goes bad. Supporting functions often face the brunt first. But then, things didn't look as if they would stop at managers. So, I stopped reading newspapers. Depression was catching up—both economic and mental.

MNCs were hit, but so were the Indian mid-sized companies, especially export-oriented and banking industries. What people didn't realize was that some Indian companies were more dependent on the dollars than the MNCs, who had operations in several geographies so that they could distribute the risk. Some Indian companies had a limited clientele, and hence dependency on these clients was very high.

Perception was everything. People needed to work and also to look busy. The manager's eye was extremely critical and harmful lately.

Selling the perception was also important internally for the organization. Management never divulged the details of the company's health with the employees. As far as we were concerned, everything was blissful. Managers always smiled. I guess they too realized that panic was the worst tonic. What we were unsure of, though, was whether they were doing anything to save our jobs.

"Do you think we can survive this, Bhoopal? The thing is, we hardly get time to search or apply for other jobs elsewhere," JD asked one evening when we were out for our only coffee break together that day. "And you know I have to leave."

"Work might ease next year," Bhoopal replied. "But nobody knows, JD, and you know that well." He didn't say much about the leaving part.

We just had to make peace with the uncertainty, the ambiguity, and the pressure.

"There would not be any promotions this year, I guess," Raj remarked.

"Forget promotions—the incentive is to save jobs," Yogi jumped in.

"So, when do you want to leave JD?" Suman asked solemnly, "How is the marriage plan shaping up?" I knew he wouldn't leave this.

"This year-end, maybe," JD looked at him. Her eyes were silent but full of undisclosed yet undeniable feelings. "I guess it's time!"

A couple of months more to go—time would just fly away. One day you are family, the next day you are out. Bhoopal looked at JD and then at Suman with incredible empathy. Something inside him felt very vulnerable now—but Bhoopal never spoke. He didn't that whole evening.

○●○

One good thing about life is that it speaks volumes even when we are busy ignoring the comprehension of it.

JD reported late to work the other day. She looked distraught.

"Pressure is increasing on Dad. Sudeep really wants to get married by year-end."

"Why is he asking you to come to Kolkata? Can't he wait or take a job here?" Bhoopal asked.

"Both our parents are in Kolkata, and I wanted to move to Kolkata anyway. Shift me to some project in *FORDIT*, Kolkata office. It makes sense."

"But look at the work, JD? Can you not stay back till Feb at least?"

Though that was true, it felt strange to see the ever-supportive Bhoopal of all people stop her because of work even though he knew the gravity of the event.

"What are you saying, man? This is a question of someone's life," Suman intervened despite himself.

"I know, and that is the very reason why I would like her to stay back. Why make rash decisions? Besides, we really don't want any disturbances in our team right now."

Maybe it was the work pressure, but that made no sense to me. Apparently, it didn't to Suman either.

"What's she got to do with the whole project pressure thing? She is done. Let her go," he retorted.

"Suman, the dependencies on her are high. We are all neck-deep in work. Is there any time left for hiring a new person and proper delegation of her work? Will any of you be able to take a 20% increase in the workload? Don't even try to say yes—you are all already at 110% due to *(unpaid)* overtime. Hence the ultimate decision to transfer or stay back on the bench is kind of dependent on me. Kanchan will ask me what we should do. Should we allow her transfer, or should we let her stay on the bench? And I will say *NO*—none of it." He looked down and then up directly in her eyes. "...looking solely at the project requirements. I am so sorry, JD, but I can't help it!"

JD sat very silent—but one could see from her stiff body language that she was really angry. "So, the only option left for me is to quit the job?" she said finally.

"No, that doesn't count as an option either. If you quit, you will not find any work outside—jobs have all dried up. Besides, you won't even get an experience certificate without serving the notice period *(of 3 months)*, as you will be leaving before the notice period ends, and the management is certain the project needs you right now. So, the best way is to stay back and continue for some more time till things sort out."

"But... if you agree, there shouldn't be a problem." JD looked shocked by Bhoopal's approach.

"Well, I have a responsibility for other people too, and I don't see how I can allow you to leave at such a short notice that too when we are so much in the thick of things."

JD tried to find her voice and argue, but her voice was quivering with tension, stress, and anger.

"We all know, Bhoopal, that the new project vacancies in our company come by the year-end or at the beginning of the new year. Now if I stay back working until February end what chance on earth do I have to ever change to a new project in Kolkata over the next year? Do you promise me in writing that you will get me transferred to Kolkata in March? Can you? So basically, this is just getting me stuck and ruining my life."

"You, for sure, cannot leave immediately without serving the notice period of 3 months."

Suman tried to soothe things and the tone of the conversation, but he didn't do great at it. "This is pure blackmailing, bro. Her interest in the project is over, and she has every right to leave. I don't know why you are doing this," he said softly.

That just did it—Bhoopal snapped.

"Oh, c'mon, guys. You know well why I am doing this—to save all your jobs. The project can't go through any such issues right now. We need to deliver and deliver on time. From my side and from the point of view of my role, I can't allow any of you to leave immediately. Personally, all my sympathies are with JD."

JD had a short laugh. It was filled with hollowness and pain.

"We thought you going to management would change things; instead, all you did was become one of them." JD said spitefully. "Speaking their language with us, huh?"

"Try to understand JD..." Bhoopal was never good at justifying his actions, and I knew that even if JD did give him a chance, he would fail miserably while at it.

"What is it that you don't know, Bhoopal? I am no longer interested in my job, or the money you guys are paying me. You still want me to slog for your project and your deliverables. My father is old; I have no mother. He is under stress to get me married to this guy he found with great difficulty. That guy is all demands, and the least I can do is to be in Kolkata this year-end for marriage. What is it that you still don't know, huh? You can help me, but all you do is hold my well-deserved work certificate at ransom and compel me to work. You, of all people, are doing this to me?" JD had started to lose all sense of logic and patience as her volume increased dangerously.

"Stop it, JD! Get a grip!" Bhoopal said in an uncompromising tone, but his eyes amply foretold that he was in pain. This was clearly not his cup of tea.

"At least say you will think about it, dude!" Suman tried to convince Bhoopal.

"I already have, Suman. There is nothing more to it. JD, just convince Sudeep to keep patience," he said, averting her eyes, which sparkled with the pain of betrayal.

"You don't need to worry about me anymore, sir. I will see what I need to do. Thanks a lot for your great concern and help!" JD lashed out sarcastically, fuming with anger.

She got up and walked away.

We dared not look at Bhoopal. His face shone with an iron resolve and also with hurt and pain. He avoided our eyes. Suman too sat down, looking at the floor somewhere, and finished his tea quietly. As for the rest, nobody made even a single sound.

I sighed at the sadness of it. We wanted to build bridges, and instead, all we ended up with, were more walls. I silently finished my cup and moved back to my work. But I worked in all sadness, and that did affect my productivity.

○●○

In the coming week, lots of such incidents and rumors from other projects came to the forefront.

A pregnant lady was sent onsite for a month despite her initial hesitation just because she had signed the no-objection form for onsite travel a year ago and had *'erroneously failed to plan'* her pregnancy. Medically, as per the company policy, she still could work for a few months before she could take the maternity leave and she had no particular complications so theoretically she was a *fit-to-fly* case for a few more months. The project manager was insistent due to the *'sheer indispensability of the resource'* to that particular assignment.

We would often take a simplistic view of the situation and react to the *'injustice'* passionately.

"How could he, I ask? Are they humans or not? Sheer demonic management this is," Raj lashed out with venom and spite.

Somehow, I would always feel all his objections were meant as taunts to Bhoopal, who had gone all silent after the other day's conversation. He would now seem closed and would respond only when asked. He would speak very politely and softly to all for work but would go totally uncompromising over noncompliance or non-submission of deliverables.

This was his new side, which we never knew till now.

JD, on the other hand, was avoiding Bhoopal, and so would not come to the one-off tea sessions we would go to as a team. Suman, sensing this, would stay away too, citing some work.

Bhoopal would come simply because he didn't want to avoid the team. But then the spontaneity and the humor were missing. Raj would ask about some technical or official doubts, and Bhoopal would clarify those for all to understand. If there were any specific queries, he would promise us assistance, but then that was about it.

"There is something that I didn't ask Bhoopal the other day though I should have," Piyush said to me.

"What?"

"I want to give *GRE* examination and do *M.S.* in Preeti's college, if possible. I want to leave this damn place too, as soon as I can."

"Oh, man. Not again! Not now!" My sinking heart told me this would lead to another unpleasant situation.

"I don't know, bro. Lately, my GF's been behaving weird—real weird. Somehow, it's like parting ways. There is nothing to talk about; there's nothing to discuss. Conversations seem strained, like she is trying her best to be patient while answering my questions. I have never been able to gain the acceptance of her parents. I am quite sure they are searching for a boy for her. What if she loses her interest and faith in me and says yes to this other guy? I can't sleep at night with this thought. It's like I have lost the key to her heart. She's gone cold towards me."

I knew exactly what he was talking about.

The girl moved ahead, the guy got left behind, and at some point, both stopped comparing notes. The boy still harbored feelings, and the girl went practical, or maybe she found somebody else. I didn't say it—it was too obvious.

"But you aren't even interested in research or tech., and no offense, but your vocabulary is horrible," I tried to show him some reason.

"Doesn't matter. I have to crack the examination some way." He was becoming irrational.

"There is no time for all this, man. Just let this time pass. Stop stressing yourself."

He had gone to a different world altogether—it was then that I saw the red-tinged eyes and the strained veins on his forehead.

"I find it very difficult to relax these days—it's like a constant feeling of uneasiness—like something is not right—not correct. Something is critically uncertain. I don't want to lose her. I am scared. The thought doesn't let me sleep."

Okay, so he was describing my state of mind as well—ah, the insecurity! Welcome to the Insomniac Club, buddy!

I just patted his head slowly.

○ ● ○

November was ending. It was the beginning of December.

Work was going well, but there were rumors floating that a test was in the offing sooner than we thought—one to check our proficiency levels in our competencies—from the point of view of talent mapping. I heard it first from Prabhu. This tied to the generic mail that the HR had sent to all, earlier.

"My PM's idea it was," Prabhu said.

"Don't go by their words, mate. Along with credit, people steal ideas as well," said I.

"Either way, he says he suggested it to the higher management and HR then adopted this initiative."

"How do you get all this news?"

"I heard Mitali talk to someone about this, or someone told Mitali about this."

"What the hell! She never told me! And why are you spying on her?"

"No-o, I am not...didn't...I," but I wasn't paying attention to Prabhu's words. All my mind was playing with was the sheer lack of communication Mitali and I had and why we weren't doing anything about it.

The need of the hour was patience though, to make sure not to overreact, to be diplomatic, suave, and understanding, and to make sure we weren't having fights over petty issues.

'Why on earth would you not tell me?' I felt like screaming. I guess my nerves were tired and I was reaching the end of my endurance. What about ordinary friendship? Some appreciation, some consideration, some acceptance, some indulgences? Why this complete lack of faith in me?

But obviously, I didn't want to hurt her. So, I said nothing of the sort.

I pinged her, and all we talked about were little ordinary things, some simple happenings of the day and life, simple enough to be ignored and yet important enough to be talked about. I guess life bonds people through shared ordinariness and not through out-of-the-world moments.

Somehow, we had restricted ourselves to just some clandestine encounters. Not acknowledging each other in public was but one of the ways to surround ourselves with guilt. Never working out our public encounters; was it a complete lack of interest in each other's public persona, or was it just a way of lying to ourselves cleverly?

By the end of the day, I did call her and ask, though. "Are we going to have a test for evaluation?"

"Oh, yes! Completely forgot to tell you. Neeraj told me this has been in talks for months now, something internal and confidential."

I tried to avoid my surprise and hurt.

"What is the gravity of this test?"

"I would say, if it actually happens, immense! Just ensure you do well; the rest is in the dark."

"When will it be?"

"Soon, in case it does."

"Can you please be a little more specific?" I was getting a little impatient with her roundabout answers.

"I would tell you if I knew." she reacted.

"Well, you didn't tell me about the test in the first place."

"I told you I *forgot*!"

"Very convenient. Anyway, thanks for the info," I replied sarcastically.

"Whatever, dude. I don't want to feed you rumors, but it might be this month itself. By month-end maybe."

"Well, I have already thanked you, but then, I guess I can thank you again."

"My pleasure!" She reacted sarcastically.

"By the way, is this your PM's idea?"

"Might be. But then tell me, is there any way of ever finding out whose devil mind this is?" she asked simply.

Made sense! I hope Prabhu learns to stop exaggerating.

I called the HR department to see if they had any information about the date for this mysterious test. They reacted negatively.

"We will let you know. Who told you, by the way?" The HR guy asked shrewdly.

"Some rumors. Heard some random groups chatting."

"Okay, but please don't spread things like these around. People bug us all day."

So obviously, then, in a couple of days, almost everybody knew about it.

"You know it too?" Yogi asked me.

"I know it," I said.

"But there's been no news."

"This is a hoax. There's nothing visible to us or communicated to us. Just forget about it," Bhoopal said with absolute confidence when asked.

"But have you confirmed with Kanchan?" Raj.

"I have. She herself told me to tell you this—to not believe any sort of rumors. We haven't been told anything!!! For that matter, nobody knows anything," he added.

"Are you sure, man?" Yogi asked cautiously.

"Absolutely," he said, but then his voice wavered a little from the sheer weight of uncertainty as he added quietly, "At least for now!"

○●○

I started staying back in the office a lot from then on. Working late nights was just one of the ways to ensure that I didn't miss out on the late-night chats. Lots of people were staying back more and more, and work hours would continue till late every night. Everybody seemed gluttonous for work.

People would not be given laptops, but they deserved one. I guess we deserved one too. Work from home was not allowed though, from a data security point of view.

My productivity was down, but I was fulfilling my share of assignments by stretching the time component.

My brain had gone dysfunctional with all this pressure, and I found it really difficult to think or put in high-quality thoughts. *'Work for the sake of it'* was fast becoming my motto. Going home late at night was one thing, and coming back on time the next day was another. I would find it difficult to wake up on time for the office and would hence come late and stay back late—the vicious cycle. Life was in the doldrums.

Raj would often give me company while working late. He would start watching some Telugu movie while working, after people had left. Sometime around 1:30 a.m., he would ask me to accompany him for a tea and smoke. Smoke was just for him; it was an incredibly cold December.

He would be at his most open during that smoke and just during it. He wanted to marry like all 27-year-olds; he needed a better job, more money, and had a secret crush—the same routine story. He wanted to move to Hyderabad as well.

"What do you want to do in life?" he asked me once as he made a puff of smoke. My mind wandered again, thinking about how I had seen girls smoke a lot in the smoking corners, more so during the evenings when the light would recede.

As for the question, maybe he meant it career-wise, but for me, it was a question occupying a wide spectrum.

It was not an easy question to answer. I was 22 and had my whole life ahead of me.

What was it that I wanted to do? Everything for that matter!

I wanted to go places, earn in dollars, have a great reputation, be great at whatever I did, have a great body, and have a great girl. That reminded me of Mitali and how most probably I was in the last phases of losing her and how I would do anything to not lose her, yet I would, and it automatically brought a lump in my throat and moistness to my eyes.

What did I want in life? All I wanted was to be with her and love her. This was happening increasingly these days; no matter what the context, my thoughts would automatically wander towards *'us'*. I knew I was nowhere near achieving this dream.

"I want to be happy and have a good life," I answered unpretentiously. That was all I wanted, hence the ambition, hence everything.

He let out another puff of smoke and looked at me shrewdly.

"Love-related matter? You took a while to answer, and I was paying close attention to your face. You seemed to be in an incredible pain. Those eyes of yours don't lie."

I just smiled, "I must be homesick. I just need to go home. Can't seem to remember the last time I went."

"Want a puff? It relaxes things."

"I can't, and I don't."

"Well, don't tell me you have never. Learn how to—one should experience everything once for good reason. Here!"

I wanted to resist, but then I should be aware of what smoking is.

"Fine. What's to lose?" I took the cigarette and looked at him.

"Okay, take a puff in with the mouth, breathe in entirely, let it stay in for a couple of seconds, and slowly let it out through your nose. Don't do it too fast."

I did exactly as he said and let out a cool puff of smoke.

"Yay, you are a natural," he clapped. "An applause for the initiation."

I took another puff, then another, and I knew I had enough. I put it down and crushed the butt.

"Already?" he asked, wide-eyed.

"I am done." I smiled widely. "I wanted to start and quit on the same cigarette!"

"Good. Now, never come back down this road. It isn't a good road." He smiled and offered me chewing gum.

"Thanks. I needed those puffs, though. Really did. But I don't know how people manage when they smoke regularly. It smells so bad."

"Ah, enough curiosity; else, take one and find out for yourself."

"Not worth it. Let's go."

"Once, try getting laid too. It's the solution to all the problems in life. Just one answer to all of life's bullshit!" he winked. "And I am pretty sure, after doing it, you won't wonder what people like in it! It leads to a new set of problems, though."

Sigh, how true it was for me in lieu of the past events.

"Started preparing for the test?" Raj asked.

"No time! You know how many assignments have piled up. Did you start?"

"No, *yaar*. We don't even know if there is a test in the first place."

We went past some people who were leaving the office in a hurry.

"Weren't you to stay back, Manish?" Raj asked one of his friends from another project.

"Check your mail. There's a surprise!!" He winked in panic and left.

We rushed to our workstation.

"Look what we have!" said Raj after checking his mail. "By God! This is strange."

We had received an email exactly at midnight from HR about a *'Proficiency Test'* to be conducted by a third-party vendor next Monday. The curriculum would be shared with us soon, but it would be based on what we were technically trained on during our induction.

"Today is Tuesday. It's less than a week from now," I said. Raj tried to control himself; his eyes were red with anger. Our brains were in no condition to give a test. We could barely think beyond our work these days. I clutched my head.

"*Chalo*, let's leave. Fuck work. I want my sleep," Raj said, fuming. What about the work? He read my thoughts.

"Leave it, man. Just go home. There is no transparency left in this organization," he said, clenching his teeth. "Just go home and revise whatever they have trained you on."

I couldn't sleep that night despite my exhaustion. It seemed like I was fast becoming a chronic insomniac.

○●○

"There is just no time to discuss the existence of this particular test now, is it? I guess it has been put together in a hurry to test that our resources are well aware on their domain basics. No choice but to just accept it and prepare accordingly. The way I see it, there's nothing more to it. Clearly, we are out of the information loop too, Kanchan," Bhoopal said to Kanchan. She wanted to clarify with the senior management after our volley of questions on the issue.

"I am sorry, guys. You know, I wouldn't do this on purpose," he said, turning to us.

"What is the impact of non-performance in this test, Kanchan?" Raj asked.

She didn't reply for some time, well aware that her words may not reflect reality, nor was she completely aware of it. She was still in shock at being overridden.

"Let's just say I would like none of you to underperform in this test. I will confirm the curriculum. Hope they tell me that at least."

We returned to our desks, confused and dazed. I sat back and looked at my computer screen blankly. The emails pouring in from onsite asked if I could complete the work a little earlier than the deadline, thanking me for my efforts in advance. I saw the emails on *LEAN* from Kanchan, the messages from the CEO congratulating us on the last quarter's poor results and encouraging us to support the organization to face the challenges of the present time with positivity, and then the present mail from HR for a test to be conducted soon despite the work overload. Three different command centers were asking different things from a single resource at the same time, and I wondered if they understood what they really wanted or what the future held for IT as a whole.

Whether we were ready at all? Maybe the over-recruitment for showcasing the headcount availability to our clients was finally pinching the company somewhere.

I opened the online documents shared with us during the induction, but my brain seemed to refuse to retain the information. I sighed, took another sip of my coffee, relaxed back in my reclining chair, put on my headphones for some soothing songs, and closed my eyes to the worries of the world.

10.

Mitali's version:

I saw the stupid mail the following day. What the fuck! People working for 4-5 years in the organization would have to undertake a test now on something they had learned years ago. Was this a joke?

What was the significance of this test anyway? How seriously or non-seriously were we to take it? Project managers knew nothing, or so they would say. Delivery managers would disclose nothing. HRs would give disgusting responses on how this is something any organization is well-justified to test at any time.

The test was mandatory for all employees!

I called Neeraj. He said the test was super-important. The company can interpret the results in whichever manner they feel is right. Tricky!

As for the new project opportunity for me, he had spoken to his manager, and I was to come to Delhi for an interview. They would discuss the job role if the interview went well. There was to be a small telephonic technical round before this in-person interview. I wanted to hug him right then and there!

This was super news—finally, a ray of hope after months of sheer bullshit. But according to the company policy, I couldn't have changed my project without my project manager's approval and blessing.

I didn't take even a moment to think. I was at my project manager's desk in a jiffy.

"How are you, Tanmay?"

"Great," he said with a plastic smile. "Tell me."

I wanted to say my thing while he had that smile, and I was hungry for the satisfaction of seeing it wane.

"I want to shift to another project. I have been referred, and they are enthusiastic to have me if I clear the interview. Wanted your blessing to go ahead."

He didn't disappoint. He went from being visibly happy to visibly grim.

"Are you sure? We need you here. The dependencies..."

"...are very low. Delegation is not a concern here at all, is it? Anyone can do this stuff. There are enough people that the project lets go anyway; one of them can be routed here. But for me, opportunities won't wait."

He was out of things to say.

"I will ask the project manager of that project to speak to you in person. The interview decides everything. You can then transfer me directly. I needn't even come back for the formalities. I am sure they would want me to join immediately," said I.

Internal transfers can be super-quick if the project manager cooperates.

I would find some way to shift my luggage from Pune to Delhi but that was all for later. Right now, he was still giving me a weird look through his glasses.

"What if you don't clear?" he asked.

"Then I return."

"In the same role?" He stressed on that.

"Yes."

"Great," he said. "Try. Let's see. All the very best!"

He returned to his screen without his smile. Maybe he had started thinking about the new resource to be allocated already. On my part, I wouldn't have taken the risk of annoying him if I wasn't hell sure of converting this opportunity.

Deepa asked me when I returned, "Do you think he will cooperate?"

"If he accepts to let me appear for an interview, he can't control anything later. I have my past year ratings to prove that I did well in this project." I smiled triumphantly. "...and he has accepted to let me appear."

"Congrats!" Deepa hugged me as my mind rejoiced at my good fortune. I was so happy I even replied to Ami's messages out of sheer generosity, owing to my happy mood.

I am going to Delhi, damn it! I would become a developer—my elated mind rejoiced. Both the technical round and the in-person interview would be held sometime after the test. So, I had a week ahead of me with an additional overhead of clearing a test with a mysterious curriculum.

Ami's version:

The following week was weird. Assignments never stopped, but Bhoopal took most of the load. He would try to relieve us before 10 p.m. in the night by taking chunks of our assignments so that we could go home and read something for the test. He would stay back late. I wondered if he was even preparing for this test.

The thought of taking leaves crossed my mind. But no, they wouldn't be allowed. Sick leaves weren't possible either. People would need to be extremely selfish to do so because even if they managed to lie and convince their manager to give them leave, that meant their assignments would go to somebody else, leading to extra pressure for that person.

Did we read? I tried. Trying isn't the same as succeeding, though; there were too many things to read and too many damn books. Our batch seemed to be doing a great job at studying. I heard from Prabhu that the group was doing night-outs at Abhinav's place.

He called me sometime after midnight.

"Dude, we should totally do the same. It's difficult to study alone. Let's just study together." Prabhu proposed. "Come on, I have you, and you have me."

"I can study with Mitali too."

"She is ready to let you inside her house and stay late at night? Seriously?" he smirked.

"I haven't asked her yet."

"Stop messing around with me! When are we meeting?"

"Please let me sleep," I said, clutching my pillow.

"Sleeping won't solve your problems."

I dozed off, thinking I would wake up in the morning to read. That morning never came. It could have, if only some idiot hadn't invented the snooze functionality in the alarm. I woke up late as usual and wondered if I should ask Prabhu if he read something last night or if I should still ask Mitali if she could teach me a few things.

I messaged them both.

○●○

As I went to work, I knew another day was wasted from a preparation point of view—impossible to study at night and just as impossible to wake up in the morning. I don't know if anybody was studying for that matter; nobody looked sleep-deprived, but everybody looked tense.

JD and Suman had started going out for coffee together. We still went out in the same group. Bhoopal had stopped accompanying us. I never received any replies to the messages I sent to Mitali and Prabhu that day.

As the chill in the air intensified, the tea machines too stopped giving free tea. Quietly, that same Thursday, they were replaced with paid machines, and we were distributed swipe cards. Since these cards would never work properly and the taste of tea wasn't that good, people would take the lift and queue for half an hour to get a tea from the tea stall (*serving hand-made tea*) in our cafeteria. I wondered if the electricity units spent on the lift and productivity hours lost per employee were lesser compared to the loss of providing people with a few cups of free tea every day—so much for the cost-cutting initiatives!

I messaged Mitali sometime late Friday afternoon: '*Can we please study together tonight? I promise we will just study. I need some help with the syllabus.*'

She messaged back. '*I don't think so. I don't trust you on that. Besides, I like to study alone! Message me in case you get stuck over something.*'

'*Please? I am serious. We would only study.*' I begged.

'*Have a good night!*' was all she messaged back.

As I stood at the bus stop that Friday evening, waiting for the company bus, I decided to study during the weekends, to write a few codes at the very minimum, and to read the things that were taught to us. I also made sufficiently ambitious and impossible plans—I will do a night out on Friday and finish the first reading that night itself.

As I sat in that dim-lit company bus along with all the others, I could feel the chill—of the atmosphere and the one emanating from the hearts of my fellow passengers. That Monday we had to prove our worth. No one spoke much. I felt tired and drained. I felt alone. As I rubbed my eyes, my phone rang. It was a call from Prabhu.

"Hey, buddy! You left?"

"Yes, man! What are your plans?"

"Listen!" He lowered his voice dramatically and started whispering. "Come to my place tonight to study."

"Nopes, you carry on, I have other plans."

"What plans? Mitali?"

"Nopes, man." I would keep feeling a sharp pain of loss every time her name was spoken.

"Okay, do you have a computer at home with a C compiler installed?"

"No." I didn't like that approach—the logical cornering of my plans. I could see where this was going.

"And do you find it very interesting to study alone? It makes more sense if we discuss and then explain to each other."

"I like to study alone," I said, taking a leaf from Mitali's book.

"Right. I assure you, as soon as you go home tonight, you are going to sleep. You will wake up late tomorrow and will immediately descend into a state of depression and self-hate, frustrated over why you never listened to me and wasted last night. Then you are going to call me, and I will say I studied and finished three chapters. You, as usual, will slide into that mood of self-pity over Mitali and waste the whole day tomorrow because you won't be able to focus on those thick, uninteresting books and links. By evening, you will be panic-stricken and will call Mitali to please help you, and she will reject you again. After 10 minutes of thought, you will call me back and beg me to help you with the syllabus. At that time, I will just smile over the phone and say..." He took a moment to breathe heavily over the phone.

I assumed it was anger.

"'*Fuck off*?'" I asked, already angry; my eyebrow raised.

"I would say, *'Fine, you are always welcome.'*" Prabhu said.

I sighed. That seemed about right except for the last part. I would never call him and beg, no matter what.

"So, what do you say?" he asked.

"Sure. I will come by your home tonight. Please ensure it isn't an issue."

"I will start cleaning the room now so that there is some room for you to sleep. My roomie has quit!" he said gleefully and cut the call.

I messaged Mitali in reply to her last message. *'I am stuck over you! What should I do?'*

As expected, I didn't receive any reply.

○ ● ○

"I can't understand what this code means," I said in a tired tone to Prabhu. I had reached his home around 9. We had had dinner and had started studying by 10.

"Let me see." He spent a moment but couldn't make sense of it. "Sorry, but I too never understood recursive functions. This is clearly Sasidhar and Balaji's domain."

We looked at each other silently; none of us really had the strength to focus either. Finally, he said, "Ask Mitali. No other way."

"Right," I messaged the query to her.

"Will she reply back?" He asked.

"She should if she is home, hasn't slept, or..." I began defensively.

"Or if she isn't on another call," he said quietly but mercilessly, never taking his eyes off my face while noting my expressions.

"She will reply, dude, don't worry," but my voice faltered as I said it.

I wondered if our query was worth the pain of asking her.

My phone rang. It was her message.

'You are studying the wrong things. It will be an MCQ (Multiple Choice Questions) test. Just focus on functions, coding fundamentals, small codes, and protocols. It will be a tricky test, so revise the basics. And Ami, stop wasting your life on me. You and I can never happen. Just move on <reply to your last message>'

"What is it?" Prabhu asked. "Why has the color of your face suddenly gone black?"

I looked up at him.

"...and why have your eyes suddenly gone red and watery and vulnerable? Oh!" He didn't say anything.

"She said, just revise the basics. It will be an MCQ. No need to write codes," I tried to shakily cover up the situation.

"Right," he said.

I messaged her back.

'I can't do that. Please don't say that. Don't I mean anything to you at all? You choose to forget everything we had between us?'

In half a second, her reply arrived. *There never was an 'us'. I just enjoyed the attention I received from you. You can as well say that, in some ways, I used you. I am sorry. Forget me.'*

That pained me. After all what happened, I just couldn't believe it. This was a betrayal.

'Oh, come on, your touch wouldn't lie, would it? All these moments we spent together—did they stir nothing inside you? Is it even possible?' I replied. Pat came the reply.

'Let's never talk about it, okay? I have deleted all your replies. Please delete all of mine too. I feel guilty. It was a mistake on my end, and I screwed up my life. It meant nothing to me, just a way out of all my frustrations.'

She couldn't actually be saying all this!

'Do you mean to say you would have done it with anybody? Do you really feel anything towards me? Not even a little affection? What was I to you then?' It felt like my heart was being ripped apart.

'I don't know what love means. As for me, it is just a strong friendship and the culmination of a lot of moments spent together. For me, it was always going to be Neeraj. You and I can never be. It was just physical between us, and you got what you wanted. Now stop complaining and let us just stop here. I want to be fair, and I want this to end well.' She messaged me. All this, all of this had meant nothing to her!

To me, it had meant everything. It was never physical!

'Did I mean anything at all to you?' I asked her, already knowing the answer.

'I never loved you. I tried but couldn't. You were a little too sweet. That made me realize all the more that Neeraj was the guy for me. We have our distances but also the bridges to reach out to each other. I believe we can make it work. So, all the things that you and I shared are no better than lies. I do not want to keep feeling guilty over a lie.'

I kept looking at that message for some time, at its sheer unbelievability.

"You look shaken," said Prabhu, looking at my ghastly face, worried. "Did the course increase? Oh, stop giving one of those expressions that one would give after receiving the pink slip."

It took me one more moment before I could reply.

'Look, he doesn't love you. He cares about you only when he needs it. I am worried if you guys will ever be happy. Where was he when you needed him? When all of this happened? That should be reason enough to break up with him.'

Pat came the reply.

'There are a lot of things you don't know about us. Besides, I do not want relationship advice from you of all people. Just accept it and let this pass.'

What does one say on that?

"Are you going to cry?" Prabhu asked, worried now.

Then I did something I am not proud of. I begged!

'Give me another chance, please. I have time with me. I am sure I will be going for higher education in a couple of years, and things will sort out economically. There are a lot of reasons why I think we will work; our height

matches exactly, and we love chatting with each other. I know the key to your heart.'

After sending it, I realized the message had become unintentionally ridiculous.

'What the hell are you talking about? Can't you see? I am completely NOT interested. So, stop moping around. You don't stand even a 1% chance of ever being with me.'

I piled it up, taking another route.

'You are the practical one. I am just trying to give you reasons so that you won't leave my hand. So, what does he say? Just in case you guys don't work out, then?'

"Dude, why are you crying?" Prabhu gave me his hanky. "Is it the bitch?"

I didn't say anything; I just let the tears roll.

'Damn it! It is not about what he says; it is about what I say!!!! Pay some attention.' Came her angry reply.

I looked at Prabhu; his dark eyes had gone wide with pain and empathy as he could imagine exactly what was happening. He snatched my phone and started reading the messages.

"Stop being so lame, dude! Be the guy; you are not the one who should be crying. You have given it everything you can: love, care, blood, time, and resources. Tell the bitch that you will cut her lover's balls and stick them on her door if she doesn't marry you.

Be a man! Stop crying like a worthless piece of shit." He had gone visibly angry. "Go to the washroom and wash your face."

As I went to the bathroom, I sensed a weird smell permeating the dingy room—something pungent and unimaginably dirty. I choked from the sheer awfulness of the smell.

As I returned, Prabhu was typing on my phone.

"The bitch is shouting at the top of her lungs that she wants it out. Look, this is what I have written!"

'No wonder you don't know what love is. Before trying to understand what it is, try to be a good human being first. Understand that others have feelings too, and they too can get hurt. Fine, if we didn't work out, but you didn't have the decency to even acknowledge my efforts. You don't deserve love. Go fuck yourself, bitch! May your sad love story with the loser guy bloom into a royal mess! Don't forget to tell him in bed that I've already had fun with you!'

Oh, God! No. I removed lots of sentences, made it even milder, and sent it.

"Why, dude, why? You need to make her realize what a horrible person she is—make her live with it!"

"Can't," I smiled at him wistfully. I didn't have it in me to hurt her in any way. She was within her rights regarding what she was saying. It wasn't her mistake that I got involved, and hence, I was not to be angry.

I received her reply.

'Fine, let's just stop talking in that case. There's no point in continuing this farce.'

I kept wiping my red eyes while studying—it was just the extreme sadness and pain of loss. This must be what they call a broken heart!

It was painful!

"I can't look at you like this—all sad. It hurts me, you know. You need a hug. We need to hug."

"Not necessary." That was the last thing I wanted—hugging a guy!

"I am not asking you; I am telling you. Come here."

We came together into an uncomfortable hug. I don't know how long it was, and I didn't really mind it until I felt something wet on my neck.

"What the fuck was that? Did you just..." I pulled back.

"Sorry, it was a mistake. Honestly! I was sleepy. Let's just study now."

I tried to read for another half hour, till I passed out on his floor.

As I woke up in the morning, I found a blanket on me, and Prabhu was already up.

"You were shivering in the night! Sorry, it is a little dirty, but it was the best I had," he said.

"Must be the cold," I said grumpily.

"Yes! Must be that." he sighed. "Let us go for tea, and you can then leave for your house."

"We couldn't do much. Let's go home and use today properly for study," I said at tea.

"Don't worry. I am not in the mood to do anything for that matter," Prabhu said.

I went home and wasted my Sunday.

○●○

On Monday, I went to the test center unshaven and took the test sleepily. It was in the first half of the morning, the duration being a couple of hours.

There were a lot of questions, and I was so tired that I guessed through half of them—one of those times when a person is way too tired to even feel scared. I just did the best I could. There were quite a few questions whose answers I dimly knew, and I just took the best guess. Even though some questions were basic, the options seemed confusing.

After completing the online test, I realized that life wasn't any simpler for anyone who had taken the test. Some freely admitted to being dumbstruck. Nobody was in the mood to discuss, and people giggled nervously at the thought of underperforming in the test. Some like Raj went out for a smoke, some like Suman tried to laugh away the stress, some like JD just smirked, some like Prabhu looked lost, and some like Mitali looked happy.

I saw her coming out of her exam room smiling and giggling. She seemed way happier when she smiled, and I took a moment to savor the sight. I forgot my worries, but I didn't go near her. I just kept looking as she passed by me. I wondered if she was right in keeping herself away. I mean, if she could be that happy despite keeping her distance, I wouldn't mind moving away from her altogether just for the pleasure of watching her smile that way. I knew she had cracked the examination.

As she passed by me, she did see me. She tried to look through me, but that was too much of an effort for her after what had happened the night before. So, she just looked me in the eye for a nanosecond and tried to nod. My heart gave a wild beat as I knew I wanted to hug her right then and there, and I knew I would cry if I did. I didn't give a damn if I underperformed in the examination, but I was hell-scared of losing her. She took a moment to recompose herself, and in a second or two, by the time she turned the corner, she was again smiling merrily with her colleague as if nothing had happened.

"How was the test?" I asked Prabhu.

"Shut up. It went too bad to even discuss. Let's eat something," he said.

We saw Abhinav and the group happily discussing the options, and we saw Pooja walking away separately. She smiled at us.

"How did it go?" Prabhu asked her.

"It was a bit confusing," she said, smiling brightly. "Can't say which answers were correct and which weren't."

"What do you think? Was this test for the yearly appraisal or something?" Prabhu asked.

"Personally, I don't think there are going to be many appraisals this time. This is graver, dude!" She took a moment before she spoke, looking deeply into my eyes. "By the way, I resign today!"

I coughed out some words, despite the shock. "That's great. Congrats, I guess!"

She smiled. "Thanks. The thing is, I am not talking to many people in our batch and wanted to tell someone badly before putting down the paper. For some reason, I am sentimental about this end, this being my first job," she tried to smile at us, well knowing it was just a difficult thing to explain.

"So, you leave in March?" I asked.

"Yes. My marriage is in April sometime. There's time, but I would go to Dubai—my home—and enjoy some last weeks of my life." She smiled sadly but corrected herself immediately. "I mean my bachelorette life. My parents stay there; my would-be husband works as a brand manager in an MNC. I, too, probably would do an MBA and join some organization in Dubai itself."

"Escaping the crowd, huh?" I smiled at her knowingly. I was envious of people with such getaways in life.

"Quite the opposite," she smiled. "I think I will miss being part of this crowd and the job."

"Really? I am sure pay can't be the reason." I smiled again.

"They pay us pennies, man! I mean, they earn in dollars and pay us in pennies; can you believe that?" She added animatedly.

"Rupees, you mean!" Prabhu corrected her.

"I know that. I meant pennies as the proverbial peanuts, dude." She lashed out at him. "I guess, it's just the fact that so many of us are putting in so much brain to write or test some code, which genuinely impacts some industry. We are both a support industry and a knowledge industry. Despite the limitations that we mostly do just back-end work and some pretty routine things, I think I enjoyed it here. Everyone was so similar."

"And that is likable to you? Everybody being equally similar and equally boring," I asked tersely.

She smiled.

"With time, it may not, but today, as I leave, I find that this industry treats everyone equally well or equally badly. No hierarchy, for that matter," she said, taking a moment to reorganize her thoughts. "Okay, fine, I think I do find some comfort in the mediocrity and moderation of the crowd. I mean, all are earning similarly, eat the same things, do the same job, are equally cash-strapped, have similar living styles, and are afraid of a similar crisis. That so many young minds are working together on technical things and speaking a common language is exciting. The industry doesn't differentiate based on gender or age. All are welcome, and no one is indispensable. It will bid you goodbye just as easily—people come, people leave and faces change. It's fascinating—there are no strings attached. No wonder people find their comfort zones in this industry and don't want to grow at times. Sometimes they don't want to differentiate themselves from the crowd. It is strangely comforting! I find it so, and so yes, it is strangely affecting for me to leave this place and this culture. I know I did a bad job of explaining it," she sighed.

I tried to see if Prabhu understood it. He seemed to be mesmerized! He just nodded.

"I personally find it a little intimidating. You know, you are one of those very few who are resigning in the times of a recession, when companies are looking forward to laying off people," I said.

"Layoffs are inevitable in industries as dynamic as these, where requirements change every hour. If layoffs are avoided, then the trade-off will be that the attractiveness of the industry will go down in terms of remuneration and job quality," she winked.

"You seem to have put quite a lot of thought into the matter," Prabhu said, evidently impressed. I wondered if he had ever seen a girl speak so convincingly.

337 | The Little Men

"Thanks. I do find some philosophical peace in this culture, I guess," she nodded at us. "Now that I am about to leave, all I can see are the good things. Anyway, it was great talking to both of you."

"Best of luck!!" I smiled at her and waved as she left, but I knew it was a sad smile.

"Wonderful girl!" Prabhu smiled at me heartily after she left. Maybe, I thought, he was just happy that some girl had spoken to us.

○ ● ○

Nights were all similar; I couldn't sleep soundly. I missed her in my sleep and during the wee hours of the morning. I hated myself for not having the dignity to move on. But I guess, the heart has its own reasons! It keeps proving that it is more than just a blood-pumping organ, after all.

○ ● ○

The next day started on a normal note with that extra degree of chill, owing either to the winter or the state of our minds. Nobody said a word about the examination, but the sweaters were out. The warmth in the air was clearly missing.

JD pinged me on IP Messenger sometime before lunch. *'Let's go out for a tea, dear. I have a severe headache.'*

'Oh, sure, JD. Suman is coming?' I pinged back.

'No, he won't. Ask Piyush. Don't ask anyone else, please. I need some peace of mind,' she pinged back.

I sighed and locked my computer. Just in the morning, someone told me over breakfast that they were firing people for leaving their desktops unlocked. Some nameless guy got fired that morning, on the spot. Unverified reports, but why take chances given the stringent data-security measures? I guess any reason for laying people off was as good as any other now.

I asked Piyush if he could join. He too was busy, so he asked us to carry on.

○●○

"Can you please take my tea too? I don't seem to have the energy to stand in the queue. Here's the money," JD said.

"It's okay. I have money, JD. You sit in the sunshine outside."

The open terrace floor was glistening with the winter sun rays; somehow it was the only warmth I could see. She took a place at a table.

When I returned with the tea, we sat outside quietly, sipping tea.

"Why didn't Suman come?" I asked JD.

"Please don't ask. I am glad you came," she said, clutching her sweater tighter as she felt the chill.

I saw Bhoopal enter the cafeteria too and buy tea. He saw us sitting, hesitated a moment, but then came to our table and took a seat quietly. I was glad he didn't ask for our permission. That would have been awkward.

"Hi," he wished us.

"Hi, Bhoopal," I wished back. JD said nothing and just looked away, trying to look unconcerned while sipping her tea.

"Hi, JD." He just won't leave it, will he? JD nodded in acknowledgement.

"I spoke to Kanchan about your case."

JD gave him an inquiring look. What suddenly changed?

He continued, "I don't want you to be part of this project against your will. I reckoned, since so many things are changing or are about to change now, why not bring in this change too?" He gave her his philosophical smile, "And for better or for worse, let you go."

JD's eyes sparkled with hope and appreciation. "So, what does she say?"

"She said nothing; I have proposed your name. Who knows, this just might save someone else's job! We will probably redeploy someone on your spot as soon as we find the person. But no promises."

"Thanks," she said cautiously. "Thanks for trying!"

"Don't misunderstand our clashes, JD. The thing was, I just didn't want to lose you. We were such a great team! And so, I hope you understand. I knew that making your stay here would be good for you too, professionally." He smiled at her wistfully. "But I guess each to his own now."

"I would be okay, Bhoopal. Father has pinned a lot of hopes on my marriage, and it would be good for Pa and me both if I married someone financially stable."

"What about your career? I mean, do you really even like this guy? I find that sometimes Suman has a point when he fights with you," Bhoopal asked with concern.

Her voice rose automatically. Bhoopal seemed to have touched her sensitive nerve.

"You don't understand, do you? I am not finding grooms as it is, owing to my age and other family issues. Beggars can't be choosers. I have to make the most of what I have. Idealistic and emotional viewpoints, though I agree with them theoretically, don't work in real life. And I know a lot about real life, so trust me on that."

Bhoopal nodded but then continued.

"I know you have had a difficult childhood financially, but for God's sake, you have to live with that person all your life. Have you thought about it?"

"He isn't that bad, Bhoopal. Leave it. What we wish for may not necessarily be good for us, and what we actually get may not necessarily be as bad as we imagine. I have made peace with my life, and I am not going to change my decisions now," she sighed. I wondered what she meant.

But I think Bhoopal did. She stood up and started to leave.

"You want to sit for some more time? Sunlight feels really good," Bhoopal asked.

"No, thanks. I come on time, work my 8 hours, and then leave on time. That's what I do these days. You guys carry on, and by the way," she took a pause before she continued. "...don't you worry whether Suman has a point or not! He has his own reasons. So, in this matter, trust my words alone."

Bhoopal smiled solemnly. "Maybe I do know more than what you think I do, and maybe my knowledge worries me."

We witnessed an uncomfortable change in her expression as she staggered a bit, leaving hurriedly.

"Are you sure she is alright?" I asked Bhoopal.

"How would I know? Are you alright?" He asked me with an amused twinkle.

"Yes, I am."

"See, you lie as well. Similarly, so would she if we do ask her," he smiled and finished his coffee.

"Are you alright, Bhoopal?" I looked him straight in the eyes and asked.

He didn't know what to say. But he was honest enough not to evade my question.

"Strange times these are—not exactly happy. Our work now will bring us alright-ness tomorrow."

"Are you happy with the work?"

He looked at me a little irritated for asking such uncomfortable questions.

"I don't know, man. I really don't. Please don't ask such questions. These are not the times to be happy. Survival would do."

"Fine, and where do you see us going?"

He stared, not breaking the silence, contemplating whether my concern was worth sharing his insights. Finally, he succumbed to my curiosity.

"See, Amit, things are complex; let's agree on that. I can't simplify them for you; bloody, I can't even simplify them for myself. I always wanted to stay a technical guy, but management is a responsibility that seems unavoidable now. I won't deny that my confidence in the technology domain has shaken a bit, and some disillusionment has undoubtedly crept in. I mean, I am not a bloody robot." He took a moment to see if we were connecting. "Things affect me too. I am trying to help you guys here, which seems very difficult under the circumstances. I would be lucky to help myself and get away with it."

Was I hearing excuses from Bhoopal? Was he the same guy I knew once?

"Would we not see the old Bhoopal again?" I asked, straining the muscles of my heart. I wasn't ready to lose that guy—certainly not to this strange replica seated in front of me.

"No time soon. I will be going more towards management in the coming months. Technology as a field has been slightly disappointing growth-wise. In the future, assuming there is one, maybe I will gravitate back to technology," he said.

Was I sensing a touch of selfishness here, or was it just my bias towards management? I didn't have the strength to judge anymore.

"Let's go down, Bhoopal. I have work to do. Hope you do well," I said in a tone of resentment. I wouldn't know if my resentment had a base at all. As I said, I wasn't judging anything anymore!

He nodded silently without getting up. He just asked me his question again.

"Do you see some happiness for you in the future, Amit? This industry didn't really take your opinion into consideration while assigning you a particular competency; it married you to a technology while never taking your choice or inclination into perspective. I mean, you are often so tense, sad, and deeply unhappy. It worries me." I knew what the sadness was for. But I kept the focus on the topic.

"I don't know where my happiness lies. But yes, I do feel underutilized at times, and I know how you feel about this, but then I can be so much more, and yet, all I end up being is another routine guy. It gets to you sometimes. You know what the best job is?" I was feeling a prickling sensation inside me, but I continued. "One where one touches all aspects of the business—and not getting limited or staying specialized in one particular aspect all his or her professional life. I mean, I don't understand the business aspects of half the technical things I do. This cross-functionality is very important for innovation, Bhoopal, and I thought this was a knowledge industry, which can't survive or grow qualitatively without innovation. The good people are going to leave, and we won't be able to retain them. Why are we being so pessimistic about our ability to innovate? Do you, as a manager, ponder this at least?"

I would have never been this direct to anyone, but this was Bhoopal, and I felt confident he would never take it otherwise. Being technically oriented, he had the ability to stay objective and reasonable.

His eyes had that glimmer of interest as I spoke, and that passion for change flickered still, but then he sighed and looked away.

"Beats me too, dear. Don't worry about these changes, though. Maybe you will be the one to bring about this change someday; who knows? Transitions are always inevitable, and we are on the edge of one. Every churn will undoubtedly result in new opportunities. I have faith in it." I gave a hollow laugh, though I knew he said that with genuine hope.

Trust this guy to analyze all the colors in the rainbow, find out they don't really exist, and then still have faith in them during a storm, but somehow this positivity seemed fake for such times. Where was the change he spoke of?

○●○

I met Piyush at the cafeteria entrance. He was coming up to meet us.

"Hey, Suman is acting really weird today. I caught him crying in the lobby alone as I was going for a leak. He just bolted off somewhere. I tried to find him for a tea break, but he isn't around. I thought you might have seen him. He didn't even pick up my call."

"I have no clue," I said, amazed.

I took the stairs, a longer route, to come down, lest I might encounter Mitali. What was with me?

As I took the turn down to the second floor, I found Suman and JD standing in a corner. JD looked red-eyed; she wiped her tears as she saw me. Suman was red eyed too, but he was too conscious to be caught in a weak spot. He wished me cheerily.

"Hey, Amit. Wassup bro? What are you up to?"

"I'm good. Are you...? Are you crying?" I asked aghast.

"Yes. Quite scared for the exam results," he smiled as he lied. I realized I had just gatecrashed a vulnerable moment between the two.

"Piyush was searching for you. He still is."

"Oh, I forgot to message him. I was in Kanchan's cabin at that time. They have decided to throw me off our ship. I am supposed to leave by the end of this month." He grinned bravely at me.

"What do you mean?" I just couldn't believe that.

"Kanchan has asked me to go back to the bench after this month-end as the project I was onboarded for was an anticipation project, and the anticipation that the project might come is now over. Bloody idiots!" he replied. "I will be on the bench without pay for an uncertain period of time, which in present times means I am as good as fired. Matter of time!" I didn't know what to say.

"What did Bhoopal say?"

"Bhoopal has no say. He wasn't there; this is a decision from the higher management. When the ship is sinking, the best thing to do is to jettison all the unwanted stuff first, and that's exactly what they are doing. I am a cost and a liability. They can't afford to keep guys like me around anymore."

I looked at JD. She just wiped her eyes silently again. She was going through a rough patch herself. I didn't have the heart to comfort either of these guys—for a moment, I felt like crying myself.

"Come, let's go to the loo, Amit. I will catch up with you, JD. Take aspirin—it will make you feel better," he wished JD, and then put his arm around my shoulder. She just waved at us.

I walked down the stairs in disbelief. As we opened the door to the ground-floor lobby, a gush of chilly wind hit us. That's when I felt an intense craving for the warmth of that guy beside me. I couldn't stop my eyes from getting moist. Then, suddenly, the moistness turned to tears.

"Hey, what happened? Are you crying too? Oh God!" He hugged me. "I am not dying, brother."

But I was, and I felt I needed him. I hugged him back.

We went inside the loo and stood by the counters.

"Let me lighten your mood a little. Have you heard of this theory called the leak theory? No? Okay. If you notice, the entire toilet is empty, and you haven't stood exactly next to me to leak. You took the alternate counter. What does that tell you?"

"That I am logical."

"Really? Why didn't you stand beside me?"

"We all need our space. Why cram next to each other? Why make each other uncomfortable?"

"That wasn't the reason. Think deeper."

I shrugged my shoulders.

"Dude, you are straight. If you had taken the place very next to me, it would have meant you are gay."

"Whoa, aren't you jumping the gun here?" I asked him

"Not really. I might be wrong, but there is no reason why that person should stand right beside me unless he has no other choice. Unnatural affinities are divulged unconsciously."

I pondered over it a little. I couldn't see the logical steps connecting the hypothesis to the conclusion. But Suman seemed sure.

"You should talk to Bhoopal about your case. He might be able to help," I suggested.

"I will. He isn't around," he said as he moved on to wash his hands.

"Suman?" I asked.

"Hmm?"

"What's between you and JD? I have never seen her this wrecked."

He stopped washing his hands for a second, but only a second as he looked me in the eyes.

"Okay."

"Did you tell her that you love her?" I asked him.

"I don't need to." he said simply.

"Well, sometimes one needs to say it. Don't leave so many things to assumptions," I was concerned.

He just smiled, "You still don't get it, do you?"

"I do get it. It is difficult. But for God's sake, have some mercy and say it."

He sighed and turned to me. "Remember that lady I lost my virginity to?"

"Yes? What about her?"

"I lied. It wasn't her." He looked me in the eye. "It was JD."

"Huh?" My jaw dropped.

"Yes, we've been together for a while now. There is no reason why I should tell you this, but I know I am leaving, and you might never find out unless I tell you." He winked at me, and he resumed cleaning his face in the mirror. "She knows I love her, perverted though I seem; she is my first and last and always will be, and she knows it all too well."

"And yet she leaves!?" I asked sullenly.

"Yet she leaves." He smiled at me. "...so do I. Let's ensure they don't use my absence to make her stay longer. That's my only agenda with Bhoopal. Last night, I had a fight with her over her would-be husband. She is not going to stay back—no matter what."

So, JD saw no future with Suman and was leaving. Bhoopal knew this.

○●○

We waited for Bhoopal. He never came back to his workstation. Kanchan wasn't there at her desk herself.

"They might be in some meeting," Suman said to me. "Let me know if you see him."

"Sure will," I said to him.

I saw JD working silently, her eyes swollen yet still rapidly moving across the screen. I went to her.

"Are you okay?"

"Yes, perfectly," she said, giving me a discerning look. "You?"

I smiled at her. I got a call from Prabhu.

"Dude, people have started to get e-mails," he said.

"E-mails?"

"People got a mail from HR this afternoon saying they underperformed in the examination and hence this would be their last day in the organization."

"You sure?" I tried not to crack on the phone.

JD stopped her typing fingers for a moment and looked at me apprehensively.

"Yes, at least 5 people in our project. We are a project floor of 300 people. They are in a meeting with the HR."

"And?" I asked.

"And Mitali isn't one of them. Don't worry," he said.

"No, I mean, did they confirm the action against them?"

"They aren't back yet," Prabhu said.

"Fine. Keep me updated," I exhaled a cold sigh of panic.

"What?" JD asked.

I explained the situation to her quickly and rushed to check if I had received any such mail. I hadn't. I looked around quickly to see if anyone had received any such emails since everybody seemed to be working on the computer. No one seemed hassled. JD told me to keep the news to myself and not create unnecessary panic.

There already were assignments in my inbox. I just shrugged away my doubts and worked, but I continued checking the inbox every 5 minutes just to be sure. Nothing ever came. Kanchan never came back, nor did Bhoopal.

For some minutes, I even wondered if this was a figment of Prabhu's imagination. I wanted to talk to him and meet him to see if what he was saying was the truth, but it wasn't safe to waste time and get caught while doing it. I wouldn't have wanted Kanchan to catch me wasting time. I called Prabhu again, but he said he was busy and that we would talk later.

○●○

That night, I had dreams of loss. It was becoming colder even without the fan. I woke up and kept glancing through the window to see if the world outside my room made any more sense. It was just as quiet. In the night, I received random messages from Prabhu. As I stood there alone, I intensely missed Mitali, so intensely that I cried a little. But I didn't call her. I no longer existed for her.

○ ● ○

The next morning, I waited near Kanchan's workstation to talk to her. She seemed under stress and looked sleep deprived. She saw me standing.

"Oh, Amit, it's you. Right, hmm," She took her fingers near the sockets of both her eyes and took a moment to ponder on what she wanted to say. "Right. Can you please call everyone for an urgent meeting in the conference room? Like right now? Please assemble in the room."

I called everyone to assemble in the room. Bhoopal wasn't in his seat. She passed us as we were entering the room and said, "Give me a moment. I will just wash my face and be right back." When she came back, she looked stretched.

Something was definitely not right.

"Something happened yesterday," she said, looking at us. "Do you remember the instruction that was shared about the new security measures installed on the client port to ensure no unverified software is downloaded? Well, there was a breach. Proxies were used to download some software a few days ago."

I looked around to see if anybody would come forward. Nobody did.

"This instance was reported, and the client did a precursory check to find the person responsible. It was found that Bhoopal did this last week."

I felt my breath stop. It must have been during the exam week when he would stay back late at night to complete our assignments.

"We had a discussion with Bhoopal on this subject yesterday. He has accepted. Last night, at around 2 a.m., I received a call from onsite asking him to suspend him with immediate effect. I called him and told him so. He would not be coming to the office today onwards."

She looked around. Nobody reacted for a while; it was too much to take. We couldn't imagine our project without Bhoopal; he was single-handedly managing so many things. Suman was the first to react.

"Surely, the client overreacted. This doesn't sound like a lot. I am sure you can talk it out with them and get him back. He is indispensable."

"Obviously, I did try to talk it out. They haven't relented. This might take some time," she said. "Maybe weeks, maybe more. We don't know. In the meantime, I have asked Raj to take over the responsibilities that Bhoopal had on him."

She looked around again.

I raised my hand, "I have a question."

"Please don't be so formal, Amit, just ask!"

"You never told us that the results of the examination held would be used against people to fire them."

"Excuse me?"

"Some resources were fired last night from the *INSITE* team based on the results."

Kanchan looked at me dumbfounded.

"You know this, right?"

She took a moment.

"This initiative is not being routed through the managers. We aren't directly involved. Earlier, it was thought that maybe just the new joiners or senior-most managers might be given additional training based on the exam results."

"This isn't about training, is it? Nor is it just about the new hires that are being fired; it's also about people who have been working for quite a few years. Apparently, HR didn't even consider the project manager's recommendation before firing people."

"I will talk to them. And I am sure they wouldn't have taken action unless the scores were abysmally low for people in their position and experience. Also, I am sure they would consider the dependencies involved while making such decisions," Kanchan said.

JD spoke, "So basically, you are saying, resources like Suman and Bhoopal with no dependencies need to worry."

"Nobody needs to worry. Not until the information gets clear. Believe only the news that comes from me. Rest all are rumors," Kanchan said before leaving.

We came out of the conference room in a haze.

"Should we call him?" I asked the group.

"I don't think so. He wouldn't want to talk right now. Maybe later," Raj said.

I looked at Yogi and Suman. They too nodded, asking me to keep it low for now.

"Not the best time, buddy," Piyush said, pressing my shoulders.

Normally we would have taken a tea break to discuss it, but times were such, we all just went to our workstations and worked.

○●○

Yogi later informed us that Bhoopal would download software from the client port regularly; it was just recently that the client had gone serious by installing the filtering software forbidding access to these sites. Bhoopal used proxies, never realizing that the client would track him and take this whole breach so seriously. I glanced at Suman; he looked at me distraught and just gave a shrug.

Mitali's version:

I, too, heard it. Just before lunch, some people from our project got an email asking them to leave the company—what a way to rock somebody's world!

Yes, it was a shock, but it wasn't completely unexpected, was it? I was more shocked by the abruptness of it.

I didn't know these people directly—they weren't from my immediate sub-team, but I could imagine their state of mind. Each of them had a small, half-hour meeting with HR. They were asked to immediately deposit their ID cards and vacate the premises by the end of the day. I don't think anyone had very high dependencies on them. None of us did—that was how the project was designed.

"Hey, Raghav," I asked one of the people who had just returned from the meeting and was emptying his desk. People came to console him and ask him questions about whether he was fine. He was my age, had a similar experience, was unmarried, and the event seemed yet to sink in. So, he was smiling gracefully and was pretty normal.

Good! He would need this cheerfulness now.

He looked at me. This was the first time I was talking to him.

"Hi," he said, bending down to check the papers in his drawer.

"Hey, sorry to hear what happened. This was a shock. What do they say? Any chance they might reconsider?"

"I tried, but they seemed pretty closed about it. I asked our PM to intervene—he gave good feedback and tried to convince them to retain me. It didn't help much."

I shook my head.

"But I don't get this. Did you fare that badly on the test?"

"I don't know. They haven't shared the score. I was working late at night on the Friday before the test and couldn't do much over the weekend," he said, stopping his work and coming closer. "My guess is that we might be in the bottom 5-10%. We aren't the only ones; people from the other projects have been called too; it's just that we would never find out who all. We are just the first wave; it's not stopping here. This continues."

"But... But I thought only the new hires would be affected. It makes more sense to release them instead of people already in the projects."

"As you know, joiners come in batches. This year, there are a few more batches joining us over the course of the next three months. From what I hear, the joining of these later batches has been delayed indefinitely. New hires will probably go, the not-so-good ones anyway, but then so would the rest of us. HR thinks the company has over-hired and the company needs *streamlining*. I hate that word—HR used it so many times in the meeting."

"Oh, hmm." I took a moment to contemplate, biting my lower lip.

"So, how are the others taking it?"

"Not so well. A lady fainted or at least acted so. One middle-aged gentleman is reported to have shouted at the HR. None of these antics helped them. Once you submit the ID card, it's over. Time to go!"

"So, what now?" I asked him as uncertainty loomed large.

"Well, I need to make some changes in the CV and will re-upload it on the placement sites. Patience would be needed. It never takes less than 3-6 months, does it? It might take even more now."

I muttered to him luck. He took his small money plant with him as he left in due time that day.

○●○

That was a wake-up call for me. I must leave this place before this place leaves me.

I immediately took steps. I got the project manager's number from the email Neeraj had sent me regarding the project in Delhi. I called this manager to discuss the details of the interview to be held. His name was Alok Mehta, and he was working on that telecom project in Delhi as a project manager for a couple of years.

"Good, you reminded me," he said. "Let's have it on Friday at 4:00 p.m. afternoon if it is convenient. We already had a small technical round with you telephonically, so now it makes more sense to meet you in person for the next round. Will you find a flight on such a short notice?" he asked.

"No problem, sir. Please mail me the details. I will be there."

"Mitali, one more thing. This interview/conversation is just to ensure that you are the right person for the project. But you will get a confirmation only after you get me a relieving mail from your current project manager in *INSITE*. Think they will agree to it?"

"Alok, we are not a project with very high individual dependencies. It might take a few days, but I would convince my manager for an approval and early relieving date. I would join you after year-end in the worst-case scenario."

"That would be good enough. Best of luck," he said happily over the phone. He sounded like a good guy. I was perfect for this role; the interview was more or less a formality given my credentials. I was quite sure I would ace it.

I messaged Neeraj I was coming and booked the tickets. I informed Tanmay, my PM, asking him for about a week's leave starting Friday.

I informed him about the interview. Given my special situation and because we had adequate backups in our project, he agreed.

And then, as I relaxed back in my chair, for a moment—just for a moment, to be specific—I missed Ami. I felt he should know this too. It was important for him to forgive me and forget me, as I was leaving him forever. I prayed that he would never find out that I was leaving, but for sure he would find out someday, and I wanted it to be a little easier for him.

I wasn't worth it—worth so much pain, but that guy will never accept it, ever! In times like these, I would realize how entangled our lives had become, and it would make me wish we had never met.

Oh, God! I was overthinking again. I took some anti-depressants with water and closed my eyes.

Ami's version:

The next few days, it was chaos.

By lunch, some person or another would receive an email stating that they had underperformed in the test and that their skill sets were not in line with the company's expectations. People were edgy, desperate, and tense, yet strained and polite with managers at the same time. The managers were polite with the delivery managers. The recession hit everybody, but the exact numbers were never known.

No set pattern was seen; experienced people with higher expectations from management for future growth seemed more in the exit numbers, though.

We were tense continuously, well knowing we were completely dispensable. Even the indispensables like Bhoopal were dispensable. JD said we were like chickens ready to be slaughtered, currently stuffed inside our cubicles. Who will go first was part of luck, so no point in thinking about it. Sooner or later, we will all be gone.

That day, I was working on my computer as usual, stifling my yawns and struggling to keep my eyes open. I received a call from Kanchan on the extension.

"Hey, can you please come into the conference room? I have something to discuss with you," she said in a professional tone.

"Sure, Kanchan," I mumbled and kept down the receiver, only to find myself dripping in a cold sweat. I looked around. People were working silently. I guess I was next. They don't need to know. I smiled at myself as my mind imagined a few chicken quacks coming through my heart and tummy.

I wished Kanchan cordially as I entered. She was typing something furiously. "Please have a seat and give me a moment."

I sat down carefully, observing her reactions and wondering what went through that head of hers as she decided on someone's fate. She gave me a weird look of discomfort, maybe to ask why I was staring at her. I moved my eyes away.

"Are you alright?" She asked me.

"Why? Yeah. You called me?" I asked back.

"Oh, yes," she replied, closing her computer and turning to face me.

"Do you like your work?" She asked.

"Yes, of course, Kanchan. I love it," I lied to save my job.

"As you know, things are pretty dismal in the organization and we are trying for optimum utilization of the resources. I am offering you an opportunity because I have noticed that you are a quick learner."

I nodded my approval vigorously. Utilize me better and pay me more.

"Now, you asked me a few months back about cross-learning opportunities. There's one slot in the project on the top floor in automotive, which represents a window of opportunity for you. As of now, you are only half-billable in this project *(I didn't know that!),* only as a buffer *(because you are a trainee and not completely ramped up yet).* By buffer, we mean additional assistance to the team." She paused to look at me.

I nodded vigorously for her to continue for a while.

"So, I was thinking of making you a buffer in that project too, so that you become completely billable from the company point of view. You would need to shift between the projects and would need to handle assignments for both projects," she grinned at me wide-eyed, happy at her wisdom.

So that's what goes on in her stupid head. I sighed as I realized my curiosity had vanished and I was disappointed.

"See, I want to help you people get in slots so that the organization has a strong reason to retain you and at the same time increase your productivity." I sighed again. By cross-learning, I meant to improve the quality of work and not the quantity of work—too late to debate now.

"When you said I was to fill a slot, you meant to say a person in that project was let go and his slot is vacant now?"

She blinked twice to wonder if I had the right to be asking such intrinsic questions.

"You can say that," she said, playing with her hair.

So, I would be doing a whole guy's job in that other project and a whole guy's job in this project, and I would be getting paid one guy's pay. They were cutting my salary by half and then expecting me to thank them for it.

Bloody, this is how they want to increase productivity now! I bit my lips to control the growing nervousness.

"Wow," I said sadly.

They were now redeploying the same resources to multiple projects so that the costs of hiring and training new people were saved. They would never let go of people who could cross-function in this manner—it was just a huge cost-saving. So basically, Kanchan was giving me an opportunity to save my job.

I stared into her eyes—those confused, tired, but enthusiastic eyes that were nudging me to get persuaded, say yes, and close the conversation. Fall in line, they asked charmingly but unapologetically.

"Do I get some time to think?"

"What's to think? What can be better than this?" she asked, typing again.

"I would need some time, Kanchan," I said, pushing for my space.

"Fine, tell me by evening without fail. Then you can begin tomorrow onwards," she said, taking my consent for granted.

I thanked her and left the room.

○●○

"So, what are you planning to do then?" JD asked me. "Work two shifts?"

I gave her a tired look of disdain. She smiled again and continued.

"Go, bloody, tell that lady that it is not possible for you or anyone else to work in this manner."

"She would say it is unprofessional," I said, stroking my chin.

"Okay, then, go back to my question," she said.

"Hmm, I see the stalemate," I said, wondering.

"In that case, go back to my suggestion," she said without stopping her work or even looking at me.

"Give me some time, will you?" I was exasperated and got up to fetch a coffee.

I called Bhoopal that evening from our company extension. I was concerned and worried for him. He had done so much for us, but none of us had even called him under the pretext that it wasn't the right time and that he wouldn't like it.

The ring went on for a few times and finally got answered by a gruff voice, "Hello."

"Hey Bhoopal. How are you?" I asked whispering.

"Fine man," he said with a hollow laugh. "How is everybody?"

"Not so good—there is tremendous pressure these days due to that test. Thankfully, nobody got terminated yet from our team."

"You mean except me and Suman?" He laughed that broken laugh again.

"You guys are suspended for the time being. They would soon be bringing you back. Things are in the doldrums without you, Bhoopal." As I said that, I realized we all missed his style of working. "They have no option. They must take you back. The project needs you."

"Thanks for your passionate vote of confidence," he chuckled. "But it is not so easy. I would suggest you guys keep no such hopes. You are on your own now. Be very careful. Stay alert." His deep voice still had that tinge of concern.

"What about you?"

"Been searching," he said abruptly and went silent.

I, too, said nothing much then. It was amazing how little I had to say. I just hoped he would understand everything left unsaid.

By evening, as I left, I gave my affirmation to Kanchan for joining the new project. JD's question, *'But can you do it?'* kept bugging me all the while.

And then, as I was about to leave, I received a message from Mitali.

I called Prabhu to discuss it, and he invited me over to his place.

Mitali's version:

I messaged Ami that I was leaving the next morning, quite possibly forever. The reason I was informing him was that he shouldn't be shocked when I do. I received no reply; just the way, I received none when I messaged Neeraj that I was coming to Delhi.

The flight was in the morning. If everything went well, the transfer should ideally be immediate. Not much notice period hassle for the internal transfers. The fact that we didn't have many dependencies might work out well for me. I would put my manager's own words in his mouth—no reason why I should stay back to train my replacement.

Prabhu's version:

Ami called me regarding the latest sky-load worth of shit that had befallen him. Apparently, the bitch was leaving for good. It was a cause for celebration, but the fool thought otherwise. I asked him to walk over to my humble abode with something to eat as I went down to a bar to get bottles of cheap liquor.

An hour later, he walked into my place, completely disturbed and upset. He was restless and supremely distressed—who the hell asked him to fall in love? His heart ached, and so did mine. He was ready.

I just pulled out the packet of green stuff and offered him some. He seemed confused and asked me all sorts of pediatric questions.

"What is this?"

"You are ready to explore the freedom of the mind. This will set you free from all your walls. You need to see the world differently; you are too weak to do that for now. So, you are going to need this!"

He looked at the material, dumbfounded.

"It is okay. I am not asking you to pay me. Thank me later."

"You are into drugs?" Something seemed to have crashed inside him—the CPU, maybe?

"It's called weed; you can also call it pot, or if you so prefer, Mary Jane. Start with this."

"So, since when?" His mouth had opened wide like the :O smiley. It was funny.

"Since always. Oh, c'mon, you should have sensed it long back. You remember some of the early incidents when we met? About Puru?"

"Yes?"

"You see, Puru was never beaten up on the bus. He fell on the pavement while walking. I imagined the version I told you and convinced him too. When a person is into such stuff, memories are fuzzy and can be rewritten. Days later, I realized that it wasn't that way. Puru and I used to do this stuff together. Due to some complications over money, he hates me. Or do you remember, say, the incident where I was asked to leave the room when my roommate tried to set me on fire?"

"Yes?"

"Apparently, that shit never happened. He found out that I was into drugs and threatened me to leave. I was the one who attempted to set the place on fire and, in the process, injured myself. Sometimes it is hard to separate the dreams from the reality, you know. That's the best part about this," I smiled.

"You concocted a version for me?" He looked shaken.

"This is just mixing dreams and fantasies with reality. Some stories are better than ugly realities—at least more entertaining," I said cheekily.

Before I knew what happened, he punched me in the eye.

"You lied to me about everything, you devil—every damn thing—that thing about Madhura. Or say the fact that Pooja is interested in me, or that Mitali loved me, or that I deserved somebody—somebody who would make me happy. Damn it! The stupid dreams! The whole damn thing! You lied!" He kept hitting me as he cried, or were they my tears? "Nobody likes me. Nobody loves me. I have no future. Nobody even considers me human enough to love me, and that's the truth. You get me—that's the ugly truth and the full reality of life. I am supposed to die unloved."

"You want to know the ugly reality of life? I will tell you," I said, wiping my own tears, which I didn't even know had started pouring. "Reality is, I love you!"

He stopped for a moment, his reddish, strained eyes looking at me with wonder.

"And nope, not exactly in a brotherly manner!" I looked deep into his eyes. "I guess I am gay."

He blinked and sat on the floor, clutching his head.

"I started diabolically. I wanted to disappoint you in love by using your loneliness as a trigger so that maybe, when you lose on all fronts—maybe just maybe—you would see me as your soulmate for all seasons. Can girls do things we would happily do for each other? We are seriously beyond them!" I said, placing my arm on his shoulder, which he shrugged away.

"So, you succeeded. I am broken, and so are all my beliefs." Those tired, unslept eyes looked at me with such pain that I felt my soul weaken. I wanted to kiss those tears off his eyes.

"But then, somewhere in the middle of all this, I realized I loved you too much to betray you. I knew you needed these beliefs and that you trusted me; I wanted you to be happy," I continued.

He didn't look at me.

"You let me fall for her? That was cruel!"

I sighed. He was taking a simpler explanation of the happenings.

"Einstein says, never oversimplify things. Look, I never pushed you into falling in love with her—quite the opposite. I never wanted you to get serious. Love, I guess, in many ways, is a journey than a destination. There is nothing to achieve and nothing to get. Just experience it and move on. You did taste it, didn't you?" I touched his cheeks longingly. "It tastes bitter; it hurts; it dehydrates us." I wiped his tears.

He looked at me, but his heart was elsewhere. It roved, and the person it was with, was stomping on it.

"Yet, I wanted it for you. When it started, all you wanted was to make her happy. To love without expectations is indeed awesome. I wanted you to go for it and get hurt while you did so. It is the most amazing, pure, and beautiful thing in the world—to love without expecting anything in return. I knew it wouldn't end well, and yet I wanted it for you because, while at it, you were happy. But then... then you started to think that it should never end, that she should love you back, and that is an expectation too. You started making her unhappy with these expectations. That was wrong—not the expectations, but then the promise was they would never be part of your chemistry, was it not?"

He tried to object...

"Was it not? That was the time to let go of her. Her happiness lies somewhere else, mate!! It's high time you stop trying to superimpose yours on hers. Let go." I rummaged my fingers through his hair with a touch of longing. "Just the way yours lay somewhere else, and I let go of you, didn't I? Well-knowing we can never be, tell me, did I not?"

I kissed him on the cheeks. He was way too dazed to object.

"But you never liked her, did you?" he asked me. "She's a bitch, a slut!"

That was a discordant note, and it hurt my ears. He was angry and hurt, and somehow these words are the only ones a guy can use when he is too troubled to express his incredible yearning.

"Never judge anyone's character. You can never know what went through her mind as she made her decisions. We all have our reasons, don't we?"

I hugged him again, and I don't know how long we hugged, but it was better than absinthe. I am sure I saw some fairies.

Mitali's version:

Early in the morning, I waited at my bus stop to catch the bus to the airport. It started raining. December rains are unexpected and surprisingly cold at the same time. But I invited the cold drops on my skin; they gave me goosebumps. Delhi would be just this cold now, perhaps even more, minus the rains.

As I waited there, I found there was someone else too at the stop, sitting on the bench with his dirtied formals, red tired eyes, and frail shivering body.

It was cold; he should have at least worn a sweater, and we both had no umbrella.

I took a seat next to him.

"I thought that I might be able to meet you here considering your flight time," he said as I sat.

"What were the chances? You should have called me," I reasoned.

"I thought you would never pick up my call," he replied in a choked-up voice.

The lightning thundered, and the rain increased in volume as the sky went darker, causing the roads to go quieter.

"I would have this time!" I said softly.

He kept his hands on my midriff and clutched me tighter. I tried to resist; he let go.

His hold had gone weaker; I wondered if he had eaten anything last night. I didn't ask. But he took my hand in his.

"What is it, Ami?" I asked him silently praying for the bus to come to the stop as soon as possible.

He kept looking down for several moments, avoiding my eyes. I was afraid he might start crying. Maybe I felt like giving him a gentle hug, but I didn't.

He pulled out a small box from his bag; it was wrapped.

"Your farewell gift," he mumbled. "If it is to end, I want it to end on a happy note."

I gently opened the untidily wrapped box. There were some chocolates, a book on Linux, and an envelope.

"Thanks," I said without giving away that I was touched.

"Keep the envelope for later," he said to my relief.

I opened one of the chocolates and offered him half. We sat silently, watching the rain pour, the droplets making strange and beautiful puddles on the road, as we munched on our chocolates. There was nothing left to be said. Silence was enough.

Minutes later, I saw my bus arriving. "I need to go."

He let go of my hand. But as I boarded the bus and saw him one last time, I felt he hadn't let go of me and probably never will. I wanted to read the contents of the envelope but let it be in my bag—maybe not now, maybe never!

However, that evening, even as I met Neeraj and even when he kissed me, my thoughts kept coming back to the image of that guy who waited for me in the rain. I had always wished Neeraj would be that guy. It isn't a nice feeling to be the cause of someone's misery.

Ami's version:

I thought of ways to manage my sorrow but could come up with none. I had never been wounded so badly, so fatally, by the very person I loved.

I contemplated suicide for a few moments but then dropped the idea after thinking of my parents. It's not my life alone. There are lots of threads that pull our heartstrings.

I called my mother and talked to her for hours, but as soon as I finished the call, the pain resurfaced. Then I thought of calling Pooja to see that smile of hers. It had the power to make people forget their pain. But she was a distant stranger, and the void grew more vacant. And when I had exhausted all the options with the powers to heal, I called Prabhu.

He never broached the topic but kept tiptoeing around it in all lightness.

He can be funny! At least he cared enough to try.

Mitali's version:

In the evening, I did open the envelope. It was a poem, but of course—his preferred way of expressing himself.

ANYTHING FOR YOU, MA'AM!!

It all started with an inevitability;
I knew I wouldn't commit nor would you;
Maybe that's the reason I let off my guard,
And thus the attachment grew.

But attachment grew more than I bargained for,
To a point, you became my necessity;
And I found myself sucked in the whirlwind so fast,
I never realized what happened was a possibility.

It was a mistake, a blunder, on my part,
Cos I always knew your limitations and mine;
Even now I accept it's my problem, not yours,
So trust me, I need no help... I am fine!

But let's see why it happened in the first place,
What exactly made me fall for you;
Was it the trust, your innocence, or your beauty?
Or was it the connection I shared only with you?

I don't remember how it all started,
Believe me, I never intended it to happen;
Just know... your beauty wasn't the reason,
Nor was my passion.

Do you still remember the times we shared?
The everyday chats during our daily chores,
You unknowingly touched my heart a million ways,
It had just never happened to me before!

You were my long-forgotten dream come true,
You were like me in so many ways;
I could trust you for accepting me as I am,
It was almost like the end of days.

I shared for perhaps the first time,
my heart, dreams, and my soul;
I knew I was going to lose you someday,
But I still bared open my core.

Guess you taught me to risk myself,
For what I knew won't happen again to me;
Maybe you find me strange now,
Still, it's just the way things were, as I see.

Is it a crime to care and love?
Why then I don't feel guilty for my actions,
What you mean is something so personal to me;
I am almost oblivious to all moral sanctions.

I mean no harm, no trouble, no anger,
It's enough for me if you know,
Don't bother to even give me a reply;
I know you won't, and I don't want a row.

But all you did was to categorize me in your list,
as yet another loser moron, who failed yet again;
I was reduced into a caricature in a list so long,
I had lost all my uniqueness, for you in your brain.

Oh, if only I could do the same.
Find a category to categorize you into;
I tried, but for you, no category ever matched,
So I created one just for you.

You might have met many like me,
But you see, you were the only one I met;
Can you empathize with what I really mean?
Again, I know it's something you can't really get!

You haunted my sleep when I tried not to think of you,
Loneliness hit me at all times without warning;
There was no one I could look up to for relief;
I got up in writhing pain every damn morning.

Seems, I need to escape my dreams to escape you,
Which depends on how cleverly I lie!
A lie so convincing that it covers every damn feeling;
I lose yet again, but at least I can smile.

If this lie is what it takes to keep you happy,
Then so be it—a liar I am;
Truth won't knock on your door ever again;
I will take care of it—anything for you, Ma'am!!

My breath went rapid. I turned the page. Also present was a letter written untidily, as if in a hurry...

'Dearest Mitali,

I don't know what to say as you leave... You take a part of me with you. Every breath of coconut oil and jasmine, the view of white flowers in a full moon, hugs, or the computer books you always referred me, but I never read, are going to remind me of you every single time.

And I would remember you fondly and miss you wistfully. I do not have to kill that part of my heart; I realize I have to treasure it. I promise that. It was a beautiful thing to love you and will always be.

This gift is because I feel proud of you—for all your achievements till date and for those soon to come—and I probably won't be around to applaud. Try not to think of us as a mistake—rather, as you once used to say, let it stay something special.

I know it once was!

Try to keep those memories alive. Have a happy life, and that would ensure that I am happy too. I realize I will never ever be happy if I am responsible for your unhappiness.

There will always be millions of things to say to you, but somewhere I have to stop on a happy note.

Everything that started well should end well; this deserves a good end too.

So there, Ma'am! Life is short anyway. I wanted to know you better, and it was one of the happiest experiences of my life (and no, I did not select the wrong girl!).

Remember me as a friend who couldn't quite make it to your heart even though he gave it his best-ever shot!!!!

Let it have its own fair space in your heart, won't you? After all, don't I deserve this little indulgence of yours? '

○●○

It was very difficult to say how I felt, but I couldn't sleep well that night. I muttered him an apology and imagined him saying something that I knew only he could: *'I forgive you as my own!'*

11.

Ami's version:

As I went to the office the next Monday, Raj met me in the hallway to inform me of the two assignments waiting for me in my inbox.

As I was sitting in my chair, I got Kanchan's call to remind me that I was supposed to meet the other project people by 12 p.m. to begin the Knowledge Transfer (KT) process. She had put in her word to the project manager of the new team.

The project was on the same floor as *INSITE*, and while I took the staircase, I wondered if I should wait a while at the project door of *INSITE*—just to see if I could yet again see her working from that pillar near the entrance of her project area.

I did stop, and I did take a look—she was gone, once and for all, but the acceptance wouldn't come. While *INSITE* was on the left, my new project was on the right, on the same floor.

There seemed to be a general feeling of disarray about the zone, and I needed a lot of directions to get to my destination. For some reason, everybody seemed restless. After calling the project SPOC[20] a couple of times, I could locate the team cubicles. The team members were seated with no awareness of the chaos, and

---

[20] *Single point of contact.*

their subdued manner alone hinted that their general lack of motivation, tinged with sadness, went well with the general atmosphere of confusion and boredom in that space.

PM came forth to wish me with a wide smile, "Hi, I'm Vijay. I'm glad to meet you. Kanchan told me a lot about you." I wondered if he was just being polite or if Kanchan had indeed been at her hyperbolic best. Neither case seemed charming enough to enquire further.

"Thank you, Vijay," I said.

He was a guy of around 32 years with a thick, bushy mustache. It was a small team of 8-10 people—some marriageable bachelors, 3-4 tired-looking girls, and a married PM—but no interesting faces, if you know what I mean. They were all friendly. The relatively senior guys gave me a briefing.

It was an engine control project again, based on the *AUTOSAR*[21] standard, this time with a focus on newer technologies and complex functionalities to be embedded in the ECUs[22]. I was given documents worth 5 GB to read within a couple of days. They were in a hurry to make me productive in a week. That would be asking too much considering the pressure I had from my former project, but I said nothing. I guess when the going gets tough, the first thing that gets punished is the

---

[21] *Automotive Open System Architecture.*
[22] *Engine control units.*

innocence—excuses were for better times. This was all about survival.

○●○

I took the docs and came down to my desk.

I saw Yogi walking out of a conference room with Kanchan—he looked distressed.

As I started working on the assignments sent to me by Raj, I realized JD wasn't around. I waited for her; she would have something wise to say about the final goodbye between me and Mitali. I never shared it with anyone, but I thought telling her would only make me feel better. She would understand.

As I took a look again, I saw her coming out of the same conference room, carrying her handbag. She walked leisurely, smiling gently at everyone, while taking her own sweet time to reach her place. I continued working. But she didn't go to her place; she came by my chair and placed her hands gently on my shoulder.

"Lot of work today?" she asked softly.

"Yes, ma'am. Raj gave me two assignments to complete by the evening."

"How's the new project? You liking it?" she asked.

I turned around and smiled at her.

"This pen drive is loaded with that project data, to be finished reading in the next few days. They expect me to work like a mule."

"You allow it!" she smiled.

"What were you guys discussing with Kanchan?"

"She was scolding Yogi, for not coming up to the level of expectations even after years with the project. He is expected to perform better and reach the ranks of a team lead. Project demands it—assignment loads are increasing."

"Everybody is leaving one after the other. It's difficult to sustain the project load. Only we people are working."

"You people," she said, smiling.

"Now, I know you don't work, but let's say we work as a team," I said, smiling.

She sighed and smiled. " *'You people'* it is. I am done. I'm out."

I just looked at her as if she had stomped on my heart—she had, figuratively.

"What the hell..." I spoke.

"I flunked the test," she said, smiling. "Got the mail in the morning."

I looked at her for a moment, wonderstruck. "By coincidence, or on purpose?"

She smiled. "Does it matter? I wanted to leave, and I guess they gave me a getaway themselves. Besides, this could save one of your jobs."

"What do you mean?"

"I wasn't the preferred separation, but Piyush and you were. You guys were lucky we seniors left first," she ruffled my hair. "Bhoopal told me this when I called him the day he left. I think he wanted you guys to leave before you got into the thick of things. He hoped you would do something worthwhile if you left in time. Only Suman had faith that things would work out for me somehow and now they have."

"Don't tell me Suman asked you to underperform!" I said this as my eyes widened.

She smiled slyly and winked, "Why would I ever tell that? Besides can't I figure it out myself?"

I relaxed back in my chair. "So, marriage with Sudeep now?" I looked at her longingly—that pretty, friendly, lovely face and those comforting eyes that I was going to miss terribly.

"I don't know. I don't love him; I don't like him. He's just exploiting our situation by being in a stronger position himself. I wish I had the courage to say no," she said, lost in the uncertainty of her future.

"I wish you had the courage to say yes to Suman," I looked at her eyes; they had become vulnerable at the mention of that name.

She wiped a tear and said nothing—who said girls don't have feelings? I laughed at myself. "He loves you like hell. I am sure you will find a way to make ends meet—the question is, do you want to lose someone who truly loves you just to make ends meet? He will take care of your father too." I would have given anything to see them end up together. She could feel me; I knew we had that connection.

"Why did you resign if not for marriage?" I asked.

"I would go back to my father. He's alone and lonely—I would probably become a lecturer in my city and stay with him. He's been facing rough health and needs me more than ever," she said, looking outside the tinted windows by our desk. "Besides, I have totally lost my interest in this place—slogging it out and making a so-called career," she said, rolling her eyes. "If nothing else, I would start anew."

Those words could only have been uttered by someone free.

"And you leave me alone?" I said with heartbroken eyes.

"Aww," she said softly and gave me a gentle hug. "You, my dear brother, need some time to come to peace with your desires. Take that time and forget your lack of confidence. You have it all. Break through your frustrations."

"Alright. alright," I said, giving her a hug again. "I will. When do you leave? I wish you wouldn't go. Please don't go," and before I knew it, I broke down completely.

It had been too much for me—too much to take. I was losing the people I loved, one after another—was I a human or what? I cried for several minutes, hugging her inconsolably as she continued to pat me, concerned for my emotional well-being.

She took me up to the cafeteria for a warm cup of coffee.

"Enough breakdowns, Ami. You need to be stronger. Stop crying, or you are going to lose everything you worked so hard for. Whatever it is, you will come out of it," she looked at me, still surprised at what I must have gone through and was going through—but she never inquired, only gently patted my hand.

That touch of affection broke me down again as I took out my hanky to cover my face.

"God, you are such a crybaby," she said, hugging me. "Are you going to let go of me or not? I can't leave if you don't smile for me."

She left that evening alright, but, by then, I had cried my eyes red. Those tears were for each of the people I had longed for, loved, and lost, and she was one of the last. I didn't know if we would ever meet again.

I called Prabhu after a while and went to his home. I was afraid of myself while alone. My cousin was after my life for the monthly expenses; he had called me three times since the evening. I transferred the money to him through *NEFT* while Prabhu prepared a delicious cup of tea for me.

I was grateful to him for not asking any questions, for saying nothing, and for just being there, standing quietly, waiting for me to take a sip, as I sat by the window with his cup in my hand.

"It's good," I smiled gratefully.

"You are getting dark circles just like me, but mine are due to something else," he said, touching my eyes. "Grief is like cocaine, baby. You can't seem to get enough of it now. What's the difference left between us?"

I gave him a sharp *'stop being a prick'* look. I needed softness and solace, not Socrates. "Alright alright. How was the day?"

"The day was great. The new project guys want an instant ramp-up from me. It is never going to happen, but it was funny to see the hope on their faces. Kanchan seems to have served them a lot of bullshit. Poor them!" I chuckled sipping my smoking tea.

"At least you are safe. We are under a constant fear of an instant let go. I have already started taking backups of my data and files, just in case I am too affected the day I get the mail. Mental torture completely."

"But tell me something—why aren't they coming up with the entire list of the desired attrition at one go?"

"Maybe to not create internal panic, to exploit, to keep backups in case business improves, to cut a good story in the media—they would do it step by step lest the shares fall. Any or all of them," he said, sipping his tea.

"Hmm," I nodded.

Our CEO was scheduled to appear on CNN-IBN for an interview soon—more specifically for a *'CEO's day off'*.

"I doubt if they can keep financial troubles away from the shareholders for long." I said.

"Business is affected, no doubt; cost-cutting isn't for nothing. There's no smoke without fire, and that fire is under the CEO's ass," Prabhu said, washing his cup. "Yet, watch him smile ear-to-ear on the interview as he declines any sign of trouble for the organization. That's one tough job I say—to smile when one's ass is on fire," he chuckled.

I smiled. That night, sleep was peaceful.

Mitali's version:

Friday was fruitful. The interview had gone well. I was convinced I had cracked it. Alok informally told me he was happy and that he would share a formal email in a few days.

It was the following week's Wednesday evening.

I was dining with Neeraj at a restaurant in the upscale Karol Bagh area. Neeraj had purchased a brand-new blue sedan and had taken me on a long drive all over the city. He had started maintaining a stubble and looked a shade wilder than how I remembered him. Perhaps it was all for the best—he had become more carefree, and the bug had bitten me too. He wanted to have tequila shots, but I warned him against it; after all, who would drive us home? Just dinner then!

"So, what are your plans for the night?" He winked at me.

"No plans. I stay in the hotel, and you go home," I said, smiling.

"That is not what you want," his eyes twinkled.

"Hmm," I spoke. "Not so fast, mister. Let's have food first."

"As if we will go to your hotel after dinner?" he said, faking a cute temper tantrum.

"You never know!"

He passed me the menu card.

"What are your thoughts about live-in?" he asked me out of nowhere.

"You are asking me to come live with you?" I asked, bewildered.

"You never know," he said, looking at me intently.

I laughed nervously, "Obviously, I wouldn't mind it at all. But why wouldn't you marry me, and we stay together, for like, *ever*?"

I instantly regretted going fairy-tale-ish in the last few words. I wasn't a girl anymore. Also, what about his parents?

"Look, marriage is not on the cards for me—at least not in the next few years. We never know; why not have as much fun as possible while at it? I would be with you almost completely over the weekends. I can't on weekdays, as my parents would be here."

"I don't get you." My nostrils must have gone red as well. I couldn't breathe. "I really, truly don't!" My heart begged silently for a kinder word.

"I don't think my parents are going to accept us!" he said sullenly.

"And you tell this to me now?" I said putting down my mocktail.

"Well yes, I mean, I did talk to them about us, but they clearly told me not to entertain any funny ideas for long!" He said it in a concerned tone. His parents wanted him to marry within their community.

"Don't worry, we'll convince them." I smiled.

"I don't get it. What's with marriage?" he said, shrugging his shoulders. "Can't we just be together and stop planning what may or may not happen two years from now?"

"Obviously, that's not possible. I don't have two years. I am 26." My eyes had gone wide. "And... and... I love you!"

"I know," he smiled as we ordered dinner. "But the question is, why drag marriage into the equation?"

"Don't you want to spend your life with me?" I asked, fingers crossed.

"I can only talk about the next two years. I would suggest you don't keep any false hopes," he said unapologetically.

"What's the issue?"

"It's just very difficult. The troubles we would face would be much greater than the joys of marriage, Mitali. The point would be lost!"

I bit my lips to ponder what would make him try harder—should I cry, or should I just offer sex? I was more comfortable doing the first.

"I would want to meet them before I accept a no," I said with finality.

He sighed and mumbled an acceptance. But that wasn't the point; I wanted him to convince them and conclude.

"Maybe we should both think of a..." I was going to say something, but his phone rang. He excused himself for a minute and walked away. It took him 15 minutes to return the *call from home*. He looked jauntier than usual when he returned.

Our starters had arrived and so had the rest of our food.

"Anything the matter?" I asked. He just shrugged.

"Pass me your phone," I said normally.

"What for?" he asked defensively.

"Just want to see something," I said, stretching my hand.

"Sure, check in the car. Have some more curry with your rice," he said, changing the topic as he passed me the curry.

As natural as he was at it, I knew something wasn't quite right. But I ate silently.

Ami's version:

I rubbed my eyes again.

The project was asking too much of me. To read so much was not humanely possible. While the team was supportive, the extra pressure of performing more had started to take a toll on my brain nerves. My retention power had drastically gone down, and I had been drinking way too much caffeine. It didn't help, but since when were the addictions meant to help?

Mitali lingered somewhere inside my mind still; maybe my hope clung to her. "Is it true that when we lose someone we love, a part of us dies with them?" I asked Prabhu as we stood at the terrace parapet, drinking coffee.

"I don't know. Medically unverified," he smiled a little at his own joke. "But maybe we do. My pa took a huge chunk of me with him," he said nervously.

"I long for her man; I wish I wouldn't, but I do," I said, my heart sinking.

"It will fade away. Give time some time." He made sense, but the feeling of loss wouldn't go away.

Prabhu turned to me. "Maybe like you, she lost a part of herself to you too—a missing part of herself that she will keep searching for, all her life. That part now belongs to you, and she can never have it back. Just maybe you are compensated for your loss, and you can use that part as a replacement. But the question is..." he said wisely, sipping his coffee. "Would you want to replace something pure like your heart with something far more insincere that was hers?"

"Do I have a choice?" I asked sadly, wondering if hers was insincere or far purer.

"You don't," he patted me and threw the paper cup down the terrace.

"Don't litter the premises. They spend so much to keep it clean," I scolded him.

"I don't care. Everybody's leaving. I know I am not too far. It's surprising I am still here."

"You aren't as dumb as you think."

"I am. Trust me."

"Okay, let's move," I said, throwing my cup down too.

"Ami?"

"Yes?"

"If I do leave, would you take care of me?" he asked. I didn't know what to say. "Would you feed me and my mother, man? I am afraid of dying of hunger."

"Nobody's going anywhere," I whispered, denying the possibility and leaving tomorrow to destiny.

"Okay, forget about me. If I do leave, do you promise to take care of yourself? I wouldn't be able to do that anymore, you see," he asked earnestly.

He was always there, wasn't he? Dear ole' Prabhu, I couldn't imagine my life without him. He was the last straw of support there was for a guy like me with no hope.

"Promise me, you will take care of yourself. Do it for me!" he said, holding my hands. "You would, right?"

I gulped down an avalanche of emotion as I nodded approval mutely, trying not to break down again.

Mitali's version:

He was standing at a liquor store counter, paying for vodka.

I think he intended to have a liquor party in my room. I wondered if it was really necessary.

It was Thursday evening. We could have just talked; after all, we had met after so many months.

I was alone on the road outside the car, and a lot of other people had started to stare at me as I stood nervously hugging myself. I felt out of place, and I wanted him to make the city homely for me. But I was missing that connection; maybe we needed to warm up for a while.

His phone rang again. He had forgotten it in the car itself.

I reached through the window by the driver's seat to grab the phone. I was about to call him, but his mobile featured the name of some girl as it buzzed merrily. I imagined the merry part in the tone of the buzz as my mind went through all the chasms of suspicion and terror. It took moments for me to realize it was still ringing in my hand.

I pushed the green button and just *'hmm'*ed.

But the lady on the other end was clever.

"Aunty?"

"Hey, hi." I cleared my throat and collected my thoughts. "I am Neeraj's sister."

"He has a sister?" the voice exclaimed on the other end.

He didn't.

"I mean cousin," I clarified.

"Oh, hi... is Neeraj around?"

She asked possessively as if she missed him, or was it just me imagining so? It was still enough to bring out the bitch in me.

"He's out with his girlfriend," I said, decisively.

"He has a girlfriend?" the voice exclaimed again.

"Yeah, everybody knows this. They are doing well—one would say, marriage is on the cards," I said coldly, like a surgeon.

"What the...?" the voice on the other end shrieked. "That can't be!!!"

"What do you mean, *'That can't be'?*" I jumped on her. "Of course it can be."

"But..." The voice faltered dejectedly.

"But what?" I snapped.

"Neeraj had me meet Aunty last month. She completely supported our relationship." The voice was on the verge of tears.

I felt the earth shift beneath my feet. "Excuse me!" I literally took a moment off to see whether it was. Nope, it was just my head whirling.

"So, what else did he tell you?" I asked her coldly, returning to the speaker.

"Lots of things! What would you do, knowing all that he tells me?" She asked in a moist tone.

"What's your name?"

"Neeta," she said. "You know what? I am sure there is some misunderstanding. I will talk to him. When will he be back?"

"There is no misunderstanding, Neeta," I said softly as I took a moment off to gulp down my grief. "Trust me on this! He will just tell you another story."

"Excuse me. Who's this?" she asked, surprised.

"The other girl," I said abruptly, before cutting off the call.

I took a cold, deep breath of panic as I stood on that road, completely numb, just looking at him. I wondered if the guy I was looking at would do this to me. This was the guy I'd loved.

There was nothing to be discussed, nothing to be asked. Things were crystal clear. Meanwhile, the phone had started to ring again.

I didn't have it in me to even look at him as he sprinted towards the car. I hate conflicts—what was there to talk about, I mean?

Things happened more or less in a haze then.

I simply called for an auto and sat in it.

Neeraj came out running, trying to stop the vehicle.

I looked back to see if he was following the auto. I was way too angry, and it would have been even more infuriating if he had followed. I would have hit him.

But he did nothing of the sort. He just stood on the road, silently looking at us. Then, I saw him slowly move towards the car and attend that call.

By that point, the auto had made a turn.

"Ma'am, where to?" asked the bewildered auto driver as he saw me crying.

It was nighttime, and I should not have gone back alone.

But I was too devastated to care. Thankfully, the driver was a kind guy.

I reached the hotel and cried. I hoped he would call and come up with a good justification—I would have been more than happy to be proven wrong.

There was some hope that he would try. The night was spent looking at the mobile, expecting it to ring any moment, thinking of all the things I would shout at him, all the while remembering the moments we spent together and how, by the end of it, our relationship had reduced to this—a hopeless mess.

I imagined him in another girl's arms and tried to visualize her face from her voice. She had a beautiful voice, better than mine. I am just an owl, I thought, as I sobbed hoarsely.

I tried to imagine if he loved her more, or if she was more beautiful.

After some time, I just wondered if he ever loved me! But suddenly, I couldn't think of a single time when he had actually said it to me.

Was it just me hyper-reading between the lines to fill in my loneliness? Imagining stuff that wasn't? Oh, God! I felt my head spin some more.

Later in the night, my thoughts turned to the infidelity I myself was guilty of and whether I had the moral right to question him in the first place. As I cried endlessly through the night, over the fork in the road my life had come to, I realized it was time to say goodbye to the idea that he was.

By morning, my decision was taken.

At 10 a.m., I called Alok to ask him about the result of the interview and my fate. No emails this time—way too time-consuming a process.

He communicated that it would take a while for them to come back, and they would let me know as soon as possible. By 4 p.m. in the afternoon, I was on my flight to Pune.

All the while, I deliberated on if I should call him just to tell him that I was leaving, and I wouldn't return—for probably, like, ever!! Even if I did get the new project, I wondered if it was possible for me to work together with him after what had happened.

The dream was over! I was sure that Neeraj wouldn't care.

Mentally, he had accepted the fact that his game was up, or maybe I wasn't even worth the effort of lying anymore on his part. Maybe, what we had wasn't worth saving!

When things end, they hardly make a sound. My head was throbbing with pain owing to a lack of sleep, and I searched my backpack desperately for my pills.

As the plane took off, I looked down at the fast-minimizing homes and lanes in Delhi, trying to find a car in blue rushing like crazy to the airport. I wondered if that car was his, and then my brain laughed at myself, well-knowing it wasn't, it couldn't!

I giggled at my innocence, wiping my tears. Funny, it was! I wish I knew why some people loved my 'brain'—it went overboard all the while in overthinking.

Ami's version:

I looked at the code to see where the error lay. It was an inefficient code.

First of all, there were too many unnecessary variables.

Second, there were *'goto'* statements.

Third, the logic wasn't optimal.

Fourth, the code jumped from program to program unnecessarily.

Hence, error-finding was a headache. It was a mess generated by an inefficient mind with the sole purpose of torturing me.

Now, this code was to be plugged into the whole, and it would disturb too many programs in the library. A good code is like a surgeon's knife, a chess step, or a merciless mercenary. It has to be a clean kill.

I checked who the programmer was. It was some lady onsite. I sent her an email to set up an evening call for requirements traceability. I discussed it with Raj, and he asked me to tell her to make the code crisper, or else further extensions to programs would be very difficult. This was an invitation to bugs, unless corrected.

As my understanding of the role had evolved with time, I had realized that we had the authority to not accept inefficient codes after highlighting potential issues to the developers. If something wasn't fitting in well, we weren't to let it pass through. I was quickly reaching the point where I could appreciate a good code and differentiate between programmers based on how clean their code was.

So, I hated Alex and loved Joanne; I would try to prefer her assignments more. I was turning into a connoisseur of the art of coding. It was like coffee for me; the code had to be written just right. Sometimes I would wish I was a developer and be given the opportunity to write codes that would be a tester's delight. I am sure testers have a secret crush on some developers. The love-hate relationship is always there. By and large, it's all about the art of thinking right. Programming is all about that.

After I was done with a part of Raj's assignment, I took the stairs and walked up to my second project for the ramp-up. I was nowhere near the expected level, and it made me smile.

As I passed *INSITE*, I stopped for a moment and, as usual, as a force of habit, peeked in, expecting to see her working. And to my surprise, she was! I blinked.

It was her! I felt like barging in and hugging her outright. But I knew better than that. I was smiling from ear to ear—too happy to be surprised and too happy to breathe.

I called Prabhu. "What the fuck?"

"Excuse me?"

"I am outside... outside your floor!" I screamed in glee.

"Oh!" he said coldly. "Don't you have work or something?"

"How is she here?"

"She? She who?"

"Mitali."

"Oh, there's some mistake. She isn't here. You are daydreaming. Get a coffee and be on your way."

"Dude!" I shouted in irritation. "Out with it!"

"Alright, I understand. I am as surprised as you are. She hasn't spoken a word since morning. I didn't tell you on purpose," he said. "I don't want you to keep any hopes of any sort. When it's over, it's over. It's dead; let it stay dead. We are living people. And don't you come in to meet her or anything. Keep some self-respect, you crawling worm. Get lost," he said, ending the call.

I was way happy, though. I looked at her intently; she was trying to act normal. As I turned, I saw Prabhu standing right beside me.

"You would never learn, would you?" He gave me the look of a policeman.

"Something isn't right. She shouldn't be here," my voice expressed concern.

"Maybe, but it means nothing to you now. Don't contact her; don't attend her calls. Right?"

I said nothing and moved back.

○ ● ○

That evening, I pinged Joanne for some small talk.

'Are developers cold people, Joanne?'

'Not at all. Why do you ask?' She pinged back.

I wrote back.

'There is this developer lady I like, who writes incredible codes just like you but is insanely cold to me. We were previously together for a short period of time.'

For a moment, there was no reply.

'What do I do?' I asked again.

It took another moment.

'Make her see the bug in her logic. If at all she's a good developer, she'll probably change☺'

I smiled. *'That's easier said than done.'*

'If there is a bug, I am sure you would find it.' That was sweet of her!

'There's a small complication.'

'There always is...' she wrote.

'This is different. She has always been committed to someone else.'

'Woah, wait a sec... are you telling me she still displayed interest in you?'

'Well, yes.' I hesitated.

'Dude, what happens if we plug in a bug-ridden code into our running programs?'

'Code bombs in production. The entire thing crashes.' I stated cautiously.

'Well, why then, my dear friend, do you still want to plug her into your life?'

I was stunned, completely out of words.

'Give it a thought, Ami. C ya,' She replied and logged out.

12.

January '08:

Mitali's version:

My first day back wasn't easy. It never is.

The latest news was that Yahoo might lay off around 1000 employees as it had failed to clock the requisite performance in the last quarter.

Things feel cold, people feel cold to you, and even the weather was cold. I felt sick inside and left early, in a couple of hours. It was difficult to say if I was feeling unwell or angry or depressed or frustrated or, well, all of the above.

The second day was even worse.

My project manager had an inkling of what might have happened, probably! He gave me weird looks, and the teammates who knew about my plans gave me curious glances.

I hadn't received any assignments by then. So, I went to meet Shankar—the team lead. He promised me one by lunch. I purposely didn't look at Prabhu. I didn't want to see his reactions— as a rule, he was way too unsubtle to surprises, and I wasn't in the mood for any more dramatics.

I was also sure he would have within seconds passed this message to his good-for-nothing pal yesterday itself, and I was afraid of way more drama from him. It is tiresome after a while.

So, I spoke little and just concentrated on reading the articles. I didn't want to see anyone or talk to anyone about anything!

I skipped lunch; didn't feel like being in a sea of people chattering and munching. It would have drained me more. The less the people talk to me, the better it is.

As promised, by afternoon, I had an assignment. I worked on it slowly, taking my time to try to enjoy it a little, while at it. It was far too traveled a road—all the nooks and corners were known. That meant the joys were few, yet I nibbled on it simply because it took my mind away from my thought demons.

Neeraj hadn't called or messaged. He had been completely aloof. What was the truth? More importantly, did I still care about it? He had left me to imagine a version for myself. I smirked! I had lost interest in shifting to Delhi. It's a different matter that one shouldn't let go of an opportunity so great, but somewhere the spark was lost. Most importantly, I didn't have it in me to see *him* again.

My hand stopped typing for a while, and it shook, as I took a moment to sigh deeply to let go of my frustration at doing something so mind-numbingly dull.

It's fucking frustrating, and I felt guilty. I didn't feel like facing Ami. I would end up betraying myself. I shouldn't be in this place—doing the same work, facing the same people, and living the same life. That wasn't the plan. It wasn't supposed to go this way.

Then I did something I had done a few times over the years. I got up and walked to Tanmay's cubicle to meet the same old monster. It was unpleasant to see that face again.

Tanmay Mukherjee had been the project manager of *INSITE* for the last 1.5 years. He was promoted and shifted to *INSITE* from some other project. Though supremely analytical and strong in technology, he was largely non-existent for us beyond the KRA discussions and leave approvals. Technically, the team lead was enough for all our needs.

He was working on something. I just stood there for a while and asked, "Tanmay, can I talk to you for a moment?"

He looked up and smiled, "Sure, Mitali. Pull a chair."

I pulled up a chair and smiled at him. "Tanmay, as you know, I have been part of *INSITE* for quite a while..."

He interrupted me, "Three years, correct?"

"4 years and 11 months."

"Okay, great... continue."

"Yes so..." I collected my thoughts. "So, I am sure I was retained because I was good at what I was doing. It has been a great experience."

"Yes?"

"But now there comes a stage where one reaches a saturation point in terms of learning. Nothing is unknown. So, it would be great if you could involve me in the development aspect of a project that is both challenging as well as necessary for a senior person like me to remain engaged."

"I am slightly confused. What about that opportunity we had a talk about?"

"It..." It took me a while to say that. "It didn't work out!"

"Hmmm," he smiled at me. "You should have started with that. Come, let's grab a coffee."

He swiped his card at the machine and got us coffees. "Coffees these days aren't so great, are they?"

I couldn't agree more. "It's way too strong and burnt. One coffee is enough to get acidity," I shared my honest opinion.

"Yeah, earlier coffees were simpler and better-tasting," he said, holding his cup. "Okay…"

I cut the small talk. "I have been following this request for quite some time now. I had been asking Gagan (the earlier project manager) before you joined. He asked me to keep my patience and upgrade my knowledge. It's been a struggle, but I kept reading various technologies to gain perspective. I have read Java, Dot-Net, and C++. I am sure I have cracked the exams that happened. I aced technology certifications that I did from my pocket—just so that I get an opportunity to work on the next step of technology, which is coding. I have learned all there is to learn in testing."

"I see." He seemed stuck for words. "I know you are great at technical skills. It's the other skills I am worried about."

I was flabbergasted. "What other skills?"

"Team skills. You don't seem to gel well with the people around you. That is one of the reasons you never became a team leader, despite your seniority."

"People around me keep changing, Tanmay. I do talk to my team and all. But we have very different mindsets, and I find it difficult to make small talk." Then suddenly, an idea clicked. "But if you think so, maybe I could be trained on it. Besides, I didn't want to be a team leader; all I ever wanted was better work."

Managers, normally, are sentimental about trainings. They find it extremely empowering to facilitate the development of team capabilities.

"Fine, hmm," he said, taking another sip and pondering. There was nothing to ponder, except maybe the training cost, which is another sentimental area for managers.

"Tanmay, I believe there is a new project coming up in the embedded healthcare device programming domain that needs C++ developers, business analysts, and Java developers to a degree. If you could shift me to that project..."

"It's not coming."

"What?" I reacted rather indecently.

"Well, yes, it went to IBM Bangalore."

Another opportunity gone!

"Our rates were the reason?"

"Nope, our experience, infrastructure set-up *(which we lack!)*, cost, and technical skills portfolio were the issues. There simply isn't enough that we bring to the table to secure new projects."

Now it all made sense...

"Oh, so that's why the organization took this exam for assessing and improving the technical skills of people!"

"Yes, there is no customer demand without a strong technical team in the current scenario. People who aren't strong in the domain or technical knowledge aren't useful to the org anyway; clients won't pay for them. They are being replaced or removed. We need knowledge and experience and may not necessarily have the time or resources to invest in people for ramp-up. People in the current ongoing development projects are well-trained and settled, so...yes," he said, taking an awkward pause.

We took another sip. "So, about my request?"

He finally looked me in the eye. "We need you here in this role, Mitali, as we decided and you agreed upon during our last chat, at least for now. If something crops up, be certain; we will let you know."

Would that day ever come? Frustration welled up inside me. It was an empty commitment.

"But... how long, Tanmay? How long? I keep coming and keep getting rejected. These conversations are not new to me. I have 5 long years of these conversations behind me."

"This isn't a rejection. You are safe here. Right now, all we want is to cut the dead weight and sustain ourselves. Think about floating for now. With time, your demands will be considered."

He was in no mood to do anything about it. I guess all he was concerned about was not moving the set pieces too much lest they get noticed by clients; if clients do notice, they won't pay. Ultimately, clients shouldn't get pissed off due to all this migration of resources. All this was fine, but what was my mistake? Why me? I had reached a point where it was too much to take.

"Tanmay, I must confess..." I tried hard to control my words and pitch. "I am seriously uncomfortable and extremely discontented with my work, and that too after trying so hard—so very hard—to ramp up my skills. Some of this is pretty unfair to me and my career. Management changed, but no one did enough to help." I hoped he could sense the pain in my words and eyes.

Instead, he decided to take it as an offense. There was an instant disconnect, and his tone changed too, as he spoke rapidly and in a matter-of-fact way.

"It is something that I can't help you with, Mitali. All I can do is explain the scenario and expect you to let sanity prevail for now. Being a senior person, you are expected to know that much."

I bit my lip, lest I abuse him, and drank the insult, hoping my high-strung nerves would cool down. If he was on a short fuse, so was I. I wished I could tell him that he wasn't doing me a favor. I wished I could say I was only asking for what was mine, rightfully mine—a fair opportunity to prove myself—something I had earned by slogging day and night on this project.

I wished I could ask him to be human, but then was it too much to ask of a techie who spends 12 hours a day watching a computer screen for years and probably lags in understanding of human dynamics? Look who's talking? I smiled at myself.

The coffee was over, and so was the conversation.

○●○

While returning, I saw Prabhu looking at me aghast, or maybe it was his normal way of reacting to someone's distress. He always would catch my vibes freakily well. Something about him, as I said, was very forgiving and relaxing. That aura could heal wounds, soothe the spirits, and was endearingly gentle on the nerves.

I walked to him and stood looking at his blank, horrified face. "Coffee?" I made an effort to smile in order to make him feel welcome in my company. It was a poor attempt; it just made him blink.

"Yes," I repeated sharply. "I am talking to you. Coffee?"

"Sure, why not?" He locked his desktop hurriedly and accompanied me.

"You want to come for a brisk walk up at the cafeteria?" I asked.

"I don't mind."

Ami's version:

I had been trying to concentrate, but I couldn't. Something just didn't feel right. It pained me to ignore it, so I messaged.

'Are you alright, Mitali? The thing is, I know you aren't in the best of spirits, and it bothers me. If you think a conversation will help, we should. Better still, why not meet?'

It took moments for her to reply.

'I am great. There is absolutely nothing that you need to worry about. I don't want to talk about anything, and it would be much better for both of us if we never meet again.'

'Look, I know this...all of this. But you must understand, I just want you to be really, really happy. ☹ I messaged as I wiped a tear. I expected no reply back, but it came.

'If you really want me to be happy, don't ever contact me again! I mean it...'

Cruelty!

'You know, you would never be able to understand me. I would have never hurt you. Ever. What's with meeting once? I would take care not to say or do anything that hurts. Please ☹?*'* My hand shook as I typed. My helplessness was getting the better of me. I steadied myself and messaged again, *'Fine. I won't contact you now. But you know what? I deserve better than this!'*

Why must she abuse her power over me all the time? That was it, then.

I messaged Prabhu soon afterward, telling him about the incident.

His response was typical.

'Let her go, buddy. You have your whole life ahead of you. Why waste it on someone like her? Find someone else. Move on.'

I mean, I understand the logic of it, but it doesn't stick. I was angry with myself as I suffered in silence, exasperated with my clinginess as the tears wouldn't stop.

The mobile vibrated again. It was her message.

'Yes, you do!! So, do you let go of me now?'

I smiled sadly and messaged...

'Is there anything left to let go of, ma'am?'

Mitali's version:

We walked leisurely to the lift and then to the cafeteria, hardly chatting. We then stood at the terrace parapet, drinking tea and watching the traffic.

"How do you do?" Prabhu whispered.

"Alright." I politely smiled, avoiding his gaze.

It was approaching evening, and the highway in front of our building was buzzing with traffic—the road was flooded with red from the reflection of the taillights of the cars leaving the offices.

"Neeraj got a new car?"

"What makes you ask?" I asked heatedly.

"Nothing. I think you mentioned it in passing before leaving."

"Oh. I might have. Yes, it's a Honda."

"Hmm," he nodded. "So, you miss Ami anytime?"

Such an inappropriate question to ask—no respect for tact.

"Nope." I kept looking at the cars doggedly.

"Ahh, it's alright," he shrieked comically and tossed his paper cup off the terrace. "He's an easy guy to forget. Good for you!"

That wasn't the case, but I kept quiet as my attention went elsewhere.

"Yes?"

"The cup! The damn cup. Stop throwing it around," my eyes flashed with a hint of explosive anger.

His eyes went sad. "I wonder when people will learn to only consider things that really matter and leave out the rest... So, what did Tanmay say?"

I was surprised to see him catch the drift of my thoughts, or had he been monitoring?

"Nothing."

"Is he allowing you to move yet?"

"Delhi is over," I said with finality.

It surprised him.

"On the personal front too?"

"Yup."

He didn't probe it further, but I think he understood without asking.

"So, you want to shift to development?"

"That was the idea. I can't go on the backfoot now, can I? I have 5 years behind me. Can't start afresh. Means nothing to the organization though...no easy opportunities in sight, they say."

"Right," he sighed.

No one spoke for a moment.

"He missed you a lot!" he said slowly. "Hope you know."

"I do," I said, feeling that twinge of guilt again.

"It would make him feel awfully nice if you... you know... let him help you. He wouldn't misbehave. I would explain him not to. He would be alright."

"There is no turning back, Prabhu. There's no hope for us now."

He turned to look at me with disapproval.

"Oh, come on, isn't life all about hope? Without hope, there wouldn't be any reason left to live. Do you love him enough to make an effort at least?"

I sighed and turned away.

"I invested too much of myself in Neeraj... didn't work out. Now see, I am broken and scarred and... and Ami is the last person who deserves me like this." I spoke with whatever integrity I was left with. It hurt to speak. "And yet, for some moments, I wonder if I should go back to him, might help reduce the trauma he's going through... just to help..."

He interrupted me and smiled. "You *don't* love him! I was afraid of this. It's not about Neeraj."

"...But maybe being together would heal the ache..." I went on.

"*Now don't do that... Don't do that at all.* Why would you want that? Half a mercy never helps." He took a deep breath to let go of his bottled-up anxiety, even as he avoided my eyes. "If you are so sure you don't love him, then it's not going to work; please *do not* talk to him. Please don't show him hope, you see... such a hope will hurt... and don't worry about breaking his heart. There's no nice way of breaking a heart, I mean. It's got to hurt. Let it hurt, then. It's already broken as it is; what do you care? Leave him and let him live as well. That's the best you can do to help him. After all, why should anybody run after mirages? Tell me, at what price for him?"

I gulped down my emotions as I stood helplessly by his side, completely alone and lost.

"I just want this pain to end," I muttered, and before I knew it, I broke down. "My life is messed up... completely! I ruined it. I have failed at everything."

I used my hanky to cover my eyes. They get red way too easily. Prabhu looked at me with incredible empathy, but he didn't try to comfort me. In moments like these, I wish I could hug Ami—a *good for nothing* guy but someone who loved me. I had never been loved that completely, ever!

It's too sad that we weren't meant to be.

"Call your parents to stay with you for a while," he said.

"Yeah, right," I smirked. Not everybody is born with such strong support systems.

Prabhu's eyes were wide with pain as he tried to feel it.

"You know I have something that will help reduce your pain. It isn't the most recommended of the ways, but it is instant."

I blinked at him incredulously.

The mobile in my hand beeped.

'Are you alright, Mitali....' It was Ami.

I smiled sadly. Life is full of such cruel quirks; sometimes it's important to be unkind in order to be kind.

He would be much better off without me, just like everyone else who managed to save themselves from being dragged down by not being there for me when I needed them. I need not burden anyone now.

○ ● ○

I reached home in a trance and found myself aimlessly wandering my place, touching my things and books gently. Probably ate nothing that night, don't remember.

I was in pain with an unbearable emptiness and numbness churning inside that had nothing to do with starvation.

After a while, I sat down on the bed deep in thought and searched for what the future held for me, or was it all hopeless? A black cloud of meaninglessness seemed to emerge. When no answer came to my mind, I got up and paid rent to my owner uncle that night itself.

Finally, as I rested on the sofa, I opened my bag.

○ ● ○

Sometime that night, I lay on the floor watching the flowers fall down the jasmine tree. I could see them through my open door. They fell randomly without any noise, but that silence was deafening, almost intolerable. I would have loved to have a chosen one of them for my hairline! Damn, it's such a drag to get up for a lazybones like me. The ground was cold, and it only grew colder with time. At some point in time, though, I realized it didn't matter! That chill was beautiful and pure, just like those flowers!!

13.

Ami's version:

It was a disturbed sleep, full of an ever-growing, little understood anxiety that had me drenched in an ever-increasing sweat. As if something wasn't quite right, as if something horrible was on the cards.

My morning was disturbed by a phone call from Prabhu. He was shrieking, but I mumbled to him to be quiet and that we would talk later. Mornings were for passionate clinginess to sleep as the sand of time slid away with every snooze of the alarm clock. I would hate bidding goodbye to the temptress in my eyes, not this soon...

He called me up again, but all he did was shriek incoherently; maybe it was due to my sleepiness or his nervousness.

"Please don't shout," I said, trying to calm him down. "Slowly, buddy, one word at a time... yes... try... yes... you can do it." I woke up and sat on the edge of the bed with a heavy head.

He stopped, and I could hear his heavy breathing on the phone. "*MITALI!*" he said.

"Yes?" I spoke. At least now I knew the topic of the conversation. I got up very slowly to fetch my brush and toothpaste.

"She is... no more!" he sighed.

"Excuse me??" The brush fell into the basin.

"Dead... yes," he repeated in a super-calm voice now. "Don't freak out. Be calm."

I had lost my words. I just stood clutching that instrument, praying for a kinder word from the other side.

"Are you okay?" he repeated in that voice, which felt like that of a newsreader reporting the morning news of a thousand deaths in Afghanistan in a pleasant tone.

"Buddy, are you alright?" He asked loudly this time, honking me back to consciousness. "I am coming to your place right now. Details when we meet. Don't try anything stupid. In fact, I am on the way already and have called you from the auto. Don't play the TV."

I just went back to bed and closed my eyes, hoping my world would black out too. It was important not to think anything, and sure enough, after what felt like a thousand years, I heard the sound of the doorbell.

○●○

In half an hour, Prabhu ensured a million times that I don't cut myself, that I stay away from anything sharp, from electricity, and even from my own shoelaces. He got me ready, and I hadn't asked him a single question, so he chattered ceaselessly about something

I don't remember a word of. I wondered how he could manage to get so much material to speak of, under the circumstances.

"First things first, check if there are any missed calls from her number."

As I checked with shaking hands, there were some 10 missed calls from Prabhu in the last hour, and thankfully, none from her.

"I want to see her." I mumbled foggily.

"Good! We will... but priorities first. Would you like to dig into a hot, smoldering cup of tea? To help you with the shock!"

○ ● ○

We sat in a café at around 11.30 a.m., where he ordered tea for both of us. I watched out the window, dazed. Seeing people move gave some hope to my diverted mind that the gravity of the situation wouldn't sink in. Tea felt good against the throat.

"One more?" he asked.

I waved my head slowly in denial.

"Say something," he said softly.

"No," I croaked in reply to the previous question.

I never asked him the details, but he still started as if it was the first thing on my mind.

"She is no more. The body was found this morning at around 7 a.m. Strangely, the door was open; her house owner discovered her unconscious. She was rushed to a hospital but was declared spot-dead. The exact reason for her death is not yet known, but it's a suicide. They have found a suicide note."

He paused to look at my facial expressions. They hadn't changed.

"It's in the news. A couple of people messaged me as well," he said, just to clarify he wasn't imagining things again.

It was in the news, alright! It played ruthlessly on and on—a software engineer was found dead at her place, unable to deal with the job stress; she committed suicide.

"And there's a complication," Prabhu said meekly.

"Yes?" What can be more complicated than this?

"I might be responsible!!"

"Huh??"

"Yes!"

"What the..." I said, standing up.

"Sit down," he said in a panic-stricken, heavily controlled tone that cracked at the seams. "We are in this together, man! Don't you dare desert me!"

He was on the brink of insanity, and I reminded myself not to make any sudden movements lest he blows up.

"She was under tremendous pressure yesterday, so I gave her weed for the night. If she had it, she would be in a dissociative state. I don't know what she did later, but now she's dead!! I don't know what triggered her. Never for a moment, I felt she would do this," he said, looking deep into my eyes and clutching my hand, putting his integrity behind every single word.

I looked at him with awe.

"Tell me what to do now. The exact steps!" he said with wide eyes full of panic and fear. "If you say shit, I shit."

I wanted to shout at him and strangle him with my bare hands. I wanted to tell him to go die. "What do you want to do?" I asked, clutching my forehead. "Okay, first, calm down and let us both breathe.

Why can't I breathe, dammit?" I was having an overwhelming urge to puke.

The newsreader carried on mercilessly…

'…*These suicides are increasingly being associated with high levels of stress in the software industry, which people find difficult to cope with. Extended work timings, competition, insecurity at the job, politics, stringent deadlines, as well as family and financial pressures for quicker growth, are leading to such stress levels. There has been a slew of suicides in the past few months as the severity of the recession keeps on increasing. The changes in the ever-dynamic software industry and client interactions are also contributors. It sure looks like the high salaries aren't without their share of tension. The pattern is witnessed more in ambitious age groups of 24–30 who are at the crossroads of major decisions in their lives while expecting ideal outcomes…*'

Then there was a local politician in his sixties who shared his opinion on the incident when interviewed by a reporter outside his

428 | The Little Men

office: *'At this age, everything gone wrong in life seems like the end of the world; it wasn't so in our generation. This generation is way too fast in expecting growth. There is a false sense of urgency, which is a byproduct of these materialistic times.'*

Another invited interviewee, a psychiatrist, added, *'Sometimes the tendencies are always present. Stress just contributes to the last step. The said girl was possibly clinically depressed for quite a while...'*

It had all stopped making sense to me. It all seemed so hyper-real— things that couldn't possibly be happening with me, yet they were. Every person who gave up was a different person. Insanity must be having its own individual reasons.

She was a rational being, not an emotional fool like us. Why did she do it?

The newsreader, meanwhile, went on, *'... The surprising element is the suicide note. It was a cryptic message:* **'And sometimes the pain belittles our joys!!'***... Nothing else did the note say.'*

My heartbeats weakened with tension. Prabhu stopped my chain of thoughts.

"Do you think there is a need to worry? Will they reach me?" he asked, massaging his heavy heart.

I just clutched my forehead and concentrated on breathing properly. At some point in time, her loss was going to sink in, leading to devastating emotional ramifications.

But till then, just breathe my boy!!

○ ● ○

We didn't go home or to the office, but we did visit her lane to find it hounded by the police. Her place was quarantined. I never could catch up with her parents—would never know how they looked. I wondered if Neeraj was around, but I didn't see anyone like him. I also couldn't see her one last time!

○ ● ○

That evening Prabhu met me for snacks at the cafeteria with wide, confused eyes.

"Everyone is scared, mate. They had an urgent meeting this afternoon. The company is paying for *INSITE* project people to see a psychiatrist, apparently to help us."

"Finally..." Too little, too late.

"Nothing of that sort." He came closer and started whispering. "It's just... if you ask me, it's just that they just want to see who's at what level of insanity, and if somebody seems susceptible to suicide, they will remove that person immediately. This has been such a scandal for the company. Don't trust anybody!" he said with weird delusional eyes looking around him with paranoia.

I pressed his hand to comfort him, as we both promised each other we wouldn't try anything stupid. It made my tummy churn, but to be able to survive this, it would be important not to let it get to you.

○●○

As I reached home, my cousin confronted me.

"Hey, do you know a person from your company committed suicide?" he asked, munching on his chips.

"Yes." I said gruffly.

"You knew her?"

"Kinda. She was a friend's friend."

"Oh," he didn't speak for a few moments. "So, any idea what went wrong?"

"Not really," I said, lying on the bed and closing my eyes. He had a wish to discuss the matter, so he hovered by my bed for a minute.

"Must be the recession. Anyway..." He fetched his diary. "You got to pay me 1150 bucks for the maid's salary. Here's the calculation. 150 extra for you this time; you borrowed from me last month and never paid it back."

"Hmm, fine," I said without opening my eyes. I couldn't remember when I borrowed that amount. Just go away, I prayed!!

"And you are to clean the bathroom as well, this time. It's way dirty," he added.

"Sure."

He scratched his potbelly and left the room. Ordinary people with ordinary thoughts!

What was wrong with it, you say? It had the stench of a rut. It smelled of falling in line and the death of all ideas. Yes, it reeked of death—of me and of her.

I closed my eyes to blacken the world.

Something inside me was rebelling. I wanted to tear apart my cover, my limitations, and the boundaries and break every single rule devised by man and applied to humans—just to defy those stupid conventions.

And before I leave, I wanted to burn down the whole office building. I would burn it all, and I would make sure all the assholes burn with it, the low-minded, high-browed, good-for-nothing, back-enders—people who believed in controlling the lives of people they were responsible for, by being jerks and by abusing their privileges.

I hated my new work, I hated my old work, and I hated myself. I had lost everything, forever!

And for good or for bad, she shouldn't have left like that. She didn't once think about how I would take it. I deserved it—some consideration, some thought. I bloody did! She just gave up and left me alone. There's only so much a man can take!

'What's fucking wrong with you? Why can't you let it go? Just relax, will you?' In my dreams, I heard Prabhu yell, *'She never loved you, and now she's dead.'*

But then I distinctly heard her whispering in my ears, asking for my leave. I knew it was a dream, but it was so vivid it made me cry, and I said I wouldn't let her go. I flatly refused.

She smiled and kissed my cheek, but she went away, nevertheless.

I woke up crying, and then I just wept inconsolably till morning. For all the pain she inflicted on me, I loved that damn woman, and she just never truly got that!

Life isn't fair, but will it stop boasting about it for once?

I despised her for leaving me alive for witnessing this day—a day without her.

It was betrayal and abandonment of the highest order.

○●○

By morning, my decision was made. There was nothing to learn from the new project. This ramp-up for being a buffer in both projects was way too much effort, and I was no longer interested. It was unfair. There was but one thing left to do.

I woke up early to see, for probably the first time, the horizon looking beautiful with the early morning lights. As I stood by my window, mesmerized, I wondered why on earth I would miss that every morning.

It felt important not to sleep now. It felt important to get ready and reach the office on time.

I walked to my desk in a hurry and opened my computer, waiting impatiently as the Lotus notes replicated, bringing in new mail. There was one from an id *'gonewiththewind@yahoo.co.in'*. Lotus was meant to filter spam, so I opened it, hoping it wouldn't be one.

The mail literally blew my socks away. I hurried to call Prabhu's extension; he wasn't there. He wouldn't be—more than half of the office would be sleeping at 9 a.m.

It was an email from Mitali.

'Dear Ami,

    It starts thus:

> *I feel life receding with every breath I take,*
> *My heart freezing and darkness seeping in,*
> *I hope pain will be gone with hope this time,*
> *As I still search for some happiness, in the void within!!*

I wonder, if life could be given another try,

But then aren't memories cruel, cruel butterflies?

They are pretty, but can one be truly happy as they chase?

And sometimes the pain belittles our joys!!

The entire poem is just for you!

You know the last hour is a funny hour. It's strangely empowering and peaceful. I experienced freedom for probably the first time. But one doesn't know what to do with the time.

So yeah, I thought of calling my parents but didn't feel like it.

Thought of calling Neeraj, but he isn't worth it.

He doesn't love me. You were right!! So, it's fair that you know this.

I wanted to abuse my boss, but this phone call would ruin his life, so I didn't.

So, I spent my last hour writing a poem. You always wanted me to write one, didn't you? This would be my first and final attempt at poetry... hope it's decent☺. Be kind!

This poem, you see, is dedicated to you!!! It's for you!

I wanted to call you but then thought that you would be sleeping and would get worked up later. I know you!

Yet, you deserved a goodbye; after all, in your own words, everything that started right needs to end right.

I don't want to go into why I am doing what I am doing.

Biased as you are, you might never be able to make sense of why I had to go; besides, I am not so sure I can explain it myself!

Remember that scary dream of mine?

Let's just say the walls of my room caved in on me, and I couldn't open that bloody door in time! It's alright, I guess. It's okay to not know all the answers! There are many answers I have searched for all my life without any luck.

But this isn't supposed to be an excuse; I am sorry, really am!

Ami, is it fine if we leave it at that? Since we both know that we will always disagree on this☺!

I spent the last several minutes thinking of you.

Strange for me, it seems you did mean something after all ☺. I can say this with whatever little hope I can feel inside me. As you rightly said, we would always have a million things to say to each other, but somewhere all this, all of this, needs to end on a happy note... **for you***!!*

P.S:

And please tell Prabhu that the stuff he gave me tastes like dogshit and, in all probability, is dogshit, so I didn't take it. It's strange how low life has brought me!!

I am taking an overdose of my anti-depressant pills... am afraid of my body not getting found for days, so keeping the door open. Keep this mail private but use it in case of trouble.

By the way, try to leave caffeine; it makes you jumpy. At the same time, don't take it ultra-seriously as my last wish or anything, just saying ☺... hate these postscripts but things just keep popping up in my head.

Follow your heart, Ami; it knows its way to happiness!!! It was great knowing you too. I hope you find that magic again. Try not to forget me, and yet you must. I would want you to! Just for once, dear... do not look back :) ciao ☺

Yours,

Mitali '

I sat stunned for what seemed like an hour. She had auto-timed the mail.

It's strange how people care! She took pains to try to make it funny, but instead ended up making it creepy, and after reading something that creepy, she wanted me to move on. I chuckled as tears rolled down freely.

○●○

Moments later, I drafted a mail keeping Kanchan and my HR Manager in CC.

'Dear Kanchan,

I want to quit my job in order to explore new opportunities.

Consider this my first day of the notice period.

It was great working with you. I will always remember gladly all the things I learned from you and the team.

Thanks & Regards,

Amitarth '

There! Simple! I knew Kanchan wouldn't take it well, not in this situation. I locked my computer and went up to the cafeteria for a breakfast alone. I didn't feel like facing her.

That's when the phone rang: *'Please meet me asap.'*

And moments later, *'And please don't leave before meeting me!'*

Present Hour.

On returning, it was funny to see Kanchan look at me with blazing eyes, but I was too tired to care. I had no energy left to feel nervous.

Prabhu called me a couple of times, but I didn't pick up. There wasn't much to talk about anymore. My resignation would freak him out, and if not, Mitali's mail most certainly would. Kanchan came by my place for a word.

"I received your mail." Her voice was tinged with sentiment. "What's with the sudden decision, huh? By the way, are you alright? Your eyes are really red."

"Yes, I am perfectly fine, Kanchan." I tried to smile at her.

"Let's have a chat for a while after lunch," she patted me and left.

"You wouldn't be able to ask for leave during the notice period. Do you know this?" said Piyush after the initial rush of their surprise receded at coffee. "You should have taken leaves and then resigned."

"Did she say anything about the notice period? Or is it the usual three months?" Raj asked, concerned.

"No idea. The discussion is after lunch," I said.

"Hmm, be assertive, and don't over-justify. Say whatever you feel like," he said with a supportive smile. "And after you are done with her, make sure the assignments reach me before the status call."

"Of course!" I sighed. The show must go on!

○●○

"So, you are leaving!?" It took an effort for her to smile. We were in the conference room having the mandatory exit interview—an opportunity for her as the project manager to convince me to rethink.

I nodded.

"What happened?"

"Would the notice period be of three months?"

"You shouldn't be worried about the notice period and all. What about the dependencies on you, Amit? We can't just let you go," she said in a hurt tone, as if it were outrageous to think she would take it that easy.

I smiled.

"You have Bhoopal and Suman. I guess now might be the time to call them back."

"Hmm," she said, taking a moment to ponder. "I didn't tell you something. Bhoopal is out, officially! He put down his papers a while back, and I have accepted them. It's been two weeks, almost. He is not interested in participating in the inspection process."

I was stunned.

"And Suman?"

"Suman is there. Let me ask him if he's interested," she said, nodding in agreement.

"Glad!!" I was happy. This might improve his chances of getting a decent girl, but that reminded me of JD, and I couldn't help but sigh.

"Let me see," she said, leaning forward on the table. "So, tell me, why this hurry to leave? That too, now?"

I didn't respond. It felt nauseating. What prompted me? Mitali's death? Money? Pay? Frustration? No onsite?

"I want to explore new opportunities."

"Yes, I read that in the mail," she smiled. "There are none! What is it really about?"

"I would take some time out to prepare for higher studies."

"And what will you study?"

"MBA."

"But isn't the *CAT* exam done for the year?"

"I will start preparing anyway."

"What's the matter? Done with technology?" she smirked.

"Yes," I said unapologetically.

"Just because I didn't let you shift to development?" she smiled.

"Yes," I repeated.

"I couldn't do that. It isn't my fault. It's the recession," she shrugged, looking at me wonderstruck. "Besides what did you do to prove yourself?"

"Hmm, maybe," but where was the time left for me to prove myself after such strenuous assignments?

"This is immature. We are in the business of managing a business. When will you understand, for God's sake?"

"Is all this just about building a business?" I asked.

"What else?"

"When will we transcend?"

"Excuse me?"

"You heard me."

"Why should we? Requirements govern our decisions."

"I mean, we definitely built a knowledge organization here, but when will we build a knowledge culture? There are people who are genuinely interested in programming for the love of it. This curiosity is not always based on business requirements. Why should business requirements be a bottleneck for creativity or innovation? Why should interest suffer?"

"Where are we taking this?"

I paused for a moment to let her query gather gravity.

"Why are we content being an outsource service provider?"

She sighed.

"You know the answer. It's profitable, and that's how we get business based on the cost-benefit we provide."

"Well, no wonder then that we are affected by the recession to this extent. Our dependency on clients and their business *'requirements'* is too high." I continued.

"Obviously, because these businesses need external agencies to do some work for them that isn't core to their organization," she smiled smugly.

"Why the f... sorry... heck, are we happy being in that role is what I am asking? Does sustainability not appear anywhere in the equation? How many *Finnacle*s did we innovate in the past several years? Can we generate business? Can we be pioneers in something? Anything?"

"And why on earth would we need that?" she asked, frowning.

"Why wouldn't we? Why couldn't an idea like Google have originated in the Indian software industry? Why are there research labs separately, but programmers or people with interests are prohibited from thinking or getting in motion? Is the frustration in people because somewhere we are trying to control their minds and the natural instinct for intellectual growth? Have we built a culture where ideas flourish? Where innovations happen?" I continued. "For example, why shouldn't a person be given an opportunity to cross-learn? Is it possible for one to just walk into another project and learn? Shouldn't there be a programmer's club in the organization where everybody can learn and participate, and interested people are rewarded with off-the-hook projects for the development of something innovative? Innovation can't prosper unless people cross-learn and learn from each other. The human mind is too rebellious to stay happy doing just one technical aspect of a job all its life, Kanchan. I wish you would get that. The mind would want to see the other side too, and it would want dreams and challenges. Doing similar kinds of assignments all my life is not why I did my engineering. There's so much innovation happening globally but we are nowhere. Must we compromise on the quality and the level of work we do to survive, as a rule?"

"In the ideal world..."

I didn't let her finish her sentence.

"The world isn't ideal. But how organizations deal with their resources during a calamity tells a lot about their culture. If business requirements govern everything, then we will never be able to rise above them, and one day the business requirements will ask us to die and become irrelevant. Present jobs are because clients don't need the best, just something cost-effective. But then, who guarantees the irreplaceability, the indispensability? When do we revolutionize the innovation industry? When will we be on the cutting edge? When will we be allowed to do the first level of thought?"

"Hmm, there are these aspects present in our industry even now. There are people working on innovative projects. It's not all rotten," she said, playing with her hair.

"That's an assumption. We don't even know. Shouldn't the genuine interest of one person be enough? Why should there be just a chosen few somewhere trying to make headway in innovation? Are ideas a monopoly of select heads? The real question is, why can't it be a culture? And forget innovation; why not go for invention? Something new altogether that can really impact the world."

"And what about everyday work?" She looked at me with a continuous smile. "Who will do that?"

I smiled as well, just to match hers.

"We want to do good work and earn good money while doing it. Is it too much to ask? Tell me, why can't so-called top-notch companies in India take up building the next-gen operating system? Do we not have enough engineers, enough infrastructure, enough bandwidth and enough time? Right now, we all are slaves to the business. At this very moment, there are a number of people on the bench, Kanchan. Can they not participate in such activities? And do we not want people to rise above their projects in learning? If not, then why the hell do we have these exams to test our knowledge, and how the hell do we expect to get more business based on our knowledge? Why do we expect people to be knowledgeable when we do not value knowledge?"

"We do..."

"We don't. A person getting fired for not having knowledge is a negative reinforcement; instead, a person getting rewarded for having knowledge is positive. Is interest rewarded? Tell me that. We can only perform at our best if we work without fear."

She didn't immediately reply.

"Look, I don't run this organization," she said, frowning. "Neither do you. So, all this is hocus-pocus as far as we are concerned."

"That's accepted. We all are just small wheels, mere mortals, but respecting an idea, a curiosity can indeed make a difference."

She chipped back. "But then, are all ideas important, Amit? Be truthful now. Even they need to be checked for their quality, subjectivity, and practicability."

It was humbling that question, but it was an obstacle I no longer intended to respect.

"Ideas and dreams are very useful, Kanchan. Flexibility is the backbone of a knowledge-based culture. People like to manifest themselves through an idea; look around you for live examples. Gandhiji did so with Satyagraha; Steve Jobs did that with designing." And inadvertently, as the images of Mitali and Prabhu floated at the back of my mind, I whispered solemnly, "And sometimes the death of an idea or of a dream is equivalent to the death of that person itself, in more ways than one. I will pray that the idea and dream of this industry never die!!"

No one spoke for a while.

"So do you have any other questions?" she asked. Her interest was waning.

"Lots of them. This may sound lofty, but don't you feel the IT industry is losing its one-shot opportunity to bring about a knowledge revolution in the country? We could have been so much more. And say, what do we plan to do if the recession keeps repeating year after year? Would we just be slipping deeper into the hole? Or would we ever be willing to take the bull of innovation by its horns? No other industry is so full of possibilities; we can have each kid coding at their homes; we can make them a treasure trove of product ideas even before they join us." My volume kept increasing, and so did my breathlessness.

She laughed broad-mindedly, maybe to indicate that she wasn't the best person to be asked such questions. She was a wife, a mother, a bread-earner, and my project manager—nothing else.

I grinned back.

"Okay, there's one—a very important one."

She sat attentively. "Go on."

I cleared my throat.

"Do I get leaves in the notice period?" I smiled.

She went in a thoughtful mood.

"No, but I will try to get the notice period reduced, since I clearly see you have lost your interest in continuing. No promises though!"

She couldn't let it go at that.

Concern resurfaced; she looked deep into my eyes and asked,

"Are you sure of what you are doing, Amit? It's impractical, sad, and suicidal in these times!"

I didn't have a good answer to that, but a man's got to do what he must do. There was no turning back.

"Thanks for your concern, Kanchan. Somehow, I just feel my heart's not in it anymore and I can't help it. I am sorry! Please just get Suman back, okay?" was all I could say. From the look in her eyes, I was sure Kanchan wondered if my mental health was sound.

As I threw my cup of coffee in the dustbin and as I tripped a couple of times over the conference phone wires in the room, I realized I was high on caffeine as usual, without even realizing it.

What did Mitali expect anyway? For all our best intentions, getting rid of such habits was never going to be easy.

That evening, Kanchan informed me on my leaving date. It was the same date I had joined a year earlier, with a notice period of approximately two months.

14.

February '08: GitHub founded.

The notice period is supposed to be like a honeymoon, yet often it is anything but. I slogged the most in my last months. Somehow, Kanchan ensured the pressure on me never waned. I was still given opportunities, a window into the soul of routine.

I worked as usual, in spells of ennui and creative outbursts. I avoided going home simply because of the fear of being alone. At night, I still suffered from sudden bouts of extreme longing for Mitali, leading to a collapse of my tear ducts, and I would weep inconsolably yet soundlessly for several hours till morning. I prayed the coldness in my heart would end.

I replied to her last email with J.M. Barrie's words.

'You know that place between sleeping and awake, that place where you can still remember dreaming? That's where I'll always love you. That's where I'll be waiting.'

She will be missed, I am sure, for the rest of my life!

Somehow, I was becoming even more of a recluse and had started avoiding Prabhu. I just didn't feel like seeing him. Everything about him reminded me of her; besides, his intentions towards me were questionable. I think he could get this; he never forced his company on me from that point on.

I had stopped writing, and he could sense it. *'There can be no creativity without happiness. Work it the other way around. Start writing.'* He would message.

The recession had stopped bothering me, and I would keep reading random articles and applying to the weirdest technical profiles from the company till late at night.

I informed my parents about the decision, and they weren't happy. They wanted me to work, stick with the organization, slog, and be unhappy for money. Unfortunately, that seemed like a difficult arrangement to me now. Whatever it was that I wanted, I was sure that continuing here wasn't it.

I still used to have lengthy philosophical chats with Joanne.

'You know there is no best way of writing a code—it can be written in several ways.' She would say, *'But there is always an optimum way of writing it—which consumes the least resources. Similarly, there is no one best way of living life, but there is an optimum way of living it—by being happy. Good code is just like life, Ami. Would you agree? You've got to stay happy, no matter what!'*

That was logic, alright! And just like it is with writing good code, I needed to practice.

○●○

It was a month now, and there was no news about my replacement. I had waited with patience and with bated breath. Finally, I received Suman's call one morning.

"Hey, Amit, how are you, buddy?" boomed his enthusiastic voice on the other end. It was still just as heartwarming.

"Yay!" I was happy.

"Can we meet in the cafeteria now? I mean, if you are free for a while," he asked. I could sense glee in his voice.

"You are in *FORDIT*?" I exclaimed.

"Absolutely!!!"

"So, Kanchan got you back?" Great news! I was delighted.

"Umm, no," he hesitated. "She did call me, but I declined the offer."

"Whyyyyy?" I screamed. "You need this!"

"Thanks, *re*. But the real reason I came was something else. I am leaving Pune. I got a job in analytics at an FMCG organization in Hyderabad. I will be shifting soon. I thought of meeting you guys before leaving," he said sheepishly. Fast moving consumer goods sector was still doing relatively well.

"Congrats!" I croaked as I felt the grief of parting ways again. My South-Indian friend was returning to South India.

"Umm, Amit, just one more thing," he said.

"Yes?"

"There's a lady with me. Try to behave yourself around her," he stuttered. "This lady is my wife!"

"Are you kidding me!?" I screamed at him.

"Just come up, will you? Get everybody along."

We all huddled up by the stairs as we didn't have the patience to wait for the lift.

Finally, as we stormed in, we saw him sitting at a table with a girl with pretty flowers in her hair. Raj took a moment to bend down to catch his breath, and I walked slowly towards them with the entire intention of punching Suman. To hell with his instruction to behave myself around her!

As I reached their table, they both looked at me, and I stared back in utter surprise. So did the others who stood with me.

"Holy Mother of God!" Raj screamed.

"Should I slap him, or will you from my side?" Yogi whispered as he stood next to me like a zombie.

"What's wrong with them?" Piyush also nudged me in shock.

"Are you guys for real?" I said, my voice wide with amazement, as we walked towards them, trying to smile. We had our hair standing on end.

He stood up to face us.

"Hey, are you not going to punch me or what? You can, I mean!" said Suman with his usual nonchalance. "But not here, guys; we have the lobby for that. Let's not embarrass ourselves."

He motioned at the lady dramatically. "Guys, meet Mrs. Nandamoori. Be polite, please. I have a good reputation with her."

And then our surprise just exploded.

"JD!!" we screamed as we hugged her.

"You bastard!" Yogi slapped Suman's back with a broad grin. "What did you do with my sister? What's all this?"

"We got married!" JD smiled ear to ear, her forehead all pretty with bindi and her hair with jasmine. She glowed in happiness. "We had a court marriage last week."

"And none of you felt it was important to invite us?" I asked.

"We didn't know how you guys would take it!" Suman said it smilingly. "And we were basically in a hurry."

"Yup, he wanted to shift in a week, and we decided to skip the pain of parting. I guess, I just can't stay away from this loser." She hugged him affectionately.

"Yup, sooner or later, we both will shift to Hyderabad anyway!" he said, smiling.

JD pulled him away. "Who the hell is shifting to Hyderabad?"

"I mean, we will, right? You are my wife now," he exclaimed, wide-eyed.

"Absolutely not, you idiot! We will shift to Kolkata with my father. For the time being, it's alright, and we'll get your grandmom to stay with us in Kolkata as well," she said with such dominance that only a wife can.

"Hell no, woman! We are going to listen to me. You keep forgetting who's the man here. You are my property now," he said, equally childishly. What a wrong note to hit!

"Hell, you would, you chauvinist pig! If you want me to be the mother of *your* children, you so bloody will!"

"Uh-oh," Yogi sniggered. "It looks like somebody skipped all the important discussions before marriage."

But I smiled happily. They both looked so brilliant together.

"Yeah, so we haven't told our parents yet. But who cares? We are just 26. They will take time, and what if they never accept? So, we simply got married. We have a lot of time to tell them. I could have waited, but Madam was in a hurry." Suman smiled carefreely.

"Good for you. What if my mood changes after going to Kolkata, huh?" she nudged him. "So, I kept delaying the whole plan of going back to Kolkata."

"You guys just love fighting with each other, don't you?" Piyush said it mischievously.

"But I don't get it. What about Sudeep?" I asked JD in private.

"I didn't feel that he could love me as much as my father could. Suman is the only guy who came close, you see. I guess something inside me would have died if I had let him leave," she said, her eyes sparkling with happiness and tears. "So yes, my father is still piling it up with Sudeep, but in a month, I am going to break that farce. Good, I didn't marry for the wrong reasons," she said proudly, glistening. She had gone softer after marriage. Her eyes looked at him with incredible affection. "I guess he will never earn as much as Sudeep, but he's still my man! We will make it work!"

Touchwood—I prayed for them. It's so great when people find that happiness in faith! Till the time they left, they were bickering over which city they would shift to, yet the only thing they were certain of was that they wanted to stay together forever—*the only thing that mattered!*

○ ● ○

In the afternoon, Kanchan informed me that they would look for a fresher to replace me or else some buffer from another project. But I guess they were no longer happy with buffers; they wanted a stable, complete resource for the project. Since the workload would go down a bit at the beginning of the year, it was possible to comfortably absorb my absence. It was better to include a fresher as a replacement, someone whose joining had got delayed due to the recession.

○ ● ○

There was an annual party arranged by the enthusiastic folks in our trainee batch to celebrate our work anniversary at *FORDIT*. A mail was sent to the common Yahoo group for all, and people were asked to confirm if they couldn't participate—default participation was expected.

It had been quite a year. We were the first batch to experience a recession in the recent times. We had our tiffs, but we had lost some of us as well—at least five by the last count, including Puru. It was time to re-bond and celebrate our times.

Somehow, people weren't in the mood to keep grudges. So, Bala and Sasi invited me twice to the party when I casually ran into them in the cafeteria. Rohit smiled at me in the lift, and Abhinav too started a conversation with me when we happened to meet at the cafeteria to inquire if I could make it. To top it off, they asked me if Prabhu could join as well. I hadn't been in active touch with him for quite a while now.

The economic slump was still going strong, and layoffs hadn't completely stopped. Maybe they never will from now on! The company was going to have regular examinations to ensure that people justified their retention.

○●○

I went up to meet Prabhu and to ask him about the party. There was still half a month until the event, but hey, we had a chance to regain some respect in the eyes of our fellow mates. It was an exciting prospect. He wasn't at his desk.

I waited a while, but he didn't show up. After a while, a person came by and occupied Prabhu's seat. He didn't know Prabhu. Nobody did. I felt my anxiety growing and looked around for a possible change in his location. He just wasn't there. I could tell that his aura was missing.

Things cleared up when I asked his PM, Tanmay. Prabhu had left the organization a couple of weeks ago based on the examination scores. He was asked to leave that very same day.

"But why, Tanmay? You could have put in a word," I cried at the manager.

"I wasn't too enthusiastic about it myself. He had gone too weird. Better to save someone else's job who respects it more," he said with a half-apologetic shrug.

I tried to call Prabhu, but the ring kept going. Thankfully, he hadn't switched off the phone. I had to take an early leave that evening to visit his place. By the time I reached his place, it was 8 o'clock in the night. He was no longer staying there.

He was gone!

I wouldn't deny that I was supremely disturbed. I kept calling and messaging him. By the time I reached my home, it was 10 p.m. at night.

My cousin waited at the door for some reason. "If you are leaving, give notice to the owner and clear your accounts with him before leaving."

Right! More notices. Somehow, I expected nothing more from him. I told him I had already done the needful.

○●○

At midnight, I was lying on my bed, feeling half empty and half awake, when I received a call from Prabhu's number.

"Hello!" said the solemn voice on the other end.

"Where the hell are you?" I inquired back.

"I'm at my sister's," he said, breathing heavily. "I had a faint hope you wouldn't find out I left."

"Good try! Except I tried to find you for the batch party we have on our anniversary. There's still half a month. You would come, right?"

"I may not be able to."

"Try at least."

"I am leaving for Bhubaneswar tomorrow."

"What...!!!!"

"Mother needs me, and I don't feel like staying back. It's impossible to find jobs. I have tried."

"You only tried for two weeks." I said, astounded.

"Yes, and I want to cut my losses. I will go to Bhubaneswar and try from there. My sis has no intention of keeping me with her, and I have no money to survive alone."

"How much do you need?"

"It doesn't matter anymore. I am leaving tomorrow afternoon," he said, his voice breaking with the expectation that he wanted to hide. "Try to come. No stress!"

"But with all these assignments..."

"I understand... I would love it if you could make it, though; maybe we can meet one last time! For old time's sake!" He sighed. "Don't stretch!"

We stayed silent for a long time on the call. It felt incredibly sad.

"Sure, dude," I said, clutching the phone and trying to control my fast-debilitating morale. "There is no way you are leaving without meeting me one last time."

The next day, after lunch, I left the office and arrived at the station half an hour before his train departure and called him.

"Come to *Comesum* restaurant on platform no. 1," he said. "My train's delayed by a couple of hours. Waiting for you."

I relaxed and took my own time to figure out the location.

I saw him sitting at a table with tea for us. He stood up to greet me.

"I thought I would never see you," he said, hugging me.

I hugged him back.

"How much time do you have?" he asked.

"Not very long."

He chuckled. "You look so scared. You are in the notice period, dumbo. Fuck it!"

"Can't. Status call at 5."

"So?"

"So, nothing," I said, drinking down my fear of possible absences and resulting conflicts.

"Yeah, right," he said, giving me an amused stare. "I am sorry!"

"I can't believe you were about to leave without telling me. I thought we were friends," I was furious.

"We are," he patted me. "Don't you ever question that. I just didn't feel like disturbing your hard-earned peace. You had finally gained some stability."

I smiled at him. "Hmm, how have you been doing?"

"I'm fine," said he. He didn't look fine. He looked battered and bruised. But if I knew him even a little by now, I could be certain he wouldn't let the topic stay.

"Would anyone believe I arrived at this station with so much hope a year back?" he reminisced looking back at the din of the platform.

"Didn't we all? I asked solemnly, "So, what now?"

"You say! Are you finally away from her thoughts?" he asked as he put his palm on mine.

I pulled my hand back.

"Oh, come on," he said, withdrawing his hand as well.

"Yeah, I will try to get a new girl, and everything will be alright," I said, trying to stress the point about my orientation. "And some more money, maybe."

"Life is not about money and sex. It can't be."

"True. But they do take up the most mental space," I said.

"Not for everyone. Have you learned nothing from the mess we got into? It's all about the things we decide to pursue. Spend life pursuing something worthy—every moment. Life is more about how one wants to live it. It's a conscious decision." He sighed. There was so much to say and so little time. "See, Ami, maybe you and I will never win a Nobel Prize or pass out of an IIM[23], and maybe we will never reach the impossible heights that we and our parents want us to reach. Life, then, will reach a fork where we will have two choices: to be happy nevertheless or to be unhappy for everything that our life, our parents, and our limitations took away from us. I know you blame your parents, just as I know I blame mine. I could have been so much more if only they had raised me properly or if I had the right things going my way. Neither can I change the situation, nor can I go back. So should I be happy and compromise on my dreams, or should I stay loyal to them and be unhappy?" he said, opening out his arms to a question. "It is very easy to be happy and equally easy to be unhappy. Logically, we do

---

[23] *Indian Institutes of Management are highly coveted.*

know our chances of success are better when we are happy, but still, we fret."

He looked at me to see if we were connecting. I nodded.

"Just be happy, mate. There is no journey to happiness. It was a mistake—a blunder, you know. Happiness is now, here. Just be illogically and unreasonably happy. Let it be a habit. That's all there is to it. Stop searching for happiness," he said with his brooding eyes looking down as they went through the haze of the present, scanning the past to check if every suffering we went through was worth it. But then, at what point do we decide if a person is successful? Life is a long journey, and success and failure are part of the game.

"But our dreams? They stay still, *don't they*?" I asked.

"The way I see it now; be happy we have them. Stop thinking and start working in that direction. Maybe one day, someday, we will reach somewhere nearby. May you find happiness every second as you tread on the path to them," he smiled at me widely, but his smile was sad.

He was just like any other guy after all, anxious at the ups and downs of life as he would see his mind, body, and intellect not supporting the beauty of his dreams. But he was my brother, and I knew we were in the same boat. "Now smile for me. You wouldn't want me to leave on a sad note, would you?"

I smiled and hugged him. As he pulled back, I saw my shirt wet at the shoulder. He was crying—the very same person who once said it was a weakness.

"Oh, c'mon, you know how it is. I am scared that I will never see you again. I am scared of leaving everything behind. I am scared of living a life without you." He wiped his eyes with his shirt. "Every day I have felt a pang of guilt for not being the person I always dreamed of being. It is a guilt I have lived with for almost half my life. People go superficial or stop taking themselves seriously when confronted with such guilt; unfortunately, I couldn't do that either. It takes a lot of courage to smile under such circumstances, but then we want this courage. That is a battle we can't afford to lose because all these smiles add up to happiness, and the weak don't deserve to be happy, only the strong do. That's Darwin's law."

I remembered Darwin's law differently, but then this wasn't the time to nitpick. It was a time to get the broad strokes from a guy who was trying very hard to use his hands and voice in a weird manner to desperately convey his message, but only his eyes succeeded in putting forth the story. It was a story of pain, guilt, and loss, but also of hope, aspiration, and life. I couldn't help but feel a lump in my throat.

"We need to find our happiness in the life we live. True perfection is always imperfect," he said. Maybe he understood the unattainable. We had both tasted it once.

I glanced at my watch.

"Guess, it's time for you to leave," he said with a tinge of longing.

"Would you like another hug?" I asked, "You know, some happy memories to remember me by!"

"I tried to stop myself. Don't blame me," he just plunged forward and hugged me passionately, drowning me in a sea of non-chaste hugs and kisses on the cheek as he broke down into uncontrollable sobs. "I don't want to leave you. I never ever wanted to!"

I didn't stop him. Probably this moment meant much more to him than it did to me, and maybe, it deserved to go his way!

"Life has a way of never working out the way we thought it would, isn't it? This particular end had to come," I said when he finally loosened his hold on me. But that only made him grip me tighter.

And then, as I could see it all ending, I lied.

"Don't worry. Nothing ends. It's all in the mind." I gave him a small peck on the cheek before leaving without looking back.

15.

O ver the course of the next year, lots of things changed. Piyush broke up with his girlfriend and, thankfully, gave up the idea of clearing the *GRE*. Apparently, the pain of the breakup was easier to endure than the pain of mugging up *Barron's*. Great was the idea of not trying to match up with his lady love in vocabulary. He soon lost touch with her and is now happier.

Yogi seemingly achieved some expertise in doodling with stocks and moved away from Venky's opinions when his expertise started clashing with Venky's, often with higher profitability. Profitability here would mean losing a lesser amount of money. He's also making genuine efforts to move out of the company; I can say so as whenever we chat, the topic always shifts to how difficult it is to get jobs. Meanwhile, from what I gathered, Kanchan took it upon herself to mentor him for the team lead role, which meant he no longer espouses long coffee breaks to the team and finds them rather *counterproductive*.

Raj is in the organization and is trying to improve his status with better money and a better role. The last we chatted; he was still searching for a bride. I think it has more to do with his giant paunch and red, scary liquor-affected eyes than the money, but I know better than to indulge myself in the honesty of letting him know my unflattering opinion. I am most supportive.

Suman is in Hyderabad, and JD is in Kolkata for now. But since I know JD, I also know this peace is temporary. Someday they are both moving to Kolkata all right! She's also preparing for *M.Tech.* and is teaching at a small private engineering college in Kolkata. Suman, meanwhile, is finding his footing in a new industry, and it seems to be a rather steep learning curve. The good part is that they told JD's father, and he accepted grudgingly. Some weekend, when Suman gets time, he'll tell his family as well. Suman's hidden fear is that his family will find JD too independent and, hence, intimidating. My only hope is that JD will make things happen. It's an inconvenient arrangement for Suman to keep finding excuses to visit her every other weekend.

Prabhu is still in a dream world and keeps asking me at random times in the night if I am happy. He is yet to find a job, and our contact has gone down. We still chat sometimes, though—mostly about happiness and guilt. Somehow, we both still struggle with guilt if we ever find ourselves stealing happiness for a few fleeting moments over random small nothings.

As for *FORDIT*, well, it sustained the impact. Contracts with key clients got renewed, and the office building still stands, but the organization neither grew nor diminished over the years. It was, is, and probably will always stay a medium-sized organization. People moved, but the culture continued to be the same!

○●○

As it later turned out, we were still in the early stages of recession in Q1'2008. *Lehman Brothers* did go bankrupt eventually, in September 2008.

The root cause for the financial crisis in this case, as we know now, was excessive mortgage lending to borrowers *(in the US)* who normally would not qualify for a home loan, which greatly increased the lender's risk. This caused the housing bubble to burst and affected markets world-wide. It's insane how inter-related global economies are!

There was a speculation of a double-dip recession in 2007–09, although a W-shaped recession thankfully did not end up occurring.

The recession started around December 2007 and ended sometime in the third quarter of 2009, after around four quarters of decline.

○ ● ○

Regular expansions and contractions of an economy are part of any business cycle. Contractions can lead to a recession. Recession often starts at the peak of a business cycle and ends at the dip of the same cycle when the next expansion begins.

In every recession, economic activities take a hit, profits fall, stock markets go bearish, unemployment increases, consumers cut back on spending, and companies make fewer investments.

Sooner or later, economic recovery follows a recession like one season follows another. With time, Indian industries recovered too.

Psychological and economic factors can also make a recession linger longer. There are studies that suggest that over-enthusiasm leading to risky investments during economic booms and deep pessimism in downturns can cause recession to persist.

Some studies say recessions are probably inevitable as they correct market imbalances.

So, what do we do in a recession? It is good to have multiple sources of income. Invest in yourself and learning; never take a single day of working life for granted; avoid risky investments; try to keep patience; and avoid panic.

But most importantly, we should take care of our own mental health and that of the people we care for. The least one can do is to be considerate towards the people we work with, those we work for, and those who work for us. I am sure there might be a way to care for our people without sacrificing profits—it is not necessarily a trade-off.

A recession might also be a time to focus on innovation or innovative inventions. Preparing for the next downturn, anchoring on value, growth, people, and a customer-centric approach might help organizations outgrow competition in the long run.

Realistically, one can just balance theory with practicability as best as possible. Let's try to not sacrifice one for the other entirely though!

Last Day.

I packed my bags in the morning. Few things always get left.

"Send it all back home via packers and movers," my father said on the phone.

My cousin stood at the door, looking at me with some impatience. I paid him his dues. Accounts were settled. I was hardly sad to lose him as a roommate. My train was the next day.

My last day in the organization was a low-key affair. I would rather not talk about it. The AC felt colder than usual, and I felt something sinking inside me; it must be my heart. I was nervous to bid goodbye to this safe, protected world inside and set foot again in the desert outside. Money at the month end would be sorely missed.

I roamed the floors wordlessly and nostalgically, clicking pictures of the places and corners I had shared a history with. People I loved were gone, but then the memories were mine and shall remain. But those were empty moments without the people who made them, a desperate attempt to grab some of the quicksilver through the veils of time. I don't know how to look at the past, I guess. It has slipped away, yet it teases with an unearthly hope of re-living it, which, quite frankly, is meaningless.

In the evening, I found myself on the terrace of the posh sky-facing lounge our batch people had booked for the anniversary party. The place was filled with joy and warmth as the sky buzzed with crackers that our batch had arranged. The ambiance had a subtle lighting that provided a soothing effect, and the temperature was pleasantly cool. It was a genuine celebration where people hugged, chatted, and laughed heartily at jokes they couldn't hear in the din. They didn't care; it was all about smiling. For once, I didn't miss Prabhu.

At dinner, we sat, as was the tradition, around the giant round table and made fun of each other—of the romantic linkups, the scares with the layoffs, the funny goof-ups, and our vicious biases towards each other. Finally, it had all come down to this: a happy dinner where we were just glad to be together. Pooja was still there and looked lovelier than ever. She was in a bright yellow salwar, and our eyes kept meeting. The connection was unmistakable.

As the night advanced, individuals began to disperse, and the table gradually emptied. I walked over to the private water cooler area situated at the back of the terrace to quench my thirst; the numerous cocktails had started to affect me. Pooja too stood by the cooler talking on her phone.

"Hi," I nodded.

She nodded too as she whispered something at the receiver and finished the call.

"Boyfriend?" I asked, smiling.

"Mother," she smiled. "I was feeling strange with so much noise."

"It's a pleasant surprise to find you still here."

"Yes. A week more for me," she said. "When are you leaving?"

"It was my last day today! I leave for my hometown tomorrow."

"Oh," her face fell; the news stunned her. "Of course... They would be happy to prepone your exit since it's voluntary. What now?"

"I don't know, seriously don't," I said, looking at her. I took a pause. "Won't you call me for your marriage?"

"It's in Dubai." She smiled nervously. "To tell you the truth, I never wanted to get married so soon. It's around, and I can't even believe it. It's crazy, and by the way, he isn't my boyfriend. It's arranged. There are so many things... leave all that!"

"Well, maybe I'll come if you do invite," I laughed, but I knew the ultimate: "...Maybe."

Crackers illuminated the night as we both looked up in unison. It was a sight to see them burst out in the sky beautifully, lighting up our faces with a rainbow of colors.

She looked at me longingly, like she was looking at me for the last time. Some stories are perhaps destined to stay unfinished. She nodded one last time and started walking back to the table.

"She is hot!!" Mitali whispers. Sky lights up again, and I find her right next to me sipping cola.

"Wait... what... The way I know you, you are straight." I raise my eyebrow in a frown as I take a moment to glance at how beautiful she looks without her specs.

"Dude, why me when you could have gone after her? Just look at her!" she says, with a cute pout of disbelief.

"Cos I was madly in love with you and am," I reason it out gruffly. "You, of all people, should know."

"I get it, but you know what?" she smiles affectionately and whispers knowingly in my ears.

> *"You will always be weak enough,*
>
> *To stay in love with me,*
>
> *And yet, I now realize,*
>
> *You are also strong enough... to let go and move on!"*

"Not bad..." I was a bit shaken at her fast-improving poetry skills, or was it just me imagining a poem there?

She chuckles like old times. "It's just you and your stupid head, silly.

I am long gone, and she leaves soon... and don't you worry as far as we go..."

"Please don't..." I find it unbearable to let her go.

She touches my cheeks. "Look...

> *What's important is that you cared enough to make me live,*
> *Our crazy dreams you didn't forget,*
> *You did live a part of them and of me,*
> *and they will live through you, so don't you regret!*

Truth doesn't matter here. After all, this is your story, and a bit of mine too, isn't it? End it well! Promise me, you will!"

She plants a soft kiss on my cheek, and then, just like that, she leaves—soundlessly, wordlessly—as if she hasn't changed my life, as if nothing ever happened at all.... but she never forgets to take away that one part of mine, which is only hers!

In return, she leaves for me a sense of loss and a dollop of guilt for not leaving caffeine—her gifts for the lifetime!

I wonder at what point one can say the story ends!

"Listen," I said, raising my voice unknowingly. As Pooja turned back and concentrated on what I was about to say, I spoke the very first thing on my mind.

"Look, probably I am supposed to say and do lots of fluffy things before I reach the bottom line, but you see, I don't have any more time. It's like this," I sighed deeply, "I really like you!"

She seemed surprised but did a good job of hiding her smile. "Oh, that's such a nice thing to say to anyone. I like you too. You are a nice guy."

"No, not like that." I didn't want any more misunderstandings, and so, before I knew what was happening, I inched closer, leaned forward, and kissed her gently on the lips. This was as simple as I could keep it, you know—means to an end—the best self-expression possible in those few moments, probably my last ones with her.

That touch was full of longing, as it was unhurried. It meant a lot of little things, and she deserved to know them all, every single one of them.

"I meant that." As I moved away, I found her looking thoroughly shaken with shock but thankfully not scared. She struggled to find words to utter.

Several moments passed. She stood silently. As soon as she regained her composure, she looked around to see if we were alone—we were!

"You can slap me, you know. It was not a *'neat'* thing to do." I tried to say something. In fact, I was expecting a slap. I had no idea what to do in case of an awkward silence.

"Probably I should. You are such a terrible kisser," she said, trying to keep her cool.

I just stared at her and gambled with my chances. "Or maybe you can teach me how to do it the right way. I wonder if this might help." I said it breathlessly without giving her time to think. "Let's play this game. Here's a coin: *heads*, you slap me; *tails*, you teach me.

I would close my eyes. Whatever you do, surprise me!" And before she was ready, I closed my eyes and tossed it high.

I could hear the metallic clanking of the coin as it cut through the air. It was a sound I never wanted to end. But it did, and the coin landed on her palm with a thud. More than anything, I wanted it to be a surprise. I closed my eyes tighter.

Sure enough, in some moments I sensed her hand on my cheek, but it was warm. Seconds later, I felt her lips on mine!

The next day, as I was leaving, I got a call from her. "I am so sorry; I don't think I can come to see you off. I thought about you most of the last night and slept late. I couldn't wake up on time!"

"I understand; wish you could! We could have met, you know, one last time! Would have been so great to have a coffee together."

"But we will stay in touch, right?" she asked, her words trying to undermine the uncertainty.

"Probably not! I would like to remember you as I saw you last night. If it has to end, if it must, I'd prefer it ends this way."

"What?" I could hear her voice cracking. "But... I should have seriously slapped you. The coin said heads. I thought, what the heck!"

"I bet you didn't even check what the coin said," I said, smiling. "And by the way, I am just kidding. We will stay in touch."

"I really hope we do. I always knew we could be good friends," she said affectionately.

"Yes, we will be good friends!" And to my surprise, I found I was still smiling. Probably for the first time, I knew a fun fact that Prabhu didn't regarding friendship and love.

With the right girl, it was possible to have the right mix of both!

Epilogue.

This was it, then!

I stood at the railway station, waiting for my train, with a cup of coffee in my hand. My phone vibrated.

I thought it was from Prabhu, only to remember a moment later that he was already gone. Who now?

"Hello," said a deep voice on the other end. It could only be one person.

"Hey, Bhoopal," a smile spread across my face.

"JD told me you were leaving. Last day?" he asked.

"Yes. I am at the station."

"Where will you go?" he asked tonelessly.

"Home."

"So then?" He inquired sarcastically, "Hell-bent on leaving technology? *MBA* huh??"

"It's the other way around. Technology abandoned me," I chuckled sadly.

He didn't find it funny.

"Interesting," he paused. "The thing is, in that case, I am here to confuse you a bit with my proposal."

"Tell me!"

"I am working with a startup in Bangalore as a contractor. It's something new and unfigured till now, but I am excited. This startup is the first of its kind in India. We need people who are interested in technology as well as in the business aspect of things for this particular idea to work. I thought you might be interested."

"What would I need to do?"

"Anything or everything, starting from website design to inventory control strategies, and all of it would be linked to results. Nothing is pre-decided, whatever the business needs. You would be able to see your technological input being translated into sales. The business interfacing of technicalities is much stronger, Amit. We might be on the edge of a revolution here. These are the early stages, and there's a lot to be explored. The exact roles are not clearly defined right now, but you will get more exposure and time to learn. We are going to hire more contractors, and I immediately thought of your name when the company put down that they would be looking more for the right approach, analytical skills, and quick learning abilities than the computer coding skills *(which can easily be learned by a mind with a good aptitude)*. It's a new business model. What do you say?"

"Umm, it appears scary, Bhoopal. Is this some fancy US idea, like credit cards? I don't want to get into something I may never be able to come out of. And during these recession times..."

"Look, in every calamity lies an opportunity," he whispered. "Ever heard of this term called e-commerce? Search Wikipedia. It's going to be big, and you will be able to stay in touch with technology. It might just be the kind of work you are searching for.

There are always risks. The question is, are you willing to risk some?"

It took me just a moment—a single moment—to answer Bhoopal's question. "Of course, I am."

"Just because there is a recession it doesn't mean we stop growing; it just means we start growing in new areas and in new ways!" Bhoopal said and smiled.

Incidentally, that's exactly what the Indian IT industry did *(post some soul-searching)* after the recession ended in 2009; it grew in new destinations, different service lines, and different sectors with better diversification. The Indian financial industry, too, is now considered more resilient, focusing on sustainable growth with limited risk. As the Indian risk appetite improved, it eventually led to a dynamic start-up ecosystem a few years later.

"I trust your vision, Bhoopal."

"Great. Come to Bangalore. They don't need any big IT programmers, not right away. I am sure we will be able to find some analyst profiles for you. It's definitely worth a shot if you're interested. They are also trying for funding, which will help the organization scale up like a dream."

"But where exactly am I to come?"

"*Flipkart, corporate office, Bangalore.* I will message you the complete address in a while. It's in Koramangala. Interviews start next week. You can apply online on the company portal first, but

I might be able to get you a shortlist and a call. The only thing is that you need to be around to grab it in time."

"How soon?"

"It's Saturday today; how soon can you come? You can stay with me for a while. You might need to wait for a few months, for things to work out. Meanwhile, feel free to pursue some quick professional courses to ramp up your skills and try elsewhere as well. A person like you can ramp up quickly. So then... what do you think?"

It was March of 2008. The sun smiled as brightly as ever. It beamed with unlimited hope—the very same hope that flickered inside me still—of returning to things that I was itching to do. I threw away my cup of coffee in a dustbin.

"I have heard great things about Bangalore. Cool. Expect me by Monday," I said, smiling as I walked away to the ticketing office. I needed a new ticket for whichever train was next. My parents probably won't be delighted!

On the way, I took a moment to ponder, searched my pockets for a pencil, and scribbled on the current ticket in my hand.

> *Sing along to the tune you believe in,*
> *Your heart knows the rhythm blue,*
> *Maybe that's not what the world wanted to hear,*
> *But then, wasn't your audience always you?!!*

I took a final breath; one filled with life and memories. I glanced back once, only to find Pooja waving at me from a distance.

I wondered how she made it so quickly and if it's really a dream. She walked towards me briskly and pointed at the *Comesum* coffee shop on the platform, the one where I had last met Prabhu. That made me smile and glance at my watch.

We had time—quite a lot of it, actually—for what was to be our first and last coffee together!

She went to Dubai, got married, and soon lost touch. Fortunately, or unfortunately, that's the way time works! The old fades away quietly once it has paved the way for the new. I just hope that I remain a faint happy memory in her thoughts, just as she continues to be in mine.

As for me, my love for coffee later graduated into a love for *filter kaapi* in *'Namma Bengaluru'*!

---

[i] *Flipkart started in the last quarter of 2007, right at the beginning of the great recession. Then a fledgling startup, it grew by leaps and bounds later. Though technically it wasn't the first e-commerce startup in India, the e-commerce journey of India truly began with Flipkart against the backdrop of the recession, as Bhoopal had once said: an opportunity in the heart of peril.*

Printed in Great Britain
by Amazon

60502866R00271